The Warrior and the Enchantress
Diana Sherrill Richards

Bright Star Romance—Athens, AL
ISBN: 978-0-578-82018-7
Library of Congress Control Number: 2020925493
Title: *The Warrior and the Enchantress*
Author: Diana Sherrill Richards
Digital distribution | 2020
Paperback | 2020

This is a work of fiction. The characters, names, incidents, places, and dialogue are products of the author's imagination, and are not to be construed as real.

The first book in the series:

The Brotherhood of the Heart and Sword

The Warrior and the Enchantress

Dedication

This book is dedicated to my wonderful husband Randall Richards, for all the encouragement and help he's given me in my book and seeing my dream come true. I am very proud of my Husband, my very own Warrior. He served in the Navy Fleet and later as a Seabee in the Navy Reserve.

Thank you, my Husband, my Love, for the many things you do. I love you!

Most of all thank you God the father, the son Jesus Christ and the Holy Spirit who I love and give thanks to everyday. I owe everything to them.

Thank you to my son, Justin for all the love, joy and happiness you've brought into my life over the years. I am so very proud of you. I love you!

Thank you to my brother Mike Sherrill, who has a heart of gold and my sister-in-law Shawn. Thank you to my Aunt Mary Sherrill Lawrence who seems more like a sister than my aunt. All of you have listened to me go on and on about my ideas for my book. Thanks again, I love you all!

Chapter 1
England
March 1062 A.D.

The battle cry sounded, as Lord Belgar led his men to battle against the advancing raiders. Their numbers were much smaller since the fever struck last year, and many of those who fell to it were warriors. Now the raiders rushed upon them, and it seemed they were outnumbered nearly two to one.

Lord Belgar's warriors clustered together with their shields, swords and spears raised for the coming battle. In wave after wave, the attack fell on the brave men of Holdenworth. The warriors stoutly resisted, but became wearier with each onslaught.

Sensing victory was at hand, Vorik, the leader of the raiders shouted out a challenge. Lord Belgar was glad to face this raider one on one in order to spare the lives of his men. He bravely stepped toward the challenger as the battle raged all around him.

This was the opportunity Vorik had been waiting for. Instead of sounding a long blast to halt the battle, Vorik raised a signal horn to his lips, and blew three quick blasts to call for an ambush.

Raiders lying in wait rushed into the battle toward where Lord Belgar stood on open ground. His warriors stood beside him, and tried desperately to defend their Lord and village, but it was all for naught.

Belgar, Lord of Holdenworth was slain by the hand of Vorik the Merciless. His lifeless body lay on the cold ground, his life blood seeping into the soil that he had fought and died for. The land had been passed down through his family for four generations, and he had loved it dearly. Belgar had been a great warrior. If only he had more men, and had not fallen into Vorik's cowardly ambush, the battle would have ended quite differently.

Fright washed over the women and children huddled in the great hall, but there was a look of determination on Serina's face. Serina was Lady of Holdenworth, and determined to show no fear, regardless of the raiders that were certain to come bursting into the hall at any moment. The first thing she did was to see to her daughter's safety.

"Listen closely, Chanity," she said, cupping her daughter's face in her hands. "You must run quickly now, to your hiding place between the walls in your chamber. Do not come out, whatever you hear, or whatever happens. Promise! Promise me now, Chanity!"

Tears streamed down Chanity's face, and flowed over her mother's strong, loving hands. "I promise, Mother," Chanity said, then she dashed up the stairs toward her bedchamber.

Chanity ran to her chamber, removed a secret panel, and crawled inside. She carefully pulled the panel back in place, watching as the last sliver of light vanished. She lay there blinking in the darkness as the sounds of battle ebbed, and soon the horrible sounds of looting began.

She was terrified when she heard the raiders enter, and begin to search her bed chamber. She prayed they would not find her, and was relieved when they finally left. Her relief soon turned to worry, as she thought of her mother facing the raiders. Chanity bowed her head, and silently prayed her mother would be safe.

After the looting was over, Chanity heard the raider's laughter, and the screams of Holdenworth's women coming from the great hall. Through the door, she heard the voice of her mother Serina in the hallway outside her chamber.

"Unhand me, filthy swine," Serina said, but her oath was cut short by a loud slap. Chanity longed to go to her mother, but remembered the promise she made. She was only ten and two, and did not fully understand all that was happening.

Sadness descended on Chanity like a blanket, and she cried herself to sleep thinking about her mother being struck, and the death of her father.

Chanity dreamt of her father and brother, and the argument they had when her brother announced he was going to fight for King Edward. Belgar supported Edward, and had fought for him in various campaigns. Belgar thought Gerald was too young, and should wait another year before going off to battle. Gerald was insistent, and he left to join Edward's men on the day he turned ten and six years.

Even at his youthful age, Gerald was nearly as large a man as his father. He proved his abilities in the training field, and had even bested some of Belgar's most skilled warriors. Gerald had dark brown hair like his father, but did not have his green eyes. Those he inherited from their mother Serina; eyes that sparkled with the color of the clear blue sky. His striking looks and bold demeanor captivated all the girls in the village, who adored him and sought his favor.

Suddenly the scene of her dream shifted, and somehow Gerald and Belgar were together again, but were now engaged in a furious battle. To her horror, she saw a warrior strike her father down, then slay her brother. She awoke with a cry, relieved at first to find it was only a nightmare. Eventually, reality sunk in, and she realized her father was dead. Chanity lay weeping in the darkness, until sleep finally overtook her again.

The next morn, Chanity awoke to the sound of her Mother's voice calling her name. "Oh Chanity, you must have been exhausted," Serina said softly.

Her mother had removed the small panel and crawled inside the hidden chamber without even awakening her. She lay on a pallet of fur pelts, and Serina lay down alongside her.

Chanity was so glad her mother was at her side. She threw her arms around Serina and hugged her tightly. Serina gasped, and Chanity realized her mistake. Some small rays of light illuminated the darkness, enough so she could see the left side of her mother's face was bruised and swollen. There were also some bruises on her neck and a small split on her lip.

Serina saw the worry in Chanity's eyes, and reassured her that everything would be alright. "Things are much calmer now, Chanity. For now, you may come out and play in your chamber, but if you hear someone coming up the stairs, run back to your hiding place. Things will settle down in a fortnight or so. Soon you will be able to come out and sleep in your bedchamber again. Here, I brought you some food and milk. I must get back to the great hall before anyone realizes I'm gone." Serina kissed her on the cheek, then quickly left.

'Twas a long two weeks that turned into three, and then four before Chanity was able to sleep in her bed chamber again. She missed playing outside in the sunshine, but most of all she missed going to her favorite spot at the cliff. Serina did not trust Vorik or his men, so this meant Chanity had to remain hidden away in her chamber.

Each morning, Serina saw to the preparations for the men to break their fast, then would slip away to see Chanity for a little while. Alma or one of the other serfs would cover for her in the great hall while she was away. Serina brought porridge and berries with milk, and talked with Chanity as she ate. She spoke of how things were going in the great hall, and about the happenings in the village.

Lord Belgar and Lady Serina had always treated their serfs well. In return, the serfs were loyal to them, and worked hard to bring in the crops and tend to other chores that needed doing. Now, with Vorik as Chieftain, the serfs were abused by his men, and the harvest had been greatly reduced. Serina was once the lady of Holdenworth, but now was a slave herself.

When Chanity finished breaking her fast, her mother pulled her into a warm embrace and kissed her cheek before leaving the chamber.

After a while, the bruises Serina received from Vorik disappeared. Still young and a beauty, she was a score, ten and one years. She wed Belgar when she was just ten and five years. Gerald was birthed a year later, and then Chanity four years after him.

Chanity hoped she would be as beautiful as her mother when she grew up. Serina's hair was very pale blonde. She had eyes as blue as the sky on a sunny day, and lips the color of a rose. Chanity heard people refer to her mother as a regal beauty. She had high cheek bones, long thick lashes, a delicately shaped face, and a smile that warmed the heart.

Once she overheard a guard remark "Lady Serina has curves and a bosom to set a man's loins afire." Chanity skipped over to him and asked, "What do you mean my Mother set a man's loins on fire? He must have done something really bad for my Mother to have set him on fire. What exactly are loins, anyway?"

The guard scowled, grumbled, and told Chanity not to be sneaking up on people or eavesdropping on their conversations, but she didn't hear him. She had already skipped out of earshot, on her way to watch the new kittens playing by the stable.

Later that evening, Chanity asked her mother the same questions that she had asked the guard. Serina blushed, then sternly told her to never mention that to anyone again, especially not to her father.

The fame of Serina's beauty and strength spread from village to village. Through the stories and songs of the skalds, the tale of her beauty spread throughout all of England.

Vorik saw the respect the villagers gave Serina, and knew he must somehow make an alliance by marriage. He had forced her to share his bed from the day he slew Belgar, and claimed the victor's share of the spoil. Her beauty and strength were without equal, and he was certain she would bear him a fine son.

Vorik hoped Serina would resign herself to her fate, and wed him, but her fury had only turned to a cold, bitter anger. He gritted his teeth in anger and wondered why she had to be so stubborn. After all, had he not proven he was the stronger man, even if by treachery? Vorik began to watch Serina carefully each day, determined to find some way to convince her to change her mind.

Vorik's careful watchfulness was finally rewarded. He noted Serina busied herself early in the morning, then slipped away once everything had been set in order. She always seemed to have a morsel of food when she departed as well. Vorik was convinced she was slipping extra food to someone, and was determined to discover who that someone was.

One morning he stumbled into the great hall, grabbed a hunk of bread and some mead. He made a great show groaning about his aching head, then wandered unsteadily back toward his chamber. Serina was relieved to see him go so soon. Usually she had to wait some time until she could slip away. She quickly gathered up some fruit, porridge and milk. With a quick nod to Alma, Serina made her way to Chanity's chamber.

Serina entered the room, and closed the door behind her. Chanity sat quietly on her bed playing with her doll, until her mother set the trencher on the table.

Chanity went to her mother and hugged her tightly. Just as she sat down to break her fast, the door flew open and Vorik burst into the room. His glowering gaze swept the room, searching for the person Serina was sneaking food to. His eyes alighted on Chanity, who was frozen in place by his sudden entry.

Vorik was dumbstruck for a moment, and Serina prepared herself for the fit of rage he was sure to unleash. Suddenly Vorik howled with laughter, laughing on and on till he was near out of breath.

"Oh, this explains a good many things, wench." Vorik said, gasping for air as he gestured at Chanity. "Tell me, who is this sweet young lass you have squirreled away for many a day now?" He asked, looking like a fox that had just cornered its prey.

"Why, you should be ashamed of yourself keeping her locked in here like this. And look at this pitiful morsel of food. Poor lass, it's a wonder you are still alive."

"I can take care of my daughter just fine," Serina spat back at him.

"Aye, aye, I'm sure you can," Vorik replied smoothly. "But come; we should speak privately, and discuss what else you can do to ensure your daughter's safety."

Serina knelt by Chanity, and told her she would return in a few moments. Vorik marched from the room and Serina followed, knowing exactly what Vorik had in mind.

Once they were alone, Vorik declared he would protect Chanity, only if Serina would agree to wed him. Serina reluctantly agreed, knowing the fate that would befall Chanity if she refused. She knew how ruthless Vorik and his men could be, even to a child.

Later on, Serina spoke with Chanity several times, and tried to explain why she had to wed Vorik. Serina hated Vorik, and knew Chanity felt the same. With Belgar's death, and no word from Gerald, Chanity was all she had left. Serina would do whatever she could to see to her daughter's safety.

On the day she and Vorik were to wed, Serina felt dreadfully ill. Vorik repulsed her, and she loathed him. Serina found herself frowning with despair as she entered the great hall.

"Can't you at least try to smile a little, Serina?" Vorik asked angrily. "This is the day we are to wed. I know you have better gowns than that rag you have on. Go back to our chambers and put on something else. I want your hair brushed out, and hanging loose. And when you come back, you had better be smiling, or you will pay later in our chamber. You will not embarrass me in front of my men."

"What have I to smile about Vorik?" Serina asked. "That I get to wed the man who slew my husband? The man that forced me to bed him on that very night! The man who is still forcing me!"

Vorik seized her face roughly with his hand. "Do not speak so loudly, and do not say such in front of my men, or you will regret it Serina," Vorik growled. "Do you think my men will respect me if I let you talk back to me? You better learn that I am Lord here now, and Belgar has long since passed. Besides, I'm not forcing you to wed me. You're doing that for your child's protection. It's best you remember that. Now go before I get angry, and be quick about it."

Chanity saw the pain and anger in her mother's eyes when Vorik spoke Belgar's name. She knew it hurt her mother deeply to hear this vile man even say the name of the honorable man he cut down in cowardice. Even though Serina tried to convince her otherwise, she realized now that her mother was wedding Vorik for her sake.

Chanity went to her side, and asked if she could look through her gowns to help find one. Any excuse to get her mother out of Vorik's horrible presence.

Now, left alone to his thoughts, Vorik closed his eyes and thought back to the night of the raid. Serina stood there like a golden-haired goddess, her chin held high, eyes aflame, with dagger in hand demanding to know why he had done this. It did not go well for her at first, but he kept her to himself and ordered his men not to touch her.

Vorik was glad he found out about her daughter, else Serina would never have agreed to wed him. She showed strength and courage most women did not. He admired Serina, but would never tell anyone how he felt, least of all Serina. He may admire her, desire her, but he would never love her, and knew she would never love him.

The rest of the morning passed uneventfully, and the wedding hour finally arrived. Serina stood with Vorik, and buried her anger deep inside. During the vows she pretended it was Belgar standing there, and remembered the day they wed, so many years ago. Perhaps remembering that day would help her get through this one. It seemed to drag on forever, but what did she care?

She dreaded going to the chamber and having to lay with Vorik as his wife. She would never think of him as her husband. Belgar would always be her husband in her heart and thoughts. Perhaps Vorik would drink too much, or go find one of the young village girls that wanted him. At last the ceremony concluded, and the feasting began.

As Serina expected, wine flowed freely at the feast. The hall was laden with food aplenty, and there was even a skald wandering about that Vorik had hired to sing his praises. Though it was early, Serina slipped away from the feast and headed up the stairs.

On the way to her chamber, she stopped to bid Chanity a good night. Her heart ached, as she tried to explain again to Chanity why she married Vorik. Whatever her reasons, she must explain so Chanity would not feel guilty, or think it was somehow her fault. Serina held Chanity, and softly sang a song she had always loved. She gave Chanity a hug and kiss, bid her sweet dreams, then went to the master chamber.

The moon hung high in the sky when Vorik came stumbling up the stairs. Serina's prayers were answered, for Vorik came to their chamber heavy in his cups and passed out on the bed. With Vorik asleep and snoring away, she felt her anxiety ease. At least she didn't have to deal with him on this sorrowful night.

Her grief set in, and the tears she had been holding back for so long flowed freely. She cried herself to sleep, thinking of Belgar, and wondered if Gerald was alive. She missed her son greatly, but it was fortunate he was not there, for Vorik would have slain him also. This day had brought back many bittersweet memories.

Chapter 2

When Vorik woke the next morn, he found Serina had already gone downstairs. Scowling, he quickly dressed, and went to break his fast. Vorik spied Serina in the hall, as she helped the servants serve meals and clean up. Vorik took his seat, as one of the servants brought out his meal.

"You will stay in our chamber until I arise, Serina," Vorik demanded, glaring in her direction. "The serfs can certainly manage on their own without you playing nursemaid to them. Besides, it is your duty to birth me a son. I'm sure you would rather do so in our private chamber, rather than display our coupling in the great hall."

Serina glared back at him, but said nothing. After Vorik's warning about watching her tongue, she would put nothing past him. He might even make good on his threat to take her in the great hall for everyone to witness.

Later that day, Serina went to see Alma's sister Etta the healer. Etta looked up from her work at the crucible as Serina entered.

"Etta, you must give me more herbs to keep from getting with child," Serina pleaded. "The supply you gave me is getting low, and I am sure that oaf will be pawing at me night and day now that we are wed. He is demanding a son, which I will never give him."

"Don't worry my dear," Etta replied, taking a bundle down from a high shelf. "I gathered these for you already. Here is some powder for Vorik as well," Etta said, with a sly grin on her face. "Just place a pinch in his mead or wine, and you will find he will not be nearly as interested, or even able to bed you."

"You have my thanks, Etta," Serina said with relief. "Vorik thinks he has won by using Chanity against me, but I will never bear him a son, and Chanity is safe at last."

A month after the wedding, Vorik received word that his Aunt Gunnora was in ill health and no longer able to care for his daughter

Marla. He sent a woman from Holdenworth along with his most trusted men to get Marla, and return with her. Vorik commanded his men to load the long boats for trading on the journey there and back.

Marla was glad when she heard her father had sent for her. Her life had been one of tragedy and loneliness. Her Great Aunt Gunnora was stern, and could even be cruel at times.

Marla didn't know much about her mother Marta. What little she did know came from Vorik's boastful stories, and Aunt Gunnora's cruel words.

On one of his visits, Marla asked Vorik if he would tell a story about her mother. Vorik had no desire to talk about Marta, but saw the pleading in his daughter's eyes. Normally he wouldn't give in to her pleading, but he was heavy in his cups.

Vorik spoke of how he found Marta in a raid on a homestead in Normandy before coming to England. He bragged about the loot captured in the raid, and how he mercifully brought Marta with him to care for her, since she had apparently been abandoned.

"Ah, your mother was a beauty for sure," Vorik told her. "She was very attractive, with dark eyes, black hair and ivory skin. Unfortunately, she died while birthing you."

A few days later, Vorik told Marla he had to depart to look after one of his holdings. Marla begged to go with him, but Vorik declared it was too dangerous, and told her she would just get in the way.

Marla awoke early the next morning, and hurried to see her father one last time before he left. The house was strangely silent, and no one answered her calls. She ran outside just in time to see Vorik and his men fade out of sight.

As soon as Vorik disappeared, Marla heard her aunt coming up from the stables. "He's finally gone at last, is he?" Aunt Gunnora said angrily. "Why, I barely have stores enough for the two of us without trying to feed him and his men. Not to mention those awful stories!" said Aunt Gunnora, rolling her eyes.

"But I liked his stories, especially about Mother," replied Marla.

"Of course you would, dear," said Aunt Gunnora. "But I must tell you the real story of what happened to your mother. Your mother was not abandoned by your grandparents. Marta was left to care for her younger brothers while her parents visited a nearby village for a couple of days. Vorik charged in on a raid, and demanded all the valuable goods in exchange for sparing the homestead. Marta's brothers were but lads, and they ran out to confront Vorik. In a fit of rage, he struck them down with his sword."

"Marta begged Vorik not to take her, since she was the only daughter, and now the only child her parents had left, but he seemed not to care. She cried for days after Vorik took her from her home. She wasn't crying for the horrible things she would have to endure, but for the grief she knew her parents would go through."

"Not long after he took her, she became with child. Your father lied about how he found your mother, but at least he told the truth about her dying while birthing you."

Marla could barely believe what she was hearing, but the words had a ring of truth to them. "How did I come to be here?"

"Your father could hardly be expected to wag you about the countryside, now could he?" Aunt Gunnora asked. "He hired a nursemaid, but that was just for the journey here. Once you arrived, Vorik asked me to look after you. He promised to return when he could, but you see yourself how sparse his visits are. The nursemaid placed you in my arms, and you have been here ever since."

Gunnora was glad Marla was still too young to ask any probing questions. The last thing she needed was Marla discovering the house was actually Vorik's holding in France. Moreover, she was well paid, in addition to having the home to live in. The nursemaid was to have stayed, and seen that Marla was well taken care of. However, Gunnora was greedy, and dismissed her on upon arrival. She pocketed the money that Vorik set aside to pay the nursemaid.

Gunnora refused to watch after the babe herself, and instead put that responsibility on one of the servants. She decided to make up some tale if Vorik should ask what happened to the woman.

Gunnora did not want the responsibility of raising a child, and thus had never had one of her own. When Marla arrived, she had no choice but to look after her, because she lost most of her coin on some bad investments. Since Vorik needed her to watch after Marla, she could count on staying at the estate, as well as coin for the household.

Though Marla was his only child, Vorik had no real love for her, but he did feel a responsibility toward her. He had only seen her a few times since he left her with his aunt. The last time he saw Marla was two years ago, when he visited France and stayed a few days at his family home. Marla was growing quickly, and looked like a smaller version of her mother.

The expedition to get Marla went well, and two months later, Marla arrived at Holdenworth. She ran to hug Vorik, but he just patted her on the head, and asked about her journey.

"I was ill at first, but after a few days I got used to the rocking of the longboat. I fared quite well after that," Marla explained enthusiastically.

Vorik snorted and scowled when Marla mentioned being ill. He could not abide weakness in anyone, not even a child. He lingered with her for only a moment, then left to see what was gained from the trading expedition.

Serina saw the disappointment on the child's face and tried to speak with her. Marla ignored Serina, and demanded to see her bedchamber.

"This is your new step-sister, my daughter Chanity. She will show you to your chamber," Serina said, introducing the two girls.

"Follow me," Chanity said, then headed toward the great hall.

As they walked along, Chanity tried to engage Marla in conversation.

"You are but Vorik's step-daughter. I am his true daughter by blood. I'm sure you know stepsisters are not real sisters. I was told all about you on the voyage here," Marla said sullenly.

Chanity stopped in her tracks, and glared at Marla. "He is not my father, nor will he ever be," she replied angrily. Chanity knew she had sounded harsh, so she tried to change the subject. "What is your age", she inquired, hoping to find something in common between them.

Marla gave her a surly look, and replied, "ten and one".

Chanity returned her glare, and said "I am ten and two, so I am a year older than you."

They walked the rest of the way in silence, till they reached the chambers on the second floor of the hall.

"This is to be your bedchamber. It is next to mine," Chanity said, as Marla entered her room.

"Would you like to play later?" Chanity asked, softening her voice. Marla gave no reply, and shut the door before Chanity had a chance to say anything else.

In time, Chanity learned that Marla was very bitter and vain. She constantly demanded her way, and ran whining to Vorik when she didn't get it. He never gave in to Marla's complaining though, nor questioned Serina's authority, because he did not want the responsibility of dealing with his daughter.

Marla did not realize Vorik hated her whining. When she complained to her father, it made him ignore her even more. She even began making up lies about Chanity, so Chanity decided it was best to avoid her.

Serina saw that Marla felt ignored by Vorik, and tried her best to be nice and show kindness. Marla shunned it most of the time, but Serina wasn't the type to give up easily. She continued to speak pleasantly to Marla, and do her a kindness at every opportunity. She asked Chanity to try and be nice to Marla also, and pointed out that she only acted out because she wanted her father's love and attention.

The next three and a half years went by quickly. Chanity stayed busy helping her mother with the responsibility of running Holdenworth.

Over the last two months Serina seemed tire more easily. She developed a raspy cough that would not go away. Her breathing became labored, and she looked quite pale. Serina stopped by Etta the healer's cottage to get some herbs to treat her cough. Etta listened quietly as Serina described how she had been feeling.

"I've got just the thing for you," Etta said, handing her a small bundle of herbs. "Just pinch a bit off, and make a tea. Drink it twice each day. It should help ease your cough."

"Thank you, Etta," Serina replied with relief. "I just hope I start feeling better soon."

"I'm sure you will, dear," Etta said reassuringly. "I'll speak to Chanity, and tell her to make sure you take your herbs each day."

"If you speak to Chanity, she will watch over me like a mother hen"

"I'm counting on it, Serina. And who could watch over you better than her?" Etta asked, smiling.

Serina left the hut, and shortly after, Etta went to speak with Chanity. Chanity was busy helping the serfs prepare for the next meal. She made small talk with Chanity until the serfs left and they were finally alone. "Your Mother just stopped by for some herbs. I had no idea she felt so poorly," said Etta with concern.

"Aye, I've been hounding her for days to go see you, and today I finally had to insist. Were you able to give her something to help?"

"The herbs will help her cough and breathing. As with any illness, she needs rest in order to recover."

"I spoke the same to her as well, but now I see I must insist that she let me take on more of her responsibilities," replied Chanity.

"You are a good daughter, Chanity. I hope she gets better soon," Etta said, taking Chanity in for a hug. "I'll be in my hut should you need me, and I'll bring more herbs as they are needed."

A few days passed, but Serina's health continued to decline. Vorik's normally ill temper was worse than ever, for he could not abide illness or weakness. He finally suggested Serina move into her own chamber, or with Chanity, so someone could look after her. This made Chanity and Serina very happy.

Serina was grateful to be away from Vorik, for she loathed him. She had been taking herbs to keep her from getting with child, and slipping herbs in his drink to keep him from wanting to bed her. Fortunately, the herbs she gave Vorik had their intended effect, and he had not bothered her much after they wed.

Since she became ill, he had not tried to bed her at all, so she was able to stop taking the herbs. She stopped giving him herbs as well. She knew he would be bedding the wenches from the village, but she did not care. Let them have his brats.

Vorik had often voiced his disappointment in Serina, because she still had not given him an heir. He complained bitterly about his lot in life, and that he could not pass on all he had managed to acquire to a son. During his rantings, Serina would secretly smile to herself, knowing the herbs had worked.

Chanity noticed Vorik behavior as well. He had been going to the village to visit the wenches, but then began bringing them to the master chamber. Sometimes they stayed the night, and sometimes he made them leave, but he never treated them well, or cared for any of them. Chanity thought him heartless. How could he ever love anyone?

14

Four months after Serina fell ill; Chanity took on almost all the responsibilities of running the great hall, as well as seeing to her mother's care. Holdenworth Manor was the largest farmstead in the region, and it demanded much of her time and attention. Alma helped as much as she could, particularly when Chanity had to stay with her mother. Marla was of no help at all, unless she was ordered by Vorik, which was not very often.

Marla did enjoy giving orders, and had once struck a serf for not obeying her command quickly enough. She knew to never make that mistake again, and the memory of Serina punishing her was still fresh in her mind. Sick or not, she knew she would have Serina's wrath to deal with. Marla may have been the image of her mother, but at times her manner was more like her father.

By the tenth month of Serina's illness, she was skin and bones. She coughed constantly, and her breathing had become very labored. Nothing Etta gave her seemed to help.

One night before bedtime Etta met with Chanity, and told her she had done all she knew to do, but the herbs were not helping. Chanity felt much sorrow in her heart, knowing her mother would not be with her much longer. She could not imagine her life without her mother.

It was no surprise to Chanity, when she awoke the next morn to discover her mother had breathed her last during the night. She fell to her knees and wept like a babe. Chanity cried until there were no more tears left for her to shed. How she could go on without her mother, Chanity wondered silently to herself. When both her parents were alive, this place had been her home, but it seemed foreign to her now.

When she had turned eight, Chanity was promised to Simon, a neighboring Chieftain's son. Their parents had been good friends for years, and lived in a neighboring village close to Holdenworth. Simon was two years older than she. They were friends, but had not really spent much time together. The year before Vorik's raid, Chanity's family received word that Simon had succumbed to the fever that had taken so many of Holdenworth's people. Now Chanity felt devastated. She had no future, and nowhere to go. She felt truly trapped at that moment.

How she wished Gerald had come home. She used to dream he would return and avenge their father's death by slaying Vorik. Since he had not returned, Chanity and Serina assumed he was slain in battle, or had succumbed to some illness. He had left about a year before the raid, and in years following there had been no word from him.

Charity sat in a chair by her mother's bedside, and held her mother's hand, while looking at her lovely face. She did not know how she was going to get through the days without her loving mother. She couldn't dwell on her own loss at the moment, even though her heart felt like it was breaking. She needed to be strong, and see that her mother received a proper burial. She knew Vorik did not believe the way they did, and would not care if her mother's grave was blessed or not. Chanity took one last look at her mother, and the only thing that kept her going was knowing at least she was at peace now.

Chanity went down to the great hall and told everyone that Serina was no longer with them. She sent for the Priest to bless her mother's grave. Alma, Etta and Chanity saw to preparing the body for burial. Afterward, Chanity returned to her chamber to be alone in her sorrow. Alma brought Chanity's meals up so she could have the privacy she needed to mourn her mother's passing.

Before Serina passed, Alma promised her that she would watch over Chanity. Even though Alma was a servant, Serina had thought of her like family, and Chanity felt the same way.

The next morning, Chanity went into the great hall and found the priest had already arrived. She was relieved that he arrived so quickly, since he sometimes traveled to other villages. Some of the villages were three days' ride away. Occasionally he stayed a week or two, before returning to their village.

On the day of the burial, they were blessed with a glorious sunny day. The color of the sky reminded Chanity of her mother's beautiful blue eyes. It hurt knowing she would never again gaze into those eyes, see her brilliant smile, or hear her laughter, at least not in this life.

Everyone she loved was gone now. First, her brother Gerald, then her father, and now her mother. She had liked Simon, but had no real love for him. Chanity had only seen him a few times while growing up. She knew one day they were to be wed, but did not really know him that well. Chanity did not mourn much after his death.

Their parents had made plans for Simon and Chanity to spend time together so they could get to know each other. This was to take place the year before they were to wed, but that time never came. Simon was only ten and three when the fever took him.

As a child, she daydreamed about being wed and having children, but never really imagined Simon as her husband. Chanity wished he was here now, so she would at least have hope of a future. She wanted to run as far as she could and never look back, but now there was nowhere to run. She had never felt this hopeless before. The Priest began the ceremony, startling her out of her thoughts and back to the moment at hand.

After the burial, Chanity felt more exhausted than she ever had before. She returned to her bed chamber at once, not wishing to be around anyone. Alma brought Chanity her meals and checked to see how she was doing, just as she had the day before. Chanity tried not to show her grief, but was sure her swollen eyes and face gave it away.

When Alma left, Chanity lay back down on her bed and stayed there the rest of the day. She cried again until she had no more tears left to cry. It was late that night when she finally went to sleep, but it was not a peaceful sleep. Her dreams were not good ones, so she tossed and turned through the night.

The next morn, Chanity went down to the great hall and worked harder than ever. She began before the sun rose, and did not stop till long after dark. The only way she could sleep, and not think about all she had lost was to work to the point of exhaustion. Chanity continued the grueling routine for nearly two months until her grief finally eased, and she was able to cope with all she had lost. She finally let up on herself, and stopped working so hard. Soon she began sleeping through the night, and her nightmares began to fade.

Chapter 3

The next month went by smoothly. Chanity continued sleeping and eating better. She even gained the weight back she lost after Serina's passing.

One morning, Chanity glanced at the mirror as she was getting dressed. All her gowns were getting too tight in the bosom. Her body was filling out and she was getting curves in places she did not have them before.

Chanity looked across the room to the chest that she and Alma had packed some of her mother's belongings in. Tears came again as she thought of her mother. She stepped over to the chest, and lifted out one of her mother's gunnas. She pictured her mother wearing it, and smiled through the tears. She could almost hear her mother say, "Come now, Chanity, 'tis time to get dressed, and start your day."

It was hard at first, but after she put the gunna on, it made her feel closer to her mother. It felt as if her mother's love wrapped around her. She could not believe it was a perfect fit! When did she grow up? In that moment, the realization struck her that she was no longer a child.

With her mother's gunna on, she glanced again at the mirror. She had always resembled her mother, but she could not believe how much she looked like her now. She had her mother's pale blonde hair as well as her delicate feminine face. The only feature she had of her father was his emerald green eyes. Her pale blonde hair enhanced the green of her eyes, making them shine a little brighter as the two colors complimented each other.

A few days later, she noticed Vorik watching her in the great hall while she helped serve the meals. She hoped Vorik and his men would not notice the changes in her body, but realized she should have known better than that. She tried to avoid looking in his direction, but when she did; his eyes were always upon her. It made her uncomfortable the way he openly stared at her body. She had always loathed him, but now her revulsion reached new heights.

Chanity decided to take care, and make sure she was never alone with him. She hated Vorik more than anyone she had ever known. Her family's belief was that you had to forgive to be forgiven. Perhaps after his death she could forgive him, but what of her soul if she died first? She decided to talk to the priest about this on his next visit.

Chanity helped Alma clear away the remnants of their meal until Alma finally insisted she retire for the evening. "You have done much more than your share, lass," Alma chided. "Besides the only thing left to do is for me to take the scraps out to the hounds."

"But I don't mind helping," said Chanity, smiling.

"I see what you're up to, lass! You'll feed them the scraps yourself to win their affection away from me," Alma replied laughing.

"We both know they favor you far too much for a few scraps to change their mind," Chanity replied. "I guess I should get to bed, for sunrise comes early. "Thank you again, for all you did for my mother, and for me."

"It was my pleasure lass," Alma replied. "Now off to bed, with you! You look exhausted!"

Alma picked up the scraps and went outside. The hounds were eager for their meal, and raised a mighty racket as Chanity turned and made her way to her bed chamber.

Chanity was nearly to her door, when Vorik suddenly stepped out of hiding and grabbed her. He must have been watching and waiting from his own bed chamber across the hall. Vorik grabbed a great handful of her hair, and twisted her head toward him in an attempt to kiss her.

As Vorik's face neared hers, Chanity could see the lust raging in his eyes, and pulled away. She felt Vorik's other hand groping toward her breasts. With a surge of strength, Chanity pushed away from him with all her might, freeing herself from his grasp for a moment.

Vorik looked her up and down. "I see my little stepdaughter is all grown up and no longer a child. Maybe you can give me the heir I want since your mother failed to do so," Vorik said as he lunged forward, pinning her against the wall.

Chanity struggled with all her might to escape, but it was in vain. She was still struggling as Marla came up the stairs.

Vorik looked back to see who stood behind him on the stairs, and saw Marla with a flickering candle in her hand, and an angry look on her face. He stepped back from Chanity, but still held one of her wrists firmly in his grip. He glared at Marla for interrupting his attack, but her eyes were locked on Chanity.

"Now that your mother is buried, I see you wasted no time trying to get my father in your bed," Marla said with disgust. "Did your mother mean so little to you? You are desperately trying to marry my father like your mother did, so you can be Lady of Holdenworth."

"You know better than that," Chanity said angrily. "My mother was Lady here before he ever came. She was a Lady, and you best remember that when you speak of her, Marla. She only wed to protect me, and Vorik knows this to be the truth. Now unhand me, Vorik" she said with a demanding voice.

To Chanity's relief and complete surprise, Vorik released her. She went swiftly to her chamber, and barred the door. But not before she heard Vorik angrily tell Marla she better not ever interfere, or interrupt him again.

Later that night, Chanity heard her door rattle, but Vorik gave up when he realized it was barred. A little while later, she heard a young serf laugh as she entered Vorik's chamber. From the sound of her voice, it was one of the serfs that Vorik bedded while her mother was sharing her room. It certainly had not bothered her mother though. She was relieved to be away from him.

When she awoke the next day, Chanity knew she had to get away to think. She could not stay there much longer and remain a maiden, for Vorik was sure to defile her. She must conceive a plan to escape, and find a place she could go. With Vorik as Chieftain, he could do anything, or have anyone he wanted, so she no choice but to leave Holdenworth.

She had not been to her favorite spot at the cliff in a long while, but needed to go there now. It had always been a place where she could go to think, dream of the future, or just escape for some solitude. Chanity moved carefully so as not to be seen, and quietly slipped away from the great hall.

The cliff was a short distance from Holdenworth manor. Chanity could easily walk there without becoming overly tired. It was nestled in trees and boulders, making it virtually invisible from any vantage point. The cliff protruded a good distance over the sea. There was no beach below, only the pounding waves and surf.

The ledge was high above the water, and gave Chanity a wonderful view of the sea. Beaches were visible on each side of the cliff during low tide, but they were a great distance away. From the cliff height they looked close, but to walk there took a good deal of time.

The top of the cliff was not her favorite spot. There was actually another ledge beneath that one. The second ledge could not be seen, except from the sea. Even from the sea it was scarcely noticeable because of the overgrowth. Trees, vines and bushes had found their place, growing around and down the ledge, hiding a small cave from sight. The only way to get to the lower ledge was to hold on to trees and bushes while climbing down a small narrow path. The path was overgrown, so unless someone knew it was there, they would never find it.

Her brother found the lower ledge while playing one day. He went to the cliff with a new wooden toy their father had carved for his seventh birthday. He played for a while, but then to his dismay he accidently dropped the toy over the edge. He thought it was lost forever, but was delighted when he peered over the side and saw it nestled below. When Gerald carefully climbed down the path to retrieve his toy, he saw a cozy secluded ledge just under the cliff! It was a boy's dream come true, and he kept the place a secret for a long while.

When Chanity turned seven, she was even more adventurous than Gerald, and would follow him everywhere. Gerald was careful to keep the ledge a secret, but Chanity's curiosity got the better of him. She secretly followed him one day and discovered the hideaway. It became their favorite spot.

Chanity enjoyed the ledge even more than Gerald. Everyone at Holdenworth had chores to do, even the daughter of a Lord, but after her chores were done, she would slip away to the ledge and stay most of the day. Her brother would get bored after a while, and she would have the ledge all to herself. She pretended the cave was her home, though it was only the size of a room. Outside the opening was a large flat rock that was big enough for a grown person to lie down on.

Having escaped the manor, Chanity reached her favorite spot and lay down on that very rock. When she was younger, she would gaze up at the sky and try to see images in the shapes of the clouds. Sometimes she would daydream of the future, and wonder how many children she would have when she grew up, but most of all she enjoyed just sitting and looking out to sea.

Chanity wished this were just a carefree day, like when she and her brother were young. Unfortunately, she had serious problems to think about. Somehow, she had to leave Holdenworth, but did not know where to go. The only people she knew outside of her village were Simon's family. Perhaps they would take her in, since she had been betrothed to Simon. That seemed to be her only hope, but she worried their village had been raided as well.

She decided to wait until evening, just before sup. That should give her plenty of time to slip away. She prayed Vorik would not come searching for her. Whatever her choice, she could not go to her chamber this night, for Vorik would surely be lying in wait.

For a moment, Chanity thought to ask one of the servants to stay in her chamber and bolt the door. Vorik would think she was still in her chamber, and that might give her more time to make her escape. But if Vorik broke through the door, he would surely punish the servant, so she dared not risk that.

Chanity made her plan, and carefully thought through what she must do. The first thing she had to do was pack her belongings, and food and drink for the journey. She would place as many of her clothes as she could in a cloth sack along with some provisions. Next, she had to prepare her horse. Lily should be saddled and tied at the back of the stable, ready at a moment's notice when the time came.

If the guards questioned her, she would tell them that she was taking garments she could no longer wear to the needy in the village. She did not like to lie, but was desperate to get away, and didn't see that she had much choice.

Chapter 4

With her escape plan complete, Chanity climbed back to the upper ledge and began walking back to the Manor. She was still a good distance away when Vorik stepped out from the trees. Chanity stopped, frozen in place on the path. Vorik dropped his mail hauberk to the ground and thrust his sword beside it. He began advancing on her, with lust blazing in his eyes.

Chanity backed away, but before she could run, Vorik leapt upon her and knocked her to the ground. "Unhand me Vorik" Chanity ordered, but it did not work this time.

"You are not getting away from me again, wench" Vorik said with assurance. He pinned her with his weight, grabbed her gunna, and pulled it up over her waist. Chanity struggled to pull her gunna back down, but Vorik ripped her under garments off. He held her down with one arm, and pushed his breeches down with the other, exposing his manhood.

Chanity fought him with all her strength, but to no avail. As Vorik was about to enter her, she heard a mighty battle cry, like she had never heard before. Suddenly, Vorik was jerked from her and tossed a few feet away.

She looked up to see a mighty warrior, ready to kill. As he looked down at her, his facial expression changed from rage to desire. He gazed down at her, and looked her all over from head to toe, lingering on her womanhood.

Chanity suddenly remembered her predicament, and jerked the gunna down to cover herself. It was far too late though, for the warrior had already seen her unclothed from the waist down. Embarrassment took the place of fright, and she felt her cheeks burning.

Vorik was stunned by the warrior's sudden attack, and realized his mistake at dropping his sword so far away. His eyes flicked past the warrior to where his sword protruded from the ground. The warrior could have killed him instantly, Vorik thought to himself. What was his purpose in waiting?

The warrior saw Vorik look toward his sword. Finally, the warrior broke the silence. "Vorik, do not worry, I am no coward like you. I will defeat you in honor. I want you to realize, as your life blood is seeping from you, that my family has been avenged. My uncle was Marta's father, who you left grieving after slaughtering both his sons. Then you took his daughter away, the only child they had left."

"What kind of heartless beast are you?" Derek asked while looking at him disgustedly. The lads were not even old enough to defend themselves properly. You proved yourself a coward, sneaking in to attack while their parents were away. I have searched for you since I was old enough to avenge them. Now you will pay for my family's grief. Get up, retrieve your sword, and prepare to die, Vorik. Your time here is over."

Vorik rose, and pulled his sword from the ground as he turned to face his challenger. "You make many a proudful boast, but we shall see if your skill with the sword matches that of your tongue," he declared, as the two began circling each other.

"Tis no boast, but a simple fact that I shall avenge myself upon you." The warrior stopped circling, closed the distance between them, and with a clash of steel on steel, the battle began.

With Vorik occupied, Chanity realized this was the perfect opportunity to escape, but could not take her eyes from the battle. She wanted vengeance for her father's death, and wanted Vorik to pay for making her mother's life miserable as well. She wanted to see him suffer for all the pain he had caused her family. If this warrior could somehow slay Vorik, perhaps she could get over the anger she still felt deep inside her heart.

Vorik tried all of his tricks in the battle; clever feints, followed by furious attacks. He sometimes even appeared to drop his guard to lure his opponent in, but the warrior countered every move. It was becoming clear to Vorik that this warrior was not only very skilled, but also quite clever.

Chanity watched as the warrior moved with assurance and power as he stepped in to attack. She had never seen anyone battle with such incredible strength and speed. The warrior was taller, more muscular and leaner in the waist than Vorik. He also appeared much younger in years.

The sound of the battle echoed all around, and the warrior's men began to gather in. Vorik's men emerged into the clearing as well, and both joined in battle. Soon the clearing was full of warriors, except this time Vorik and his men were the ones outnumbered.

Vorik knew he was no match for the Norman warrior, and now was tiring fast. He should already be dead, but the warrior was toying with him like a cat playing with a mouse before going in for the kill. The warrior was keeping him alive, punishing him so he would have to struggle for his life. Vorik ached all over from countering the warrior's massive blows. He was also bleeding heavily from several cuts he received. The warrior seemed to enjoy watching him suffer, as he added more and more to his pain.

Finally, Vorik fell to his knees, and the warrior cried, "this is for my uncle, his wife, and their children" as he drove his sword through Vorik's heart.

Chanity watched Vorik's lifeless body fall to the ground. He lay on the cool earth, his life's blood seeping into the ground, just as her father's had done. Relief washed over Chanity at that moment, as she fell to her knees. After four years of loathing and tolerating Vorik, he was finally gone from her life forever.

The warrior left Vorik's body on the ground and turned to battle Vorik's men, but not before he spied Chanity and saw that she was alright. He didn't have time to go to her, for there was another of Vorik's men advancing to attack. He dispatched the attacker quickly, and saw the battle was coming to an end.

The warrior and his men had won the battle, with hardly any losses. What few of Vorik's men were left had been severely wounded.

The warrior gave orders to seek out Holdenworth's holding cells, to lock Vorik's men up, and to see to the wounded, after his own men were seen to.

The warrior glanced down at Chanity, and noticed how pale she had become. As he reached to help her up, her hand trembled in his. "Are you alright, wench?" he asked.

"Aye, but don't call me wench," Chanity said a little harsher than she meant to. As he helped her up, she began to smooth out her wrinkled gunna, and brush the dirt and grass from it.

In a softer tone, she said "My name is Chanity, Chanity of Holdenworth. My father was Lord Belgar, who was Chieftain here, before that beast Vorik took his life. I am glad you slew him, for he deserved to die. I have dreamed of this moment for over four years now. I feel my father has finally been avenged."

"Then you may thank me now, Lady Chanity."

"What is your name Sir Warrior, or should I have said, Sir Knight?"

Derek laughed at that, taking some of the seriousness from his face. "Some of my men call me Sir Derek, while some just call me Dragon. My name is Sir Derek, though I should say Lord Derek of Holdenworth now."

"Then I thank you, Lord Derek." Suddenly, she realized he was now Lord of Holdenworth, her home. She was now his slave, but she had rather be a slave, than to have Vorik as their Chieftain. She also realized she should be afraid of this man, but for some reason she wasn't. Strange as it was, she felt safe with him, or maybe she only felt safe since Vorik was no longer living. But exactly what would this new Lord be expecting of her?

He had an image of a fierce dragon on his shield. The dragon was a fiery red, with bright green eyes nearly the same color as Lord Derek's. She had to admit he had the most amazing green eyes she had ever seen. They were not emerald green like her own, but a lighter green that almost had a glow to them. His skin was tanned by the sun, which made his light green eyes stand out even more. His tawny hair was thick, sun-streaked and hung down just past his shoulder. It was wavy at the end, even though it was tied back with a leather cord. A strand of hair had come loose during the battle. Chanity had a strong urge to smooth it back with her fingers, but knew better than to act on it.

Now that she had a closer look at him, she thought he was the most handsome man she had ever seen. She felt nervous, and self-conscious of how she must look. It was the first time in a long time that she had cared about her appearance. Usually, she tried to look disheveled so Vorik and his men would not take much notice of her.

Derek was taken aback himself, and did not know what to think of this brave and beautiful enchantress. She was the most enchanting woman he had ever met. She had spirit for sure, and certainly spoke her mind when he called her wench. She didn't even run away when the battle began. Chanity must have wanted to see her father's death avenged. Some might think that foolish, but Derek though it brave.

He had never seen a woman stay and watch a battle before. When combat began, they ran away in fear. His men knew not to harm a lady, but what if it had been someone else who had raided? She might have been taken on the spot or slain.

As they stood there, he took a long look at Chanity, taking in every detail. He noticed that her eyes were a darker green than his, but her hair enhanced her eye color, making them shine bright. Her hair was pale blond that reached down to her waist.

From the first moment he saw her, he thought she was beautiful. He remembered how she had looked as she lay on the ground with her hair flowing freely around her. She had looked like a true enchantress lying beneath him.

His memory went back to that moment, remembering her unclothed from the waist down. It was clear she was more than just a lass, she was a very well-formed young woman. He could picture her shapely legs going up to her womanhood. The sight of her had excited him to the point he had to cover himself with his shield so as not to frighten her.

He hoped she was still an innocent, but didn't think that possible with Vorik and his reputation with young wenches. Marta was proof of that. At least he saw she was not going to let Vorik take her willingly. That spoke something of her morals.

Chanity noticed Derek was deep in thought, then blushed when she considered what he might be remembering. She knew the look of wanting on a man's face. She had seen it many times on Vorik and his men. Vorik warned his men with death if they ever dared to touch her. Her mother had even wed Vorik to prevent that. Vorik's men feared him and knew to follow his orders.

"What brings you to Holdenworth, Lord Derek?" Chanity asked.

"I came to slay Vorik to avenge my uncle and his wife. He slew their two sons, and took their only daughter Marta, leaving them childless. I was told he had raided and claimed Holdenworth, so I came to take it from him. As a second son, I must obtain my own lands. I heard Holdenworth was the largest farmstead in the region, with the richest crop lands. I sought King William's permission to take Holdenworth from Vorik, and came as soon as he granted it," Derek explained.

"Do you fight under King William's banner?" Chanity asked.

"I do not fight in battle as much anymore, but still go to King William when I am needed," Derek said. "I mostly help him plan battle strategy now. King William did not mind me settling down, because he felt he owed me for saving his life. This endeared me to him, and he trusts me completely."

"How did you save his life?" Chanity asked.

"In the heat of battle, one of William's guard was slain. An adversary saw an opening, and suddenly attacked William. I had no time to parry, so I threw myself in front of William and took a sword to my side," Derek explained. "T'was a deep wound, and went across my whole side. Infection set up in the wound, and I nearly succumbed to the fever. While my wound was healing, I helped King William plan battle strategy. William was pleased that I had a natural skill for it. Several months passed before I regained my strength enough to return to battle. Since I recouped, I have not been bested while training in the list."

"How long have you served King William?" Chanity asked.

"I served him for eight years, from the time I was ten and six till now. He was Duke of Normandy when I first joined him, before being crowned King of England," Derek answered.

"So King William granted you Holdenworth for the life-debt?" Chanity asked.

"The life-debt is but one reason why William sent me to take Holdenworth from Vorik. William knew Vorik could not be trusted. He placed a spy amongst Vorik's men. The spy informed William that Vorik withheld bounty and coin from his raids. Also, William wanted more loyal followers on English soil, now that he has taken his rightful place as King of England." Derek replied.

"I knew Duke William had been crowned King of England, but why was he not crowned after King Edward's death?"

"Word must be slow to reach Holdenworth. I am surprised you have not heard of what transpired," Derek exclaimed.

"I never sat at the Lord's table when Vorik was alive. I tried to avoid him and his leering men, so I didn't hear much word from beyond our borders," Chanity explained.

"William was illegitimate, so his cousin Edward claimed to be the rightful king. To make peace with Duke William, it was rumored that King Edward promised he would make him his heir, since he was childless. This seemed to settle things between them. Duke William still had other responsibilities to see to in Normandy and France at the time. But when King Edward died, Harold Godwinson was appointed as the successor instead of William. Duke William contested the throne, and defeated Godwinson at the Battle of Hastings. That is where I took the sword that was meant for William. Godwinson was killed in that battle and Duke William was crowned King the following December on Christmas day."

"Thank you, Lord Derek, that explains much," Chanity said.

"Now that you have heard my story, perhaps you could tell me if any of Vorik's house still live," Derek asked.

"I heard that his wife Marta died while giving birth. I did not know she had been taken unwillingly by Vorik until now. Two months after Vorik wed my mother, he brought his daughter Marla here. She was ten and one year at the time, and has been here for four years. Vorik never spoke of Marla's mother or uncles. I learned what little I know from Marla herself.

"So, Marta's babe lived then, a daughter, who is here at Holdenworth?" Derek asked.

"Aye, she lived, and is here," replied Chanity.

"Our family heard rumors she died while trying to birth her babe, so we assumed the babe had died also. My aunt and uncle will be happy to hear they have a living granddaughter. They have been sad and alone for these past ten and six years. I will send word to them that she is here with me. I cannot take Marla to her grandparents now, for 'tis my responsibility to see to the harvest and get Holdenworth ready for winter. By the time we finish, the water will be too icy to take her to Normandy," Derek said.

Derek could not believe he had been standing speaking to this lass for such a long time. He felt like he could stay and talk with her all day, but needed to see to his men after the battle.

As he looked around, it seemed as though they had taken care of things without him. He had never just forgotten what he was doing or what was going on around him while speaking with a lass before. Chanity was truly mesmerizing; he could get lost in those eyes of hers.

What was wrong with him? Derek thought to himself. Why had he let this young lass enchant him so? He was a warrior, not some wet behind the ears lad. Why was he being so nice to her? Most raiders would have just taken her, and done to her what he had rescued her from.

Even though he would like to throw her over his shoulder, and head for the master chamber, it would have to be with her approval. From what he saw of her encounter with Vorik, she did not give her approval easily. Her fighting spirit didn't keep him from wanting her though. He had wanted her since the first moment he laid eyes on her while she lay half unclothed on the ground.

He didn't have to take a woman by force, for there were many willing ones. Long ago, he gave strict orders to his men that they were to never force a woman while under his command. He could not control what they did on their own, but he could while they were with him. He knew most of his men were good men and felt the way he did. They were warriors, not pillagers.

For some reason Chanity didn't want to leave this man. She felt safe with him. Maybe it was because of his great size and strength, or maybe because he had just slain Vorik. However, her duties were waiting, so at last she turned to make her way to the great hall.

"You and your men must be hungry after a long journey and battling Vorik and his men," Chanity said. "I will see that Cook starts preparing the sup. Knowing her, she has already begun."

She walked to the Manor, and upon reaching the door, she turned back to give Lord Derek a smile. He was still watching, which pleased her greatly.

Chanity gathered everyone in the kitchen to tell them what had transpired outside. She told them of Vorik's death, and that Sir Derek was their new Lord. She gave an estimate of how many warriors were with Lord Derek to Cook, so she would know how many to prepare food for. After getting things settled in the kitchen, she went in search of Marla. Chanity was not fond of Marla, but she should be told gently of her father's death.

Chanity found Marla in the hall, and told her that Vorik had fought hard, and died an honorable death in battle. Marla sat stoically as Chanity gave her the news. She did not shed a tear or show any emotion. Finally, she rose, lifted her chin and headed up the stairs without saying a single word. Chanity never got a chance to tell her about her grandparents. Perhaps it would be best if Lord Derek told her about them.

Cook did not have much time to get a meal prepared for that many men, but meat was already roasting, so she decided to put it in a stew to make it go further. Alma and Elspeth helped chop vegetables and added them to a pot simmering over the fire.

Soon the stew was done. Cook was pleased with the hearty flavor of the meaty vegetable stew, especially since it was prepared on such short notice. It was served along with stewed apples, sliced cheese, and fresh baked flatbread, smoothed with butter and honey. Cook was good at seasoning foods, and knew just what to add to make a tasty meal. She made sure Holdenworth was well stocked with herbs and spices, as well as wine, mead and ale.

Derek entered the hall and took a seat in his rightful place in the beautifully carved Chieftain's chair at the head of the Lord's Table. His men followed soon after and sat in their usual order. Bram was second in command and the most trusted of all the men, so he sat on the bench to Derek's right. Ortaire was third in command, and sat beside Bram. Derek trusted Ortaire and Bram equally, but Bram was the more serious of the two. The three of them talked and carried on like brothers as they sat at the table.

In short order the meal was served, and the men dug in with a hearty appetite.

As they ate, Chanity was surprised to see Marla come down the stairs smiling, as if nothing had ever happened. Amazingly, she fetched her meal and sat down right beside Lord Derek. Several men had to slide down the left bench to make room for her.

All the tables had a long bench on each side, and there were several tables where Marla could have sat down. Chanity was amazed that Marla had such gall to sit with the new Lord without his permission. She had not even been informed he was a relation to her yet.

During the meal, Marla kept laughing and batting her eyes at Derek, outwardly flirting with him. Derek was clearly uncomfortable with her attention. Finally, he was able to tell Marla they were related, and that her grandparents still lived.

Chanity busied herself helping Alma, Anna and Elspeth serve food and drinks. It seemed they were constantly working to refill mugs with wine, ale or mead. This allowed her to overhear much of the conversation with Marla.

Chanity approached the main table with a fresh pitcher of mead to fill Derek's mug. Marla was merrily chatting away, but as Chanity drew near, Derek lifted his hand to silence her for a moment. Chanity reached for the mug, but Derek caught her hand in his. "Chanity, you have been working too hard. Everyone has had their fill. You have served us well, but you should sit and take your meal," Derek said, releasing her hand.

"Thank you, my Lord," Chanity said, then went to fetch a bowl of stew. Elspeth stopped to sup as well, so Chanity sat down beside her at her table.

Marla resumed her banter, but Derek held up his hand to silence her a second time. As Alma walked by, Lord Derek stopped her. "Tell Lady Chanity I wish for her to sit with me," Lord Derek ordered.

"Aye, my Lord," Alma said, and went to do his bidding.

Lord Derek rose as Chanity approached, and held out his hand to where Marla was sitting. "Slide down, Marla," Derek commanded. "I have a great deal to discuss with Lady Chanity, and the hour is getting late." Chanity glanced at Marla and saw the rage seething in her eyes as she slid down to make way.

"The food is delicious, and plentiful, considering the short amount of time there was to prepare it," remarked Derek.

"My thanks," Lord Derek. We will prepare a feast for you tomorrow night, to welcome you as our new Lord. My apologies, but there was not enough time for Cook to prepare it this evening."

"My thanks to you, Lady Chanity. 'Tis very kind of everyone to go to such trouble to welcome me. I will send some of my men out hunting for fresh meat at first light on the morrow," Derek replied.

Derek was more than a little surprised at the warm welcome he received at Holdenworth. Vorik must have been reprehensible as Lord here. Most raiders were hated, not welcomed. No one, not even Vorik's own daughter seemed upset about his death.

"Who has been overseeing the great hall?" Derek inquired.

"I have, and my mother before me," Chanity replied. "I took over during her illness, and it has been three months since she succumbed to it."

The sorrow in her voice and the sadness in her eyes were clear to Derek. It was obvious Chanity was still grieving over the loss of her mother. He wondered if she even stopped working long enough to let herself truly mourn her mother's passing.

They sat in silence for a moment, as Derek looked around the great hall. It was the cleanest great hall he had seen since leaving his parent's home. It had a nice smell from the fresh rushes on the floor, and there were no dust or cobwebs anywhere. He also noticed there were no hounds inside, which his own mother had strictly forbidden as well.

"You have done an excellent job of taking care of the place, Chanity," Derek remarked.

Marla made a gruff snorting sound, stood up at once, and left without a word.

Derek was puzzled at Marla's sudden departure. She was in such a good mood when she first sat down. Perhaps she was having a tough time dealing with the loss of her father. He hoped she was a kind person for her grandparent's sake. They had been through so much the past few years.

Derek was just turning back to talk with Chanity, only to see her getting up as well.

"I regret I cannot stay to speak with you, Lord Derek, but I must prepare for the morrow," Chanity said as she excused herself.

"I suppose I should as well when I'm through speaking with Bram and Ortaire," Derek agreed regretfully. "Fortunately, we will have plenty of time to speak later."

"I look forward to it, Lord Derek," Chanity replied, with a smile as she headed toward the stairs.

Chapter 5

Before going to her bedchamber Chanity stopped by the master chamber to make sure Anna had prepared it for Lord Derek. She looked around the room and saw that everything was in order. As she turned to leave, Chanity was startled as Derek entered the room.

Derek saw the embarrassment on her face, and it was clear that she was nervous at his presence so close to her. "Chanity, you do not have to be afraid of me," Derek said soothingly. "'Tis not my way to force an unwilling lass to my bed." He put the palm of his hand on her face to gently caress her cheek. "I can imagine what you have been through with Vorik and his men. You are safe with me, as well as with my men."

"I was not harmed by Vorik or his men," Chanity replied. "Vorik guaranteed my safety, on the condition that my mother agreed to wed him. He kept his word until last night. He caught me as I went to my chamber, but Marla interrupted his attack."

"Today I went to the cliff to think, and devise a plan to escape. I decided to escape this very night and was returning home when Vorik took me by surprise. He grabbed me, and forced me to the ground. I was so thankful when you threw him off me. You stood there like a tale from a fable, where the knight in shining armor rescues the damsel in distress. Though at the time, it was more nightmare than fairy tale. Thank you again, for what you did," Chanity said, sincerely.

Derek gently stroked her hair as she spoke. It felt so soft in his rough hands. It came as a great relief that she had never been with a man. He gazed down into her beautiful eyes and then rubbed his thumb softly across her bottom lip.

Chanity closed her eyes and enjoyed the sensation he was causing. Suddenly, he drew her into his strong arms and kissed her. His kisses were soft, and feather light. She felt so safe in his warm embrace. She had never been kissed by a man, but with him it seemed so natural somehow. His tongue traced her lips, before he nibbled on her bottom lip lightly with his teeth. He kissed her again, but much longer and deeper this time. Chanity felt sensations in her lower body that she never experienced before. She knew she should break this spell and go to her bedchamber, but she did not want to leave.

Derek felt the heat of his passion stirring. He knew he should stop this before he went too far and then could not stop. He had never felt so enchanted by anyone before. She was beautiful, kind, and easy to talk with. He could get lost in those green eyes of hers. When she looked into his eyes, it was as if their souls were connecting. She was an enchantress, who had him spellbound.

"Perhaps you should go to your chamber before this goes any further," Derek said. "Thus far we have done nothing amiss, though I must admit, I enjoyed it very much. I wonder if you enjoyed it as much as I."

"Aye, I did enjoy it," Chanity replied, a little reluctantly from embarrassment. "I have never been kissed by a man before," she admitted. "Vorik tried to kiss me but I turned my head and refused to allow it. I really must go to my chamber now, Lord Derek. I bid you good night."

"I bid you good night as well, Lady Chanity," Derek said, as he gently kissed her forehead.

They smiled warmly at each other, then Chanity pulled away from his embrace. She felt almost light headed from their kissing as she walked to her chamber.

Chanity closed her door, prepared for bed and curled up in the covers. The day had been a whirlwind of activity. First, she planned to escape, was attacked by Vorik, then heroically rescued by Lord Derek. Now it seemed she could think of nothing else, except what had just happened with Lord Derek.

She had been so affected by him and his kisses. Chanity wondered what went through Derek's mind when he found her in his bedchamber. What must he think of her, since she let him kiss her and offered up no resistance? Should she have stopped him, she wondered? She knew if she could go back to that moment, she still would not have stopped him.

She had truly enjoyed his kisses, and being held in his strong arms. It was the first time she had felt safe in years. The sensations she experienced while Derek kissed her were amazing. She enjoyed the sensations, but they alarmed her at the same time.

Her mother had explained a lot to her about what took place between a man and woman. After Serina first became ill, she sat Chanity down and spoke with her about it. Chanity was grateful for her mother's foresight. However, her mother did not tell her about the sensations Lord Derek caused her to feel. She hoped that was normal. Chanity finally drifted off to sleep, remembering how she felt with Derek's arms wrapped around her.

Not far away, in the master chamber, Derek tossed and turned on his bed. He could not go to sleep for thinking about Chanity. He tried not to think of her womanly body on the ground the first time he saw her. He would never forget how beautiful she looked lying there, even in her unkempt state. He could not blame Vorik for wanting her, except that she was his step daughter and Vorik had promised to protect her.

As Derek thought of what Vorik had tried to do, he wanted to slay him all over again. This lass had only been in his life one day, yet he felt as though he had known her a lifetime. What was it about her that affected him so? Derek went to sleep thinking of her, and she was his first thought when he awoke.

Chanity awoke the next morn from a bad dream. In the dream Derek kissed her and held her tightly, but when she opened her eyes it was Vorik! Instead of feeling secure in Derek's arms, she was trapped in Vorik's. She woke herself struggling to get out of his embrace. She kept telling herself it was just a dream, and laid back on her bed relieved. Vorik could never harm her again, thanks to Lord Derek.

Thinking of Derek caused Chanity to take extra care dressing that morning. Usually she pulled her hair back with a leather cord and put on her mother's oldest work gunna. Today she put on her mother's nicest wool gunna and brushed her long hair. She braided the front strands and pulled the braids to the back leaving the rest of her hair down.

For years Chanity dreaded leaving her chamber. Now, she felt like a bird freed from its cage. Chanity opened her door, and went down the stairs with a smile on her face, and an unburdened heart.

The hall was bustling with activity that morning as the servants prepared food for the men to break their fast. Chanity helped place the meals on trenchers and take them out to the men. She needed to speak with Lord Derek about what her duty was, now that he was the Lord of Holdenworth Manor. She looked up to see Derek walk in the front door, and realized he had been up even before her.

Derek took his seat at the Lord's table, and looked around to see Chanity disappear into the kitchen. She returned with a trencher of ham, eggs, and hot bread with butter and honey. As Chanity placed the food before Lord Derek, Marla came rushing up, sat down beside him, and began chattering away. Apparently the discussion about her duties would have to wait until another time.

Chanity fell into the task of serving the meal, going from table to table, and back and forth from the kitchen. After everyone had a trencher, she started refilling mugs.

Derek stopped her as she passed by the Lord's table, and bade her to stop and break her fast. Chanity fetched a trencher of food, and sat down at a table nearby. Derek rose from his seat and asked her to sit with him. This time Marla slid down the bench without being commanded, but her displeasure was clear as she moved over to make room.

"I want you to join me at every meal, Chanity," Derek said as he sat down. "I enjoy your company and our conversations."

"But she is a mere servant, and should be serving us, instead of sitting," Marla complained. "Besides, she has no right to this table, since her mother and father are no more. I have the right because I am your relative by blood."

Derek's face flushed with anger at Marla's words. He stood at once, and a silence fell across the hall.

"I am Lord here; I will say who is a servant and who is not. Chanity's parents were Lord and Lady here, so she will be treated as a lady. She will not be treated as a servant or serf, so do not suggest such nonsense again. As for you, you will make her duties less of a burden. Chanity has too many responsibilities for one person, but she does not complain, and everything is in order. Family or not, everyone has responsibilities here. As of yet, I have not seen you do anything. From this moment that is going to change," Derek commanded as he slammed his hands down on the table. "Do understand Marla?"

"Aye, Lord Derek" Marla replied, with a stiff smile. He could see the hidden fury in her eyes, but she dared not utter another word. After a few moments of pouting, Marla left the table and headed for the stairs.

Derek glanced at Marla, and realized exactly where she was headed. "Marla, do not go to your chamber," Derek said sternly, as his voice halted her in her tracks. "Seek out Alma and see what she has for you to do. Chanity will instruct you on what your daily duties will be, when we are finished with our conversation."

Marla trudged back down the stairs, and reluctantly headed to the kitchen to find Alma.

Chanity liked Lord Derek even more after what he said to Marla. She was happy he put Marla in her place. Vorik had done so a few times, but not very many. If it had been anyone else besides Lord Derek who had raided Holdenworth Manor, things might not have turned out so well. During raids, most women and girls were bedded forcefully, and some even slain. She was thankful to the Lord Almighty for sending Derek instead of someone like Vorik. She was also thankful for his timing. If it had been a moment later, she would have lost her innocence.

It was harvest time, and everyone pitched in to help, including Derek and his men. Their only break was at the noon meal, and they continued working until nearly nightfall.

Chanity occasionally caught herself looking across the field hoping to get a glimpse of Derek. She pictured how handsome he was, and how well built. She remembered being in his strong arms, and his lips softly kissing hers. Even the thought of him could stir sensations in her body. Finally, she stopped her fantasizing and went back to her duties.

At last nightfall came, and everyone headed to sup. To Chanity's amazement, Marla was again at the Lord's table trying to flirt with Derek as they ate.

Chanity sat at her place beside Lord Derek. She felt so tired from the work in the field, she was almost thankful Marla talked enough for the both of them.

Though Derek paid Marla little attention, Chanity wondered if he could be attracted to her. It was not uncommon in noble families to marry their first cousin. Of course her mother had been Derek's first cousin, so Marla would be his second.

Marla asked many questions about Derek's home, her grandparents, and his service to King William. She constantly laughed and batted her lashes at him. Chanity felt her anger rise at Marla and realized for the first time what jealousy felt like.

Chanity rose to help the servants clear tables, but Derek laid his hand on her arm. "You have done enough for the day," Lord Derek said. "You know you're supposed to sit with me. Stay and speak with me awhile. Marla can take over for you. She and the servants should be able to clean up without your help."

Marla stood reluctantly after Derek's comment, and glared at Chanity before walking away. She headed for the kitchen in a huff, but did what she was told.

"Would you mind telling me about some of Holdenworth's history?" Derek asked. "I would enjoy learning of its past."

Chanity went into great detail, telling him all she knew about Holdenworth's beginnings, all the way up to his arrival. Then she told him about the nearby village, and the crop arrangements with the serfs. They did not speak long into the night, for everyone was tired from a hard day's work. Soon they bid each other good night and went to their chambers.

Derek lay on his bed, and quickly fell into blissful slumber. For several hours his sleep was calm and restful, then his dreams turned wild and dark. In one dream, he walked through dim woods, and suddenly heard a woman's scream. He searched everywhere for the source of the sound, but in vain. The dream troubled him so much that it woke him from his slumber.

Now awake, he heard the sound again! It came from Chanity's bedchamber across the hall. He grabbed his sword and burst through his door, only to run headlong into her bolted door.

Derek struck the frame with his hand, and called for Chanity to unbolt the door. He was about to bash it down, but was relieved to see her open the door. Derek rushed inside and looked about for an intruder. "What happened?" he asked.

"Lord Derek, I am sorry I disturbed you. I had a bad dream and screamed out before I awoke," Chanity explained. "Ever since Vorik attacked me I've been having horrible dreams. I suppose it was just the shock of what almost happened to me. Again, I am sorry I disturbed your slumber, my Lord."

"Chanity, 'tis understandable to have bad dreams after what Vorik tried to do. He came so close to hurting you. Don't be sorry for waking me." Derek saw Chanity's eyes go wide, and her mouth drop open. He looked downward, and realized that in his haste to get to her, he had donned no clothing.

Her downward gaze embarrassed and excited him at the same time. He quickly grabbed one of her fur pelts to cover himself. Apparently Chanity had arisen in haste as well, and wore only a thin chemise. Chanity's hair flowed down to her waist, and her shapely, full breasts were nearly visible through the thin fabric. Derek wished he could reach out and take them in his hands, but knew he might not stop there.

Chanity realized how scant her clothing was and took a step back. The candlelight cast a soft glow, giving Derek enough light to see her form through the chemise. Before he knew what was happening, he took her into his arms and kissed her softly at first, but then his kisses grew more adamant.

Derek pulled Chanity tightly to him, and mindlessly dropped the fur pelt. He felt himself brush against Chanity, and wanted her so badly that he hurt from the need. He knew he must stop this, but had no desire to do so. He put one hand in her hair and deepened the kiss. This kiss was more demanding, and his tongue went into her mouth. She froze for a moment when his tongue entered, but it felt so wonderful that she did the same.

Derek felt his passion grow stronger. He must stop now, before he went too far and could not. His lips lifted from hers, and he held her close, breathing in the jasmine scent of her hair.

He finally forced himself to release her, and bent to get the fur pelt. Derek covered himself, then kissed her on the forehead just as he had done the last time. "I bid you good dreams Lady Chanity," Derek said. He embraced her once again, then headed for the master chamber.

Chanity bid him good dreams as well, then closed and bolted her door. He had really stirred the sensations in her body this time. She didn't understand everything that was happening to her body. She wanted something, but didn't really know what that something was. She didn't understand her body or his. His manhood had grown bigger while she was watching it. Her mother had explained about that, but she really didn't understand all of it. She hoped she remembered right what her mother had told her. It was fascinating to see it grow while she watched it, but the size worried her.

She realized that men must have different sizes, because Derek's looked bigger than Vorik's. She had seen Vorik's one time, but only for a quick moment before she looked away. When she saw Derek unclothed she had no wish to turn away. She felt slightly ashamed because she had stared at it in fascination. How did something that size fit inside a woman? But women birthed babies, so they must stretch somehow. She wished her mother would have explained things better. She lay back on her bed and finally fell back to sleep, this time to better dreams.

Derek went back to bed as well, but he could not get Chanity off his mind. For the last two days she was all he could think of. No female had ever enchanted or bewitched him so. He wanted her with a hunger he had never felt before, though he knew he could not bed her unless they were wed. It would not be fair to her. If she married after he had taken her, her husband would resent her for not being pure. He could not stand to think of anyone being cruel to her.

As much as he wanted her, he could not marry out of lust. He wanted to wed because of love like his parents. He wanted someone he could laugh with. Someone he could share happiness with for the rest of their days. He wanted a true love that would last a lifetime. With Chanity, he felt so much unbridled passion he would have to avoid her until his lust settled down. He didn't want to give her false hope or hurt her. He decided to busy himself with the harvest and preparing for winter. The activity would ease his lust and give him time to get to know Chanity better.

Everyone worked hard the next month. Soon, the harvest was gathered, the wood chopped and stacked, and the winter meat supply preserved. The last task that remained was to repair the roof on the manor and outer buildings so they could handle a heavy snow.

Bram took two dozen men and organized the repair. Even so, it required four full days to complete the work of patching and reinforcing the many roofs of Holdenworth. The largest task was the work on the manor, which took a full day to repair. Another day was devoted to the large outbuilding that housed many of the guards, serfs as well as the hounds and other animals. The roofs on the serf's cottages, smokehouse, stables and privy were reinforced as well.

The large outbuilding was rare for a village such as Holdenworth. Serina had insisted Belgar build it after they wed. It provided a place to house the guards, hounds and other animals, while keeping the great hall uncrowded.

Chapter 6

Derek was grateful that all the winter preparations were finished. He had seen Chanity from time to time during the harvest, but they were too busy or tired except to speak for a few moments at a time. The powerful desire Derek had for Chanity had faded somewhat, just as he hoped. Perhaps now he could begin courting Chanity properly. Derek finished his meal, and then headed for his chamber.

As soon as Derek crawled into bed, he heard a knock. Derek rose from his bed to find Bram at the door.

"A messenger from King William just arrived," Bram announced.

"My thanks, Bram, I'll be down shortly," Derek replied, and closed the door to get dressed.

The messenger informed Lord Derek that King William would be arriving in two days, and would be accompanied by fifty of his men. The King and his advisor would each need a bedchamber, and room in the great hall for twelve of the King's personal guard. The rest of his men could stay in outer buildings, if need be.

Derek saw Alma in the hallway, and stopped to speak with her. "Spread the word that King William will arrive in two days," Lord Derek ordered. "Tell the servants to begin preparing on the morrow. I will let Lady Chanity know as soon as I see her."

Derek wondered about the reason for King William's visit. There had been considerable unrest after William's coronation, so he could be seeking his share of Holdenworth's plunder. Vorik had raided Holdenworth only four and a half years before, so surely William knew there was not much to be had. They had discussed that very matter a day or so after William was crowned King of England.

The King's coronation was on Christmas Day, and Derek was in attendance. Two days later, King William gave him permission to take Holdenworth from Vorik. He only asked that Derek remain with him few more months, so he would have time to consolidate the throne.

Vorik had fought for William when he was Duke of Normandy, but Duke William never really trusted him. Duke William placed a spy among Vorik's men to make sure he received his rightful share from raids. Vorik suspected this, and made sure to surrender the proper amount most of the time. Vorik watched carefully, but could not figure out which of his men was the spy. Eventually, he became too confident in his underhanded dealings with Duke William and was caught.

As punishment Vorik had to give up his entire share, and pay more besides that. Vorik would have forfeited his life, were it not for the intervention of his father. Vorik's father was a loyal French ally of Duke William, and because of that loyalty, William conceded to spare Vorik to preserve the alliance.

Vorik's father contributed much to the Duke's cause in exchange for his son's life. Vorik was stripped of his Knighthood and banished from Duke William's service. His father made Vorik leave France, worried that Duke William might change his mind. Vorik journeyed to Normandy, and through riotous living gambled away all the funds he had acquired.

Derek continued to serve the Duke faithfully, and put his life on the line so that William would be King. After he recovered from his near-fatal wound, Derek broached the matter with King William, who gave him permission to take Holdenworth without a second thought. Now more than ever, the King needed Lords in England he could trust, and he trusted Sir Derek with his life.

On the way back to his chamber, Derek stopped at Chanity's door to let her know of King William's visit. He raised his hand to knock, but paused for a moment. It had been a constant battle the past month avoiding being alone with Chanity.

He wanted to do the honorable thing, and court her properly. If he was alone with her again, he might not be able to control himself. It had taken all his will power to break away the last time.

Derek wondered how Chanity was feeling. She might have realized he was avoiding her, and this would surely hurt. The bad part was she was an innocent who didn't realize how she was affecting him. He could not take Chanity without being wed to her, and he could not wed her without love.

Over the past month he had worked hard and tried not to think of Chanity, but it was in vain. He thought of her every moment of the day and dreamed of her most nights. How could feelings this strong be anything other than lust, not love? Each time he had held her it felt so wonderful, and her kisses were unbelievably pleasurable. She was an enchantress to be sure.

Derek lifted his hand a second time to knock, but was surprised as Chanity came up the stairs.

"Did you want something Lord Derek?" Chanity asked.

Her voice sounded so sweet, and her smile made her look even more beautiful than usual. Derek's heart beat quickly in his chest. Just being in her presence made him feel like a young untried lad, instead of a man almost a score and five.

"I was just coming to tell you that King William will be here in two days," Derek replied. "I am going to let him use the master chamber while he is here. I will use the spare chamber at the end of the hall. Ortaire will stay in the great hall to make sure there are no problems amongst the men and so William's advisor can have his chamber. Bram will stay in his own chamber as added protection for you as well as Marla."

"We will begin preparations at first light on the morrow, and send out hunting parties to bring in fresh game," Derek continued. "There will be fifty extra men to feed, so the hunting parties and kitchen help will be busy for the entire visit."

Chanity looked troubled for a moment, but tried to hide it with a smile.

"What distresses you Chanity?" Derek asked. She hesitated, but Derek insisted she tell him.

Blushing, Chanity explained, "I have heard him called 'William the Bastard.' People talk of how cruel he can be."

"During wartime there are bad things done and spoken on both sides," Derek explained. "There is always conflict. Each side feels they are in the right. Sometimes you have to pick the side that shares in what you believe in. I know King William is a good man, and he deserved to be crowned the rightful king. 'Tis why I fought as his knight for eight years, and will still join him when needed."

"With that said, I know he will have some new warriors with him that I do not know, so be cautious, Chanity. Be sure to bolt your door at night, and do not go outside unless escorted by one of my guards. You and Marla will be assigned a guard to watch over you at all times. I do not expect any trouble, but 'tis best to prepare for it just in case."

Their eyes met, and neither could look away. Derek leaned in and was about to kiss Chanity when Marla cleared her throat to make her presence known.

"Haven't I come upon this same scene with you and another man Chanity?" Marla asked. "You seem to be making a habit of this sort of thing."

"Of course you did Marla," Chanity said, smiling sweetly. "I never thanked you for saving me from being taken forcefully by your father," Chanity added, with an intense glare in her eyes. She usually ignored the mean things Marla said, but this time it was just too much. She had never been a violent person, but this time she wanted to slap Marla in the face.

Derek noticed Chanity's eyes were more a brilliant green than usual, and they seemed to be shooting green daggers. He could not blame Chanity for being upset. What Marla said was inexcusable.

"Tis best you take your leave to your bedchamber, Marla" Derek said gruffly. "You should get your rest, for you will surely be up at sunrise preparing for King William's visit."

Marla spun around and stomped off to her chamber without another word.

Derek apologized to Chanity for Marla's remark. "I am afraid my uncle and his wife are going to have a hard time with her. I hope they will not spoil her worse, but unfortunately, I'm sure they will. She is their only grandchild, and all they have left since they lost all their children because of Vorik.

"Both Uncle Marten and Aunt Tilly took the slaughter of their children hard, but Aunt Tilly took it worse. She locked herself in her room and refused to see anyone but her maid and Uncle Marten for over two years. Sometimes she could be heard talking to her children as if they were there. One day she finally emerged from her room and started living again, though she was never the same. I just pray Marla will be good for them."

"Now Chanity, I must bid you good night, since it grows late and I am weary," Derek said with a smile. He almost started to gather her up in his arms, but realized he needed to keep his distance since he almost kissed her earlier. Tomorrow would surely be a difficult day and he would need his rest. But as weary as he was, it would be hard to fall asleep this night, for his thoughts would be of her.

Chanity smiled in return and bid him good night as well. She bolted the door and readied herself for bed. She could not sleep for thinking of Derek, and wondered what she had done to cause him to avoid her.

She had thought of herself as a grown woman, but it seemed there was much she had to learn. She thought they had started having tender feelings for each other, but perhaps she was only one with those feelings. She felt like a foolish girl who thought someone cared for her, only to be ashamed and embarrassed.

In the two days after Derek arrived she had begun to believe in fairy tales, and imagined that her knight had come to rescue her. But this was no fairy tale with hope of love ever after. She was all alone in this world, and had to accept that. With a saddened heart she fell asleep.

Derek and left the hall early the next morn. He wanted to inspect Holdenworth one last time before King William arrived. As his gaze swept over the grounds, a feeling of pride filled his heart. The hall, out building and stables looked sturdy and well kept.

The soft fragrance of beeswax greeted Derek as he reentered the great hall. Every surface gleamed and sparkled in the warm candlelight.

Derek was grateful that Chanity had overseen all the work in the great hall. She had a special touch, and knew how to set everything in its proper place.

All was finished and prepared for the King's visit. Even Marla had done her part after he ordered her to help. He was proud of all they had accomplished, and would compliment them that night at sup. But for now he needed to go over his ledger so it would be up to date.

Later that evening, Derek rose from his seat and bade all gather in the great hall. "Everyone has done a fine job readying Holdenworth for the King's visit," Derek declared. He held his mug high in the air, and raised a cheer; "Thanks to one and all for your hard work, and long live King William." The men followed suit and held their mugs and wineskins up high, shouting "long live King William."

Exhaustion caused them all to retire early that night, and soon the great hall was quiet. Chanity went up to her bedchamber early, but lie awake in her bed, unable to sleep. She kept puzzling over why Derek continued to avoid her. He spoke to her at the table, but the rest of the time he seemed to ignore her. At last sleep came, and Chanity drifted off to her dreams.

That night Derek was awakened by someone slipping into his bed. As he roused from sleep, the first thing he thought was that Chanity desired him as well, and wanted to bed with him. The slight figure bent over him, and he could tell she had on no clothing. She kissed him, and he put his hands into her hair and pulled her close. Suddenly, he sat up and pushed her from him. He could tell by her kiss, her scent and hair that this was not Chanity! Derek leaped out of bed, and grasped a poker to stoke the fire. The glowing embers revealed the shape of Marla.

Marla looked Derek up and down admiringly, causing Derek to grasp a pelt to cover himself with.

"Why would you come to my bed?" Derek demanded. "We are family and I have no desire for you."

Marla walked seductively toward him, not at all shy about her nakedness. "I think you are very fine to look upon Lord Derek, and I want to know how to pleasure you," Marla said boldly. She threw her arms around his neck, and pressed her young body against him, as her lips sought his.

"Stop this now, Marla," Derek said, sternly, pushing her away from him a second time. Marla's fur pelt lay on the floor where she discarded it. Derek grabbed it off the floor, wrapped it around her, and led her roughly to the door. "Go back to your chamber," he ordered. "Never come into my bedchamber again."

She tried to protest, but Derek closed and bolted the door. Marla suspected that if it had been Chanity, Derek would not have made her leave. She had been unsuccessful in seducing Derek, but there was still some mischief she could carry out. The pout on her face turned to a sly smile as she formed her plan.

She quietly eased over to Chanity's door, and made some small noise to draw her out. Marla heard Chanity stir in her chamber and quickly stepped back to Derek's door. She wildly mussed her hair, and leaned against the frame as if she was just departing Derek's chamber.

Chanity opened her door, curiously looked out in the hall and spied Marla. Marla smiled a lazy smile, and let the pelt fall away from her shoulders so Chanity would see she was unclothed.

"Well, it seems I'm the one he wants and desires now," Marla smirked.

"Why do you hate me so, Marla?" Chanity asked. "I have tried to be kind to you since the first day you arrived here. We could have been close like sisters, but you never wanted to be close to anyone. I feel sorry for you, because you have no feelings or kindness in your heart. You are heartless just like your father was when he was alive."

"Oh he had a heart alright, for you and your mother," Marla replied. "On the trip here, his men talked of your mother's great beauty and how Vorik fawned over her. They also spoke of how he protected you and threatened anyone if they touched you. He never protected me! Instead he left me with that crazy old widowed aunt of his."

"Aunt Gunora had men suitors there constantly. One tried to touch me in the place that is forbidden every time he got the chance. I told my aunt what he did, but she just laughed, and told me that men will be men. The next time I complained about him she said that I was a foolish little girl. Then she slapped me, told me to keep my mouth shut and demanded I stop enticing him. I had to ask someone what enticing meant. Vorik cared enough to see you protected, but he didn't care what happened to me. So why should I like you? You had the love and protection of my father that I always dreamed of having."

"Marla, he did not care for me either," Chanity countered. "The only reason he protected me was so my mother would wed him. After mother was buried, he tried to bed me. That was only because of his lust, not because he cared for me. If he had cared for me like a daughter, he would never have done such a thing."

Marla's face was blank and expressionless as Chanity spoke. It seemed nothing Chanity said would change Marla's mind. Chanity sighed, hung her head, and returned to her bedchamber.

She could not understand why Derek desired Marla. He had always been firm with Marla, and acted toward her like a father. Most of all Chanity wondered why Lord Derek was avoiding her now. She missed him holding her, not to mention his kisses. What she missed the most was feeling that someone cared for her. She should have known that no one could have feelings for her in such a short time.

As she lay back down she could not stop thinking about what had just happened. She felt so foolish for believing Lord Derek could care for her, and even more foolish because she cared for him. The thought of him caring for Marla that way was like a wound. Although she was jealous, she did not want to be. She had always seen jealousy as a weakness, but could not keep from feeling it when it came to Derek. Chanity drifted off to sleep with Derek still in her thoughts.

Chapter 7

Soon, the morning of King William's arrival was upon them. Everyone except for Marla was up before sunrise making the final preparations. When Marla finally came down to the hall, Chanity told her to go help Alma, while she and Anna went to see that King William's chamber was ready. They went upstairs to the master chamber, and Chanity began tidying up. Anna gathered Derek's belongings and moved them to the chamber at the end of the hallway. Chanity was nearly finished cleaning when she heard someone enter. Thinking it was Anna, she turned to speak, but saw Derek standing there instead.

"I didn't mean to startle you, Chanity," Derek said. "I just wanted to remind you once more to be wary of King William's men. Most are good men, but some are not to be trusted." Their eyes met and neither could look away. He stroked her cheek with his hand, but Chanity pulled away. All she could think of was Marla coming from Derek's bedchamber.

"I am sorry my Lord, but I must get the bedchambers prepared for King William and his advisor."

Derek could tell something was bothering Chanity, but didn't have time to discuss it at the moment. He left his chamber, reminding her again to take care and be watchful. Perhaps she was just worried over William's visit, or maybe she was upset because he had been avoiding her the last month.

It troubled him, knowing he might have hurt her feelings. Even if he had, it would be better to have distance between them now. He refused to lead her on, only to break her heart when he found his true love. They needed time to get to know each other better if he was to know how he truly felt about her. He resolved to explain things to her after King William left.

His thoughts were broken by the sound of a horn, announcing the approach of King William to the outer gate. Everyone quickly gathered in the great hall to welcome their King. Derek, Bram, Ortaire and six of Derek's best warriors went outside to welcome King William to Holdenworth.

King William dismounted, and met Derek with a warm embrace. "Tell me, how is the new Lord of Holdenworth, my loyal friend?" he asked.

"I am well, Majesty," Derek replied, smiling broadly. "Welcome to Holdenworth Manor. Come inside and let us break our fast while we speak. I'm excited to hear of your travels."

Derek opened the door, and everyone in the great hall shouted "Long live King William" as the King entered.

William looked around the clean, spacious hall. The tables were laden with food and drink, and there was a crackling fire on the large hearth.

"You have an excellent stead, Lord Derek. I'm surprised you were able to bring in the harvest and finish the winter preparations in such a short time," King William declared.

"Thank you, Majesty, but I'm afraid I played only a small part. Let me introduce you to Lady Chanity, who is the real reason I have been so successful thus far," Derek responded, as he motioned for Chanity to approach.

"Pleased to meet you, Majesty," Chanity said, as she curtsied.

"Lord Derek tells me you are mainly responsible for all this," King William said with a smile.

"Lord Derek gives me too much tribute, Majesty," Chanity said blushing. "'Tis truly due to the hard work of everyone at Holdenworth."

"I'd like to hear more of Holdenworth from you and Lord Derek."

Derek pulled the Chieftain's chair out for King William, then took the seat to his right. Chanity sat beside Derek, and Bram beside her. After Bram, sat four of the King's personal guard. William's advisor sat on the King's left, followed by Lord Jacot, the King's commander and his two guards. Derek motioned for Marla to sit next, followed by two more of the King's guard.

"Why are there so many guards at the table?" Marla asked, before any introductions had been made.

Lord Jacot turned and looked at Marla sternly. "We seven Knights make up the King's guard. We are always by his side except when he sleeps, but even then we are close by."

Derek apologized for Marla's interruption. He explained she was still young and had not yet been to court. Derek went around the table speaking the name and title of each person, leaving Chanity and Marla for last.

"Chanity is the daughter of Lord Belgar and Lady Serina, the former Chieftain of Holdenworth, before Vorik's raid. She became Vorik's stepdaughter when he forced Serina into marriage."

When Derek introduced Marla as Vorik's daughter, he noted the sudden change in the King's countenance. He went on to explain that Marla was his cousin Marta's daughter, who he came to avenge. King William knew the story well, and nodded his head so Derek would know he understood.

After King William finished his meal, he spoke of his travels and accomplishments in Normandy and France, followed by his adventures in England. He noted Chanity was an intelligent young lady. He was amused by her wit and wisdom, though some men didn't find these traits appealing in a woman. To him, anything was better than hearing about the latest fashion and such that most ladies wanted to talk on and on about. When Chanity spoke, it was clear she knew her family's history and part of the country well. Whenever William broached a subject, she listened and asked shrewd questions afterward. He could tell she was truly interested in his travels and conquests in England.

"Thank you for telling me more of Holdenworth, Chanity," King William said pleasantly. "In truth I have heard much from afar. The skalds often mention the beauty and grace of Lady Serina in their songs and tales. If she was as beautiful as her daughter, then surely there was no competition for her beauty in all of England."

Chanity blushed at the compliment, and murmured "Thank you, King William."

"'Tis but the truth, and I am certain we will be hearing stories from the skalds about the beautiful Lady Chanity soon," King William replied, smiling.

King William observed that Chanity's charm had affected several of the warriors tonight. Lord Derek seemed to glow when he watched her. It was clear that he was smitten with the beautiful lass, but Lord Jacot seemed to be as well. Even his champion knight, Sir Garth was eyeing her.

Garth was a mighty warrior, but he had an ego and temper to match. He hated Derek because some of the men had snidely suggested that Derek could best him in battle. William hoped Garth didn't try to continue his quarrel with Lord Derek or attempt to use this lovely lass to start trouble. He had enough to worry about without strife amongst his men.

The evening wore on, and drink flowed, it humored the King to see Derek so jealous of Chanity. He could see the anger on Lord Derek's face, and even hear it in his voice when he thought someone paid Chanity too much attention. Derek had always hid his emotions well, so this was a surprising turn of events. He cared for Derek like family, and hoped he would settle down and take a wife.

Marla seemed the typical young lass, and talked of frivolous, boring matters. At first she tried to dominate the conversation, but finally left the table in a huff because she wasn't getting the attention she thought she deserved. William was glad when Marla departed. She reminded him of her pompous father. A few minutes after Marla left, Chanity rose to excuse herself as well.

"I enjoyed our conversation very much, Majesty. I realize though, you have important matters to discuss with your men."

"It was a delight speaking with you as well, Lady Chanity, which we will do again before I leave," the King replied. William had really enjoyed her presence, and wanted her to stay, but knew his men would be distracted by her beauty and charm.

Chanity curtsied to the King, then headed toward the kitchen. King William looked around the table, and noted every eye followed her as she left. Lord Derek surely had his hands full, for she was truly delightful.

"Lady Chanity is perceptive, for I do have some matters to discuss," King William said to the assembled men. "In order to maintain a stable foothold in our newly acquired lands, each Lord should construct a fortified castle. England needs castles like Normandy. These fortresses are the heart of my strategy for my conquest of England. They will provide my Lords and troops with strong defensive structures to guard against any Saxon bold enough to try thwart my plans for England."

"A fortress would surely be a deterrent to any enemy attack on this land," Lord Derek agreed with enthusiasm.

"Sir Bram, you have much experience with castle plans and layout. Would you have enough time to draw them up while I am here?" King William asked.

"Certainly, Majesty," Bram replied.

"I have never seen anyone better at sketching and planning castle defenses. Your work at Hastings was admirable. The castle there could never have been constructed in such a short time without your planning and intuition. You are needed here with Lord Derek now, but I hope you will join me again someday. You are one of my best knights."

"I will consider that, and give it a great deal of thought, Majesty," Bram replied. "Majesty, if you're finished with me, I will begin sketching the plans.

"Thank you, Sir Bram," King William replied. "By all means, please proceed with the plans."

As the King and his men discussed strategy, Chanity helped the servants clean up and serve drinks. It seemed the men drained their mugs more quickly with each passing hour.

King William continued to speak, and as the evening turned into night the women were still refilling mugs. Chanity grew uneasy at the way Garth kept openly staring at her bosom. He had begun gawking at her long ago, even before they took their meal. Finally, she became so uncomfortable with his overt attention that she asked one of the other servants to serve his side of the table, while she served Derek's side.

The night grew later still, and it seemed as though it would never end. Chanity became overly warm from the roaring fire on the hearth, and from dashing about filling mugs. She decided to go outside for a bit of fresh air, but watched to make sure that her guard followed. As Chanity headed for the doors, she was relieved to see that the guard had indeed arisen, and was following her outside. She stepped out into the cool air, turned to the rose garden and took a seat on a wooden bench.

The roses were still in bloom, and had not yet succumbed to the cold. Their scent lingered in the air, and she breathed in the sweet fragrance. She loved the rose garden and the smell of the roses. She had spent a great deal of time here over the years.

The night was beautiful, with a full moon and stars filling the sky. As a child she loved to star gaze, and would sit outside until her mother beckoned her to come in. The night sky and its stars had always intrigued her. After her father's death, she and her mother had occasionally ventured out to the garden at night, but those times were few and far between.

As she sat remembering the past, she heard the doors of the great hall open and close, and turned to see who it was. By the torch light she could see that Sir Garth had emerged from the hall. He looked around the courtyard until he spotted her, then began walking toward the rose garden. Garth's eyes gleamed as he approached, taking in every detail of her. He reminded Chanity of Vorik, which made her even more cautious of him.

"'Tis not safe for you to be alone, Chanity, with so many men about," Sir Garth said.

"I'm not alone. I have a guard coming this way as we speak," Chanity replied, with venom in her voice.

The guard had been checking the area around the garden. Upon hearing the opening door and Chanity's voice, he approached to see who she was speaking to. He relaxed somewhat when he saw Sir Garth, and walked over to join them. By the time he was close enough to see the alarm on Chanity's face it was too late.

Garth swung a mighty fist at the unsuspecting guard. The blow caught the guard right in the temple and knocked him out cold. "He's not much of a guard, is he?" Garth said laughing. "Your wellbeing is in my hands now," Garth exclaimed, grabbing hold of her.

Chanity tried to scream as panic overcame her, but Garth's lips covered hers before she could do so. He grabbed her into a tight embrace, and his muscular arms nearly squeezed the breath out her body. Garth violently kept trying to kiss her and cover her mouth, as she struggled to get away. She realized she had to do something to make him release her, before she passed out from lack of air.

The only thought that came to her was to bite his lower lip, and she bit as hard down as she could. Garth jerked his head back suddenly and pulled his lip from between her teeth. He released Chanity from his crushing embrace, and she gasped air once again.

Garth grabbed her arm in rage and drew his hand back to strike her in the face, but quickly stopped when he felt something press against his manhood.

"Release her now, or you will never enjoy another woman again," Derek ordered, as he pressed harder against Garth's manhood with his sword. Garth grudgingly let Chanity slip from his grasp, and she ran to Derek's side.

Derek lowered his sword, and Sir Garth turned to face him, glaring.

"Is there a problem here?" King William asked as he approached.

"Lady Chanity, did he harm you?" Derek asked with concern.

"Nay, Lord Derek, I am fine now," Chanity answered.

Bram helped the guard up, and was about to ask if he was well, but the man only held up his hand and shook his head. It was clear he had been taken by surprise, and was too embarrassed or afraid to say anything against Garth. Bram would question the guard later when Garth wasn't around.

Derek looked at Garth with fury in his eyes and repeated the King's question, "Is there a problem here, Sir Garth?"

"Not at the moment," Garth answered.

"Let us see that it stays that way," King William ordered, as he gave Sir Garth a warning glare. "I have enough battles to worry about without my men trying to battle each another."

Derek sheathed his sword, but gave Garth a warning. "If you have a problem with me, then take it up with me, not a mere lass that can hardly defend herself."

"Ah, Lord Derek, 'tis naught but your strong mead, which I clearly have partaken too much of," Sir Garth replied with a small laugh. "Pardon me to take my leave, and retire to bed," Garth said, giving a devious smile as he departed.

Derek followed protectively behind Chanity, as everyone returned inside to speak of future plans and battle strategy.

As Derek took his seat at the table, he noticed Lord Jacot had drawn Chanity to the side, and was speaking with her at a table nearby. Lord Jacot rested his hand on the back of her shoulder while they spoke. He liked Lord Jacot, but at the moment he wanted to take his sword and remove that hand from her shoulder. "'Twill be many weary days trying to keep the men away from Chanity," Derek thought to himself.

Derek rose from his seat and loomed over them as they spoke. "Lady Chanity, I think Alma needs your help in the kitchen," Derek said, as he glared at Lord Jacot.

"Aye, my Lord," Chanity said. She excused herself, and then went to the kitchen to search out Alma.

"Lord Derek, she is truly an enchanting Lady. You will have your hands full the next few days keeping the men away."

"I was just thinking the same thing as I watched you with her," Derek said harshly. "She is an innocent Jacot, so remember that."

"Chanity seemed quite upset when she returned from outside, and I was merely consoling her," Jacot explained, with humor in his voice.

Jacot glanced at his friend's face and was quite pleased with the contortions he saw as Lord Derek struggled to compose a response. He wondered why Derek had not claimed her, as it was plain to see he was in love with the lass. Plain to everyone but Derek himself, Jacot mused. He had always thought his friend wise, but now Derek seemed to flounder about like a longship without a steerboard.

Perhaps a few more honeyed words with Chanity would ignite enough jealousy to break through that stubborn heart, Jacot thought, with a wry grin on his face.

"Of course, Lord Derek," Jacot said deferentially. "The lady is an innocent, not to mention beautiful and wise as well. Even King William seemed impressed with Chanity after he spoke with her." It seemed his plan was working, for Derek glared at him furiously.

Derek had enough of Lord Jacot's praise of Chanity. "We should get back to King William before he grows tired of our neglect," Derek said, irritably. "I know he wants to speak with us about his upcoming journey across England, and where he wants the castles constructed."

They returned to the Chieftain's table, but the hour was indeed late, and everyone rose to depart to their chamber, or to take a pallet in the great hall. Some men were staying in the outer buildings, so they headed outside. After the King departed for his chamber, Derek bade everyone a good night. Lord Jacot clapped Derek on the back, and bade him good night as well.

The next three days were as Derek foresaw. Every time he glanced Chanity's way, another man was scrambling after her, vying for her attention. He had never been so vexed in his life.

Garth kept his distance from Chanity, but he continued watching her with either lust or contempt in his eyes. It was if he lusted after her, but detested her as well. Garth's lip still showed signs of Chanity's bite. It was swollen and had a bluish hue underneath. Derek noticed Garth rubbed at it often, and he glared at Chanity with loathing as he did.

Then there was Lord Jacot, who was constantly at Chanity's side, and always seeking her attention. It sorely burdened him to see that she enjoyed Jacot's attentiveness. He wished he could declare a tournament then and there, and take all the men out one by one. When William and his men left, he would be overjoyed. He wanted Chanity all to himself, like it had been before the King's arrival.

Derek was so lost watching Chanity, and dreaming of the tournament he longed for, that he didn't notice Bram approach.

"Lord Derek!" Bram said loudly.

"There's no need to yell, Sir Bram," Derek said, eyeing him strangely.

"'Twas the third time I called your name, Derek. I began to wonder if I would ever get through to you," Bram explained.

"I'm sorry, Bram," Derek replied. "I was just lost in thought. What did you want to discuss?"

"Exactly this, Lord Derek," Bram said, gesturing toward Chanity. "I've seen you staring at Chanity with longing in your eyes many a time. Why do you not just wed the lass?"

"Because I must love the lady I wed."

"Then wed Chanity," Bram replied.

"Are you saying I love Chanity?" Derek asked.

"Only you know what is in your own heart and can answer that question," Bram stated. "I would wager my life that you do. Everyone else seems to think you're in love with the lass. You guard her like a mother hen protecting a chick and try to flog anyone that gets too close. When you look at her, you stare at her with yearning in your eyes. If I had to guess, you probably think about her day and night."

Derek knew Bram was right, and felt foolish for not knowing his own heart. This beautiful, sweet, enchanting lass had captured his heart. He must speak with her soon and let her know how he felt. He could only hope she felt the same way about him.

He looked back across the hall, where Lord Jacot was regaling Chanity with another poem. Apparently, he would have to wait for another time, for at the present, Jacot seemed to have her spellbound.

In truth, Chanity was enthralled with Lord Jacot's unrelenting attention. He took her mind off what happened between Derek and Marla. He made her laugh when she was with him, and she could tell that he loved the sound of it. He quoted poetry to her, which she enjoyed immensely. He was always very kind to her, and she enjoyed their conversations.

Derek carefully sought an opportunity to speak to Chanity, but the King's time at Holdenworth was short, and he had much to discuss with his men. Besides, it seemed whenever Derek had a spare moment, some other suitor was trying to whisper in Chanity's ear.

A few nights later it seemed he finally had the chance. He had just finished discussing next year's plantings when he spied Chanity crossing the hall, heading outside. The new guard assigned to her followed close behind. Derek rose, and was about to follow, when King William summoned him.

Derek made his way to the Chieftain's table, and gritted his teeth at the sight of Lord Jacot accompanying Chanity and the guard out the door.

Chanity made her way outside with Jacot following close behind. Chanity headed over to the rose garden, and the guard stepped off into the shadows where he could watch unobtrusively from a distance.

The stars shone brightly that night, and Jacot pointed some of the constellations that he knew. As they talked about the stars, Chanity looked up toward Jacot, and he pulled her into his arms and kissed her. It was a long, sensuous kiss that she enjoyed immensely. She thought Lord Jacot handsome, and his kiss felt wonderful, but he just wasn't Derek.

Jacot noticed the guard was coming over, and he released Chanity. He gave the guard a stern look, and the guard went back to where he had been standing.

"I'm sorry Chanity; I should not have kissed you without your permission. I know how you feel about Lord Derek."

Jacot also thought of a beautiful young countess back home and felt guilty for kissing Chanity. There had been other women who tried to capture his heart, but they didn't mean anything to him. Under the star filled sky, Chanity had reminded him of her. She did not look like his young beauty, but being under the stars reminded him of their many nights star gazing together. He had never even got to kiss his young lady, but he imagined it every night before drifting off to sleep.

"'Tis alright, Lord Jacot. Derek does not share my feelings. I know I must seek a life without him," Chanity said with a sigh.

"I think he does share them," Jacot said. "Be patient Chanity, I'm sure Derek is already starting to realize his feelings for you. That much is clear by the way he guards you constantly, and glares furiously at any man who dares give you any attention. If Derek's eyes could shoot daggers, I as well as a few other men would be in our graves right now. If King William wasn't demanding Derek's attention, he would be outside glaring and imagining running me through with his sword."

Jacot wondered if he would still feel the same way about his young beauty when he saw her again. It had been so long since he had the chance to visit her. She was only ten and five years of age the last time he saw her, but so very mature and wise for her years. She was ten years younger, so he had to give her a chance to grow up. She was always so carefree, happy and laughing.

Jacot smiled as he remembered back to all the mischief she unintentionally gotten into as a child. He thought he knew her well, but before he realized what was happening, she transformed into a beautiful young lady.

The more he thought of her, the more his guilt grew. How would he feel if another man was kissing his young beauty? He felt tremendous anguish at the thought of another kissing her. He wanted to be the one to give her that first kiss. He had tried to kiss her on their last night together, but her mother interrupted before he could.

"Is there something troubling you?" Chanity asked after Lord Jacob had grown quiet for several moments.

"Nay, I was merely lost in thought," Jacot replied, but never spoke of what he was really thinking about. He stayed with Chanity until she was ready to go back inside and did not try to kiss her again.

There was only one young lady that he wanted to be kissing at the moment, but she was far away. She would be turning ten and seven years soon, so he had to decide if he was ready to settle down. If so, he had better claim her hand before someone else did. He also didn't want Chanity to start having feelings for him because she thought Derek didn't truly care for her.

"Come along Chanity, I will see you safely inside," Jacot said, as he motioned for the guard to follow.

Derek couldn't hide the anger on his face when he saw Chanity and Jacot walk in together. Her guard should have been the one at her side. As soon as he finished his conversation with King William, he headed for Lord Jacot. Jacot saw him approaching and told Chanity to go, because he needed to speak with Lord Derek in private. He wanted to make sure Derek wasn't foolish enough to say something out of anger he would later regret.

Just as he expected, Derek confronted him as soon as Chanity walked away. "How dare you be alone with her outside and especially at night?" Derek asked, with clenched teeth and an angry face.

"How could we be alone Lord Derek, when you assigned a guard to watch over her?" Jacot asked. "But I warn you, he is not a very good guard, and I only stayed to see her safely inside. I will confess I did kiss her, but only once, and 'twas not because her guard stopped me, for he did not. It was because she has deep feelings for you. Given time, I could change her feelings for me, but as you know, I haven't the time. If you do not ask her to wed there are plenty of other men who will.

"There is one other matter I wish to discuss with you," Lord Jacot said, with concern. "'Tis the way Garth has been staring at Chanity. One moment he eyes her with lust, then another moment with hostility. It is rumored amongst the men that he likes to be cruel with his women, especially when he beds them. Beware of him, my friend. He intimidates the guards because he is the King's Champion. If I were you, I would assign several guards to keep her safe while he is here. One or two guards do not stand a chance against him."

Derek was angry and disappointed in himself for not realizing Chanity needed more than one guard to keep her safe. Derek was also angry at Lord Jacot for kissing Chanity, but he also heard the concern in Jacot's voice. Derek wondered how strong Jacot's feeling were for her, and hoped Chanity didn't have feelings for Jacot. There had been rumors around camp that Lord Jacot was smitten with the daughter of an Earl and Countess from another part of England, but Derek wasn't for certain who she was or if Jacot still cared for her.

How could I have been so foolish? Derek pondered. He hadn't treated Chanity very well the last month or so. He convinced himself it was to avoid hurting her later on, not realizing how he was hurting her now. Bram and Lord Jacot had finally helped him realize his feelings for Chanity. Still, he wondered if she had wanted and enjoyed Lord Jacot's kiss. The bad part was he couldn't blame her if she did since he had avoided her for so long.

"You know Derek, if you had claimed her, I would never have sought her out. You shouldn't have any anger toward her or I," Jacot said.

Derek knew Jacot spoke the truth. "'Tis my fault to bear," Derek said, without any malice in his voice. "Thank you for warning me of the peril Chanity is in, my friend. As for me, I will tell Chanity of my feelings before the night is over. I must have looked the fool, not realizing I love her, when everyone else saw it. Perhaps she will still agree to wed me, even though I've been so foolish. She enchanted me from the first moment we met and has held me enchanted ever since."

Derek clapped Lord Jacot on the back, then left the great hall to search for Chanity.

Later that evening, Garth boasted of his plans to his friend Edmond as they sat drinking in a quiet corner of the hall. "I have decided to wed Derek's wench. I'll ask the King's permission in the morn after we break our fast. Since my older brother was slain in battle, father is demanding an heir. He declared that if I remain with King William instead of returning home, then I must wed and sire a son. I despise Lord Derek, and it will please me greatly to take his wench for wife."

"Now that I consider it, I despise that wench of his as well. She will regret biting my lip and shunning me, when other women yield to me without hesitation. It will be fun bringing her down a few notches. Soon, she will grovel at my feet," Garth said angrily. As he spoke, he rubbed his lip, which still greatly pained him.

"What will Bertha think if you wed this beautiful wench?" Edmond asked. "She has always been possessive of you. Think of the hostility you will bring into your father's house."

"Let me worry about Bertha," Garth said. "She is my father's servant and I can handle her. I allow her some small indulgences because she is a good bed mate. As far as Chanity goes, I don't care how hostile Bertha is to her. It will serve the little wench right for how she treated me. I am the King's Champion. I can have any woman I desire. She will soon learn she is not so special, and I will enjoy teaching her that lesson."

"If you think so little of her, and do not care for her, then why would you want to wed her? Is it only because you desire her for her beauty?" Edmond asked, with a baffled look.

Garth smacked his friend on the back while roaring with laughter. "My friend, you ask too many questions."

Garth did not tell Edmond the real reason he was determined to ask the King's permission to wed the wench. As the King's Champion he could not challenge Derek without cause. King William refused to tolerate strife amongst his men, and he could not afford to anger the King. If he asked to wed Chanity, Derek would instantly challenge him.

Garth had grown tired of the taunts of the King's men long ago. Whenever he boasted to the men of his exploits, they declared Derek could best him in battle. They clearly took pleasure in reminding him that Derek was younger, faster and like lightening with his sword. It enraged him knowing that most of them believed Derek was the better warrior.

He would prove his might by defeating Derek and taking his lady from him. He had no love for her, but would enjoy the sorrow he caused them. He would keep her with child, and torment her by forcing her to birth babes with a man she despised. Then he would laugh at the King's men who had scorned him.

Marla stood absolutely still in the shadow nearby, as she eavesdropped on Garth and Edmond's conversation. She did not know what they would do if they saw her. If she were discovered, they would know she had heard everything. She remained frozen in place and did not move until they retired to bed. She would use what she discovered to her advantage but had to wait till the opportune time. Fortunately, for Marla, she did not have to wait long, for that night her time came.

Marla had also overheard Derek and Jacot's conversation earlier and was determined to prevent Derek from confessing his love to Chanity. She concealed herself in an alcove upstairs and waited for Derek to arrive. A short while later, Derek came up the stairs to speak with Chanity.

Lord Derek was just about to knock on Chanity's door, as Marla stepped out. "If you are seeking Chanity, she was not feeling well and went to lie down."

Derek hesitated a moment, then nodded and headed to his chamber. Marla smiled in secret delight. Now Garth would request the King's permission to wed Chanity first, and would have first claim on her. Since Garth was Champion Knight the King would have to consider his claim. Then perhaps Derek would give up on asking the King to wed Chanity, since Garth was so good in battle. Most of the men were frightened of him, and Derek would probably be as well. With Chanity out of the way, she would finally have a chance with Derek.

Chapter 8

The next morning, William gave the order to prepare to depart after they broke their fast. Derek looked around the crowd for Chanity, but she was nowhere to be seen. He wanted to seek William's permission to wed Chanity, but wished to speak with her first. If he was unable to find her before William decided to leave, he would make the claim anyway.

Derek found Alma and started to ask her to check on Chanity when he saw her coming downstairs. His heart thrilled with excitement when he saw her, and he quickly went to escort her to the great hall. Just as Derek reached her, Garth stood and banged his empty mug on the table to command attention.

"As the King's champion knight and of noble birth, I claim Chanity for my wife," Garth said loudly.

Chanity heard Garth's announcement, and felt blackness closing in around her. She swooned and almost fell, but Derek caught her as she recovered.

Derek spoke quickly before King William could answer Garth. With his arm around Chanity he said, "I, Derek, Lord of Holdenworth and King William's loyal Knight of noble birth, claim Chanity for my wife."

King William was quite concerned over this situation. He could not turn down his champion knight's claim, especially since he was from a noble family. On the other hand, he owed Derek for saving his life, and he was from a noble family as well. It was obvious Chanity and Derek had feelings for each other, but Derek had not claimed her before now. Since he had not, Garth's claim had to be considered.

"As Lord of Holdenworth, I challenge Garth for the right to wed Chanity," Derek said.

"I cannot let you risk your life for me," Chanity whispered. "You said when you wed it must be for love, and you do not love me. You cannot do this for me, I will just have to learn to tolerate him," Chanity pleaded. The thought that Derek could be slain because of her was too much to bear.

"'Tis love I feel for you, it just took me awhile to realize it", Derek replied, looking deeply in her eyes. "You cannot wed him, for I love you and want you to be my wife. Besides, this is not about him wanting to wed you. Garth saw that I loved you and knew this was the only way I would challenge him. He wants everyone to know he can best me in battle because of how the King's men taunt him. Garth is vain, and yearns to prove that he is the best warrior. It is his ego that has caused this. Do not worry though, Chanity. I will defeat him."

King William saw Derek and Chanity speaking with each other, but could not hear what transpired between them. Now Derek turned and set his gaze on Garth. William thought Derek looked fiercer than he ever had in battle. It was truly a disturbing situation, and he did not want to lose either of them. Perhaps some space between the two would cool the rivalry between Garth and Derek.

"I must give this matter some thought," King William declared. "I will give my answer when we come back this way, after visiting some of my supporters and distributing the plans that Bram sketched."

This was one occasion William was glad the lords and nobles had to have his permission to wed. If any of the nobles wed without his permission they had to pay a penalty.

"I should stay and see to Chanity's wellbeing," Garth said to King William. "How do I know that he will not take her innocence while I am gone? Or she might try enticing him to her bed to get out of wedding me."

Derek's hand grasped the hilt of his sword. "Another word like that about Lady Chanity, and you will never have anything else in this life to worry about," Derek said, with fire in his eyes and anger in his voice. "Why don't we just settle this here and now?"

Garth's continued goading was clear to King William, and from the look in Derek's eye, it had to end now, or bloodshed would surely result.

"Lord Derek is an honorable man, and he would not dishonor Chanity or himself that way. If you stayed here, it would be your wellbeing in jeopardy, instead of hers. Now be off with you. Go outside to ready the men for the journey," William commanded sternly.

The two warriors eyed each other menacingly one final time before Garth headed out to ready the King's men.

"Lord Derek, I would like a word with you alone," King William said. At the King's word, everyone quickly excused themselves and left the hall.

"Why did you wait so long to claim Chanity?" King William asked. "If you had, it would not have come to this. I would have gladly given my blessing."

"You will think me foolish, Majesty," Derek replied.

"At this point you look foolish anyway, so you have nothing to lose," King William said. By the King's expression Derek could not tell if he was jesting or not.

"I did not know 'twas love, I thought it was only desire. I finally realized my feelings over the last few days after seeing Lord Jacot and all the other men seeking after Chanity's attention. Bram also pointed out some things that opened my eyes. I was about to ask your permission to wed Chanity as soon as she came downstairs, but Garth asked before I got the chance. Truly Garth has no desire for her, but the whole matter is only a ploy to force me to challenge him. He feels he has something to prove because your men chided him, saying he could not defeat me in battle. He did not challenge me outright to avoid angering you. He also realized your men would laugh knowing they goaded him into it."

"I overheard my men taunting him before," King William said. "I could see the fury in Garth's eyes. It is hard being the Champion Knight, knowing you will be bested sooner or later. Garth is pompous and vain, but he is loyal to me. I trust him with my life, but he is too hot tempered to be trusted with others. It may well come to a challenge when I return. Practice well with your sword and your jousting Derek, because he is called champion for a reason."

"I also know you love Chanity and he does not," William continued. "I have seen Garth looking at her with loathing at times, then at other times with lust. You probably already know the rumor of how he treats his women in bed, so I will not speak of it. Good luck to you, my loyal friend. Be sure to practice hard in the list," he clapped Derek on the back, then walked out the door.

Derek followed the King outside to see him off on his journey. The trumpet blew loudly, to announce the King's departure as the company left Holdenworth Manor. Derek had always known William would be crowned King of England. Thus far he had succeeded, but still had many battles ahead to have all of England accept him as their rightful King.

Derek went to find Chanity after William and his men left. He found her working as always. "I knew you would be toiling away. You work much too hard," he said, smiling at her.

Derek drew her into his arms, and breathed in her enchanting scent. She always smelled of jasmine, and her own special essence. He couldn't define it, but her scent was intoxicating. Since no one was about, he gave her a long sensual kiss that left her lips tingling.

He gazed in Chanity's eyes for a long moment, as if trying to see into her heart and soul. "I love you, Chanity. I think I have from the first moment I saw you. I was just not wise enough to know it was love at first. You are the only lady I have truly loved, so it took me awhile to realize it. You are my first real love, and will be my only love. I have been trying to get you alone for two days to tell you of my feelings, but something always came up. Now I finally have the chance to tell you all that I feel. I did not get the chance to ask you properly, so now I will. Chanity, will you wed me and be my wife?" Derek asked nervously, as he silently prayed that she would agree.

Chanity stood quietly before him and did not answer. The anguish she felt in her heart showed on her face.

"I promise you I was going to ask you before the situation with Garth happened," Derek assured her. "I came up to your chamber to ask you last night, but Marla stopped me before I knocked on your door. She told me you had turned in early because you did not feel well. I decided to wait until the morrow and not disturb you. I went to speak with you early this morning and Marla told me you were going to sleep in because you did not sleep well last night."

"'Tis strange that she would say such," Chanity replied with concern. "I felt fine last night, and never spoke to Marla. This morning Marla told me that you asked that I clean your chamber before coming down to break my fast, so it would be ready for you tonight. That was why I was late coming down to the great hall. I wondered why you wanted it done in such haste."

Derek knew Marla had been lying and was up to something. But why had she done this? He decided to seek her out and find out exactly what she was up to. Marla was a strange girl and he did not trust her. Chanity probably did not trust her either, since she looked upset when Derek mentioned Marla's name. Once again, he worried for his uncle and aunt, fearing that Marla would be too much for them to deal with.

Derek thought back over the days, trying to discern the reason for Chanity's reluctance. When they were together at the table during meals, Chanity had been extremely quiet. He knew he had hurt Chanity by avoiding her the past month and wondered if that might be the reason she was still upset.

"Chanity you still have not answered my question. Do you wish to wed me?"

Chanity looked hurt and sad as she said, "I need more time to think on it."

Derek felt the pain in his heart at her answer. He must have hurt her worse than he thought. Could it be because she has feelings for Lord Jacot now, he wondered. If she did have feelings for Lord Jacot, it was his own fault for avoiding her for so long. It saddened him knowing he had hurt her by being so foolish.

"I better go practice with the men. I have a challenge to ready myself for," Derek said with a heavy heart. Somehow he would make everything up to her. Now he had two battles to prepare for; the battle with Garth, and the battle to win back Chanity's heart. He wasn't as concerned about the battle with Garth, but he had to get Chanity to love him again. Above all, he was determined to win both battles!

Chanity needed time to think, so she headed to her favorite spot by the sea. She was so lost in thought as she walked along, that it seemed mere moments before she reached the cliff edge. She slowly climbed down to her secret spot and gazed out over the glittering water.

It was a glorious day. The sun shone down on white puffy clouds over head, and the sea sparkled with mild waves. The air was slightly chilly, but not cold. Chanity sat on the big rock and basked in the warm sun as she watched the birds fly about. She thought Derek would like this spot, and purposed to show it to him one day. He was the only person she had ever trusted and wanted to share it with.

As her thoughts turned to Derek, she remembered the hurt in his eyes when she did not agree to wed him. She wanted to say 'aye' with all her heart, but the image of Marla leaving Lord Derek's chamber with only a fur pelt kept coming to mind.

If Derek loved her, why did he take Marla to his bed? This was so confusing to Chanity. Would he still bed Marla if they wed, like Vorik did with the wenches from the village? She could not stand the thought of him bedding anyone else. She wished she had her mother to discuss this with. She missed her mother so much it was like she was missing a part of herself.

She wanted to ask Derek about what happened with Marla that night, but was that the proper thing to do? Should she ask a man about such things before she wed him? If she could not ask him, then she had to decide if she could wed him and overlook what he had done with Marla. She also had to decide if she could trust Derek not to do it again after they wed. Chanity sighed, knowing deep in her heart she could not.

Both sat at the table that night with a saddened look on their face. Neither spoke a word, but Marla talked enough for the both of them, and chattered away about mundane things. She seemed elated that Derek and Chanity were not speaking much. Marla kept smiling at Derek and tried vainly to coax him into conversation with her. Derek finally had enough of her endless banter.

"Marla, I need to speak with you privately after sup," Derek said, angrily.

"Of course, Lord Derek," Marla said beaming, oblivious to his serious tone. She looked across the table to see Chanity's reaction. She was disappointed though, because Chanity never looked her way.

Chanity stood, then left the room. Derek watched as she departed, and did not take his eyes off her until she was out of sight. It was clear that something was bothering her, and he desperately wished she would tell him what it was. When they had kissed earlier that day, she returned his kiss eagerly. He was somewhat relieved to know she must still have feelings for him.

Derek rose from the table, and Marla quickly followed behind. He made his way to a private part of the hall as Marla approached. She smiled her brightest smile and took his arm. "What do you wish, Lord Derek?" she asked.

Derek pulled roughly away from her. "I have some questions for you Marla, and you had better answer truthfully. If you do not answer truthfully you will regret it," Derek said, through gritted teeth. "Why did you lie about Chanity not feeling well?"

"My Lord, she went to bed early, so I took it she didn't feel well."

"You told an untruth, Marla. You said that Chanity told you she did not feel well." Lord Derek forcefully took her arm and commanded, "Now tell me the truth!"

"I overheard you telling Bram that you were going to ask Chanity to wed," Marla stammered. "Chanity cares for Lord Jacot, so he should marry her instead. I just want us to be together, Lord Derek. We would be good as Lord and Lady of Holdenworth."

"There is no love between us, and there will never be," Derek said with finality. "When I wed, it will be to someone I truly love, that loves me as well. You lost your father and want someone to care for you. I care for you as family, and soon you will have more family that will care for you. You will be going to Normandy. I hope that one day you will find someone you truly love."

Marla started to object, but Derek began questioning her again. "Why did you lie to Chanity this morning? I want the truth!"

Marla hung her head and confessed to eavesdropping on Garth and Edmond's conversation when Garth spoke of asking for King William's permission to wed Chanity.

"You knew Garth was going to ask King William's permission to wed Chanity and did not tell me?" Derek said, shouting with fury.

"You could have helped me Marla, and yet you did nothing. I have been good to you and given you more than you deserve. Go to your chamber, and do not come out until I summon you. I must think awhile to decide on your punishment."

Left to himself, Derek shook his head in amazement at Marla's conniving behavior. When they had started speaking, his first reaction was to have pity on her for the circumstances she had faced in childhood. Now, it seemed she had no compassion for others in her heart. She was a liar and conspirator, and so much like her father. He dreaded telling his uncle, but knew he had to warn him the next time they spoke.

Some of Marla's words seemed to have been spoken in sincerity. Derek wondered if Marla really thought Chanity had feelings for Lord Jacot, or was she just trying to get him to give up on Chanity. He would never give up on Chanity. Besides, how could he anyway? She had him enchanted, so that she was all he thought about day and night. Somehow, he had to revive her love for him so that someday they could wed.

Derek regretfully turned back to his duty of dealing with Marla. He wished she could be sent to her grandparents now, but traveling that distance was not possible with winter approaching. She would have to remain at Holdenworth until arrangements could be made. He called a servant over and bade her order Marla downstairs to accept her fate. In short order Marla stood before him with her head hung low, and a dejected look on her face.

"Marla, I have decided to confine you to your bedchamber for two weeks as punishment for the plotting you have done. If you ever do anything like that again, I will banish you from Holdenworth forever," Derek declared.

Marla accepted her punishment without a word, turned and made her way back upstairs.

For the next three weeks, Derek spent as much time with Chanity as he could, but dedicated most of his time to practicing with his sword. He must defeat Garth and prevent any harm from coming to Chanity. He would protect her and hoped she would someday be his wife.

Chanity still had not given him an answer, but he was patient. At least she smiled a lot more, and they spoke together at mealtimes. She seemed to enjoy their time together, and he always looked forward to it as well.

A few days later, Derek saw Chanity walking back from the wood. "Where have you been on this glorious day?" He asked, giving her his best smile.

"I have been to my favorite spot at the cliff," Chanity answered.

"If it is your favorite, I would love for you to show it to me one day."

"We could have a picnic there on the morrow, if you are not too busy practicing in the list," Chanity said excitedly.

"I am never too busy to spend time with you, my dear Enchantress." Derek bowed to her, then gave her his most brilliant smile. "I anxiously await our meeting on the morrow," Derek said. She smiled back at him, then headed back to the manor. Derek gazed after her smiling, until she went inside and closed the door.

That night Derek could not take his eyes off Chanity while they supped in the great hall. He leaned in close and whispered so no one else could hear. "I am looking forward to our picnic on the morrow. 'Tis our first chance to be alone and speak in a great while."

Derek thought back to their first conversation on the day he had taken Holdenworth from Vorik. He remembered how close he felt toward her, even though they were strangers. Those two or three days had been enchanting, until he began his foolishness about avoiding her. He saw a great depth of caring and trust in her eyes, which scared him at the time.

He had wanted Chanity so badly, but refused to take her to his bed and ruin her chances for a good husband for the sake of a night of pleasure. He cared for her feelings and didn't want to hurt her. Looking back now, Derek realized he loved her from that very first day. How could she have had a chance of finding someone to wed? He was so jealous of Chanity, he would have slain them with his sword.

Bram was right; he had guarded her like a mother hen watching her chick, ready to flog anyone who came near. He realized his mistake and swore he would never deny his feelings again. It gladdened his heart, knowing Chanity was his, and no one on this earth would ever take her from him. He was enchanted, and he loved the enchantress, his enchantress.

They met in the hall that night on their way to their bedchambers. Derek drew her into his arms and kissed her with sweet, tender kisses, taking care not to get over excited. His desire for her was overwhelming, and he struggled to keep from going too far. "Chanity, I love you and I am so sorry I avoided you those last few weeks. "I was so foolish for not realizing how much I cared for you. Chanity my love, will you forgive me?"

"'Tis alright that you did not realize your feelings for me. We only knew each other for a short amount of time. Yet that has nothing to do with why I could not give you an answer. I still need time to think."

"Do you have feelings for another?" Derek asked, dreading the answer.

"I only have love in my heart for one man. That man is you," she replied, smiling up at him.

Derek gazed into her beautiful green eyes, saw they were filled with love, and knew it was all for him. Once again he took her into his arms, and gave her a long sweet kiss. That one sweet kiss would be remembered by both as they lay in their own bed that night, as they fell asleep thinking of the other.

'Twas always Chanity's habit to rise early, and this morning was no different. She rose before daybreak, and practically skipped down the stone stairs, feeling happy and excited about the coming day. In the great hall there were already a few men at the tables, but Derek was not one of them. She hoped he was excited as she about their upcoming outing. She could not wait to show him her favorite place, and hoped he would find it as incredible as she did.

Chanity decided to try her best to not dwell on what happened between Derek and Marla. She wanted his first visit to her favorite spot to be special, just as it had been for her. She dreamed all her life of one day showing it to the man she loved, and then marrying him. At least one part of her dream would come true. She loved Lord Derek with all her heart, but she could not wed him. Once again Chanity put those thoughts out of her mind so she could enjoy her special day.

She busied herself helping the servants get food and drink prepared for the men to break their fast. After most of the men were finished with their meal, Chanity set in cleaning the great hall. When Marla finally made her way down, she would ask her to take over the noon meal, for she had something to see to.

Derek awoke that morning, still pondering on what could be bothering Chanity. If only she would speak with him about it. At least now he knew her reluctance was not because she loved another. He decided to speak to her again today and try to convince her to reveal what was bothering her.

After donning his clothing, he went to break his fast. He hoped the morning would go by quickly so they could leave for their outing. Maybe then she would speak with him about her worries since no one else would be around. He went swiftly down the stairs with a smile on his face, anticipating what the day would bring.

Derek spied Chanity, and they smiled warmly at each other. Both were excited about their upcoming picnic at the cliff. Chanity approached and whispered quietly so only he could hear, "I will meet you as soon as everyone finishes breaking their fast, and we get the great hall cleaned."

As they sat down to eat, Marla finally entered the great hall. Even though Derek only confined Marla for two weeks, she went another week without joining them at meals. During Marla's confinement, Chanity took her food and drink, but the next week Marla went down to get her food then took it back up to her chamber.

They were both careful not to mention the picnic in front of Marla, afraid she might want to come along. Instead they talked about the livestock, and how the weather was getting colder.

The mornings had been brutally cold over the last few days, with a blustery wind which caused it to feel even chillier than it was. The weather should be warmer for the outing, as the wind had calmed somewhat, and the bright sun warmed the air by the noon meal. Though the day would be pleasant, it was only a matter of time before the cold of winter would be upon them.

Chanity broke her fast, bid everyone a good day, and returned to cleaning up. Soon everything was put in order, so Chanity went to the kitchen and packed up the things they needed. She had confided in Alma about the outing, but Chanity knew Alma would not say a word to anyone. The last thing she wanted was some idle gossip telling tales to King William on his return. Derek felt the same, and so they were careful not to touch one another, or kiss in front of anyone.

Chapter 9

The morning seemed to wear on, but finally the time for the outing drew near. As planned, Chanity met Derek at the tree line where Holdenworth disappeared from sight. He was anxiously waiting for her, and took the cloth bundle from her hand. The happy couple walked hand in hand through the woods to the ledge.

"What do you think of the view?" Chanity asked as they drew near the spot.

"'Tis amazing, but not as wondrous as the enchanting vision I see before me," Derek replied.

Derek dropped the bundle, lifted Chanity up in the air, and spun her around. Chanity laughed as she whirled in the air. He gently put her down and held her for a moment in case she was dizzy from the spinning.

Derek stooped to unpack their picnic, but Chanity stopped him. "This is not my favorite spot. It is on another ledge beneath this one. You must climb down the path beside the cliff to get there," Chanity explained. "'Twas a secret spot of my brother's and mine."

Derek climbed down first with the bundle, then helped Chanity as she descended. He could not believe this place. He could have lived here a lifetime and never found it. Chanity and her brother must have enjoyed it so much here. "How did you ever discover the place?" Derek asked.

"My brother was playing on the cliff above when he dropped a toy. He thought it would be dashed to pieces on the rocks below, but when he peered over the ledge it was lying just underneath. He climbed down to retrieve the toy and found this secret place."

"That explains how Gerald found it, but how did you?" Derek asked with a knowing smile.

"Gerald disappeared day after day, but wouldn't tell me where he went. I followed him, and discovered his secret," Chanity admitted, blushing. "We played here many times, and pretended the small cave was a fortress. Gerald tired of the ledge after a while and wandered back to the hall or stables. Once I had it all to myself, I would lay back on the rock, and daydream of the future."

They stepped back out of the cave onto the sunlit ledge. Chanity spread a cloth on the large flat rock for them to sit on while they ate. She brought meat, cheese, bread and an apple, along with a flask of wine for them to drink.

"What was your childhood like growing up?" Chanity asked. "Did you not say that you had an older brother and two sisters?"

"Aye, my brother Olen is two summers older. We were very close while growing up. Olen is a good warrior. He fought for William for six years, until my father asked him to come home to help with our families' vast lands."

"Both my sisters are younger than I. Mirana is nearly five summers younger. She's very pretty, and acts like a lady, though she is always happy and carefree. She is a fearless rider, and enjoys riding her horse more than anything. She helps our mother run the castle, while training to be a Lady. She is betrothed to a Chieftain's son of great standing who is one of William's commanders. They would have already wed if he wasn't away so much."

"Reyna is the youngest. She is seven summers younger. She should have been a lad, since she loves to hunt and fish. She always tried to tag along with Olen and I. Of course, when Mirana weds this spring, Reyna will have to start training to help run the Castle. Mother does not how much Reyna loves to hunt and fish, or else she does not let on that she knows."

Chanity was surprised to hear they lived in a castle. "It must be exciting to live in a castle. I know of only one castle in all of England. Well, now there are two, since King William built one at Hastings. 'Tis amazing to think there will soon be castles all over England, thanks to King William. What is it like living in a castle?" Chanity asked, curiously.

"Well, there are lots of corridors instead of hallways. Some have secret passages inside. They are cooler inside than a manor house and can be drafty. The walls are thick and fortified to keep out invaders. Olen and I used to explore and play in the secret corridors.

We had to be careful to never let anyone see us going in or out. Only the family members were to know of them."

Chanity could see the love Derek had for his family as he spoke. She enjoyed his stories about his siblings and parents. It was a joy watching him laugh, as he talked about the amusing mischief he and his siblings had gotten into while growing up.

Derek reclined on his side and propped his head up with his arm to watch Chanity as he spoke. Chanity noticed his careful attention, which made her feel very self-conscious.

"I would have loved to have lots of brothers and sisters," Chanity said. "There had only been Gerald and I, except for a baby brother who only lived a couple of weeks. He passed away during the night, and my parents never knew what happened to him. I had always hoped for a sister to play with when I was a younger. Unfortunately, Marla was the closest I ever came to having one, and she never wanted to play with me."

"I was so excited when I was told Marla was coming to Holdenworth, but sorely disappointed when she arrived. My mother and I welcomed her with open arms. We did not hold it against her that Vorik was her father. Marla shunned us from the very beginning and refused to have anything to do with my mother or me."

Chanity noted the darkening of her mood as she spoke of Marla and decided to change the subject. She wanted this to be a good day, filled with happy thoughts. She laughed, and began telling of some of the tricks she used to pull on Gerald, and some he pulled on her.

Derek reached up to take a lock of her hair, and played with it as she spoke. When she finished her story and fell silent, he sat up and placed the palm of his hand against her cheek.

"Chanity, you are so beautiful. You are the most beautiful lady I have ever set my eyes upon. I have been enchanted with you from the very beginning. You will always be my enchantress." He drew her into his arms, kissing her with feather light kisses that enticed them both.

Derek moved behind Chanity and passed his arm around her. He pulled her backwards to lean against him so they could look out at the sea as he held her. "That is one of the most amazing sights I have ever seen," Derek mused.

They sat there for a long while, just staring at the ocean and enjoying its beauty. He embraced her tightly and nuzzled her neck, then her cheek before turning her gently around to face him. He kissed her with a long sensual kiss that took her breath away. They clung together for the longest time, not wanting to let go of each another.

"Chanity, please tell me why you will not agree to wed," Derek asked, with pleading in his eyes. "I am so thankful I found you, and now I never want to let you go. I want you to wed me and be my wife. If you are worried about my battle with Garth, then don't be. I am certain I can best him in battle, for I am quicker and younger than he. He is only the King's champion because some of us don't care about being braggarts. The champion always has to watch his back, because someone else is constantly striving to take his place. Once he is defeated, the victor boasts, and the former champion is left feeling like a loser."

"'Tis not the reason, even though I do worry, and wish you did not have to battle him," Chanity tried to explain. "'Tis hard for me to speak of such things with you. It has to do with you and Marla."

Derek puzzled in his mind, trying to think of what she could be talking about.

Chanity's cheeks blushed as she finally told him all that was on her heart. "I saw Marla at your chamber door with only a fur pelt wrapped around her. She told me that you preferred her company instead of mine. Then I understood why you had been avoiding me, because you preferred Marla, and wanted to bed her."

Chanity could barely get the words out and blushed heavily with embarrassment as she spoke about bedding. Except with her mother, she had never spoke of such matters with anyone.

Derek wanted to thrash Marla at that moment, and was glad she was not there, or he would have been tempted to give her backside a good switching. He had never hit a lass before, and still would not.

"Chanity, upon my honor, I give you my word, I have never bedded Marla. I woke up and she was climbing into my bed, with no clothing on. I told her to get out and handed her the pelt she dropped. I forced her out the door and told her she better never enter my bedchamber again. From that night forward, I bolted my door to make sure she never would."

"I do not know what to do about Marla, but she must be punished," Derek said. "When Marla plotted against us and lied, I told her that if she did anything else, she would have to leave. Even though this occurred before then, she still must be punished for it. I will have to think on what I should do."

Derek turned to back to face Chanity. "I know for certain how I feel for you. 'Tis my fondest dream to wed with thee, and make thee my wife. Please say you will wed with me. 'Twould make me the happiest man in all of England."

Derek was overjoyed when Chanity answered, "Aye, I will wed with thee." Then she gave him the most loving smile he had ever seen. He picked her up, held her high in the air and then twirled her about, laughing the whole time. It was the happiest moment of their lives. They knew they had to keep this to themselves for now, until after the tourney was over, and King William gave his blessing.

Even in all the excitement, Chanity couldn't help but be afraid for Derek. Derek was tall and muscular, but Garth was taller still, and heavier.

After Derek issued the challenge, she overheard his men talking of Derek's speed and skill in battle. They were certain their Dragon could best Garth. Even the King's men had talked of placing their wager on Derek instead of Garth. This helped her feel a little better, but she would be worried until it was over and done with. She had so much love in her heart for him and knew she would never want another. She had cared for him in the very beginning. Her caring turned to love very quickly as she got to know him.

Derek was not troubled by the upcoming challenge. He had not fought in the King's tournaments, but had watched all the battles with interest. He studied each warrior's strengths and weakness and tried to learn from their mistakes. He had especially watched Garth, taking in his every move. For now, he was glad the hardest battle was over, and he had won Chanity's heart.

Chanity was so glad she was finally able to talk to Derek about Marla. She hesitated to tell him, but now was relieved that she did. She knew Marla's reputation for lying, and should have questioned what she said instead of just believing her. Everything finally made sense in light of what Derek had said.

What frustrated her most was that she didn't realize Marla's deceit when she saw how Derek avoided her. It was obvious that he did not prefer Marla's company, regardless of what she said.

Chanity sighed contentedly, and once again resolved to put Marla out of her mind. "This has been a most wonderful day," Chanity said.

"It has been the most wonderful day of my life, for you agreed to wed me," Derek said, with a smile.

They hadn't intended on spending the whole day at the cliff, but evening was drawing near. They wrapped the picnic items into a bundle, then Derek assisted Chanity up the path toward the upper ledge.

After they reached the upper ledge, they embraced each other once again. The sun dipped below the horizon; setting first the ocean, and then the sky ablaze. They stood watching the glorious sunset over the ocean. This was a perfect ending to a perfect day.

The hour was getting late, so Derek led Chanity back down the path toward Holdenworth. Just before came in sight of the hall, Derek told Chanity to go on ahead and he would follow later, so there would be no wagging tongues.

As Chanity stepped down the path she heard a whooshing sound. She turned to see what made the noise, and saw Derek fall to his knees, with an arrow protruding from his shoulder. Chanity ran to him and placed herself between him and where the arrow had come. She looked at his shoulder, and was relieved to see the arrow had not pierced deeply.

Derek stood and pulled her behind him with his good arm. He looked around for the assailant but saw no one. The danger seemed to have passed, but still he shielded Chanity with his large frame as they went back to the Manor.

Some of his men spied them approaching and rushed out to help while one of the guards ran to fetch Bram. Bram led Derek inside, called for a healer, then sent for Ortaire.

Ortaire came at once and Bram explained the situation. "Lord Derek has been shot in the shoulder with an arrow," Bram told him. "'Tis not a deep wound, but you must go in search of who did this. Take thirteen of your best trackers. Send four men to the north, for that was the direction the arrow came from. Send two in the other directions. You and the other three men search the dense wooded area nearby. Send word if you find any evidence the attacker may have left behind, or where he may have escaped to."

Ortaire nodded and left at once, while Bram went out to warn the guards at the gate and walls to be on alert. He wanted them to watch inside and outside the wall as well. After the watch was well set he talked to each guard and serf, asking if they had noticed anything out of the ordinary, or anyone acting suspicious over the last couple of days. He also asked if they had seen anyone they did not recognize. His search produced no leads, but he advised everyone to come directly to him if they saw an unfamiliar face, or someone acting suspiciously.

Chanity stayed at Derek's side as the healer worked on him. Soon Bram returned as well. For the last eight summers Derek, Bram, and Ortaire and he had watched each other's back in battle and otherwise. They had known each other from their youth, since they grew up in neighboring villages.

In their younger years they were inseparable. They all went to join Duke William when they were only a ten and six years, and were closer to each other than they were their own brothers.

Derek knew he could trust Bram with his life, and now with Chanity's as well. After Garth's challenge, he had asked Bram to take Chanity to his family in Normandy if anything should happen to him. He gave Bram a letter to give to his parents, introducing Chanity and telling of his love for her. It went on to tell them of the challenge, and how Chanity would be horribly abused if she wed Garth. Derek knew they would take her in and treat her like family.

Thinking of Garth and the battle to come helped keep his mind off the pain somewhat, as the healer worked on his shoulder. At times the pain was excruciating, but he refused to cry out.

Now, Derek's mind drifted to the challenge. He knew Garth would not fight fair, for he had watched him in battle after battle during the tournaments. He studied every move Garth made, suspecting he would have to fight him one day. What once seemed a battle he could win might now be a difficult battle, if he did not recover from the wound.

Derek opened his eyes and saw Chanity watching him. He saw the worry and love in her eyes as she laid a cool cloth on his brow to ease his pain. Derek tried to tell her he was going to be fine, but she could see the pain in his face, though he strove not to show it.

Chanity was relieved when Derek finally passed out from the laced drink they had given him, and from the pain when Etta seared the wound.

Alma came up to check on them before going to bed. She tried to take Chanity's place so she could get some sleep, but Chanity refused.

"You must get your rest," Chanity replied. "You have work in the great hall, and I won't be able to help."

"At least Marla is finally lending a hand, since Lord Derek told her she would have to earn her keep," Alma said with a smile.

"It seemed everything had gotten better at Holdenworth with Derek here, but now this," Chanity replied sadly.

"Don't worry lass, I'm sure he will be fine," Alma said reassuringly, and hugged her before she walked out.

By the second night Derek was burning up with fever. Chanity had no sleep, but still refused to leave him. She kept a cool, damp cloth on his brow, and spoke to him often so he would know she was there.

Alma and Etta shared a pallet in the room and refused to leave Chanity alone. By this point Chanity was so worried for Derek she was glad they were there with her. She also realized at least one person had to be in the bedchamber with them so no untruth got back to the King.

In his fevered state, Derek repeated his speech to Bram about taking Chanity to his family if something went wrong when he fought Garth. Tears streamed down Chanity's face, knowing he had thought to see her taken care of, even if something should happen to him. She knew he loved her, but now she realized he loved her more deeply than she had dared imagine. The thought of him not being there saddened her and caused her heart to ache. She loved him more than she had loved anyone and could not bear to lose him.

Chanity prayed many prayers that day for Derek, and a chance to have a future with him. She wanted him to know how much she loved and appreciated him for the life he offered her. He had given her a future filled with love and happiness to look forward to. Before he arrived, her future had seemed dark and hopeless.

Later, Derek began talking in his fevered state again. This time he talked of a woman named Lauren who wanted to wed him. He told her he did not love her, and did not care about her wealth or lands.

After a while, his dream turned to Marla. He ordered Marla out of his bedchamber, and said she was his cousin, and he would never love her.

Next, Chanity heard him warning a man about Marla, which she guessed was his uncle. At times he mumbled and rambled so she could not understand anything he said.

Etta entered with a cup, which she handed to Chanity. "We must help him drink all of it," she said, raising Derek's head while Chanity held the cup. "It is a strong mixture that will help with his fever."

After the drink was gone, Etta removed the dry paste that was on Derek's wound, and applied a fresh mixture to absorb the infection and help it heal. Not long after, Derek fell back asleep, and Chanity dozed off on the side of his bed as well.

Etta woke Alma, and they gently lifted Chanity and laid her beside Derek on the bed, since they would be the only ones who knew. Etta made sure the door was bolted as she lay down, and Alma took over watching Lord Derek. He still had fever, so Alma kept a cool, damp cloth on his forehead.

Chanity was exhausted, so they let her sleep until she woke on her own. It was late in the morn before she stirred. She chastised them for not waking her when she first dozed off. They chastised her in return because she went for so long without sleep.

"It does Lord Derek no good for you to exhaust yourself," Alma said. "Rest now, for he will want your attention later. He is recovering, though he will have to stay in bed for several days. It will not be easy to convince a Knight, much less a Lord to confine himself to bed."

Chanity checked Derek's brow for fever. His color was better, and his body was not as warm. They gave him water and broth, in small amounts several times a day. That night he slept peacefully, and only felt slightly warm.

The next morn Chanity was relieved to find Derek's fever was breaking. He was cool to the touch, and damp all over. Derek's eyes slowly opened, and the first thing he saw was Chanity standing beside him. They gazed into each other's eyes for a moment without speaking. He loved the big smile she gave him. It was as if sunshine had just filled the room. He smiled back weakly, then closed his eyes again.

Chanity broke the silence. "I am glad your fever broke. How do you feel?" She asked.

Derek's mouth was dry even though they had been giving him water. He motioned for his cup and Chanity brought it to his lips as she raised his head with her other hand. His shoulder wound was still tender, and he winched in pain from the movement. After drinking, he tried to rise, but Chanity pressed him back firmly, and told him he had to rest a few more days.

"I cannot stay in bed," Derek grumbled weakly, but soon ceased his grumbling when Chanity told him she would be spending most of each day with him. The thought of getting to spend time with Chanity made his temper much better.

"How long have I been like this, and what of my men?" Derek asked.

"This is the fourth day since you were struck with the arrow. You had a fever for three days and nights. Etta, Alma and I have been the only ones in your chamber, except for Bram and Ortaire. Bram stops by several times each day to check on you. Ortaire comes once or twice a day, but Bram keeps him very busy. Bram has two guards outside your chamber at all times, and has ordered all the guards to be on alert, watching for anyone or anything unusual."

Derek knew there was only one person who would want him injured, and that was Garth. He understood that Garth would not fight fair, but going to this extent was cowardly. He doubted Garth did the deed himself, but probably sent one of his henchmen. Garth would make sure he was with King William when Derek was attacked so he had an alibi.

At one time Derek believed Garth was worthy to be the King's Champion, but it was clear he let it go to his head. He had became a braggart who would do anything to keep from losing his title.

The next day, Derek was feeling even better. He got out of bed and sat at a small table in his chamber. From time to time he rose and strolled around his bedchamber so his legs would not get weak. Chanity visited often, and talked with Derek as they sat at the table.

Chapter 10

O ne day as they sat together, Derek asked Chanity if she would like to learn to play chess.

"Aye," she replied, keeping to herself that she was quite familiar with the game.

Derek explained the game to her as they played. At first Derek thought Chanity a quick study, but it was not long till he realized she knew the game well. They reset the board for another game, and his suspicions were confirmed, for she won the next game on her own.

"My enchantress has played me false, and did not tell me that she knew the game well," Derek mused.

Chanity laughed and gave him a beguiling smile. Derek thought she was truly beautiful, especially when she smiled. He stood and pulled her gently to him with his good arm, thankful again that his left shoulder had been injured, rather than his right.

Chanity went willingly into his arms, wanting to hold him and be held by him. They stood a long time holding each other and enjoying the warmth. Derek kissed her brow, then nibbled her ear and neck tenderly with his teeth. He brushed his lips lightly on her skin as he moved from her neck to her face slowly traveling to her lips. He traced her lips with his tongue, and used it to part them, then slid his tongue inside to mingle with hers. His kisses became more demanding, kissing her until she was nearly breathless.

Derek held her a moment, then kissed her again. She was getting those sensations again, and she could feel his excitement against her. Her mother had explained to her about what happened with a man's body, so she knew it was natural. What she did not know, was if what she was feeling in her lower body was normal. Chanity wondered if he felt the same sensations as she did. That was the last thing she thought, for his kisses were making her think of nothing else but the pleasure they brought.

Derek finally pulled away. "I must stop before we go too far," He said. "'Tis hard, but we must wait until we wed. I want our wedding night to be special for us."

He gave her a parting hug, and Chanity stepped away to take a seat at one of the chairs beside the bed. Derek walked over and stood in front of the window. One of his men saw him standing there and gave a shout to the others. All the men came running and crowded around to look up at Derek.

Suddenly they went down to one knee in unison, struck their chest three times with their fist, and shouted 'Dragon' with each hit. Then they stood with their right arm held high in a fist and shouted, "Hail to Lord Derek."

Derek was proud of the honor they had just bestowed on him, and slowly raised his good arm in the air with his hand in a fist. The men were greatly cheered to see their Lord recovering from his wound.

The next morning Derek rose early and began to make ready to leave his chamber. Chanity and Etta bade him stay in his chamber a few more days until his wound healed. Derek thanked them for all they had done, but said he must leave so as not to show weakness to his men.

"As a Warrior, and Lord of Holdenworth I must set an example for my men," Derek reminded them. "Besides, I don't want Garth finding out I have been injured, or where I was injured."

"Are you certain it was Garth?" Chanity asked.

"It must have been one of Garth's henchmen, since no one else would benefit from my death or injury," Derek replied. "Garth will soon find he is not as cunning as he thinks. When we meet in the list I will fain injury in my right arm. I can only hope his henchman was in such a hurry to get away that he did not notice where the arrow struck."

That night Chanity told Derek she would stay in her own chamber since he was quickly recovering. She knew that remaining in his bed chamber might prove a temptation too strong for either of them to resist, especially since he was feeling better. She would miss being by his side, but it was for the best until they were wed. Besides, she suspected Garth had a spy hidden amongst Derek's men, or in the men of the village. She wished she could ferret him out, but that seemed to be impossible.

Derek inspired great devotion among his men, and they served him admirably. They frequently offered to help and volunteered for duty even before being asked. Bram had been steadily searching for Derek's attacker, as well as keeping an eye out for any sympathizers and informants Garth might have. Chanity wished she could have seen the honor Derek's men had given their Lord, but did not dare to be seen in his bed chamber.

The next morning Chanity went downstairs into the great hall just as the servants were entering. To her surprise Marla marched from the kitchen a moment or two later and started giving orders, but went to work herself when she saw Chanity.

"So you decided to help us today?" Marla asked.

Chanity merely smiled and continued on her way. It was frustrating to keep silent and not respond after all that Marla had done, but she knew Derek wanted to confront Marla, and get her response.

The servants asked how Lord Derek was fairing. Chanity told them he was much better, and would be down today. They cared for their new Lord because he was just and fair, as Chanity's father had been. After Vorik's rule, they were doubly thankful.

On more than one occasion Chanity had heard them express thanks to God that Derek arrived and released them from the burden that Vorik and his men imposed. No one was more thankful than Chanity. A moment later and she would have been ruined. Now she had love and a future to look forward to. She could not wait to wed Derek and share her life with him. The thought of their future together brought a big smile to her face.

Just then, Derek entered the great hall. "I hope that smile has something to do with me," He said, smiling in return.

"It has everything to do with you, my Lord Derek," Chanity said laughing. "'Tis a glorious day since you are feeling better."

Derek took his place at the table, and Chanity brought a trencher of food and mugs of milk so they could break their fast together.

As Marla sat down beside Chanity to break her fast with them, Derek looked down the table curiously at her.

"Marla, it has been brought to my attention that you told Chanity that I bedded you in my chamber. What say you?" Derek asked.

Marla blushed and hung her head. "I didn't say you bedded me, though I did say you preferred my company to hers."

"But you knew Chanity would think that, since you had only a fur pelt around you, did you not? Did I give you the impression that I preferred your company to hers?" Lord Derek inquired.

Marla could not bear to look Lord Derek in the eyes. "You were not paying her as much attention," she replied softly.

"That was not my question," Derek said sternly.

"Nay, but I hoped. Besides, I have not done anything since then, especially after I heard of what happened to you," Marla pleaded.

If Marla had not plotted so heinously against them, he might have more sympathy for her, Derek thought to himself. He had told Marla she would have to leave Holdenworth if she continued her plotting, but perhaps she could still be redeemed. He decided to give her one last chance.

"You have been punished for lying to me, but not for deceiving Chanity. I know this happened before, but you must be punished. There is an empty hut at the edge of the village. You will stay in it for seven nights, and take your meals there. The only time you will be allowed in the hall is to help prepare meals and clean up afterwards. If you plot, scheme, and lie again you will be banished from Holdenworth Manor for good," Derek declared.

Marla nodded her head in acceptance, picked up her trencher, and began to make her way outside.

When they were alone, Chanity asked Lord Derek if perhaps Marla's punishment was too cruel.

"Marla has never had any real discipline, and she needs to know there are consequences for her actions. I can only hope we can help change her ways before she goes to her grandparents. I do not wish to bring any more trouble upon my uncle," Derek replied.

"I know 'tis not my place to question your orders as Chieftain, but I was thinking of her safety," Chanity said.

"Yes, she must be kept safe," Derek agreed. "I have spoken with Bram, and he will place guards. The hut is being repaired and a bolted latch put in place so Marla will be secure. All she will need to do is give the place a good cleaning."

Later that morning, Chanity saw tears in Marla's eyes as she was left the great hall to go to the hut. Chanity waited awhile, then

90

walked through the village to check on Marla. When she arrived at the hut, Chanity saw Marla's face was streaked with tears.

"I guess you came to gloat over my punishment," Marta said.

"Why would I come to gloat, Marla? This is not what I wanted for you."

"Why wouldn't you gloat after all I have done? And now you have won Derek's heart so he will never desire me," Marla replied.

"I wish you hadn't done those things, but I understand why you did them," Chanity replied. "What I regret most is all the years that we could have been close as sisters, but you chose to be alone instead. I know you have feelings for Derek, but you will find someone else when you go to your new home with your grandparents."

"I do not want to go live with them. Vorik's aunt was old, and she was very cruel to me. I don't want to live with another old woman. Your mother was kind to me, but I was always afraid she would become like my aunt as she became older, so I did not let myself care for her. I suppose I will always feel alone," Marla said, as tears rolled down her cheeks.

"Derek spoke highly of your grandparents and how much they will love you. They will be so excited when you go to live with them. Your great aunt was a bad person and was cruel to you, but your grandparents will love and want you. To be honest Marla, I will miss you, and I do care what happens to you."

Marla looked at Chanity in surprise. "You will? After everything that happened?"

"Of course I will," Chanity replied. "We have been together a long time. I want you to have a happy life and find someone to love who will return your love. I want you to trust in your grandparents that they will be good to you. Chanity squeezed Marla's shoulders in a hug as she stood to leave.

"I must go for now. Just bide your time here. You will be back in your chamber before you know it. Don't be afraid to stay here by yourself. Lord Derek has seen to it that you are well guarded. Still, you should be sure to bolt the door when I leave."

As Chanity departed, Marla still looked glum, but it seemed a spark stirred within her. Chanity made her way back to the great hall, hopeful that Marla would finally change her ways.

Marla spent the rest of the day pondering over the past. Deep down, she knew Serina and Chanity had tried to welcome her to Holdenworth. She would never admit it, but she had cared for Serina. She often envied Chanity for her closeness to her mother.

Once when Marla was sick, Serina came to her chamber and cared for her. She never left her side until Vorik ordered Serina back to their chamber. Even then, Serina had Etta the healer stay with her. Serina herself would slip in a few times during the night to check on her.

She loved when Serina stroked her hair, and told her everything would be fine. Every night after Serina left Chanity's chamber, she also came by hers. She kissed Marla on the forehead and bid her good night. Marla acted like it did not affect her, but she always looked forward to Serina's nightly visit.

She had never told Serina she loved her, but wished she had. She was always afraid to love. Now she regretted not telling Serina how she felt. After Serina died, Marla cried for the first time in years. For several nights afterward, she cried herself to sleep.

Marla thought of Chanity, and knew her jealousy had kept them from being close. She wished she had accepted Chanity's friendship and became like sisters. It was too late for that though, so there was no use dwelling on it. Though her feelings about Chanity had changed much, she still resented Chanity for having Derek. She wished that Derek loved her instead, and wanted her to stay at Holdenworth. She might not plot and plan, but if she had the chance to have Derek and Holdenworth she would gladly take it from Chanity.

She thought back to all the stories Derek told her about her grandparents. He talked of how they loved their children, and assured Marla they would love her as well. He told Marla of the hard years they had after their sons were slain and Marta was taken. It must have been difficult for them when they heard rumors that Marta died while trying to birth her child. Derek told her they would have surely searched for her, if they thought she lived.

In return, Marla told Derek what she knew of her birth. She spoke of the nursemaid that cared for her from the time she was born until her father dumped her on his aunt. The nursemaid named her Marla, in tribute to her mother Marta. In truth, the nursemaid probably cared for her more than anyone else in her childhood.

As Marla reflected on her younger years she felt angry at Vorik for abandoning her, and hated her great aunt for raising her without love.

She used to resent Chanity because Vorik protected her, but now she realized it was only because of Serina that he did so.

On the night she came across Vorik and Chanity in the hall, Marla knew he would have taken Chanity by force if she had not come up the stairs. She only said those mean things to Chanity because she resented that Vorik wanted Chanity, even if it wasn't in a fatherly way.

Marla felt like she was growing up and had begun to see things as they really were. Soon she would be a half score and seven, and no longer the child she once was. As night closed in, she sat on a bench in front of the fire, thinking of her future and what it held.

Chanity went down to the great hall the next morning to see the first big snow of the winter. It was more like a blizzard, since the wind was blowing hard and snow still coming down. At night more of the men would be sleeping in the great hall because of the storm. As the snow started to fall, they slowly began to drift inside to the warmth of the hall.

She was glad the animals were not brought inside Holdenworth's great hall during the cold as was tradition in most manors. Her mother had insisted her father build a large building to shelter them along with some of the men. That way the great hall would not be over-crowded, not to mention have a nicer smell.

Lord Derek was already downstairs speaking with his men at the table. They were waiting for their trenchers to be brought to them so they could break their fast. Chanity headed straight to the kitchen to help get the food prepared.

While helping place trenchers on the table, she overheard the news that King William and his men would not be stopping by Holdenworth as was planned. King William decided to leave court early because there were other matters that needed his urgent attention. It seemed a revolt had started in a village a few days ride from London.

Derek was grateful the King took the time to send a messenger to deliver word of the change in plans. It was clear the King thought a great deal of him and took the matter of his challenge seriously. The messenger also stated that the King would come as soon as he could so the challenge could be settled between Derek and Garth.

Chanity was also relieved on hearing the news, for this gave Derek more time to heal. She regretted it would be longer for them to wed, but at least Derek would be fit for battle. She had been increasingly worried about the upcoming challenge since Derek had been wounded.

Derek saw her smile and knew her thoughts. Chanity was clearly relieved he would have more time to heal. They cared so much for each other; it seemed they knew what the other was thinking just by a glance.

Chanity saw his expression, and knew he was thinking that the wedding would be delayed. At least the delay would not matter much, for they grew closer and loved each other more with each passing day.

Since they were snowed in, Derek and Chanity passed their time playing chess. They sat bent over a table by the roaring fire in the great hall, debating their next move. Chanity had not won as much at chess since Derek found out how good she was. He carefully studied his every move, trying to beat her so his men would not taunt him so. They would get a great laugh if she bested him, and teased him endlessly. Derek enjoyed the challenge she gave him. If the men taunted him too much, he silenced them by challenging them to play against her.

Bram was always first in line to play the winner after their game. Bram's skill nearly matched Chanity's, and he had defeated her a few times. Ortaire won sometimes, but would just laugh when he lost. "'Tis always wise to let the ladies win," he would say after a loss. Even after his comment, the men would still taunt him for not being able to defeat a lass.

Marla's seven days were up, so Derek sent a servant to tell her she could return to her chamber in the great hall. Marla was so relieved to get out of the hut that she practically ran back to the hall. She had not shed a tear in years, but that changed the day she was banished to the hut. The temporary banishment opened the floodgates to the memories and fears she had growing up.

Her great aunt had always told her that if she didn't do what she said, Marla would be thrown out in the streets. It had terrified her as a child, and her aunt was so cruel Marla believed she would really do it. Now she was older, and knew her aunt would never have turned her out, because all she had was provided by Vorik.

Her aunt had acted as if she was solely responsible for Marla's care, and did not tell her that Vorik had provided for that and more. If she had known, she might not have resented Chanity as much when she first arrived at Holdenworth. On the voyage to Holdenworth she overheard the guards talking about how Vorik protected Chanity. This made her think he cared more for Chanity than her. Now she realized that Vorik cared only for himself. He paid his aunt so he could be rid of her.

Marla had always wanted her father's love and approval, but never received it. If Vorik had a son, he probably would have given him more care and attention, but she doubted he could truly love anyone. She was glad he never got the heir he always wanted. She was especially glad that Serina never had to birth him a child. She knew Serina loved her first husband until the day she died. It would have hurt her too much to have a child by the man who slew the only man she ever loved.

Long ago, Marla had overheard Serina speaking with Etta. They talked about herbs to keep Serina from having a child. Etta gave Serina some herbs for Vorik as well. Marla never told anyone and kept it to herself so her father would never find out. She didn't want him to have a son, and didn't want Serina to be hurt as well.

Deep down, she knew Serina cared for her. Vorik on the other hand, thought nothing of hitting women, beating them and even raping them. She even overheard some serfs saying that Vorik had forced a couple of the village girls. She couldn't understand why he would do so, since there were plenty of willing ones.

Marla entered her chamber and was greeted by the warmth of a fire on the hearth. She knew Chanity had seen to this for her. She couldn't understand why Chanity was always so kind. She wished Chanity wasn't nice, so it would be easier for her to sway Lord Derek. She realized there was no use wishing things were different. Chanity had Derek, and there was nothing she could do to change that. She certainly would not be plotting anything else, for she did not want to be banished from Holdenworth forever.

If she did not win Derek's love, she would have to leave Holdenworth anyway. Marla dreaded going to her grandparents in Normandy. Her only other option would be to go to Vorik's family in France, which she refused to do. Holdenworth was the only real home she ever had. She would just have to try harder to win Lord Derek.

When she went down to sup that night, she smiled and thanked Chanity for having her chamber readied for her. She hoped Derek would notice her and think her kind. She also complimented a couple of his men, one of which was Bram. Bram seemed to see through her ploy and snorted in disdain.

Bram knew Marla wanted Derek and would do anything to win his favor. He listened as Marla apologized to both Derek and Chanity for her behavior. He feared Chanity would be fooled into thinking she had changed, and decided to warn Chanity not to trust her. Derek was smart enough to know Marla was playing a game, but he would still care for her since she was family.

Bram thought of Laren, a young widow who taught Derek a hard lesson when he wasn't even a score in age but only ten and five years. He found out it was his body she wanted and not his love. Derek had adored Laren, and it took him some time to get over her. There were a couple other women that tried to win Derek's favor, but he never paid much attention to them.

Bram had tried to warn Derek that Marla had her eye on him, but he had not listened. Derek thought of her as only family and did not see that she felt differently.

Derek's enchantment with Chanity was obvious from the first day. He had never stopped to speak with anyone, much less a lass, before seeing to his men after battle. Derek seemed to forget everything around him while he spoke to her. It was as if she was the only thing that existed. Bram hoped no woman ever had that effect on him, or did he? Bram saw Chanity was special, and it would be easy to fall for a lass such as her. When Derek had a fever, he had watched as she lovingly cared for him, and never left his side. Etta had to slip a sleeping herb in Chanity's wine one night because she was exhausted, and in much need of rest. Fortunately, Chanity never realized it, or she would have been very upset. Bram smiled as he watched them, knowing they would be good together.

Chapter 11

The next night Chanity decided to entertain, and they sat around the fire listening to her play the harp. Afterwards she sat down by Derek, who complemented her playing.

"Does your family celebrate Christmas with a festival?" She asked. "My family always celebrated it until Vorik became Chieftain, then Mother stopped. I would love to start the tradition back. I always loved the festival and so did the people of Holdenworth, though no one felt like celebrating when Vorik was Lord here."

"My family celebrated with a grand feast, and it would be nice to do the same at Holdenworth," Derek said. "I don't see why we can't start it back again."

"Our Christmas festival was held on Christmas day with a great feast. The whole village was welcome to celebrate in the great hall. The village women liked to show off by cooking their best dish along with the cooks at Holdenworth. We would sing songs, and there were also skalds and jugglers to entertain."

"My parents celebrated in much the same way. Sometimes we even had a Christmas ball the day before, with people coming from a great distance away," Derek said. "On Christmas day my parents always put a yule log on the fire to burn. My mother told me they had called it yule festival when she was a little girl."

"When my grandparents were young they were not Christians. At that time, Christianity was not as common in our country. My great-grandparents believed in several gods, but my grandparents became Christians after they wed. Most people in our country have converted to Christianity now."

"My parents burned the yule log, as well," Chanity said while a smile, remembering back to those happier days when both her parents were still alive. "My great-grandparents were Christians, but I don't know about their parents. It will be so nice to celebrate Christmas again. I really missed it. When Vorik was here, Mother and I never felt like celebrating. He probably would not have allowed it anyway."

Chanity silently thanked God again for sending Derek to Holdenworth. Derek brought prosperity and joy back to her and the village. "Thank you Derek, once more for coming here and making Holdenworth a better place. You gave people hope again, something they did not have the last few years before you came."

"'Tis no need to thank me Chanity," Derek said warmly. "Besides I would never have found you if I had not came to Holdenworth."

Chanity had brought meaning and purpose back to his life. In the past, he had hopes of a loving future, but never seemed to find the right lass. Since the first moment he laid eyes on Chanity, his life had not been the same. She had enchanted him not only with her beauty, but with her ways as well. Her warmth and kindness filled his heart. Chanity seemed to have the same effect on everyone she met. All she had to do was smile to brighten someone's day.

"Will you be able to bring in game for the festival?" Chanity asked.

"I will see to it that the men hunt plenty of game," Derek promised. "That way our winter provisions will not be used. We will have a hunt two days before the Christmas festival. There will be a prize for the biggest game, and most game taken. Do you want to come along on the hunt?"

"I'm sorry Lord Derek, but I will be busy getting ready for the festival," Chanity replied.

Marla perked up at Chanity's response. Finally, it seemed this was an opportunity to spend time with Derek without Chanity getting in the way. "I would like to go on the hunt, Lord Derek," Marla declared. "I always begged my father to let me go, but he would never take me."

Derek asked Chanity if she could spare Marla for the hunt.

"I won't need her help that morning," Chanity replied. She didn't want Marla to go, but could think of no reason why she shouldn't.

"Marla, you will have to be aware at all times," Derek advised. "Sometimes a wild boar will charge at you even when you are mounted. Bram is our best boar hunter, so you can ride in his group.

He will flush the game and drive it toward my group. I will not see you during the hunt, but I hope you have a good time and stay safe."

The look on Marla's face was one of pure disappointment. "Since the hunt will be so dangerous, perhaps I should stay and help with the preparations for the festival." She hated the thought of spending her morning with Bram. Things never seemed to go her way. She knew if Chanity had wanted to go, Lord Derek would have her by his side.

Derek glanced at Chanity to see if she noticed his ploy to dissuade Marla from going on the hunt. Their eyes met, and she gave him knowing look, and a big smile. Fortunately, Marla was none the wiser. The last thing they needed was for her to feel rejected and out of place again.

No matter how many times he saw it, Derek knew he would never tire of seeing Chanity smile. He liked how Chanity's face had lit up while talking about the Christmas Festival. He enjoyed seeing her happy and excited. Happiness seemed to amplify her beauty.

For a moment he wondered what she would look like being with child. In his mind he pictured her face radiant, her belly rounded, and her long golden hair hanging freely to her waist. He had never pictured another woman with child before, but he could not wait to see her carrying their babe. It was truly frustrating waiting to wed her. He wanted to get on his horse and ride straight to King William's camp to battle Garth, but he didn't even know where William was at the moment.

Derek could not stand the waiting, but he knew the King would not approve, and did not dare disobey him. King William thought a lot of him, but if he defied him by wedding Chanity without his blessing, William would not forgive it. He could lose everything he had gained, even Holdenworth. King William might even annul the wedding and grant Garth permission to wed her. He would never risk losing Chanity, so he would just have to be patient whether he liked it or not.

Chanity's laughter brought Derek back to the moment. Bram had said something amusing which Derek had missed.

"I see you have rejoined us from being lost in your thoughts," Bram said laughing. From the look on Derek's face, he could guess at what was on his mind. The wait was weighing heavily on his friend. He felt for Derek, but it was wiser to wait on the King's blessing.

As the days passed, Bram watched his friend pace around restlessly with a scowl on his face. It was fortunate that they had not heard any news of where King William was, for Derek would surely be on his way if they did. At least Derek had time to heal from his wound and train for the battle to come. Bram loved Derek like a brother, and they had been together for years. He knew Derek could best Garth in battle, but they had plans in place if something went wrong.

Bram would take Chanity and flee to Derek's parents in Normandy. Bram would never be able to return to William's service, but he cared enough for Derek to see Chanity was safe. He would be certain that Chanity was safe from Garth, even if he had to stay there the rest of his life. He knew Derek's parents were good people and would not turn them away.

For Derek to ask this of Bram proved he loved Chanity more than life itself. Bram cared for her as well, but he knew he had to think of her as a sister, for she loved Derek. He hoped Derek would always appreciate the lass. She seemed to have the respect of all the men at Holdenworth because of her kindness and caring ways.

The next morning Chanity decided to spread the word that the Christmas Festival would be held this year. After everyone broke their fast and the great hall was cleaned, she stopped by the stable to ask the stable boy to saddle her beautiful white mare, Lily.

Her parents had given her Lily on her birthday when she turned a half score. She had treasured Lily from that day on. After Vorik's raid, her mother warned her never to tell Vorik that Lily was her mare. If he knew, he might sell the horse just to spite her. Chanity snuck carrots and apples to Lily only when Vorik was busy and away from the stables. Fortunately, he never ventured into the stables much.

Marla had ridden Lily sometimes, and treated the horse well; it was just people she was not kind to. While Vorik was alive, Chanity kept the secret from Marla as well, fearing she would run and tell him. She would never risk the chance of losing Lily just to make a claim on her. Derek would have claimed Lily, but after hearing the story he told Chanity the horse would always be hers.

After Derek first arrived at Holdenworth, he made visiting the stables one of his top priorities. He ran into Chanity during his inspection. Derek admired the horses stabled there, and told Chanity that her father had great knowledge in horse flesh and breeding. The steeds were the best he had seen in years.

Chanity took Derek on a tour of the stables and told him about each horse. They first stopped to look at Rollo, the horse Derek had chosen for himself. Rollo was sired by her father's own horse Zeus. Vorik had sent Zeus to Duke William as part of the appeasement tribute after Holdenworth was raided. Chanity had an unfavorable opinion of Duke William at the time, but was glad that anyone had her father's war horse other than Vorik.

The stable boy seemed to be taking a bit longer than usual to bring Lily, so Chanity decided to check on the yearlings in the other side of the stable. She turned the corner and saw Derek looking over the new stock.

Derek greeted her warmly, and pulled Chanity to his side.

"I was glad to discover that the stable master learned Belgar's breeding methods, so we will have fine steeds at Holdenworth for years to come. I've asked the stable master to start training the stable boys now, so they will have the knowledge when they are older."

"I've also been studying your father's horse lineage charts. With the help of the stable master, I would like to even improve upon the breeding stock if I could. So far I have been good at drawing up battle strategy but have no notion of how to plan horse breeding," Derek confessed.

Chanity watched Derek closely. She liked that he wanted to learn new things. Now he had the time, and she was sure he would find it challenging. Chanity looked again at Derek and saw he was still concentrating on the horses and evaluating the features of each.

"Sir Knight, are the horses more entertaining than I?" Chanity asked, laughing.

"Nay, dear Chanity, nothing could be more delightful or entertaining than you, my enchantress," Derek said, smiling. He was pleased that she called him 'Sir Knight', because she had called him that on their first meeting.

"I was just thinking how nice it would be to have a new interest to occupy my spare time, though there isn't much to spare. I want the best for Holdenworth and our future."

The stable grew quiet as they stood alone for a moment. Seeing no one about, Derek quickly pulled her to him and gave Chanity a kiss that left her breathless. Just as he was about to kiss her again, they heard the sound of the stable boy. They turned as he came around the corner leading Rollo and Lily.

Derek took the Rollo from the stable boy, and Chanity took Lily.

"I see you are going riding as well, Lady Chanity," Derek said smiling.

"I am going to spread the news of the Christmas Festival in the village," Chanity said as she mounted.

"I have a few things to check on, but afterward I would like to ride with you," Derek said.

Chanity was pleased at the thought of riding with Derek, so they arranged to meet at the ironsmith when she was done.

Chanity rode Lily to several cottages and asked the villagers to pass the word about the Festival. Her last stop of the day was at the ironsmith. After she told him the news, he asked Chanity to go by the cottage to say hello to his wife Nell, since she always looked forward to visitors.

The ironsmith's cottage was but a short distance away, so Chanity stopped by to greet Nell. At Chanity's knock, Nell opened the door and welcomed her in.

"'Tis so good to see you, my dear. It's been too long since you paid me a visit," Nell said. "Take a seat by the fire, and let me get you some cool water from the well."

Nell handed Chanity a cup of water, and looked her over from head to toe. "Why, Chanity, you grow to look more like your mother every day. We all miss her very much."

Nell's daughter Alice came in as they were talking. "We are blessed to have Alice back home with us," Nell said. "I believe I told you she went to stay with my younger sister a couple summers ago. My sister needed help caring for our parents since she had her hands full with her small children. My parents have both passed on now, so Alice is back home to stay."

"Chanity came by to tell us that they have started the Christmas Festival back again," Nell explained to Alice. "We always enjoyed it, and I know the whole village did as well. We are so glad Lord Derek is our Chieftain. It was hard on everyone when Vorik was here, but I know it was even harder on you and your mother."

Chanity saw Alice light up at the mention of Derek's name.

"Aye, we are glad Lord Derek is here," Alice said, with a lustful look in her eyes. "He stops by often to speak with me, and I always enjoy our conversations."

Alice deliberately swayed across the room swinging her hips, while pushing out her big bosom. Chanity scowled at the implication Alice made. She noticed Alice had definitely filled out while she was away.

Nell saw the expression on Chanity's face and turned to give Alice a stern look. "Lord Derek likes to stop by and talk business with my husband," Nell said, smiling. "Men say women like to talk, but they certainly talk enough themselves, when the subject interests them."

"Thank you for the water, Nell. I had best be going, for I have to meet Lord Derek for our ride back home," Chanity said. Chanity set the cup down, and Alice dashed out the door before Chanity had a chance to rise from her chair.

As Chanity rode up to the ironsmith's shop, she saw Derek and Alice standing together. Alice had Derek by the arm, and leaned in to press her bosom against it. Alice threw back her head and laughed loudly at some comment Derek had made.

"Why Alice, you were as fast as Lily getting here," Chanity said as she dismounted.

"Who is Lily?" Alice asked, smiling and still holding tightly to Derek's arm.

"My horse," Chanity answered, with a serious look on her face. Derek could not help but give a slight laugh at the seriousness on Chanity's face, and the look of shock and hatred on Alice's.

Alice dropped Derek's arm, glared at each of them in turn, and stormed away.

"It seems she does not sway her hips when she runs away," Chanity said laughing. She patted Lily consolingly as she dismounted. "Don't be envious of her Lily, even though she is pretty fast."

Derek could not help bursting out into laughter. Chanity laughed along for a moment, but then her face turned serious.

"It seemed as though you were having fun with Alice," Chanity said. "Did I come back at a bad time, my Lord?"

Derek exhaled, knowing it did not look good when Chanity rode up. "Chanity, I promise I had nothing to do with her grabbing me," Derek explained. "She grabbed my arm when she first ran up. I tried to pull it free, but she has a tight grip."

"I told her she had a grip like a warrior, and that was what she was laughing about. I guess that was more amusing to Alice than being told she was as fast as a horse."

They both couldn't help but laugh again, thinking of the angry look on Alice's face.

"'Tis alright, I know how she is with men. Alice has always been a flirt, just try to be less familiar with her."

Chanity remembered the gossip that had been flying around when Alice left. Some speculated she might have been with child, instead of going to help with her grandparents. Traveling to distant family to have a babe and give it up was not an uncommon way to deal with a child born out of wedlock.

She did not speak of that to Derek, because she did not know if it was true, and it was too embarrassing to have such a conversation with him. Besides that, she refused to spread gossip. Her mother taught her to treat everyone the way you want them to treat you, and not say anything about someone if it was not kind. The only exception was when someone was trying to hurt you or someone else.

"'Tis getting late. We best head back to Holdenworth before it gets any colder," Derek said. He helped Chanity mount Lily before mounting his own horse. He had grown very fond of Rollo, which was named after the first Duke of Normandy.

Chanity laughed as she quickly took off on Lily, and Derek pursued. She looked so beautiful, laughing and riding with the wind in her hair. She had a carefree and happy manner as she rode Lily.

Derek was glad he came and rescued her from the harsh life Vorik had imposed. He couldn't imagine the sorrow she and her mother felt, having to live with Vorik after he slew Belgar. He wanted to make her happy always, and gritted his teeth in determination to defeat Garth. His determination reflected in his riding, as he pursued Chanity even faster.

Rollo was extremely fast, so Derek caught up with Chanity before she knew it. "You will never escape me enchantress, and you will always be my captive," Derek shouted. He rode close, and scooped her off her horse and into his arms.

Derek slowed Rollo, and Lily cantered along behind them. "You have enchanted me, and hold my heart captive, only for you," he whispered in her ear. Chanity loved the feel of his warm breath on her ear and neck as he whispered to her. She loved being trapped in his embrace, as he held her tightly against his warm body. He kissed her neck, then her lips. The sensation he caused coursed through her whole body.

As they neared an open meadow, Derek noticed some tracks in the soft earth. He halted Rollo, and dismounted to inspect them. Just as he bent down, an arrow flew over head. Derek felt the force of the arrow as it went past, and heard Chanity scream. Derek thought Chanity had been shot through as she sat on Rollo, but was relieved to see she was uninjured. He yelled for Chanity to drop to the ground, and dove into the tall grass, thinking she would follow suit.

Chanity's eyes swept the woodline as she saw one arrow, and then another fly toward where Derek was hiding in the grass. She grabbed Rollo's reigns, and wheeled him around to catch Lily. Turning again, she placed the horses to shield Derek from the flying arrows.

"Chanity have you gone mad? Get down here before you get shot," Derek commanded, reaching up to pull her down with him. "Stay down. Now that we are shielded by the horses, I'm going to shoot some arrows in the direction these came from."

Though the attacker had probably fled by now, Derek quickly retrieved his bow and fired three arrows back into the wood.

It was strange that the arrows stopped after Chanity shielded him. Now he knew for sure it was one of Garth's henchmen.

They crept through the meadow, using the horses to shield them until they reached the edge of the woods on the opposite side. The trees would make any attack difficult if their assailant decided to follow.

Once they were safely in the trees, Derek turned toward Chanity. "Never risk your life again, no matter what," he ordered angrily. "It was very brave what you did, but you must not do it again. I couldn't live with myself if you were slain trying to save me. You are the most important thing to me, even more than Holdenworth. I can replace a home and lands, but I could never replace you, or the love that I feel for you."

105

Tears came to Chanity's eyes as he spoke. "I feel the same for you, and that is why I had to try to save you," Chanity said, wiping away the tears. "You would have done the same for me. You would not have just sat back as arrows flew around me, knowing you could do something to help."

Derek knew she was right. "Thank you Chanity, it was very brave of you, but please never do it again."

Derek and Chanity mounted and rode their horses hard as they headed back to Holdenworth. They felt better when they emerged from the woods and the walls of Holdenworth came into view. Finally, they were able to relax once inside the gates.

Derek shouted to one of the guards to fetch Bram and Ortaire right away. Derek and Chanity made their way to the stables, and Bram arrived a few moments later. Derek explained what had happened, then ordered Bram to take some men to scout the area for signs or tracks the attacker might have left.

Bram gathered four of his best trackers and headed to the place Derek described. He was determined to find Garth's henchman one way or another. He had never liked or trusted Garth as far as Derek was concerned. Perhaps Garth wanted Derek merely wounded, but one shot with an arrow could be fatal.

It was clear to Bram that Garth wanted to insure his victory by wounding Derek. He was a braggart, and wanted witnesses to see him defeat Derek in battle, proving he was the mightiest warrior. Bram thought Derek was the better warrior. The only reason Derek had not battled Garth was because he had no desire to be the King's Champion Knight.

Derek had often told Bram that he wanted his own farmstead, so he could settle down and have a family. After Derek won Holdenworth he persuaded Bram to remain, hoping he would settle with him to help oversee the place, and ensure that his family was well guarded. They had been inseparable since childhood. He thought of Derek like a brother, and knew Derek felt likewise. Though Bram had planned to rejoin William, he agreed stay for a while.

Bram and his men scoured the area until nightfall but did not find much evidence. When it became too dark to see, they headed back to Holdenworth to give Derek the disappointing news.

"Whoever this man is, he is skilled at covering his tracks," Bram told Derek. "We found nothing where you were attacked, other than a few foot prints around where he sat. Fortunately my men have sharp eyes, and were able to find tracks leading to where he tethered a horse. We followed his horse tracks to a stream, where I split the men into two groups. We searched each side of the stream till it became too dark to see, but did not find where he rode out of it."

Bram told the trackers to get their rest, for they would be leaving before daylight to resume the search. Derek and Bram sat at the table discussing the situation well into the night. At last Bram retired to his chamber so he could get an early start in the morning.

Chanity stopped Bram as he was about to leave the great hall. "Were you able to find the man or any evidence?" She asked, hopefully.

"Nay, but we will start out again before sunrise. Don't worry, Chanity. 'Tis just a matter of time to before we catch the fiend," Bram said reassuringly. "Derek told me how brave you were today, and I want to thank you. He is like my own brother, and I would not want anything to happen to him. You must take care, as well, Lady Chanity."

Chanity assured him she would, then Bram bid her good night and headed for bed.

The next day Bram and his men found tracks leading out of the stream. They followed a horse beaten path to an old run-down cottage, where it seemed the man was met by several people on horseback. Seven sets of horse tracks lead out in different directions. It seemed as if this had been well planned out.

Disappointment settled over Bram, as he ordered the men to head back to Holdenworth. The ride back was faster, since they took a path that ran by the stream and were not searching for tracks.

Bram told Derek all they had seen, and the elaborate effort the adversary had made to confuse pursuit. It was disappointing news to Derek, but he had been expecting it. He knew Garth would not have sent just anyone. He sent a man that was experienced and knew what he was doing. Someone that was smart enough not to be easily caught.

The next day, Bram came looking for Derek. "I have a plan to trap the scoundrel, but it will be risky. We know he stayed at a hut in the woods, and used it to hide out in. By now, he thinks we have called off the search. After spying the hut, I stayed well away from it, and watched long enough to know it was empty. If the henchman thinks we don't know about the place, then he might return."

107

Derek agreed, so Bram dispatched a guard to watch the place so they would be alerted if the henchman returned.

A fortnight passed before they received word that Garth's henchman was back at the hut. The guard had spied him entering right at dusk. Derek wanted to charge in and capture the henchman immediately, but Bram persuaded him against it.

"Let me place men around the hut tonight, in case he is there to meet someone," Bram advised. "We will watch closely so he will have no chance to escape."

Derek agreed, so Bram set out with his men.

Bram strategically laid out his men around the hut while the henchman slept that night. The next morn, the henchman went outside to relieve himself, and was easily captured by Bram and his men.

Bram showed no mercy to the man who had nearly killed his best friend. He tied a rope around the man, mounted his horse, and rode back to Holdenworth. His captive was forced to walk quickly to keep up. If he stumbled, Bram drug him for a distance before stopping his horse to let the man stand again. Each time he stood, Bram gave the henchman a chance to say who sent him, but the man refused to speak except to curse.

When they arrived at Holdenworth's gate, Bram stopped one last time. "You are making it harder on yourself, but that is fine by me," Bram stated. "I will enjoy making you confess. You will surely tell me what I want to know before this is over with, I promise you that. Not only is Derek my Lord, he's my best friend, and like a brother to me."

The man stood silently, staring at the ground. Bram flicked the reins and drug the man across the inner baily for all to see. The guards left his hands bound, and roughly led him away to a cell.

Derek and Chanity sat breaking their fast as Bram entered the hall. "We have the baggage you have been waiting for, Lord Derek," Bram said, grinning as he arrived at the Lord's table.

Chanity, I have something that needs my attention. Stay and finish breaking your fast." Derek said. "I will see you at the noon meal."

Chanity smiled slightly to herself as she returned to her meal. Men and their secrets, she thought to herself.

Though she felt amused at the little drama that had just unfolded, Chanity was greatly relieved as well. Bram and his men must have captured Derek's assailant, who had undoubtably returned to finish the task he started.

Derek promised to return by the noon meal, so Chanity decided to busy herself so the day would go faster. She entered the kitchen and grabbed the scrap bowl on her way out to feed the hounds.

Chanity called out to the hounds and they came quickly. The scraps immediately quietened the noisy bunch, as the hounds enjoyed their first meal of the day.

Chanity was so busy watching the happy mob that she didn't hear Alice approach.

"I see little miss high and mighty is lowering herself to serving the hounds this morn," Alice said scornfully. "I forgot though, you no longer the Lord of Holdenworth's daughter. You are just a slave, a servant, like everyone else."

"What brings you to the manor this fine morn, Alice?" Chanity asked contemptuously.

"I was bringing some eggs as usual, but I wanted to speak with you as well. I am warning you now, stay out of my way with Lord Derek if you know what is good for you."

"I will do as I please where Lord Derek is concerned, Alice," Chanity replied angrily. "You should also know I don't take kindly to threats. In fact, 'tis you that better stay away from Lord Derek."

"As I said, you are not the daughter of a Lord any longer, and I have just as much right to pursue Lord Derek as you do. Besides, has Derek ever indicated that my attention was unwanted or unwelcome?" Alice asked with malice. "So take it as a threat if you wish, but just remember – I will be Lady of Holdenworth one way or another."

"T'will be over my slain body," Chanity replied, giving Alice a furious look.

"Whatever it takes," Alice said with a sickening smile.

Before Chanity could reply, Alice grabbed her basket and strode toward Holdenworth manor.

Chanity nearly pursued Alice, but one thing held her fast. Derek had never truly rebuffed Alice's attention. If she were to openly dispute with Alice, Derek might notice her even more.

Chanity shook her head to clear her thoughts and tried to get Alice out of her mind. She looked forward to hearing from Lord Derek about the prisoner.

Chapter 12

Even though the cell was locked, Derek took no chances. He left the man's hands tied and stationed a guard outside. Derek looked the man over to see if he recognized him, but it was impossible to tell.

The henchman was filthy from head to toe and had numerous cuts and bruises. After the pain he had suffered from the man's arrow, Derek did not feel sorry for him. The henchman had no empathy for another person, since he would wound or kill for a few coins.

"He refused to answer any of my questions, so I drug him behind my horse, hoping it would loosen his tongue. Unfortunately, he didn't wish to make it easier on himself or his appearance," Bram said with a laugh.

"I see no need to introduce myself, since you knew who I was when you shot me. You do the introduction. What is your name, and who sent you to wound or kill me?" Lord Derek demanded. The man remained silent, so Derek ordered Bram to have him tied to the whipping post in the courtyard.

After the man was securely tied, Derek spoke to him one last time. "'Tis not my want to have you whipped. You need not speak your name, just tell me who sent you," Derek said. Still the man refused to answer, so Derek turned, nodded to the guard and walked away.

The guard drew back the whip and struck the henchman. With every lash, Derek asked the man who sent him, but he would not answer. After twenty lashes Derek bade the guards unbind the man and return him to his cell. It infuriated Derek that the henchman refused to answer. He did not like using a whip on anyone, even though the man deserved it for all the pain he had caused.

For a moment Derek imagined Garth tied to the whipping post, since he was responsible for all this. Or better yet, at the tip of his sword as he ran it through him. Garth, like the man he hired cared only for himself, and had no empathy for others.

"Bram, have the guards give the prisoner food and water for a few days until his body heals," Derek ordered. "Once he heals, give him naught to eat till he decides to give us the name of the man who sent him."

Derek made his way back to the great hall, where Chanity was waiting for him. "Lord Derek, what is going on? Is the man they have locked in the cell the one who wounded you?" Chanity asked with concern. "Please do not keep these things from me, Lord Derek. I heard a commotion outside and looked to see what it was. I saw the whipping post, and a man receiving lashes".

"I am sorry you had to witness that scene," Derek said. "I assure you he is alright now."

"You misunderstand, Lord Derek. If that was the man who shot you, I would have used that whip on him myself. I am not some weakling when it comes to punishment. I was a Lord's daughter, and was taught if you do wrong you must receive punishment for it. I feel better knowing the man is in a cell rather than running loose causing mayhem. Now you can find out if Garth sent him."

"You'd think it would be that easy," Derek said with frustration. "Even after the lashes, he still remains silent. He must be more afraid of Garth than he is of me. After his body heals, we will see how he does without food. I do not want him to die, especially before he speaks the name of the man who hired him. We know 'tis Garth, but King William will expect proof of his guilt."

Eight days after they stopped the henchman's food, Bram went to Derek and told him the man was ready to speak.

Derek arrived at the cell, and looked inside at his captive. The man was a little gaunt, but his welts had healed.

"My name is Turk," the henchman said. "I do not know the name of the man that hired me. A man spoke to me from the shadows as I left the stables in a village near my home. He was a very large warrior, and had another warrior with him. The warrior with him was a sizeable man as well, but not as large as the one who hired me. I cannot describe their facial features, for they were wearing helmets, and there was no moon. I'm sure they did this so I couldn't identify them if I was captured."

"The warrior said they heard of my skill with a bow, and wanted to hire me. I was told to wound you with an arrow in your right shoulder," Turk explained, weakly. "The warrior said that if I accidentally killed you, I would not receive the rest of my payment. I would not have agreed to do the task if he had wanted me to kill you, and would not have done it at all, except that my family has fallen on hard times."

"When are you supposed to meet the warrior to get the rest of your money?" Lord Derek asked.

"He told me to meet him back at the same place on the next full moon. It is two day's ride from here if you don't take many breaks. 'Tis almost time to meet him again."

"I give you my word, I will set you free if you take me to this meeting and do not try anything foolish," Derek promised Turk. "You will show up alone for your payment. We will hide ourselves and watch. I am certain that the warrior intends to kill you, and not pay you."

Turk looked at Derek in surprise. He had not considered this possibility.

"After you tell the warrior I have been wounded as he instructed, then he will not have any more use for you. If I know Garth, he plans to save his coin by killing you then and there. Your only hope now is for the man you shot to save your life. But first, I have more questions for you. Why did you come back a second time if you were to only wound me?" Derek asked, curiously.

"The first time I did not know for certain that the arrow hit its mark. Guards came close to where I was hiding, and I had to flee," Turk explained. "I was afraid some of the villagers would remember me asking questions, so I went home for a while to see to my family."

"When I returned, you did not appear to be wounded, so I decided to make a second attempt. I thought for certain an arrow struck, and fled back to the hut," Turk said.

"What of your accomplices?" Derek asked. "There were many tracks at the hut."

"I rode several paths to the hut to confuse pursuit. Later, I returned because the time to meet the warrior was getting close. I had to know where the arrow hit you, and make sure you still lived so the warrior would not kill me."

"The warrior told me I better be there the night of the full moon since he had to leave out early the next morn. He made it clear I had to be there to receive the rest of my pay, and if I were not, then my life was forfeit," Turk explained.

Derek thought quietly to himself for a moment. King William must be sending Garth on an errand soon. Garth was probably already in the area so he could meet with Turk.

Derek turned back to Turk. "Why did you take the lashes instead of telling me this before?"

"There were too many men within hearing distance, and I thought some might be in league with the warrior," Turk explained. "Any in league with him would have killed me the first chance they got. I was more afraid of the warrior, because he sought me out and knew who I was."

Turk realized that Derek's warning about the warrior killing him instead of paying him made sense. At times he wondered why he had ever agreed to do such a deed.

Now, he had no other choice but to help Lord Derek, for his life was in danger either way. The warrior would kill him if he discovered Derek was nearby, and Derek would kill him if he did not take him. Taking Derek to the place where he was to meet the warrior would at least give him a chance to survive.

Turk announced he had made his decision. "Lord Derek, if you give me your word that you will protect me as best you can and set me free afterwards, then I will do what I can to help you."

"I give you my word," Derek said, as he turned and left the cell.

Chanity had asked him not to keep anything from her, so Derek reluctantly told her what had transpired, and about the trip they were to take in three days. He thought they would not be gone but five days at the most if the weather held up.

Chanity's expression told him of the worry she was feeling, even though she would not speak of it. She knew there was nothing she could say that would stop Derek from going, so there was no use trying to persuade him to stay.

"Lord Derek, if 'tis Garth he's meeting, please take care," Chanity said with concern. "I will pray every day until you are back home safely."

Derek wrapped his arms around her, and held her in his strong embrace. He kissed her lightly, not caring who saw. "'Twill be alright Chanity, I will have many skilled warriors with me. Bram will stay to guard you, and see to your safety. Everything will be fine, my love."

"While I'm away, stay inside the inner walls when you venture out. I know Bram will guard you well. I want the gates of Holdenworth to stay bolted while I'm gone. No one is to enter or leave unless Bram gives the order."

Derek released Chanity from his embrace, took her arm and lead her to the table. "Now my love, let us share our noon meal together." He seated her at the bench beside him, then sat in his chair at the head of the table.

"What plans have you made for the Christmas festival, my love?" Derek asked.

Chanity appreciated Derek trying to change the subject, so she would think of happier things and not worry for him. They talked for a good while about the preparations that were being made.

The next three days went by quickly. On the day they were to depart, Derek did not dress in his battle gear, and only belted a sword around his waist.

There was still snow on the ground, so he tossed his warmest fur cloak around his shoulders, and strapped smaller pelts around his boots to keep warm on the journey.

Derek packed his helmet and chain mail in a cloth sack and gave it to his vassal, along with his shield. The vassal took the armor down to the stable, and helped the stable boy give Rollo a good brushing. They saddled Rollo, and tied the armor and shield on the saddle.

Derek was eager to get the journey started, and finish the matter with Garth so he could wed Chanity. He could hardly wait to wed her and start their life together as husband and wife.

The next few days would be hard on Chanity, but he would make it up to her when he returned. He wished she wouldn't worry, but knew that he would if he were in her place. Everything depended Garth's defeat.

Derek and his men broke their fast early that morning. As he sat with Chanity, he noticed she had a worried look on her face, and had barely touched her food. He hugged her tightly to him, and felt her relax in his arms. "I will be back before you have time to miss me," Derek said smiling.

Suddenly he had an idea to help keep Chanity from missing him while he was away. He asked her to take some of material she had laid up and fashion herself a gown from it. She had shown him the hidden chamber in her room, laden with expensive fabric, silver and gold. She had plenty of velvets, silks and other material in all colors to make a beautiful gown. Perhaps fashioning a gown would take her mind off what was going on so she wouldn't worry about him the whole time he was away.

Chanity walked outside with Lord Derek as he prepared to leave. He took her into his arms, and gave her a sensual kiss that left her breathless. He pledged his love for her, and hugged her tightly again before stepping away. By now he did not care who saw, for all knew he was going to deal with Garth so he could wed Chanity on his return.

Derek mounted Rollo, and gave Chanity a devilish smile. "Fair well my sweet enchantress, and take care until I return."

"Fair thee well, Sir Knight," Chanity replied, giving him a beautiful smile.

Derek saw tears starting to slide down her face as he turned to leave. He took the lead at the head of the procession, with Ortaire riding beside him, followed by ten skilled warriors.

Derek ordered the procession so that Turk was placed in the midst of the ten warriors, just in case he changed his mind and tried to escape. Derek did not believe everything Turk told him. He had always been able to sense if someone was telling the truth or not, and something rang false in what Turk said that. Bram confirmed his suspicion, and told Derek he had sensed it as well.

Chanity said a silent prayer that Derek and his men would accomplish their mission and return safely. She could not stop the tears that slowly flowed down her face as she watched Derek and his men leave. She stood watching in the cold morning air, until Derek and his band of warriors were out of sight.

Chanity felt someone take her hand. She turned to look, and was surprised to see it was Marla.

"Will you be alright, Chanity?" Marla asked.

"Aye, but please pray for Derek and his men," Chanity said.

"I prayed this morning, and will continue to do so until they return home safe," Marla said.

Chanity knew Marla still cared for Derek by the look of concern that showed on her face. Chanity had been afraid Marla would blame her because Derek left to face Garth, but Marla had surprised her. The old Marla probably would have, but she had changed a lot since Derek's arrival. They went back inside to warm themselves by the fire.

Several times that day Chanity slipped away to her chamber. Sometimes she would cry, and sometimes pray, but even then she would end up crying. She decided to start the gown Derek suggested she sew while he was gone. Chanity planned to make him a matching shirt out of the same cloth for the Christmas Festival, or for him to wear when they wed.

In a short while, Chanity had designed the gown and cut a pattern for it. She started to cut the fabric, but decided to ask Anna's help. Anna had always been good at laying out patterns to save fabric. This was her favorite material, and she did not want to waste any of it.

Anna placed the pattern on the fabric and began to cut it out, while Chanity went to find one of Derek's old tunics. The tunic would be used to fashion a pattern so that Derek's new garment would be the right size.

Chanity was glad Derek had suggested she make the gown. Maybe this would help ease her mind and relieve some of the worry she felt in her heart.

Chapter 13

As Derek rode along, he prayed that everything would go as planned, and that he and his men would return safely. He also prayed that everything went well at Holdenworth, and that Bram kept Chanity safe. He wished he could speak to King William before going on this endeavor, but he only had a small window of opportunity and had to move now.

Derek wondered how King William would react to him seeking out Garth. He knew the King valued them both, and had wanted them to settle the matter during a joust. Derek wished that would have ended the matter, but he knew Garth, and his reputation. It would not have been a fair fight.

King William created the tournaments to serve a dual purpose. First, it provided an opportunity for the men to test their skill against each other, and establish a ranking. Secondly, it allowed an avenue for quarrels to be settled under the watchful eye of the King.

Several quarrels had been settled in this manner, but this case was different. Derek had been attacked by Garth's henchman, so he was justified in his pursuit. William might not like it, but he would understand why Derek had to avenge the underhanded attack.

Derek had fought beside Garth in battle countless times before, but he had never known him to act in a cowardly manner. There were rumors of his underhanded ways during tournaments, but never anything as bad as having someone shot with an arrow before he was to battle them.

Garth might have paid someone to injure an opponent before, and the victim would never have realized the origin of the attack. One thing was for certain: Garth was a braggart, and would do anything to remain the King's Champion.

Though Garth might be cowardly, he was not foolish. Derek had to carefully plan Turk's meeting, and his encounter with Garth. Garth would be even more watchful of his surroundings, and the slightest noise or shadow would betray those lying in wait.

It did not seem likely, but Garth might have anticipated Derek would discover Turk. If Garth and Turk had conspired, they may be planning to spring a deadly trap at the meeting spot. Derek knew he had to be ready for anything. He took three of his men aside and told them to watch Turk at all times. At least one of them was to stay awake on watch while the others slept.

Derek regretted leaving Bram behind to protect Chanity, but thankfully he had Ortaire with him, along with several other skilled warriors. Ortaire had been with him for many years, and Derek knew he could trust him with his life.

Bram and Ortaire seemed like brothers to him. Though he was a little closer to Bram, he loved them both. Derek was glad they decided to stay with him to help keep Holdenworth secure. They were like family. He wanted them near, and it would have been a great loss had they left. He realized that sooner or later the day would come when they would seek holdings of their own, or return to King William. At least that day was not today, and he dreaded the thought of them leaving.

Now his thoughts returned to Chanity, and he could envision her in every detail. He imagined her wavy pale blonde hair, hanging down to her waist, her emerald green eyes, and beautiful smile. Her smile had a way to uplift his spirit even if he felt sorrowful.

He enjoyed watching Chanity's face as they played chess, as she pondered her next move. Her every expression fascinated him. She was more learned than other women, and could talk on almost any subject. She was the only one for him, and now that he met her, no other woman would do. He was so thankful to have found the love he had always wanted, and knew they would always be happy as long as they had each other.

Ortaire called out a warning that drew Derek's attention back to the moment. He had spotted a group of riders in the distance, and they appeared to be heading toward them. At first Derek was worried they might be raiders headed for Holdenworth, but then he caught sight of King William's banner. The approaching riders grew closer, and he recognized some of the men. They greeted the warriors, and asked them where they traveled.

One of the men did not have the look of a warrior about him. The leader of the company introduced the man as one of the King's advisors, who they were escorting back to William's camp.

The other warriors were about to stop and set up camp, since the sky was growing dark. They invited Derek and his men to camp with them, but Derek did not want them to begin asking questions about Turk.

If they stayed, it would be obvious that Turk was being guarded. He also did not want any questions about where they were headed. Some could have been friends of Garth, and Derek did not want to alert Garth to their arrival. Derek said they still had a way to go before dark, so the two companies parted, and went their separate ways.

Derek knew of a cave ahead where they could camp in the dry, and get some respite from the cold, since there was still snow on the ground. The company continued on their way, and came upon the cave right after dark. The moon wouldn't be full for a couple nights, but its light shone strongly enough so they could set up camp.

In short order they built a fire, and made their beds from fur pelts before sitting on the ground to eat. The men were thankful to have the cave to stay in where there was no snow. The meal was meager but hearty, consisting of dried meat, bread and cheese.

All missed Cook's good food at Holdenworth, but they were warriors, and used to living off the land when necessary. The men had become very fond of Cook, and she of them. She told Derek that he and his men were like angels after putting up with Vorik and his men. If the servants were busy with other tasks, any of the warriors and guards at Holdenworth would jump to do Cook's bidding.

The warriors ate and told a few stories, then went to their pelts to lie down for the night. Derek looked up from the mouth of the cave and saw the moon and stars shining in the night sky. The twinkling stars made him think of Chanity's eyes, and he wondered what she was doing. He knew she was probably just now lying down, and would surely be worrying about him. He hoped she had started making her gown so she would keep busy, and not worry about him the whole time. He did not blame her for worrying though. Anyone

120

would be worried for someone they loved in this situation. As he fell asleep, she was still in his thoughts as well as his heart.

The next morning, the warriors awakened at first light. They quickly broke their fast by eating some dried meat and bread. Then they packed up their pelts, and saw to the horses before heading out. It was cold when they left the cave, but all were seasoned warriors, and used to worse weather than this. All were in good spirits as they rode their stout horses down the path. It was still another day's ride if they pushed hard and didn't stop much. Derek hoped they would be there by nightfall, so they would have that night and the early part of the next day to rest. Long before the meeting was to take place, they would be in place and ready for the confrontation.

Lord Derek set a fast pace that day, but not so much as to over tire their horses. Occasionally they stopped to rest the horses, and eat a meager meal. As the day neared its end, the company was just a little southeast of London and still heading north-eastward.

"We should make it by nightfall. 'Tis not much further," Turk said.

Dusk was falling when the village appeared in the distance. They would not go into the village this night. So many warriors entering the small village would surely start tongues a wagging. If Garth suspected anything, he would bolt and leave. Derek wanted this battle over with, so they had to remain out of sight for now.

Derek had been watching for a place to camp, and was lucky to find an abandoned homestead. The dwelling had burned to the ground, but an there was a sturdy, well built stable nearby. It would be a roof over their head, and dry ground instead of the snow. Thankfully the stable was off the beaten path a little, so they could camp there and no one would be the wiser.

After a long day of riding, they were glad to stop for the night. The men tended to the horses first, as always. The horses whinnied and shook their mane, seeming relieved to be unsaddled, watered and fed.

The warriors unrolled their fur pallets, and sat around a fire as they ate their traveling rations of dried meat, cheese and bread. The mood was pensive, and there was little talk before the men went to their bed of furs. Derek told them they could sleep a little later on the morrow, since they did not have to go into the village until noon.

Derek lay down for the night thinking of Chanity. He wondered how she was feeling and how she had spent her day. She was probably laying down thinking of him just as he was thinking of her. The day's ride had taxed them all, and it was not long before weariness overtook him, and he drifted off to sleep.

Though Derek and his men planned to sleep on into the morning, they were up at sunrise, since they were used to rising early. Two of the men went out hunting earlier, and fresh meat was roasting over the fire. The aroma made them all hungry, and there was plenty for everyone.

As noon grew near, Derek and Ortaire took Turk into the village, so he could show them where he was to meet with the two warriors later that night. The meeting place was a narrow alley between a large stable on one side and a blacksmith shop on the other. A well-worn road ran in front of the smithy and stable, and there was an inn on the opposite side.

Derek and Ortaire looked around, trying to find somewhere to station themselves and the other warriors so they would not be seen by Garth and his men. Derek was not sure who would come with Garth, but from Turk's description, the other warrior was Edmond. If what Turk told them were true, Garth would not be expecting Derek and his men, so it would probably be just the two of them. Besides, Garth would not want anyone else knowing he had to injure Derek in order to best him in battle.

"Ortaire, take Turk back to camp," Derek said. "I want to look around a bit more before I head back."

Ortaire and Turk mounted, and headed back to camp. Meanwhile, Derek began searching for a place to wait and observe the meeting that was to take place.

The wood line came nearly to the rear of the stable and smithy. The woods could conceal a few men, but not the whole band. Besides, men hidden there would be too distant to observe the meeting, and could not hear anything going on.

Derek stood in the meeting spot as his eyes scanned around. The inn was close by, but there were no windows facing the direction of the alley, and Derek did not want to bring attention to himself by entering the inn. He leaned back against the stable and noticed something peculiar. The stable siding was made of bark slabs running vertically instead of horizontal, as all the other buildings were. The side of the stable was only a few feet from the meeting spot, and would be a perfect spot to hide and wait.

Derek decided to look inside the stable, and talk to the owner to see what could be arranged. The stable was quiet when he entered. There was no one coming and going, and the rear portion was completely empty. The stable owner caught sight of Derek, greeted him cheerfully, and asked if he needed a stable for his horse.

"Aye," Derek replied. "I'll need a place for my horse, and a few more. Do you have any horses boarding in the rear of the stable?"

"Nay, 'tis yours for the asking," the owner replied.

"I would like to board five horses here, but there is one more thing I would ask before I decide," Derek said.

"Ask on, sir," the owner replied, seemingly eager to have the coin in hand.

"I see there is no door in the back of the stable," Derek noted. "If you would allow me to make a doorway here in the rear side, I will agree to board the horses straightaway."

Derek noted a strange look on the owner's face, and went on to explain. "My friend and I are skilled at this sort of work. We will not mar the look of the stable. You will not even notice there is a door from the outside."

The owner could scarcely believe his ears. He had often thought about putting a small door in the back of the stable so he could come and go to the smithy without having to walk all the way around. Now, here was a man asking if he could install the door, and pay him for the trouble. "'Tis agreed then," the owner said quickly. "One coin for each of the horses, and one more if you want to put in a door."

Derek counted out the coin, and told the owner he would be back shortly to begin work. He mounted Rollo, and made his way back to camp.

A short while later, Derek returned with Ortaire. They took some of the slab siding down and fastened it to a framework the size of a small door. They put the door panel in place, and went outside to inspect their work. The slab siding looked just as it did before, and there was no sign of an opening. They had worked quickly, and the blacksmith's shop was noisy, so no one noticed the noise they made, or even glanced at what they were doing.

Derek and Ortaire made ready to return to the camp. As they were leaving, Derek gave the stable owner another two coins, telling him that he, and three of his men would like to bed down in the stable for the night. Derek told the man to keep quiet about this and he would get another coin on the morrow. The owner looked at him strangely again for a moment, then laughed.

"Don't worry, sir, I shan't tell a soul, especially not my wife," the stable owner said, jingling the coins in his hand with a mischievous look on his face. Derek did not laugh in return, but thanked the man for letting them put in panel door, and for letting them stay in the stable.

"We may rise early on the morrow," Derek told the owner. "If we leave before sunrise, I will place your coin under a stone in the corner of the stable."

Back at camp, Derek summoned Gunnar and Sean while the other men remained to guard Turk. As they gathered around Derek and Ortaire, he told them his plan.

"Ortaire and I located a stable right beside where the meeting is to take place," Derek began. "We bargained with the owner to let us install a hidden door on that side. He is unaware of our true purpose, and that we plan to use the stable to eavesdrop on the meeting and spring a trap on Garth."

"As evening draws near, the whole band will proceed toward the village. The three that guard Turk will split from the group and head into the trees. The rest of the men will go on to the stable," Lord Derek advised.

"To avoid arousing alarm in the village, wear only fur coverings and pack your chain mail and helmets in cloth sacks," Derek continued. "We will split into two groups to further avoid suspicion. "Ortaire and Gunnar will arrive at the stable first. Sean, Turk and I will follow a few moments behind."

"Once inside, we will wait until evening, then Turk will be sent to the meeting place. We will station ourselves behind the false panel. "Once Garth makes his appearance, we will thrust away the panel. I will take on Garth, and Ortaire will attack his accomplice. Sean, you and Gunnar should stand back and guard Turk. You also need to stay on the lookout for any other warriors Garth may bring with him. The other men will be watching from the woods and will join in if needed."

"Finally, we must talk of what you are to do if I should fall in battle," Derek continued, looking at each of his men in turn. "If Garth should defeat me, you must ride hard to Holdenworth and give the news directly to Bram."

Derek asked if they had any questions about what they were to do that evening. There were no questions from his men, so Derek bade them relieve the others and send them over, so he could tell them the plan as well.

The men guarding Turk were relieved by Ortaire, and came over to talk to Derek. He repeated what he had told the others, then told them of their duties. "It may take a long while for Garth to show," Derek said. "Stay out of sight in the trees, and try not to stir around much. Move closer to the stable as nightfall approaches."

After Derek finished talking to his men, he headed back inside the abandoned stable and started rubbing Rollo down. The simple task helped clear his mind, so he could focus on what lay ahead. He knew he might be going to his death, but for Chanity's sake he had to win. With renewed spirit, he felt undefeatable, and ready to get this over with. He stroked Rollo's silky mane to calm him, for he had picked up on Derek's mood and was getting anxious.

Derek could not wait to get back home to Chanity. At last he thought of Holdenworth as his home now. He thought of it as home not because he owned it or it was his possession, but because Chanity was there. She was his and he was hers, and as long as they were together, any place could be home to him.

He never dreamed love could be this strong of an emotion. He always said he wanted a true love that would last a lifetime, but did not realize how wonderful or powerful it could be. He prayed he would get to hold Chanity again, and tell her how he felt. Somehow, their love gave him more strength and determination. He looked forward to the morrow, so he could begin the journey back home to his enchantress.

The men prepared one last meal by roasting some meat over the fire, and soon it was ready to eat. They ate quickly in silence, as they envisioned the encounter to come. After the meal, Derek gave the order to saddle up the horses.

The sun peeked through the clouds, and beamed down on the frosted trees as they prepared to depart. The snow and frost made the landscape glitter like it was covered in diamonds, though it was starting to melt from the sun's warmth. The men were grateful for the warming weather, for there had been no sunshine for several days; only gloomy gray clouds that covered the sky.

The band mounted up, and their horses thundered through the snow as evening descended. As the village came into sight, Derek, Ortaire, Gunnar, Sean and Turk continued on toward the village, while the rest of the men veered toward the woods behind the town just as they had planned.

The remaining men split into two groups, and entered the stable a few minutes apart from each other. Each of the warriors concealed their helmets and chain mail in a cloth sack. Their swords were belted to their sides, and covered shields hung from the horses.

They had to cover the shields with a fur pelt so the insignia could not be seen. The dragon on Derek's shield would surely have been recognized. His reputation as Sir Derek or Dragon was known throughout England, France and Normandy. Only Garth was more admired since he was the King's Champion, though now folk were saying Derek was a better warrior.

Derek shook his head in disgust as he thought of what had caused all this. If not for Garth's oversized ego, and the goading of the king's men this might never have happened. Derek wished Garth felt as he did, and not care about what the people said.

Once inside the stable, the men tied their horses and positioned themselves by the false panel. Time seemed to slow to a crawl as the moon appeared over the horizon, and began to rise in the night sky.

Finally the time drew near, and Turk emerged from the front of the stable and went to stand in the alley to await Garth. Derek and his men put on their mail, and took up their shields and swords. They left their helmets in the bags, but kept fur caps on their head. The helmets would have obscured their vision in the darkness, and they needed to see as well as they could.

Not long after, Derek's patience and planning was rewarded. He heard the sound of two men talking right outside the newly constructed panel. Derek instantly recognized Garth's voice and was almost sure the other was that of Edmond.

"So, you showed up Turk," Garth said quietly. "We were not sure you could get away without being discovered by Derek's men. Did you wound him in his right shoulder as you were paid to do?"

Before Turk could answer, Derek and his men flung the panel away, and rushed through the opening.

Chapter 14

C hanity chose a fabric of emerald green velvet to match her eyes, and a golden shimmering silk for trim. Derek's shirt would be made of green velvet also, with gold silk and embroidery to match the colors of her gown.

She was glad she asked Anna if to help cut out the cloth. When they finished cutting out the material for the gown and Derek's shirt, Anna asked Chanity if she would like help with the sewing, but Chanity declined. She told Anna the sewing would keep her busy while Derek was away.

Anna knew Chanity missed Derek, and worried about his fate. Chanity had left to go to her chamber twice already this morning. Once while they were cleaning, and then again as they were cutting out the fabric for her gown. Anna could tell Chanity had been crying when she returned.

They used Derek's bed to lay out the material since he would not be back for a few days. Chanity felt closer to Derek while in his chamber. She tried to mask her worry, but Anna saw through her guise.

Anna prayed for Chanity's strength during this time, and for Derek's safe return. For Chanity's sake, she hoped Lord Derek would return soon. Anna and the others knew the next few days would be hard for Chanity, so they decided they would all take turns spending time with her.

The second day Chanity kept very busy. She worked all morn in the great hall, then after the noon meal she went back to her sewing. Anna offered to help once again, but Chanity declined.

"I need to keep busy, and my mind occupied so I won't worry all the time," Chanity explained.

The rest of the second day Chanity was fine, but on the third day she could not sew from her hands trembling. The battle between Derek and Garth was to be this night. Derek had told her not to worry, for Garth might not even be able to get away from his duties to meet Turk. Then all her worrying would be for naught. He lifted her spirits, and she had felt better then, but he was not here with her now.

Chanity went to the small chapel at Holdenworth. It was a recently constructed building not far from the hall. Their family had not been Christians until after her grandparents were wed. As Chanity entered the chapel, Marla walked up beside her and asked if she wanted someone to pray with. Chanity smiled, and gratefully accepted. They went to the front and kneeled at the altar. Both prayed a silent prayer that Derek and his men would return safely, then they stood and took a seat on a pew.

"Marla, I wish things were different between us," Chanity began. "I still feel like I'm your sister, even though we have not been close. There are a lot of sisters by blood relation who are not close, but I care for you, and you are family to me. Derek cares for you as well because you are his blood relation."

"Then why is he sending me away?" Marla asked sadly.

"'Tis for your sake, and the sake of your grandparents," Chanity explained. "They never knew you lived, and have suffered much loss. I'm sure when you arrive, they will surely dote on you and try to spoil their only grandchild. Even if you go live with your grandparents, you can still visit, and we will visit you also. We always want you to be a part of our family, and I am going to miss you." Chanity reached out and hugged Marla. Marla felt stiff at first, but slowly relaxed and returned the hug.

Chanity was not surprised by Marla's lack of reaction. From what Marla had told of her childhood, she had never been given hugs or affection growing up. Chanity wished she had tried harder to break through the shell Marla placed around her heart.

At the time Chanity was but a mere child herself, and did not really understand why Marla acted as she did. When spring arrived, Marla would be leaving, so she decided to do the best she could to mend their relationship now.

As they sat in the chapel together, Chanity had an idea - she would surprise Marla with a new gown for the Christmas festival. If she asked Anna to help, she would surely finish it in time. Chanity hugged Marla once again, then they returned to the great hall to clean and get ready for the noon meal.

As the day dragged on and nightfall descended, Chanity grew frantic with worry for Derek and what was about to happen. Alma, Anna, and Marla all gathered around trying to calm her.

Bram drew Elspeth to the side, and sent her to get Etta and some calming herbs. Bram was anxious himself, and wondered what was happening. Above all, Bram wished he was there with Derek. Derek and Ortaire were skilled warriors, but he worried still. Garth was also a skilled warrior, and would stop at nothing to win. Derek wound from Garth's henchman was proof of that.

Etta arrived shortly after with the herbs. She mixed them with some warm milk and told Chanity to drink it. Alma and Etta took Chanity up the stairs to her chamber. As they passed Derek's door, Chanity halted and told them she wanted to lay down in his chamber so she could feel close to him. They helped her undress down to her shift, then laid her down for the night.

Alma spoke with Etta, and offered to stay with Chanity for the night.

"Stay till she is well asleep, but 'tis no need to stay with her tonight," Etta replied. "The herbs will calm her, and give her rest as well."

Chanity nestled into Derek's pillow as the herbs began to take effect. Tears flowed down her face as she prayed for Derek's safety before finally drifting off to a deep, calm sleep. Alma watched Chanity for a few moments, then joined Etta as they went downstairs.

Bram looked up to see Etta and Alma coming down the stairs without Chanity. He met them at the foot of the stairs and asked if it was wise to leave Chanity alone as upset as she was.

"We have given her herbs that will calm her, and help her sleep. She is soundly asleep by now," Etta said. "We will check on her at first light on the morrow."

Bram thought to ask Etta for a sleeping draught as well, but he was a warrior and did not want anyone to think he was weak. He loved Derek and Ortaire like brothers, and hoped they would be safe. The women departed, and Bram sat down at the table and returned to his drink.

Bram filled his mug several times, and drank them down one after another until he felt himself begin to sway. It was getting late, so he stood and headed for the stairs. He paused at the door to Lord Derek's chamber. If Lady Chanity cried out in the night, he might never hear her from his chamber. It would be better if he stayed in Derek's chamber tonight, since it was across the hall from Chanity's.

Bram quietly opened the door, placed his candle on the table, then went to add a log to the dwindling fire. The women had gone to bed, so Bram decided to leave the door cracked so he would be better able to hear Chanity if she got upset during the night.

Bram was just about to get in bed, when he suddenly came to an abrupt stop. Chanity lie there in her thin shift that left almost nothing to his imagination. The fire must have been blazing earlier, for she had thrown off the pelts revealing her curvy form. The glow of the fire made her look radiant, and he could see her beautiful body through the thin shift.

Bram knew he should just turn and walk away, but was mesmerized by her beauty. Chanity lay on her back, with her long wavy hair spread all around her, shining like gold in the light from the candle and fire. She looked like a golden goddess, and was so beautiful that he ached to touch her.

Bram could do nothing but stand and stare at her beauty, and tried valiantly to walk away. Even though he was a strong and mighty warrior, this woman made him weak.

Chanity's cheeks had a pinkish hue, and her lips a little darker shade of the same color. Her lips looked like they were drawn up in a pout, and ready to be kissed. He had an overpowering urge to kiss her, but resisted with all his might.

He would never do anything to hurt Derek, because he was his brother whether by blood or naught. Besides, Chanity loved only Derek. He would have to keep his lust in check, and learn to love her like a sister. He would not drink heavy again until Derek returned. He hoped Derek would always know how blessed he was to have her. Not only was she a beauty, but she would always be faithful to him. He had seen in the great hall this very night how much she loved Derek.

Bram looked into her beautiful face one last time, then reached for a pelt to cover her. She awoke as he reached for it, looked up at him and smiled. "Thank you Bram, for looking out for me and

Holdenworth while Derek is away. I don't know what I would have done without you."

"Chanity, you would have done fine," Bram said as he smiled back at her. "I came to check on you once more before I went to my chamber. Now close your eyes, and go back to sleep."

Chanity closed her eyes and drifted back to sleep. Bram thought he was fortunate that her eyes were closed. He did not want her to look down and see the state he was in.

If only Alma or Etta had told him that Chanity was in Derek's chamber. Then he would have never entered, nor had to feel guilty for looking upon her. He walked out, and shut the door behind him. Since her door was not bolted, he went down stairs and ordered two of the night guards to stand by her door. He also told them to let him know if they heard her awaken during the night. The guards saw how upset Chanity was earlier that night, and nodded their assent.

Bram went to his chamber, and left his door ajar so he could hear if Chanity screamed out during the night. He remembered the way she screamed their first night at Holdenworth. He ran to her bedchamber, but Derek was already there without a stitch of clothing on, holding Chanity and reassuring her. He quietly returned to his own chamber, and they never realized he had been there.

Bram felt guilty for looking upon her, but did not get angry with himself. Derek would have done the same in my place, he reasoned to himself. Besides, it was only a glance. It wasn't as if he touched her, or let her know how he felt. He considered himself a knight, a warrior and lastly an imperfect man. Before he went to his bedchamber that night, he finally managed to convince himself that any other man would have done the same.

Though he tried to clear his conscience, Bram paid for his wrong, for he could not get the image of Chanity out of his head, and his body refused to ease.

As he lie awake, Bram thought of Derek again, and hoped all had went well. It past midnight, and the meeting would be over by now. He tried to quiet his mind, but could not help worrying for his two best friends that had become his brothers.

When they were but ten years of age, they made a small cut on their palm, and clasped hands together to signify they would always be brothers. He thought back to all the wild stunts they had pulled as young lads. The memories eased his worries a little, and gave him something to smile about. Finally sleep overcame him, and did not awaken until the rooster crowed.

The next morn, Bram dragged himself out of his warm bed, and sat up in the cold room. He gathered his clothes, and quickly dressed. It made no sense to build a fire since he would not be in his room the rest of the day. He stopped to talk to the guards standing by Derek's door.

"Lady Chanity slept through the night," one of the guards informed him. "She has not come out of the bedchamber this morn, nor did she cry out during the night."

Bram thanked the guard. He asked that one of them remain by the chamber until Chanity rose, while the other broke his fast. One of the guards nodded assent to the other, and made his way down stairs. Bram followed behind, thinking of Derek and Ortaire, and wishing for news from them. He still worried about Derek, and would continue to do so until he returned unharmed.

Chanity awoke later than usual. She opened her eyes, and looked about at the unfamiliar surroundings. Finally, she realized she was in Derek's bedchamber. Suddenly the thought occurred to her that Derek might not be alive. She quickly stood, then fell to her knees in prayer. After praying, she dressed, as the tears streamed down her face.

When the tears stopped, Chanity dried her eyes, and rubbed her face before going down stairs. As she entered the great hall, everyone grew quiet as they turned to look at her. Alma rushed to her side, led her to a table, and went to fetch some food. Though Chanity had not eaten the night before, she only picked at her meal. She sat lost in her thoughts with a sad look on her face.

Bram came through the front doors and took a seat across from Chanity, who glanced up at him with a tired, sad look in her eyes. She wore an old woolen gunna, with her half combed hair pulled back and dark circles under her eyes. She was far from the beauty of last night, or a few days ago.

Bram wished he could say something to ease her worries, but there was probably nothing he could say that would help. Only Derek walking safely through that door would truly ease her burdens. Still, he had to try something.

"Chanity, I know Derek, and he is the greatest warrior I have ever seen. He has triumphed in battles that I thought were impossible to win. He is a fine swordsman, and the fastest. People call him Dragon not only for his toughness and ferocity in battle, but also for the speed of his strike. Derek is like lightning with his sword. Garth may be bigger, but that only makes him slower. Besides that, he's ten years older, which is to Derek's advantage."

Chanity smiled and nodded, grateful for Bram's encouragement.

"Now eat, so you will keep your health," Bram said. "You don't want to be skin and bones when Lord Derek returns. It will hurt him seeing you like that. He will think you did not have faith in his skills as a warrior. 'Tis important to a man that his lady has faith in him, especially to a warrior. He also wants you to be strong so the people at Holdenworth will look to you for support while he is away."

To Bram's surprise, Chanity began eating her food, even though her hand still trembled as she ate.

Later, when Chanity was leaving the great hall she saw Alice staring coldly at her. Chanity walked toward Alice, but she suddenly turned and hurried away. The strange incident made Chanity worry even more about Alice's intent.

Chapter 15

Derek, Ortaire, Gunnar and Sean burst out of the stable and into the alley. Though it was night, the look of shock on Garth's face was noticeable in the light of the full moon.

Derek immediately attacked Garth, and Ortaire squared off with Edmond. Gunnar and Sean stood back as they had been ordered, alert in case Garth brought more warriors.

Turk leapt back from the fray, and moved to stand by Sean and Gunnar. Turk knew Derek had been right. Garth intended to kill him that night instead of paying him. He wanted no witness to his cowardly scheme to injure Derek before the tournament. Once again, Turk regretted he had made the bargain, and knew he was stupid to have gotten involved with Garth.

With a constant clash of steel on steel, Derek and Garth slashed at each other with their swords. The sounds of battle from the warrior's swords and shields sounded through the sleeping village.

Garth and Edmond had left their shields on the horses, but Derek and Ortaire wisely brought theirs. They must have assumed they would not need them, or perhaps thought Turk would suspect something was amiss.

They needed Turk to show up so they could be rid of him. If Turk had seen the two armored warriors, he might have bolted. Now they realized their mistake, as they attempted to deflect the attacks of Derek and Ortaire.

Ortaire wore Edmond down by letting him be the aggressor. His large shield protected him quite well from the other's sword, and Edmond exhausted himself trying to break through Ortaire's defense. As the tide of battle turned, Ortaire became the aggressor, and slew Edmond easily.

Garth was smarter, and a better swordsman than Edmond, so he avoided pressing the attack. He only struck to parry Derek's blows since he did not have his shield to use for protection. Garth launched a sudden attack, then tried to break away and get his shield, but Derek outmaneuvered him and blocked his way. Since Derek was the aggressor, Garth's hope was that Derek would wear himself down, but as the battle continued it seemed Derek only became more energetic.

Derek drew first blood with a savage slash, laying open Garth's upper left arm. Garth responded by bringing his sword up in a vicious attack, aiming to drive the point of his sword under Derek's chin. Derek's lightning reflexes parried the blow, but the tip of Garth's sword drew second blood, cutting Derek's face open along his left cheek, just under his eye. Derek hoped the cut wasn't deep, but blood streamed down his face.

Garth saw the injury and laughed. "Do you really think you can escape this battle alive?" He taunted. "Even if you survive, Chanity will be repulsed by you, and when I am done with your face, she will shun you."

"You do not know Chanity at all if you think she would ever shun me," Derek replied. "She was repulsed by your face without you having any battle scars," Derek said, laughing at Garth.

Garth was furious that he could not break Derek's concentration. He continued attacking Derek's right, thinking the constant pressure on his opponent's wounded side would surely cause him to falter.

Little did he know, 'twas Derek's left shoulder that was wounded. Though the weight of the shield wore heavy on Derek, he did not have to move his arm much, and kept the shield clasped tightly to him.

The battle went on far longer than any of the men had ever witnessed before. The warriors continued circling and attacking, though both were weary from battle.

As Derek circled, he noticed the ground was uneven beneath his feet. He crouched, then stepped back, hoping to lure Garth in. His opponent lunged forward quickly, seeking an advantage, but stumbled in his attack. Derek was quicker by far, and thrust his sword into Garth's neck.

The battle was scarcely over, when Turk approached to ask if he could get his coins from the pouch on Garth's belt. Derek stood there bleeding, and looked at his men. He was utterly amazed at the gall of this man to ask such a thing of the armed warrior he had wounded. Derek's men returned his look, pointedly waiting for a silent nod from Derek to run the man through.

Derek had enough bloodshed for the night. "Only retrieve the amount that was owed you," he replied. "I should not let you have any, since this was payment for your cowardly attack. If you take the coin, it had better be because your family truly needs it. I will look into this, and if I find out differently, you will pay with your life," Lord Derek warned.

Turk thought about Derek's warning, and walked away without taking a coin. Derek knew that Turk's tale of his family needing money was a lie. If only he had an arrow to plunge into Turk's shoulder to repay him for the pain he had suffered. At least Turk led him to Garth, and for that reason he spared his life.

Derek remembered what Bram had said, and realized that Bram's intuition had been right once again. He warned Derek that Turk was probably lying about his family falling on hard times. In all the years that Derek had known Bram, he had never been wrong. He had saved their lives many times. Even King William valued Bram's ability to read people, and asked his advice before trusting someone.

Derek retrieved the pouches from Garth and Edmond's belts. They checked the horses, and found large sacks of coin on them as well. Derek counted out the coin, and found the tally to be a surprisingly substantial amount. They had to be up to something nefarious to be carrying this much coin. He decided to ask around on the morrow before they left to go back home.

Derek divided the coin four ways. One quarter was shared between Gunnar, Sean and the other men that came with him. Another quarter would be split by Ortaire and Bram, though three fourths of that share would go to Bram because he had the most responsibility. Bram was charged with seeing to Chanity's safety as well as the running of Holdenworth while Derek was away. The third quarter would go to King William for the defense of the land, and his noble endeavors. Derek put the last quarter back for himself and the running of Holdenworth.

"We had best be going," Derek said, noting some of the villagers had begun arriving to see what all the commotion was about.

"This man and his accomplice have betrayed King William by plotting against the innocent," Derek announced to the arrivals. "They have been brought to justice for their crime."

Lord Derek turned to walk back toward the stable to get his horse, but suddenly felt dizzy and weak. He dropped down on one knee, and held his hand out for Ortaire to grasp. "Help me onto my horse, and we will ride back to camp."

Ortaire took one look at Derek, and saw the urgency of the situation. Not only was Derek's face slashed open, but his arm was as well, and blood still seeped from both. Ortaire bade Sean take the other men back to camp and stay there until they returned. He slung Derek's arm over his shoulder, told Gunnar to take the other, and headed straight to the inn.

After helping Derek into the inn, they had to bang on the counter several times before a man appeared. They told him they needed a room, and asked if he knew of a healer in the village. The innkeeper showed them to a room, and the warriors placed Derek on the bed. The man gave them directions to the healer's home, and Gunnarr left straightaway.

Ortaire removed Derek's tunic, found water and a basin, and washed the wounds. The innkeeper arrived with some clean strips of cloth, which Ortaire used to apply pressure to stop the bleeding. Lord Derek had lost so much blood, Ortaire worried they might be too late to save him. Derek began to drift off to sleep, but Ortaire kept him awake until the healer got there. A few moments later, the healer and Gunnar came through the open door.

She was younger than Ortaire expected, and very lovely. She had long red tresses, warm brown eyes and a curvy ample body that he found quite appealing.

"My name is Herleva, but most people just call me Leva." None of the men volunteered their name, so she opened her satchel and went to work on the injured man immediately. She did not know who the man was, but the one who came to fetch her said his Lord had been injured, and bade her come straightaway.

Before she began closing the wounds, she handed a small vial of powder to Ortaire, and told him to mix it with a strong drink. Ortaire poured the powder into a cup, and filled it with mead from his flask.

Leva bade them make sure he drank it to the dregs. Next, she went to work threading a needle, and setting everything she needed in place. After Derek drained the last swallow, she went to work stitching his arm since it was the worst, and the bleeding needed to be stopped. After the stitching was complete, she applied a dark gooey paste. "This will help heal the wound and keep away infection," She explained.

Once Leva was through with his arm, she set to work on his face. As with the arm, she stitched it closed. "The scars will be long but narrow. Since the cuts are even and clean, I was able to use small straight stitches."

Derek had passed out from the drink and pain, but awoke as Leva spoke with Ortaire and Gunnar. Turning to Derek, she said, "You are a very handsome man, so the scar will not matter much on your face. Even with the scar, all the lasses will still be chasing after you."

Derek looked into Leva's eyes and said, "There is only one lass that matters to me, and no other."

Leva patted Derek's good arm as she spoke, "Then she is a truly blessed lass." She turned to give Ortaire and Gunnar directions on how to care for their Lord's wounds.

"The wound must be cleaned to keep the infection away," Leva explained. "Apply the paste once in the morn, then again at night."

Before taking her leave, she turned again to Lord Derek. "You should rest a couple of days before trying to ride. I will check on you on the morrow," Leva said with concern. She handed a vial of the paste to Gunnar, then looked Ortaire up and down, smiling as she left the room. A few moments later, Derek fell into a deep sleep.

After Leva closed the door, Gunnar laughed softly, not wanting to wake Derek. "Ortaire, don't get too excited over her smiles. You know you were her second choice since Derek refused her advances."

Ortaire laughed softly in return. "My friend, Leva fixed her eyes on Derek only because she was busy tending to his wounds, and did not have the chance to gaze upon my good looks. After she saw my face and how handsome I was, she was all smiles. Not to mention how she stared at my muscular build."

"If you refuse her tonight, then it will be me she'll be smiling at," Gunnar teased while laughing again.

"Friend, don't be fooled. She did not appear to be that desperate," Ortaire replied, and clapped Gunnar on the shoulder with his mighty hand.

Gunnar scowled at his friend for a moment, but finally laughed along as well. He knew Ortaire had meant it all in jest.

With their jesting aside, they debated whether to send a messenger to Holdenworth with the news of what happened, or wait to see what Derek wanted to do when he awoke. Ortaire wished he had thought and asked Derek before he fell asleep. He knew Derek was stubborn and would not want to follow the healer's advice. He would probably try to leave on the morrow when he awoke. They decided to wait until morning, for it would be difficult to roust a messenger at this late hour.

"Gunnar do you think you would be alright to stay with Derek without me for a while?" Ortaire asked. "If I know Derek, this will be our last night in the village."

Gunnar caught on to what Ortaire was up to. "Go on and have your fun, my friend." Gunnar replied, smiling. Ortaire almost tripped in his haste to get out the door.

"Hold on now," Gunnar said laughing, as he halted Ortaire by the door. "You are no untried lad. Slow down before you break your neck. The wench will probably be waiting for you outside, and if not, her home is the fifth hut down the path. Now be gone with you, before your stumbling around awakes Dragon."

"You know where I can be found if Dragon needs me," Ortaire said as he gladly took his leave with a smile on his face.

As Gunnar suggested, Leva was leaning against a post outside, with a seductive smile on her face. "What took you so long?" She asked. "I was about to leave." Ortaire gave her his arm, and she led him to her home.

Ortaire would never admit it to Gunnar, but the teasing had irritated him. It bothered him that he was her second choice. Ortaire knew he was pleasant to look upon, but for some reason most of the lasses seemed to go after Derek and Bram first.

This usually did not bother him, for he always had plenty of beautiful lasses seeking his attention. This wench however, attracted him like no other had before. He reassured himself by thinking she only noticed Derek first because he was injured, and she had to tend to him.

Leva opened the door to her home, and Ortaire entered. Her home was small, and sparsely furnished. It did have a warm feeling about it, though it smelled of strong herbs. The main room had a fireplace with two wooden chairs on each side, a table with two wooden chairs by the window, and a long makeshift table that covered the length of one wall. It was a typical healer's table, with bowls and baskets that held herbs and such.

The bedchamber was small, with only a bed, wardrobe and a small table with a bowl and water pitcher. The rooms were charming, and though the place was small, it was large enough for her.

"You have a warm and welcoming home," Ortaire said smiling. "It suits you well."

"I was an only child, and was birthed in this very cottage", Leva replied, smiling in return.

She held out her arms to Ortaire, and drew him in for a passionate kiss. They stepped into the bedchamber, snuffed the candle, and fell into each other's embrace. The cottage, room and all other surroundings were instantly forgotten.

Ortaire fell asleep holding Leva in his arms. She nestled in, and felt comforted and secure. She also felt desirable, a feeling that Garth had taken away from her a long time ago. Leva was angry and hurt that Garth had shown no feelings for her when he left only hours ago. She had never been with another man other than Garth. She had finally tired of his mistreatment. His visits were sparse, and when he did stop by, he smelled of cheap women.

She loved him in her own way for the first couple years. She had been naïve, and too young to realize he didn't really care for her.

Garth began visiting after her parents had died of an illness that spread through their village. He came around saying sweet words about how pretty she was, and how special she was to him. He would also see that one of his men split wood for her fire, and helped repair her hut when needed. On one of his visits he promised that when he finished serving William, he would take her home to his family's vast farmstead.

Garth's visits could last from a few days to a couple of weeks. On his third visit he brought some wine with him. She had never drunk wine, because her family could not afford it. He poured a cup for each of them, and kept refilling her cup even though she said she didn't want more.

In a short while, she felt dizzy and a little confused. Before she knew what was happening, he picked her up and carried her to bed. She told him he needed to go, but he laughed, and started kissing her instead. She was ashamed that she had given in to his wishes. If she hadn't drunk the wine, she would never have done so.

She had heard other women talking about their experience with a man after their wedding night. Most spoke of their betrothed as a tender lover, but there had been no tenderness from Garth.

Hours ago, she finally worked up the nerve to ask him when his service with King William would be done so they could wed.

He roared with laughter at her question. "I never said anything about wedding you. How did you come to that conclusion?"

"You said you would take me home to your family's farmstead when your service with King William was done," Leva replied nervously.

"I did say that, but never as my wife," Garth replied. "You can work there, and be one of my mistresses."

Leva suddenly felt nauseous at his words. He actually thought she would live as one of his mistresses, and not as his wife.

Garth rose from the bed and got dressed. "I will see you in a week or so, after I complete an errand for King William. After I finish the errand, I will stop by to visit before returning to William's camp." Garth shook his head and laughed again as he made his way out the door.

Leva sat crying after he left, wondering how she could have been so stupid and naïve. She suddenly felt old, though she was only ten and eight years. She had only been ten and six years when he first took her. He made her feel special on his first few visits, but she no longer felt that way. Instead, she felt used like a harlot. She did not blame him as much as she did herself. What he said had been true. He never stated he would wed her, but when he laughed at her, it was almost too much to bear.

When Garth first arrived, word somehow spread through the village that the King's Champion had stayed all night with her. Her village had supported King Edward, then Harrold Godwinson after him. The villagers hated when King William's warriors traveled through. After Garth's visit, they began avoiding her when she walked down the street, and would not even speak to her.

Her mother had been the village healer, and began training Leva at an early age. Her father had passed first, then her mother soon after. By the time of her mother's passing, she knew nearly as much as her mother about birthing and healing. The villagers had always sought her out before, but shunned her now.

It had taken two months after Garth first stayed the night with her before anyone in the village would speak to her. Even then, it took someone nearly dying for them to seek her out again.

She had not even been asked to help with the last two births. Eventually, the women of the village started speaking to her again, but only in the privacy of their home. She understood, because they would be shunned as well if anyone saw them talking with her.

It was a lonely life, so she looked forward to Garth's visits even though he wasn't always nice to her. She loved him and thought he cared for her. Now, she realized he didn't love her, and her home was just a place for him to sleep when he was passing through. Not to mention he used her like a harlot for his own pleasure. He would stay a few days, then be gone again. She never knew when or if he would return.

Garth and Leva had words that night. He began putting her down as usual, so she told him to leave and never come back. It hurt because he didn't even act like he cared. He just laughed, then slapped her face.

Finally, his words and actions had caused her to lose any feelings she had for him. After Garth left, she began packing her meager things so she could start a new life in another village.

She was still gathering her things together, when there was a knock at the door. At first she feared Garth had returned, but he never knocked. She went to the door, and opened it to find Gunnar asking for her assistance.

Ortaire awoke, still holding Leva in his arms. He could tell she had been weeping. He pulled her closer against him and asked if he had hurt her?

"Nay," she replied, as tears softly trailed down her face. Ortaire had been very caring with her, unlike Garth, who was rough and demanding most of the time.

"If you tell me what is bothering you, perhaps I can help," Ortaire said.

At first she wasn't going to tell him, but he seemed very concerned, and she had nothing to lose. She decided to tell him everything. As Ortaire held her in his arms, she told him her life story.

Ortaire felt sad for Leva, and the lonely life she had because of Garth. He told her Garth lived no more, and described what happened at the stable that night. He even told her why they came to seek Garth out.

Leva listened impassively as Ortaire spoke of Garth's fate. It was unfortunate that Garth let his ego get the better of him. It even brought him to the point where he was willing to take the life of another just to maintain his position. She was sad that Garth lost his life, but there was no longer any caring in her heart for him.

"Now I have decided to leave the village, but have no idea where I am going," Leva told him. "I don't have much coin, but plan to work as I journey. I hope to find a good man like you one day, and I appreciate you listening. Just being able to talk about everything has helped a great deal. It has been so long since I talked with anyone that cared how I felt."

Ortaire felt something stir deep inside him as she told him her life story. He wanted to hold her and make everything better. He could tell she was telling the truth, and could feel her sorrow.

"I could speak to Lord Derek about you coming with us back to Holdenworth if you wish. I'm sure he could use more help at the farmstead."

"Are you sure you would not mind doing that?" Leva asked. "I am a stranger after all."

"After this night, I feel we are no longer strangers, but friends," Ortaire replied, hugging her tightly.

"I feel the same for you," Leva replied. "'Tis nice to have a friend again."

"I want you to have a fresh start when we reach Holdenworth. I will tell Gunnar that nothing happened between us except that we talked," Ortaire told her. "I had better get back to the inn. I will slip out the back way, so no one will know I was here. I do not want any of the villagers to say anything else about you, for they have said enough already."

Ortaire rose, and bade her finish packing for their journey. "Lord Derek will probably not take your advice, and try to begin the journey to Holdenworth on the morrow." While it was still dark, Ortaire left, and headed back to the inn.

On the way back, Ortaire could not stop thinking about Leva and all she had been through. It must be hard for her to just pick up and leave her childhood home. He was angry that the villagers had made her into an outcast, so that she wanted to leave the only home she had ever known.

Ortaire eased into the Inn's bedchamber, trying not to wake Gunnar and Derek. His attempt at silence was in vain, for the slightest rustle woke the skilled warriors. After they saw who it was, they relaxed again. Derek immediately fell back to sleep, still weak from the loss of blood. Ortaire apologized to Gunnar for waking him, then laid down himself.

They slept later than usual the next morning. Through Derek awakened last, he declared he wanted to journey back to Holdenworth, just as Ortaire expected. Ortaire explained what had happened to Leva, and asked Derek if she could go with them to live at Holdenworth.

"Ah, Ortaire has a lass for himself now," Gunnar said, laughing.

"Nay, 'tis not as you think, Gunnar, for we only talked a while," Ortaire replied. He hated to lie to them, but wanted Leva to be able to start her life over again.

"Well, she certainly made eyes at you," Gunnar observed. "I thought she made it clear what she wanted."

"'Tis true she had a flirty demeanor, but she only spoke that way because she was angry with Garth, and wanted to feel desirable after all the mean things he had said to her," Ortaire explained. "Besides, it would be good to have her on the journey in case Derek's wounds begin to bleed."

Derek was disturbed to hear this woman had been Garth's mistress. At first he wondered if she would try to seek revenge for his death, but Ortaire would never have asked to bring her along if he suspected such. Though he had misgivings, Derek cared for Ortaire like a brother, and could not say no to him. He told Ortaire to get Leva, and have their horses readied for the journey.

Leva had her things packed and ready to go when Ortaire arrived at the cottage. Leva's horse was smaller than theirs, and had two large baskets balanced on each side. "I have more belongings packed than I will be able to carry," she said sadly.

Two makeshift sacks made from bed linen and tablecloths sat in the cottage doorway. They held the remainder of her clothes and some small keepsake items. The large baskets held herbs and items for her work as a healer, but Leva decided to leave the rest behind.

Ortaire picked up the sacks, and carried them to his horse. "Don't worry about these," He reassured her. "I'll carry them to the inn, and we will place them on the supply horses."

Ortaire secured the sacks to his horse, and mounted to head back to the inn. Leva mounted as well, and Ortaire saw tears flowing down her cheeks as she took one last look at her home. Leva set her eyes forward, and looked at him.

"Thank you for all you have done, Ortaire," Leva said, smiling.

"I'm glad to, lass," Ortaire replied. "Thank you for saving my Lord's life."

When they arrived at the inn, Leva changed Derek's bandages and applied more paste before they set out on their journey. She was sad, but excited also. A new life awaited her, and she hoped new friends. It had been so long since she had friends to talk to and share her life with.

As she rode along beside Ortaire, Leva asked many questions about the people of Holdenworth and how they lived. Ortaire was pleased that Leva was excited about her new home.

Ortaire told her first about Chanity. "She is the lass Lord Derek is to wed. She will help you get settled in your new life at Holdenworth. She is very kindhearted and always helpful to everyone. I think you will like her a great deal"

Before two days were over, Ortaire had told her about everyone and everything at Holdenworth. He would have to think of new things to tell her about. They had to travel slow, and stay on smooth cleared paths instead of riding directly through the woods. Since Lord Derek insisted on leaving before he had recovered, he still suffered from his wounds. Everyone tried to keep Derek in good spirits, but they were all concerned for him.

At the end of one long day of riding, they decided to stay at an inn along the way. As they rode through the market on the way toward the inn, Derek asked Ortaire to stop, and eased out of the saddle. The inn was just ahead, so he handed the reins to Ortaire, and headed to a silversmith shop. The smith was tidying up for the evening, and asked Derek what he needed.

"I need a ring for my wife to be," Derek said. "It should be gold with diamonds surrounding an emerald at the center, formed in the shape of a heart."

The smith had a small collection of precious stones which he placed in front of Derek. There was a beautiful emerald and plenty of sparkling diamonds. In short order the smith made a mold for the ring. "Come by in the morn, and I'll have it ready for you," the smith told Derek.

The night's rest seemed to do Derek some good, and he awoke early the next morn. Ortaire was still getting the horses ready, so Derek ventured down to silversmith.

"I just finished setting the stones," the smith said, as he placed the finished ring in front of Derek.

The gold ring with its precious stones sparkled in the morning light.

"'Tis truly beautiful," Derek said. "It will be perfect for my bride.

Derek paid the smith as Ortaire approached. He told Derek the horses were saddled and all was ready for the journey. They made their way back to the inn, and set out again for Holdenworth.

Chapter 16

Chanity stayed busy, and tried not to worry for Derek. She finished her new gown a day ago, and now Derek's matching tunic was complete as well. She was feeling well, and had been taking better care of herself.

Bram's lecture had its intended effect. He reminded her that the wife of a Lord had to be strong, so he could depend on her when he was away. She was glad he had noticed how exhausted she was, and expressed concern about her health. Also, she had not wanted to disappoint Derek by neglecting herself while he was away.

She knew her show of strength would help their people feel more secure in Derek's absence. Chanity remembered how her own mother had behaved when her father was away, and she wanted to follow her example. Serina had been strong, wise and proud, and Chanity had admired her for it. She regretted showing such weakness at first, and was determined not do so again.

Chanity spent most of her time in the great hall, making sure all was going smoothly. There was no item that escaped her attention, and she diligently worked with the folk of Holdenworth to make their village better. She spoke with herdsmen about livestock, and with craftsmen about improvements. She talked to farmers about planting, and hunters about game.

Bram was pleased, and smiled to himself even though Chanity sometimes looked after matters that were really his duty. He was glad to see her flourish so in just a few days. Her beauty had returned, and there was no look of exhaustion in her eyes. Her cheeks had plumped again as she regained her normal weight. He tried not to notice just how beautiful she was, or how curvy she was becoming. She was Derek's and he respected that. He would love her like a sister, for Derek was like a brother.

Bram played chess with Chanity every night after they supped. He saw that her mind was still preoccupied with Derek's absence, for he bested her two games in a row. Though Chanity often beat him at chess, she always made him laugh. He enjoyed their conversations, and hoped she did as well. He remembered King William had enjoyed conversing with her even about war and strategy, topics he usually reserved for his men.

Chanity had a sincere way about her that made you want to speak with her. She always thought things through, and knew the right way to go about solving a problem. Most of the women he knew from court only wanted to talk about the latest fashion, and who was sleeping with whom. They enjoyed the latest gossip whether it was truth or falsehood. Chanity was not like any of them. She was truly an intelligent, kind and caring lass.

Bram prayed Derek was safe and well. He tried to think of how he would respond if Derek fell in battle. Somehow, he must be strong for Chanity. Deep down, he knew Chanity would be all right, for she had strength and would endure if something did happen. She would be deeply hurt at first, but she would survive it. She could easily see to the running of Holdenworth, but he would have to get her out of Garth's reach. Bram decided to put it out of his mind, and have faith that Derek would best Garth and come home soon.

The next morn, Bram was starting to get a little worried. Derek and his men should have been home late yesterday, but not even a messenger had arrived. Derek had given him strict instructions that if he hadn't received word by noon tomorrow, he had to quickly get Chanity out of England.

As Chanity came downstairs, Bram could see a difference in her appearance. Today she looked a little weary and withdrawn. Bram doubted she slept much last night. Actually, he hadn't slept well either. He understood how Chanity felt, and would speak with her about it.

Since she had just awakened, Bram knew she had not eaten, and probably would not unless he coaxed her. "Have you broken your fast, Chanity?" He asked.

Alma heard Bram's question, and rushed to get some milk and a trencher of food. She had tried to get Chanity to eat the morn before, but had failed. Alma admired the way Bram could coax Chanity into eating, or help perk her up. He had worked a miracle getting Chanity out of her sorrowful mood when Derek first left. She hoped Bram could again this time. Alma silently prayed that Derek and his men would arrive today, or at least send a messenger with word that everything was alright.

Bram saw the worry in Chanity's eyes as they spoke, though she smiled and tried to hide how she really felt. "Chanity, I won't tell you not to worry, because you will anyway. It's only natural to worry about the one you love," Bram said with understanding. "If something had happened to Derek, we would have received word by now."

"Derek gave his men strict orders to ride swiftly and bring word if something happened to him," Bram explained. "That way, I would have time to get you safely away from Holdenworth before Garth could arrive. Derek did not want either of us to worry. I can assure you everything will be fine. There are always little delays that come up when traveling in this cold weather."

"When Derek was wounded and had fever, he spoke of his plan to help me escape if he fell in battle. He thought he was talking to you, and repeated the whole conversation. I was so pleased to hear how he loved and cared for me," Chanity said.

"So you see, there is nothing to worry about," Bram replied. "You should go to your bed chamber and get some rest after you break your fast. Derek will be upset with both of us if he arrives and sees that you look weary. There are plenty here to get the work done. Besides, you had everything cleaned and ready yesterday, so there is little left to do now. You must have faith in his ability as a warrior and his skill with a sword."

Chanity thanked Bram, smiled and began to eat.

Bram began devouring the hearty meal, as he thought of all he needed to set in order so that he and Chanity could leave quickly. He already ordered the guards to be on the lookout for a messenger or riders.

If only Derek would arrive soon, or at least send a messenger to tell why they were delayed! Bram refused to believe Derek had been slain by Garth, but if Turk had led Derek into an ambush, Garth might have been able to seize the advantage.

Chanity needed to be well rested in case they had to leave quickly. Bram finished his meal and went in search of Alma. He found her in the kitchen and asked to speak with her privately.

"We may need some of Etta's herbs to help Chanity sleep for a while," Bram advised Alma. "I know that Chanity did not sleep well the night before."

"We have already seen to that," Alma replied. "Etta gave me a sleeping herb for Lady Chanity this morn. We can give slip it into her drink at the evening meal, and she should sleep a good while. She looked so weary this morn when she entered the hall. The herbs will help her sleep through the night so she will be well rested. They are nearly tasteless, so she will never notice it."

Bram was a little angered that they planned to give Chanity a sleeping draught without consulting him. If he had decided to leave that night, he would have been unable to rouse Chanity. His anger quickly cooled, for he knew they loved Chanity, and acted out of concern for her.

"After tonight, do not give her a sleeping draught without my permission," Bram ordered. "I may need her alert on the morrow."

Alma nodded her assent, and returned to her work in the hall.

Sadly, Bram began setting things in order in case he had to flee with Chanity. He did not want to think of it, but knew he had to be ready.

Bram prepared provisions and asked the stable master to saddle the horses the next morn. Finally, all was ready, as darkness descended on Holdenworth.

Bram played chess with Chanity that evening to take her mind off Derek. As they finished the game, Bram nodded slightly to Alma, so she would put the herbs in Chanity's drink. They had just sat down to sup, when the guards blew their trumpets to sound the alarm of riders approaching.

Bram and Chanity rushed to the double doors of the great hall, threw them open, and ran outside. The gates of the outer wall opened, and the torchlight revealed Derek and his men entering. Both let out a sigh of relief, but then noticed how badly Derek looked as his horse drew near. He had a bandage around one side of his face, and another around his arm.

Rollo came to a sudden stop and Derek practically fell from the saddle, but Ortaire jumped down to steady him. Chanity started to rush to his side, but a lovely red-haired wench dismounted and beat her to him. Chanity stopped still in her tracks as she saw the curvy full breasted lass with long red tresses lay her hands on Derek. Derek tried to assure the red-haired wench he was fine, but Bram could tell he was badly injured.

Bram looked to see hurt and confusion on Chanity's face. "'Tis alright, give them a chance to explain," he whispered to Chanity.

Ortaire began telling everyone what happened as they helped Derek inside, then up to his bed chamber. Chanity could not believe the red-haired wench followed him right into his bed chamber!

From the torch light, Chanity could see the wench was even younger than she first appeared. Her figure was that of a mature woman, but her face seemed young and youthful. Chanity could not help feeling jealousy even though she did not want to.

Marla heard the commotion, and arrived to check on Derek. She watched the guards bring him inside, and help him up the stairs to his chamber. She knew something was wrong, and wondered who the red haired wench was as well. Had Derek met a new lass on his journey? If she couldn't have Derek, she rather it be Chanity instead of this red-haired wench. Marla noticed Chanity's hands trembling, so she took them in hers as they listened to Ortaire explain what had happened.

Ortaire told them about the battle, and how Derek slew Garth, but was injured in the fight. Derek insisted on leaving before he was able. The healer had wanted him to wait a few days before riding, but Derek was stubborn, and left the next morn.

The journey had taken two additional days because Derek was weary, and the riding was too much for his wounds. Ortaire had insisted they rest often during the trip.

After the warriors settled Lord Derek in his chamber, Chanity, Marla and Bram made their way inside. Derek greeted them with a slight smile when they arrived, and sat up in bed to continue the tale.

"I sent a messenger from the village the morning we headed out. He was told to only report that everything was alright, for I wanted to be the first to tell Chanity that she was free of Garth," Derek explained. He tried his best to smile as he told her the good news, but the pain from the slash on his face was too much for him to bear.

Chanity was thrilled the ordeal was over, but now was more concerned about Derek's wounds. "The messenger never arrived, and we were getting worried," Chanity replied.

Derek looked in Chanity's eyes and reached for her hand. Chanity clasped his calloused hand in hers, and moved to sit beside him.

Suddenly, Derek's eyes closed, and his body relaxed as he passed out before he could say anything else.

Chanity noticed Derek's hand felt quite warm to the touch. She placed her cheek against his, and felt the heat of fever. "Marla, go get Etta quickly," Chanity said, as she felt her pulse quicken in fear. "Lord Derek has a raging fever."

"There is no need to get Etta, Leva is a healer also," Ortaire said.

"Then why has she not noticed he is with fever?" Chanity asked harshly.

"He had no fever when we stopped earlier," Leva said, with a hurt look on her face.

Chanity saw Leva was upset, and was sorry she had reacted so strongly. "She may stay," Chanity decided. "It will not hurt for both to see to him."

Leva was relieved that Chanity allowed her to care for Derek, and went back to her work. At first she thought she had made a mistake in coming to Holdenworth.

Chanity watched Leva carefully. She did not fully trust this wench with Derek, nor with his life. After all, he was a very handsome man, not to mention Lord of Holdenworth. Leva might see Derek as her way to become the Lady of Holdenworth. She trusted Derek's love for her, but sometimes women were opportunistic and took advantage of men's weakness. She decided to keep an eye on Leva for the moment.

"I'm sorry Leva. I did not think to introduce you, but everything happened so fast," Ortaire said. "Bram, Chanity, this is Leva. She has been seeing to Derek's care since he was wounded. Leva, this is Chanity. She and Lord Derek are soon to be wed. This ugly warrior is Sir Bram. Sir Bram is Lord Derek's second in command. Be wary of him, for he thinks of himself as charming to the wenches."

"It is Sir Ortaire you have to be wary of in that case," Bram replied.

Leva laughed at their jesting, and everyone noticed she looked even lovelier than before. She had a cute little laugh that made nearly everyone smile. Everyone except Chanity and Marla, both of whom had decided to be wary of her.

Leva thought Bram even more handsome than Ortaire, but that did not matter to her. She adored Ortaire's kindness from the beginning, and he was a handsome man. He had even helped her find this new place to settle down. She hoped all would be well, but kept noticing how Chanity looked at her. She guessed she would have felt the same way if she had been in Chanity's place. She just had to give everyone time to get to know her.

She knew Ortaire would speak on her behalf, for he told her he would. She owed him a great deal for his help, and was thankful he came into her life. He was a dear friend to her, and she hoped he felt the same way. She was excited about her new life and her new village, an excitement she had not felt in a long time.

Etta arrived from Marla's summons to check on Lord Derek. She and Leva spoke for a moment about Derek's condition, and the course of treatment to apply.

"'Tis fortunate Leva journeyed with you," Etta told Ortaire. "The poultice she applied surely helped keep the fever at bay. We will give Lord Derek some healing herbs, and fresh paste for his wound as well."

Under the care of two healers, Derek was up and around in just a few days. Chanity was relieved, and thanked Etta and Leva for all they had done with their healing skills. Chanity was with Derek most of the time now, and refused to leave his side for long. She even took her meals with him in his chamber. She knew some might talk, but did not care what people thought when it came to Derek's recovery. Especially now that they were to wed.

Later, Ortaire spoke to Chanity about Leva, and told her what she had been through. He asked that Chanity keep what he said to herself.

Ortaire told her how nice Leva was, but Chanity decided she would have to see that for herself before she believed it. She promised Ortaire she would not say anything about Leva's past, and would give her a chance to prove herself.

Chapter 17

With the Christmas festival and wedding quickly approaching, it seemed Derek and Chanity continually beamed with love and happiness. They could barely contain their excitement to be married at the Christmas festival.

Derek wanted to be wed as soon as he returned, but realized he needed a couple more weeks to recover from his injuries. He wanted their wedding night to be the most special night of their lives. He also wanted to make sure Chanity would not be repulsed by his facial scar, but he should have known better.

When Chanity found out he thought she might be repelled by it, she had scolded him. She asked if would he love her any less if she had accident that left her disfigured.

Derek regretted doubting her love, and pledged he would love her no matter what, and knew she would as well. He looked forward to their future together, especially now that the matter with Garth had been settled.

It did not take Chanity but a few days to realize Leva did not have designs on Derek. She spoke to him nicely while tending his wounds, but only in a friendly manner. Chanity did notice that Leva's eyes lit up when Ortaire walked into the room. Leva also seemed a little nervous when he was around, which was another sure sign she had feelings for him.

Chanity saw that Ortaire had feelings for Leva as well. She suspected as much when they first arrived at Holdenworth, and he spoke on her behalf. She noticed how Ortaire's eyes never left Leva as she walked around the room. He was always smiling as he spoke with Leva, and would seek her out when he came into the great hall.

If another man spoke to Leva or went near her, Ortaire would frown in frustration. If they touched Leva's arm, Chanity saw he seethed with anger, but held his tongue and did not say anything.

A few days later, Chanity came right out and asked Ortaire if he had feelings for Leva.

"We are but good friends," Ortaire replied with sadness in his voice.

Chanity sighed to herself in frustration. Ortaire clearly had feelings for Leva. He was denying his feelings to himself, which men and especially warriors were prone to do. Somehow they believed feelings made them weak, which was just silly. She remembered it was like that with Derek, until eventually something made him realize his feelings for her. She would have to think of what she could do to help Ortaire realize he cared for Leva.

As the festival drew near, Chanity asked Leva if she would like to help decorate.

"I would love to help," Leva answered excitedly. "Our village never had a Christmas festival, so you will have to tell me what I need to do."

After a couple days of working on the decorations they had become fast friends, and Chanity finally felt comfortable enough to ask Leva if she had feelings for Ortaire.

Leva blushed, then answered with a question, "'Tis that obvious?"

"Nay," Chanity said. "I just pay more attention to people's feelings than most." They laughed about that, then went back to decorating the mantle.

They continued talking about Derek and Ortaire as they worked and decorated. "I don't think Ortaire has the same feelings for me that I do for him," Leva said a little sadly.

"I think you're mistaken about that," Chanity said. "Men never want to acknowledge their feelings, but soon something will happen to make him see it. It may even happen at the festival. Just wait until he sees you dancing and laughing with the other men. Jealousy has a way of opening people's eyes and showing how they truly feel."

Leva hoped that Chanity was right; that Ortaire truly had feelings for her, and would come to realize it. Her life had changed so much since coming to Holdenworth. She had a small hut of her own that she decorated with the things she brought with her. She was grateful

Ortaire had brought them along, and would have regretted leaving them behind.

Ortaire had been so kind and helpful to her. He fixed everything that needed to be repaired in the hut. After that, he crafted a long table the length of one wall for her work, as well as a sturdy bed. There was a nice table and four chairs that remained in the hut from whoever lived there before. She missed the two heavy chairs near the fireplace at her former home, but could use two of the table chairs instead.

The best part of her new life was having friends to come and visit. She had several friends now, and felt so blessed. Everyone treated her well. Even the men never got out of hand around her, which she knew was because of Ortaire. She was sure he had warned them to treat her well, and she was thankful for that. She never wanted people to treat her like they had at her old village.

As she was sitting and thinking, there was a knock at the door. Leva opened the latch to find Chanity standing outside holding a beautiful gown.

"This was mine, but I did not get to wear it much before it became too short for me. If you like it, then it is yours. I'm sure it would be beautiful on you at the festival. It will need to be altered for the bosom to fit, but I have two matching strips of material to add to it. We can add the strips under the arms so it will hardly be noticeable."

Tears welled up in Leva's eyes. "Chanity, this is too nice a gift for you to give me."

"Leva, you have helped so much with the Christmas festival, as well as helping me prepare for my wedding. It was the least I could do," Chanity said. "Besides, I want to see Ortaire's reaction when he sees you dressed up and your hair done."

"Thank you again Chanity, not only for the gown but for making me feel welcome here." Leva laid the gown across the table and gave Chanity a hug.

Later, when Chanity walked into the great hall, Marla looked at her coldly. "You must have been visiting with Leva again."

Chanity was surprised at Marla's tone, because she and Marla had been getting along better.

"I went to give Leva a dress that she could alter for the wedding ceremony and festival. I just wanted to thank her for the work she has done."

157

"It is her responsibility, since she is a serf now at Holdenworth," Marla said.

"She is also my friend, Marla," Chanity stated with a frown. "Holdenworth's serfs were always treated with kindness when my parents were alive."

Marla just ignored Chanity and walked away. Finally, it dawned on Chanity that Marla was jealous of her and Leva's friendship. Marla had started out helping with the decorating, then suddenly stopped. Chanity realized it was because she and Leva had become friends. Marla felt left out, so she sulked and kept to herself instead of joining in. She decided to make an effort to include Marla from now on.

The next day, Chanity decided to go ahead and surprise Marla with a gift she had made for her. Not long ago, Chanity asked Alma to help her make a new gown for Marla. She wanted Marla to have a new gown for the Christmas festival as well. Chanity designed a gown with a beautifully colored amber velvet, with gold colored silk and gold thread to match Marla's dark hair and brown eyes.

Chanity saw Marla go upstairs after they finished cleaning the great hall. This was the perfect opportunity to surprise her. She fetched the gown from her chamber, then went straight to Marla's door. She held the gown behind her back and knocked.

Marla opened the door, and gruffly asked "What do you want?"

"I have a surprise for you," Chanity said, as she drew the gown from behind her.

Marla stood in her chamber doorway with a confused look on her face. She looked at Chanity, then at the gown, and back to Chanity.

"Derek and I thought you might like a new gown for the Christmas festival, so Alma and I made it while he was away."

Marla ran her hand across the beautiful velvet before taking it from Chanity's hands. "'Tis beautiful Chanity, and it was so thoughtful of you," Marla said, still in disbelief.

Chanity stepped forward and hugged Marla tightly. "You are going to look beautiful wearing it. I was going to wait till the day of the Christmas festival, but now you can try it on and make sure it doesn't need altering."

Marla tried not to cry, but Chanity saw the tears in her eyes. Marla turned to lay the gown on her bed as she wiped at her face.

"I will leave you to try on your new gown, but let me know if it needs altering," Chanity said.

Marla thanked her again, as she shut the door behind her. She sat on her bed as tears streamed down her cheeks. She had been so angry and jealous because Chanity had given Leva a used dress instead of her. Now, Chanity had surprised her with a beautiful new gown out of her loving kindness. Not a used one, but a new one she helped make herself.

Marla wished she could be kind like Chanity, and not always suspicious and wary. She knew she had to change if she wanted to be happy.

As Marla looked around her chamber, she suddenly remembered that Holdenworth would not be her home for much longer. Soon she would be journeying to their home in Normandy.

She worried her grandmother would be old and mean like the great aunt her father left her with. That had been such a horrible time in her life. Holdenworth seemed like her home now, even though she knew it was not since Vorik was no longer alive. Derek was a second cousin, but she was not his responsibility.

She wished he had cared for her as more than as a family member, but she saw the way he looked at Chanity, and knew he would never think of her that way. It hurt because she cared for Lord Derek, but he did not feel the same.

This is what getting older and wiser must feel like, Marla thought to herself. She was not the same person she had been a year ago. She would miss Chanity even though she had always been envious of her. Envy had kept her from being close to Serina and Chanity, when she could have been welcomed into their loving family.

If she ever found a man to wed, she could not wait to have a family of her own. Perhaps she would find that man in Normandy. Whatever her fate, she was determined to be a kinder person than she had been at Holdenworth.

After the noon meal, Derek pulled Bram aside and told him he had something to show him. "I had this made for Chanity," Derek said, as he pulled a ring from his pocket.

Bram looked the ring over admiringly. The workmanship employed by the craftsman was evident in the ring, as was the costly stones and gold. "Chanity will certainly be pleased with this," he told Derek.

Derek was glad the ring had Bram's approval. He wanted everything to be just right on the day they were to wed. Only a few more days and Chanity would be his forever. He was truly happy, and that was all because of her.

He wished his family could be there for the wedding ceremony, but he could not wait till spring. It was hard enough waiting until the Christmas festival. He wanted Chanity to have a special day, one she would always look back upon with joy. He knew his parents and siblings would love her, and be proud to have her in the family. He could not wait for them to meet Chanity, and for her to meet them.

After Derek retired to his bed chamber that evening, there was a knock on his door. He opened it to find Chanity standing there with a big smile on her face. He quickly pulled her inside his chamber and closed the door. He gave her a long sweet kiss, then hugged her tightly in his strong arms. "Lady Chanity, are you here to ruin my reputation before we wed? What will people think of me?" They both started laughing as he acted the shy virgin.

"Sir Knight I'm sure that your reputation was sullied a good many years ago. I am merely here to deliver a gift I made for you to wear on the day we wed, so your virtue is safe with me."

Chanity held out her hands and presented his tunic. Derek held the tunic up and looked it over.

"'Tis the nicest tunic I have ever seen. You did fine work on this Chanity. It must have taken you many long hours. Thank you very much. I will cherish it, since it was made by your hands."

Derek pulled her to him and gave her a long kiss. Releasing her, he stepped over to his strongbox and pulled out a velvet pouch. "I have something for you as well, Chanity," Derek said, smiling.

He opened the velvet pouch and pulled out a ring. "I want you to wear this to symbolize my love for you. It does not take a wedding ceremony for you to be mine. I will always love you Chanity."

Tears filled her eyes as Derek spoke those words while slipping the ring on her finger. To Chanity's surprise, it fit perfectly. The large emerald set in the center caught her eye first. It was surrounded by glittering diamonds in the shape of a heart. The gold gleamed brightly, and the precious stones sparkled and shimmered.

"'Tis truly beautiful," Chanity exclaimed. "Where did you find such a ring?"

"I came upon a silversmith in one of the villages just as he was closing his shop. He graciously brought me inside and laid stones out for me to choose. I told him how I wished it to be fashioned, and he worked through the night so it would be ready the next morn," Derek explained.

"I will always love you as well, Sir Knight, and you will forever be mine," Chanity replied. They shared a long sensuous kiss, then Chanity reluctantly stepped back to go to her chamber.

"I cannot wait for this to be our bed chamber. Then we will never have to sleep apart," Derek said wistfully. "I just have to be patient a few more days." Derek kissed her on the forehead, and escorted her to her chamber. He kissed her once more, bowed, and returned to his own chamber.

Derek wished he could have let her stay the night in his arms, but it would have been too tempting for him. He was a gentleman, but could only endure so much. His desire for Chanity was stronger than anything he had ever felt.

Derek went to his window and looked out, trying to take his mind off his desire for Chanity. He could hear the wind gusting outside, and snow was beginning to fall. It was a beautiful sight to see snow glittering in the torch light. He was finally a Chieftain with his own lands. He had dreamed of this for many years, but what brought him the most happiness was Chanity.

Holdenworth was a great prize, but nothing could compare to Chanity, and he would give it all up for her if need be. She was everything he had dreamed of. She was beautiful, kind hearted and intelligent.

Some men disliked intelligence in a woman, but he admired it. He also admired her bravery the day she tried to shield him after he was shot with an arrow. He hoped she never risked her life again for any reason. He was so glad they found each other. She was the true love he had always hoped to find, and even more than he could have asked for.

Chanity could not sleep, so she wrapped herself in a fur and walked to the window to gaze out at the snow coming down. Torches were sparse on the back of the manor, so she couldn't see much beyond the inner wall. Still, the torches gleamed brightly, illuminating the soft flakes swirled about.

As the wind gusted outside, she thought of how wonderful her life was now because God answered her prayers. She had prayed that someone avenge her father's death, and for someone to love that would love her in return.

Chanity had felt so trapped and alone after her mother's death. Then her knight came along, rescued her and fell in love with her. Chanity knew from the moment she saw Derek she would care for him, and that quickly turned to love. She truly loved him with all her heart, and always would. She gladly looked forward to their life together.

Chanity wished her parents were alive to see her happiness. They would be so proud that she and Derek married out for love for one another, not dowry, land or noble status.

They would also be proud she was Lady of Holdenworth, since her brother had not been able to become Lord. That had been her parents plan, but fate had not allowed it.

She hoped Gerald was still alive and well somewhere, but her hope had begun to falter. It had been too many years since he left, and they had never heard any word from him.

If he ever did return, Derek would receive Gerald into their home as a brother. Still, she was afraid Gerald would not accept Derek as Lord of Holdenworth, and would challenge him for it.

Chanity looked down at the ring on her finger and smiled happily, knowing that in just a few days they would be wed. She wanted to watch the snow, but knew she needed to get some sleep. There were still a great deal to be done before their wedding ceremony on Christmas day.

With all the work preparing for the wedding and Christmas festival, the next few days went by fast. Chanity woke up early on Christmas morn, happy and excited because it was the day Derek and she were to wed.

The wedding was scheduled to take place before the noon meal, which would signal the start of the Christmas festival. Holdenworth had a huge feast prepared for the special day. There would be a large variety of meats, since the men had been hunting for several days, and obtained fresh game for everyone.

Holdenworth smelled wonderful from all the food being prepared. Chanity thought about trying to go help in the hall, but knew the other women would forbid her since it was her wedding day. They had probably been up cooking since dawn. The aroma from the kitchen was making her stomach rumble, so she freshened up to go down stairs.

As Chanity opened her chamber door, she spied Alma coming up the stairs with a trencher of food and mug of milk. Alma handed Chanity the trencher, and spun her around to go back to her chamber.

"You have no need to go down to the great hall, lass," Alma said smiling, as she set the mug down and left.

As Chanity ate, the servants brought hot water, and filled her wooden tub for a bath. She sighed, because she had wanted to see Derek that morn, but 'twas not meant to be. It probably was for the best, because it would take a while to get prepared for her wedding.

She was nervous, but not as nervous as she thought she would be. Her mother had prepared her well for the wedding night. Leva had also told her a few details.

At Holdenworth only Chanity, Derek, Ortaire, Gunnar and Bram knew of Leva's past. Chanity knew these warriors well, and was sure they would not speak of it to anyone.

After her bath, Alma helped Chanity to get into her gown and style her hair. Chanity wanted it done her favorite way; braided around the top to the back, then tied with a ribbon, leaving the rest of her wavy blonde hair flowing down to her waist. The ribbon was green velvet mingled with gold silk, and it matched her gown perfectly.

"You are the exact image of your mother Serina, except that your eyes are green, and your hair is just a little darker," Alma told her. "Your mother would be so proud of the fine Lady you have become. I know she would have approved of Derek."

Chanity hugged Alma as a tear rolled down her cheek.

"Now don't be sad, for this is a joyous day," Alma said.

There was a knock on the door, and Marla entered with her dress in hand. "Chanity, you look lovely, and your gown is beautiful also," Marla said.

"I was just telling Chanity that she is the image of Serina, except for the color of her eyes, and her hair is a little darker," Alma said.

"'Tis true, she does look like Serina," Marla said. "Chanity, told me to come to her chamber today. I was hoping that you would assist me with my gown and hair."

"Both of us will help you," Chanity said with a smile.

They helped Marla with her gown, then fashioned her hair. They pulled her hair on top, tied it with a ribbon, and let it cascade down her back.

"You look so lovely Marla, and that gown is just the right shade for your coloring. You look more mature now with your hair like that. The men will keep you dancing all through the festival," Chanity told her smiling.

There was another knock and the door, and Leva entered to tell them it was time to go to the chapel. Leva looked lovely in the gown Chanity had given her.

"Leva, you did an excellent job altering your gown," Chanity said. "Unless you knew it had been altered, you would never notice it."

Chanity knew the dress would look good with Leva's red hair, but was amazed at how it accented her curvy figure.

"Ortaire would have to be blind not to notice you today," Chanity whispered to Leva, with a giggle.

It was nearly time for the wedding, so Alma, Marla and Leva escorted Chanity out of her chamber and headed to Holdenworth's chapel.

Derek awoke with a smile that morn, thinking of all that was to come that day. It was the happiest day of his life. He dressed quickly, then went down to break his fast and see Chanity. It was finally the day he could wed his enchantress and make her his forever. He looked around the hall, but she was nowhere in sight. Alarmed, he headed for the stairs, but Etta stopped him before he could start up.

"Lord Derek, Chanity will be breaking her fast in her chamber. Then Alma will be assisting her with her bath, and helping her get ready for the wedding ceremony."

Derek was disappointed, but went back to break his fast.

After his meal, Derek ordered water to be taken to his chamber. He bathed and shaved, then donned the fine tunic that Chanity made for him with her own hands. It was the finest tunic he had ever seen. He knew she spent many hours stitching it for him. As good as he felt now, he would feel much better once the vows were spoken, and she was his.

He was relieved as well to have finally heard word from King William. As soon as he arrived back at Holdenworth, he sent a messenger to the King telling him all of that had transpired. He included every detail from when he was wounded by Turk, to the slaying of Garth.

He wasn't sure how King William would react when he heard the news. Fortunately, the King sent back word that he was furious with Garth's betrayal, and he understood why Derek had to do as he did.

Derek immediately sent another messenger back to the King, requesting permission to wed Chanity. After sufficient time passed for the messenger to return, Derek began to worry, and dispatched another messenger. The second messenger had returned with the King's approval only two days ago.

There was a knock on Derek's chamber door, and he bade them enter. Bram marched into the room with a broad smile. "Are you ready to wed, or have you changed your mind?" He inquired. "After all, there are a good many wenches out there that will miss out on your company."

"Why have wenches, when I can have an enchantress?" Derek asked laughing.

"'Tis true my brother," Bram said.

Derek thought he saw sadness come across Bram's face for a moment, but perhaps he just imagined it.

"Etta bade me tell you it was time to go to the chapel, for everything is in order," Bram told Derek.

Derek rose and clapped Bram on the back. "Soon it will be your turn to wed, brother."

"Nay," Bram replied. "'Tis not for me. You know I am a free spirit, and will not be tied down."

Derek smiled back at his friend, but said nothing in return. He knew that a lass would capture Bram's heart one day; just as surely as Chanity had captured his.

Chapter 18

The sun made the snow shimmer like sparkling diamonds as they walked to Holdenworth's small chapel. The priest fidgeted at the front, clearly anxious to get the ceremony started. Derek proceeded to the front of the chapel, and stood facing the entrance waiting for Chanity to arrive.

Everyone fell silent as Chanity entered the chapel. She looked absolutely radiant in her new gown. More than a hundred candles had been lit, and she glowed in their light. She caught sight of Derek standing at the front of the chapel, and smiled. He looked truly handsome in his new tunic.

Time seemed to stand still for Derek as he watched Chanity approach. Derek smiled in return, and admired every detail as she walked slowly toward him. Her beauty was striking, and her smile made her even more beautiful. The green and gold gown stirred softly with her movement and accented her figure.

As Chanity reached him, Derek took her hands into his, and the priest said, "let us begin."

Everyone in attendance could see the love they had for each other as they spoke their vows. Derek repeated his vows with a loud, clear voice, and great pride in his heart.

Chanity looked into Derek's loving eyes, repeated her vows with confidence, and never faltered. Their love was unmistakable, and they never looked away from the other until they sealed their vows with a kiss.

The kiss was slightly more lengthy than the priest was accustomed to, and Derek sensed he was beginning to get nervous before their lips reluctantly pulled apart.

Now with the wedding complete, everyone followed Derek and Chanity as they made their way to the great hall.

The wedding feast was ready, and everyone filled a mug for a toast that would signal the start of the feast and the Christmas festival. Bram performed the honors, as he raised his mug, and shouted "Hail to Derek, Lord of Holdenworth."

Holdenworth's warriors and villagers shouted in response "Hail to Derek, Lord of Holdenworth."

Bram shouted again, "Hail to Chanity, Lady of Holdenworth." Again, the warriors and villagers repeated that hail as well, then let out a great cheer that could be heard far beyond the great hall. It was a grand day that no one would ever forget.

Lord Derek and Lady Chanity led off the first dance, then others joined in. They danced several dances before becoming tired. As they took their seat, the dancing stopped for a while, and jugglers came out to perform. There were three of them, and all were very good.

After the jugglers performed, a troubadour came out and silence fell across the great hall. He began a tale of Derek as a lad, who left home and kin, to fight for William. Then he began a tale of Chanity, who even at a young age endured so much sorrow, until Sir Derek had come to her rescue. He told of the battle between Lord Derek and Vorik, then of the battle between Lord Derek and Garth over the fair maiden. He continued his tale about the great love the two of them shared for each another, then ended the tale with the wedding feast.

At the last he cried out "This is not the end of their story, but the beginning." At the conclusion, the crowd shouted out a great cheer for the couple.

After they supped, a magician came out and performed some tricks that amazed everyone. Once their food settled, the music began again, and people started dancing.

Derek stood, took Chanity's hand to his lips, and kissed it. "My Lady may I have this dance?" He asked with a devilish smile.

Chanity smiled brilliantly in return as she answered, "My Lord Husband, you may have all the dances you wish." There were a lot of people dancing, but everyone's eyes were on the happy couple.

Bram stole Chanity away from Derek for the next dance. After him, Ortaire whirled her away for the next. Derek smiled, seeing the fun she was having. Derek danced with Marla, then Leva.

As Derek headed back to Chanity, Alice dashed up to him. She wrapped herself around his arm, and pressed her bosom against it.

"Lord Derek, I am hurt you have not asked me to dance," Alice said. "I will be so terribly disappointed if you don't dance with me." She ran her hand up his chest, making Derek quite uncomfortable.

Derek's eyes quickly searched the hall for Chanity. The last thing he wanted was anything upsetting her on their special day. Suddenly the music began, and Alice pulled him into a dance. When he finally caught sight of Chanity, her eyes were spitting daggers at Alice.

He could have made a scene by pushing Alice away, but decided it best to tolerate her for the moment. He kept her at arm's length as much as possible, and finally the music ended.

As soon as the music faded, Derek turned to depart, but Alice grabbed his arm and ran her hand up it. "My, Lord Derek, you look so handsome," she said with pouting lips.

"Excuse me Alice, but I want to go dance with my wife. After all, we were just wed," Derek replied, as he turned again to walk away.

Alice had other ideas, and would not let go of his arm. Seeing she was still fastened on, Derek reached down and peeled her hand away, as he looked at her sternly.

She seemed to relent for a moment, but as Derek walked away, Alice quietly called after him, "When you get bored with her, I'll be waiting."

Derek could not believe his ears. There was no getting through to her. He spun around and faced her squarely. "Tis no chance of that ever happening," Derek said hatefully.

Derek turned again, and found that Chanity had just reached him. "Husband, are you ready to dance?" Chanity asked, smiling at him lovingly as he took her into his arms. She refused to let Alice see that she was upset. Alice would love knowing she had accomplished that, especially on their wedded night.

It was clear to Chanity that Alice had no morals or decency about her, and she had her eyes set on Derek. She could tell Alice to keep away from him, but knew that message had to come from Derek. She would have to talk to Derek and let him know to be careful not to encourage her. Alice was the type of wench a man could not just be nice to. She thought every man that so much as spoke to her wanted her.

Chanity was not angry with Derek, because she saw him searching for her as Alice approached. She saw the look on his face, and knew he did not want to dance with Alice. Derek would have to be firm with Alice, or she would keep after him. Chanity wanted to pull Alice's hair out every time she touched Derek, but knew it would do no good.

Derek pulled Chanity out of her thoughts, "Are you having a good time wife"?

Chanity gave him a brilliant smile. "How could I not be having a good time while I am dancing with you, and held in your arms? I am wedded to the most handsome man in this region and probably even in the world."

"I love you so much, and I can't wait to be alone with you in our chamber," Derek said as he pulled her even closer to him. "I will not rush this for you though, because I want it to be the most special day of your life."

Chanity smiled, then looked him in his eyes. "'Tis already the happiest day of my life."

Chanity was thrilled everyone was having such a great time. She noticed Ortaire glaring at every man that asked Leva to dance. She also saw his eyes light up every time he danced with Leva. It was obvious that he cared for her. Sean danced with Leva twice, then he asked her to dance with him a third time.

Ortaire was beside him in an instant. "There are plenty of other lasses here for you to dance with. Go ask one of them," he said angrily. A little while later, he grumbled at Gunnar for holding Leva too close.

Finally, Ortaire began to admit to himself that he was smitten with her. He felt like a jealous untried lad instead of a grown man because of the way he had been acting and speaking to his friends. He knew they must be laughing at his besotted behavior when he wasn't around. At the moment, he really didn't care what they thought as long as they kept their hands off Leva.

Ortaire suddenly felt full of life, and knew it was because of Leva. He wondered if he made her feel the same way, and dearly hoped that he did. He had been happier since he met her. He looked forward to seeing her with a smile on her face each morn in the great hall, and each night he ached with the need to go to her. He knew he wasn't in love with her, but he did care for her.

Ortaire's heart belonged to another, but he knew he would never be able to claim her for his wife. She was a noble Lady and he had nothing to offer her. He would make sure to confess this to Leva before they went any further.

He visited Leva often, but never went into her home at night. In daylight hours he always made sure to carry in firewood so tongues wouldn't wag. He never wanted Leva to be shunned again like she had been in her old village. He would just have to control his urges for now.

The merry making went on until the late hours of the night. Derek wanted to go to their chamber immediately after they supped, but Chanity was enjoying the festivities so much he could not bring himself to mention it. He did not want her to be disappointed in any way on this special day.

Derek sipped lightly at his wine. He wanted to be clear headed and remember every moment of this evening. He noticed Chanity was sipping lightly as well. Alma must have read his thoughts, for he saw that she went to speak to Chanity, then the two of them slipped upstairs.

A few moments later, Alma came down stairs then nodded to Derek so he would know Chanity was ready for him to come to their bed chamber. Derek was just about to dash up the stairs when Ortaire grabbed him.

"Dragon, did you really think you could skip out on tradition?" Ortaire asked, laughing.

Ortaire, Gunnar and Sean along with two other warriors heaved Derek on their shoulders, and carried him up the stairs. Bram watched, but did not join in on their fun. They entered the chamber, and deposited him on the bed with Chanity.

Chanity blushed, and pulled the covers all the way up under her chin.

After the warriors left and the commotion died down, Derek bolted the door even though he knew no one would dare enter. "Chanity, are you nervous or afraid?" Derek asked with concern.

"Nay," she replied, shyly. "Well, not afraid, maybe just a little bit nervous, but I will be fine. My mother explained to me about what happens when a man beds a woman." She did not mention she knew there would be discomfort for her the first time. He took her by the hand, lifted out of bed and into his arms. Derek embraced her tightly, as he inhaled her scent, and felt the warmth of her body against him.

Chanity felt the strength in Derek's arms, as his hands explored her body. The heat from his body passed easily through her thin shift, and she clung to him as he started kissing her. They kissed until they were breathless from it.

Derek pulled back for a moment, then looked her up then down as he admired her body. He removed her shift so he could see every bare inch of her. The candle light and crackling fire joined to light her body with a soft glow. He drew in his breath as he saw just how beautiful she was. He had never seen a woman's body so well formed as hers. She was a little embarrassed to be the object of his hungry gaze, but she stood there proudly like a regal queen, letting his eyes roam all over her.

Derek could not stand the temptation any longer and began to undress. After he disrobed, he stood there in the light for a moment. Chanity studied his body intently, and wanted to know his as well as she did her own. His manhood was excited from looking at her even before he took off his clothes. It stood out proudly for her to see, and she looked at it with curiosity. For a moment Derek thought the sight of his member might frighten her, and asked again if she was afraid.

"Nay," Chanity answered once more as she looked lovingly in his eyes.

Derek lifted Chanity into his broad arms and carried her to their bed. He laid her down like she was fine porcelain that might break.

"You are so beautiful Chanity; you are an enchantress that has held me spell bound from the first day I laid eyes upon you. You are my enchantress, and you will always be mine." He lay down beside her and they embraced each other with excitement over what was to come.

Derek took his time kissing and stroking her body, and Chanity shivered with delight at the sensation. As he brought her more and more pleasure, she softly moaned, and pulled his body closer. Derek knew she was ready for him, and though there was some pain, both relished the moment they had awaited for so long.

He was as gentle as he could be, and gave her time to accustom herself to him. He kept kissing her, tenderly at first and then with desire. Chanity pulled him to her again, and they moved as one, their passion building with every moment. Their love making lasted a good while, but Derek was glad when he felt her desire building. Just when he thought he could take no more, Chanity cried out in bliss, as he did the same.

Derek softly stroked Chanity's face as they gazed into each other's eyes. He kissed her again, and embraced her tightly before moving to lay by her side. He wrapped his arms around her, and pulled her close, breathing in her scent.

This was the love he had wished for, but dared not imagine he would ever find. Just the thought of their future together made him smile. Before he drifted off to sleep, Derek silently prayed they would know the joy of being together for the rest of their lives.

Chanity embraced Derek in return, and sighed contentedly. Derek had truly given her a wedding night that she would always remember. He brought her pleasure that she never dreamed existed, and never wanted to do without again. She knew it was only the beginning of many nights of ecstasy that Derek would show her, and she looked forward to each night with him. She was astonished at how he awakened her desire with a simple touch, caress or kiss.

He had made her a woman, his woman and she would crave him endlessly. He was hers, she was his, and she would love him forever. She fell asleep with a smile on her lips, love in her heart, and felt secure as he held her in his strong arms.

The next morn, Derek awoke with a smile, feeling Chanity unclothed body snuggled tightly to him. Her closeness was causing an effect already. He always dreamed of love, but never imagined he would find anyone as beautiful or kind hearted as Chanity. Pride swelled in his heart as he held her close to him. She started to stir, and awoke when he kissed the tip of her nose. "Good morning dear wife, did you sleep well?"

"The first or second time I went to sleep?" Chanity asked smiling. Derek laughed, and pulled her closer. He wanted her, but thought it was probably best for Chanity to wait until later.

Derek went to the door and opened it. He peered into the hall, and saw one of the guards standing a discreet distance away. Derek bade him tell Alma to send up a trencher of food. The guard nodded assent, and made his way downstairs.

"'Tis our first day as husband and wife, so I want to keep you to myself."

Chanity smiled in agreement. "I refuse to share you with anyone else as well, husband." She was grateful Derek decided to shun the duties of Holdenworth today.

Derek took his duties seriously, but he also knew how to relax and enjoy himself as well. Besides, everything was in Bram's capable hands. Bram could take care of running Holdenworth for one day, so they could spend their time together.

In a short while, there was a knock at their chamber door. It had not been long since the guard left, so Alma must have been expecting them to send for food. They made themselves presentable, and Derek opened the door. Alma came bursting in with joy, carrying their meal. "Good morning my Lord and Lady! 'Tis a beautiful sunny day outside. Here is your trencher of food, milk and mead," Alma said as she sat it on the table.

As Alma was leaving, Derek whispered something to her, then she nodded her head and left. Chanity wondered what Derek was up to. She didn't wonder long, for she was starving, and could smell the wonderful food. Derek pulled out a chair for her, and gave her a sensuous kiss, before taking the other.

"Apparently Alma is going to make sure we do not go hungry," Chanity said as she looked at all the food on the trencher. There were several kinds of meat, along with eggs, and hot bread with butter and honey. It was plenty of food for the two of them, and Chanity thought it might be enough to feed four. There must have been plenty of meat left over from the wedding feast and Christmas festival. She was quite famished, and was surprised that she ate so much.

Derek smiled nearly the whole time they sat together. Chanity was glad to see he was as happy as she was. As a young girl she dreamed of a life like this, but after the death of her father she had given up on her childhood dreams. She decided in her heart to never give up on her dreams again, even if they seemed impossible. Who would have thought her Knight in shining armor would arrive just in time to save her virtue. Now she could truly live happily ever after.

Suddenly, there was another knock at the chamber door. "I asked Alma to send up a tub and water for you a bath," Derek said, as he gave her a hug and kiss. "I thought you would like a hot soak in the tub. I have something I have to do, but I will be quick and will return before you are through with your bath.

After Derek left, Chanity took her bath. She had just finished, and was resting in the warm water when he returned. He took her cloth and rubbed her back, then proceeded to her breast. "I have already washed there and all over," Chanity said giggling. "I was just relaxing in the warm water". Derek wanted to continue, but knew he needed to stop before he decided to take her again this morn. It was tempting, but he thought she needed a little more time since they had coupled twice last night.

Chanity stepped out of the bath to dry off. "If you don't mind me smelling pretty, I will wash off in your tub," Derek said as he undressed, and tried to take his mind off her curvy unclothed figure. After soaking for a while, he lathered his soap onto a fresh cloth and scrubbed down, then rinsed off with water before stepping out of the tub. "That should hide some of your floral scent on me," Derek said hopefully.

"I would not be getting too close to Bram, Ortaire or Gunnar, or you might not hear the end of it," Chanity said teasingly.

Derek drew her into his arms and nibbled her ear. "My Dear Enchantress, I think they may expect me to have your scent all over me after the night we had." Chanity blushed deeply and buried her face in his bare shoulder.

"You should not be embarrassed with me now since we are wed," Derek said smiling.

"I'm not really so much embarrassed with you, but what will the others think?"

"They will think we are fortunate to have one another, but we should not care what they think since we are wed."

"I will try not to be embarrassed, or worry what other people may think," Chanity said. She gave him a seductive smile and a sensuous kiss.

They went downstairs a few moments later, only to be swarmed by people wanting to wish them well. Derek whispered in Chanity ear, "Meet me outside in a few moments, but make sure you dress in warm clothing. We might be outside for most of the day." Chanity spoke with the village folk a little while, then went back upstairs to don her warmest cloak. The fur lining of her cloak, gloves and boots would keep her warm on the coldest day.

Chanity walked outside and saw Derek mounted on Rollo, with a wicked smile on his face. He reached down and lifted her in front of him. "Close your eyes," he told her, then rode his horse in a few circles so she would not know in which direction they traveled. He even took a longer route so she would not know where they went.

After a few minutes of riding, Derek dismounted, and helped Chanity dismount as well. "Keep your eyes closed, I am going to put you over my shoulder, but it shan't take long to get to our destination." She held on tight when she realized he was climbing down. Derek reached his destination, and helped her get seated. "Now you can open your eyes my love."

Chanity opened her eyes to see her favorite place, but it looked quite different. Derek had surprised her by dressing it up. Inside the small room chamber was a bed made up of straw and fur pelts. He had built a fire at the entrance of the chamber so the room would be cozy. There were pelts lying on the big rock outside, and on it sat a basket of food and flask of wine. Tears came to her eyes as she realized the thought he had put into this to surprise her.

"Don't cry Chanity, I didn't mean to upset you. I just thought you would enjoy it."

Chanity laughed. "Of course I love it. It was so thoughtful of you, to ever dream of doing this for me. It was a wonderful surprise Derek! I can't thank you enough," Chanity said, her voice filled with emotion. This must have been where he had hurried off to while she bathed and soaked in the tub. He must have asked Alma to have everything ready for him so he could set it up and get back before she finished bathing.

"You can thank me with your sweet kiss," Derek said, as he pulled her to him so she could do just that. Then he carried her to the bed he had made so they could enjoy one another once more. Derek was thankful he was able to resist her earlier that morn, as tempting as she was.

Later, they sat upon the big rock, eating their lunch and daydreaming of the life they would share. They talked of the children they would have together. Then talked about how many they wanted, how many they hoped would be lasses and how many would be lads. They even thought of some names for them.

The sun was dipping low on the horizon, and the air was growing colder. "We better head back," Derek said reluctantly. "I don't want you to get sick from the cool air." They held each other one more time while looking out to sea, then climbed back up to the ledge above.

"Derek, thank you again for bringing me to my favorite place and spending the day with me. You are so special, I am truly blessed to have you, and I will always love you," Chanity said lovingly.

"I am blessed as well to have you as my wife, and I will always love you," Derek said, as he looked deeply into her eyes.

Derek mounted Rollo, reached down for Chanity, and placed her in front of him again.

"You tricked me well by turning the horse in circles, and taking a longer route. I did not know where you were taking me."

"I know how wise you are Chanity, and you would have known our destination if I had not done so," Derek said laughing.

Chanity was glad he did not mind her being wise. Most men wanted silly females that did not think on important matters. She was glad he loved her for herself and didn't want to change her.

When they returned to great hall, they greeted everyone, then headed back to their chamber. Later that evening, Alma brought their sup to them. After they supped, they sat in front of the fire and talked. Derek told her again, about his family and told her they were going to love her.

Chanity now had a mother, father, two sisters and a brother by marriage. She was looking forward to meeting them in the spring. From all the details Derek had given her, she felt like she already knew and cared for them. She prayed they would love and care for her as well. Before Derek arrived she had been so alone. Now she was blessed with her husband and a big family. She could not wait to journey to Normandy to meet them.

Chapter 19

Over the next few weeks, Holdenworth thrived under the care of its Lord and Lady. Derek and Chanity scheduled their duties well, so they had their evenings free to spend private time together. Everyone could see the great love they had each other.

They would sneak off to Chanity's favorite spot whenever they had a sunny day. Derek teased Chanity, and claimed the spot was his now as well. This week brought a heavy snow, so they would not get a chance to go for a while.

Marla finally seemed to stop being jealous of Chanity and Leva's friendship. She spent time embroidering, or sewing with Chanity each day. She even went to search Leva out at times. Chanity was glad Marla was starting to act her age. Marla would be ten and seven the last of March, and Chanity would be ten and eight the middle of March.

Marla still did not like the idea of going to her Grandparents to live. She never openly said anything about it, but when Derek and Chanity talked of traveling in the springtime, Marla would get a sad look on her face.

Chanity noted this, and persuaded Derek to stay a few days with his uncle and aunt to see Marla settled, before traveling on to see Derek's family.

Bram was one of the Warriors that would be traveling to Normandy with them, as well as Sean and eleven others. Ortaire would stay behind to see to the running of Holdenworth, and Gunnar was to see to that everything was secure. Some of the villagers were already being trained as extra guards to replace Sean and the other eleven men that would be going to Normandy with them.

Chanity looked forward to traveling, since she had only been as far as the next two villages. Most of all, she was excited about meeting her new family and seeing where Derek grew up. He had described it so well she could almost see it in her mind. She knew he missed his family and longed to see them.

The first of February was cold and icy, but by Chanity's birthday in mid-March the waters should be travelable. They would make a couple stops to trade valuables along the way. Time seemed to fly by, and soon only a few weeks remained until they were to depart.

It came as no surprise to anyone when Ortaire asked Leva to wed. Leva happily accepted, but went to Chanity with some concerns.

"We care for each other deeply, but aren't really in love, Leva confided, though she did not tell Chanity about the Lady Ortaire loved in Normandy.

"A lot of marriages start out that way but most grow to love one another with time," Chanity replied.

"Thank you Chanity. Hearing that gives me great hope for a happy future with Ortaire. I'm glad you will be with me on my special day," Leva replied smiling.

The ceremony took place at Holdenworth, with the entire village looking on. Leva wore the gown Chanity had given her for the Christmas festival, since she had worn it only once before. She looked happy and beautiful as brides always do. Ortaire seemed truly happy as well. Chanity prayed they would have a good life together.

The middle of March came, and Chanity turned ten and eight. Alma made sure that Cook made her favorite foods that evening in honor of the day of her birth. Derek gave her a beautiful necklace and ear bobs that matched her ring.

Chanity told him they were the most beautiful set she had ever seen. She still had her Mother's jewelry, hidden in the secret chamber, but never wore them. The set Derek had made for her was her favorite because it was made from his own design, as well as his love for her.

At sup that night, Derek and Bram discussed the best route to take and what ports they should trade wares at.

Everyone was excited about the upcoming trip except for Marla. Over the last three days she became quieter by the day. When she wasn't helping with the work in the great hall, she stayed in her chamber.

Chanity felt bad for Marla, and tried to ask her about how she was feeling, but Marla denied there was nothing wrong. Then she went back to work or up to her bedchamber.

The day before they were to leave, the guards at the watch tower sounded the alarm that a group of ships were headed their way. No messenger had been sent to announce a pending arrival, so Derek readied his men for battle.

"Chanity, take all the women and children inside. Make sure all the doors are bolted, then watch outside. If you see any sign of battle, take Marla and get inside the hidden chamber. Do not come out until it is safe to do so. Either Bram or I will come and let you know when it's safe." He quickly kissed her, and started shouting orders to his men.

A flood of memories came back to Chanity of the day Vorik invaded and slew her father. She stood frozen in place remembering all the terrible events of that day.

Derek looked toward the hall for Chanity, but was surprised to see her standing in the same spot like a statue. He quickly ran back to her. "Chanity what is wrong?" He asked, but still she stood there like she didn't hear him. He shook her to bring her out of her thoughts.

Chanity finally snapped back to the present. "Please be careful Derek, I love you so, and could not bear to lose you," she pleaded.

Chanity grasped Derek so tight that he worried he would harm her if he had to pry her hands away. It suddenly occurred to him that she was reliving the day Vorik invaded Holdenworth.

"'Tis alright Chanity. Everything is going to be fine. It may just be some of King William's men arriving with a message, or seeking a place to rest overnight on their journey. Even if they are raiders, they are no comparison with Vorik and his men. We have plenty of warriors and are prepared for them. Go, so I know you are safe. Only then can I stay focused if we have to battle."

Suddenly Chanity let go. A look of determination and strength showed on her face, and she didn't look frightened anymore.

"I am fine now, Derek. I just had a memory of when Vorik came. Go now, and see to your men." She kissed him, then held her head high and showed no sign of fear. She felt fear but would not let anyone else know she felt it.

After Derek spoke to her, Chanity felt stronger and could not believe she had showed such weakness. She was now Lady of Holdenworth. Her mother had showed strength as a Lady, and so would she.

Chanity called all the women and children and commanded them to get inside the great hall. They entered, barred the doors and settled down to wait. It seemed like an eternity before the strangers arrived.

As Chanity looked outside, instead of battle, she saw Derek embracing an old man and woman. They had brought only enough men to maneuver their Dragon ship and two long boats.

Chanity and Marla looked at each other in relief that there would be no battle that day. They walked outside to greet the new arrivals and welcome them to Holdenworth.

Derek pulled Chanity to him, and said, "This is my wife, Lady Chanity and this other young lady is your granddaughter, Marla. Marla, these are your grandparents, my Uncle Marten and Aunt Tilly," Derek said as he introduced them.

Marla stood frozen as the older couple pulled her into their arms and hugged her. She finally eased a little, and hugged them back, but there was still uncertainty on her face. She could not help but remember how her aunt would pretend she cared for her in public, but was openly hostile when they were alone. Marla tried to smile and act friendly as they went on and on about how much she looked like her mother Marta.

"We were so happy to hear from Derek that our granddaughter was at Holdenworth," they exclaimed. "We couldn't wait to see you, so we left out as soon as the weather permitted."

"You must be tired and hungry. Let us go inside," Chanity said.

As they entered the great hall Chanity directed Marten and Tilly to a table, and asked Alma to bring them a trencher of food. Alma was always prepared. As soon as she saw the arrivals were visitors instead of foes, she set Cook to work warming food. Chanity had not noticed Alma was carrying their trenchers to them as she spoke.

"Thank you, Alma," Chanity said, as she placed the food on the table. "I do not know what we would do without you."

Chanity turned to see Marla heading for the stairs and stepped away to speak with her. "Marla, you must not leave now, for it would be unkind and rude. Your grandparents have traveled a great distance to see you. They will be hurt if you leave now, and they seem like good people. Can you not see how happy they are to see you? I can see how much they love you, already."

"But what if it's just an act for people to see, like how my great aunt would do in public?" Marla asked. She didn't give Chanity a chance to answer the question before she turned around and headed back to the table.

Chanity watched Marla walk away, and wondered how an adult could have been so cruel to such a young child. Vorik's aunt must have been as heartless as he had been. Now she understood why Marla had acted the way she did. She was never shown any real love or kindness before coming to Holdenworth. Chanity decided to pray Marla would come to love and trust her grandparents before she had to leave with them for Normandy.

Derek enjoyed seeing his Uncle Marten and Aunt Tilly, but he was disappointed that they would have to postpone the trip to see his parents. They could not leave on the morrow, since Marten and Tilly had just arrived. They would have to stay until his uncle decided to journey home.

As they supped, Derek asked his uncle all kinds of questions about his family and how they were all fairing.

"They all send their love and congratulations on your wedding, Derek. They wish the ceremony could have waited till spring, but completely understand. They know you wanted to wed so you could start your life together as husband and wife. Your parents were just as impatient as you to start their lives together," Marten said, smiling.

Derek saw a hopeful look in his uncle's eyes, and thought he knew the cause. Marten and Tilly had been a loving couple at one time, but after their two sons were slain and Marta was abducted, they had grown apart. The horrible destruction and chaos Vorik brought into their lives still weighed heavily upon them all. Perhaps his uncle hoped Marla would be the miracle his wife needed to be happy again.

While Derek entertained the guests, Chanity set about making arrangements for where they would sleep. She asked Elspeth to set Marten and Tilly up in her old bed chamber, since she no longer used it.

"Alma has already ordered it cleaned, just in case you should want them to stay there," Elspeth replied. One of Marten's men brought the trunks up the stairs as they spoke. "I'll see to this, Chanity. You go enjoy yourself and get to know some of your new family."

Chanity knew Derek's aunt and uncle must be exhausted after the long journey from Normandy. After they supped and talked awhile, they mentioned how tired they were. "Marla, would you show Marten and Tilly to their bed chamber?" She asked.

Marla smiled and agreed, as they stood up to be shown to their bedchamber.

Derek was glad his uncle and aunt wanted to retire to their chamber. Now they could go upstairs as well and enjoy some time alone with each other.

Derek and Chanity spent the rest of the evening lying in each other's arms, or sitting in front of the fire playing chess. They truly enjoyed their time together, and had quickly become so close they could almost tell what the other was thinking.

Derek's uncle Marten had been at Holdenworth for only a week, when Derek received a sealed message from King William asking him to come to camp.

William was at an impasse in a battle with one of his foes and needed Derek's help with battle strategy. Derek did not want to leave Holdenworth, and especially did not want to be away from Chanity. He dreaded telling her that he had to leave so soon after they wed, but he could not refuse King William. He never wanted to be away from Chanity even if it had been years since they had wed, much less right after. Though his heart ached, he had to tell Chanity now, since he would leave at first light on the morrow.

Chanity felt apprehensive when the messenger arrived, and announced he had a message from the King. From across the great hall Chanity watched Derek's face as he read the message. She could tell by the look on his face he did not like what it contained. He looked around the great hall until his eyes meet hers. She could see the anguish held in them.

Instantly, she realized the King had summoned Derek. She felt like her world was falling apart and she was going to be sick. She gripped the table and sat down on the bench. She knew she had to be strong, so Derek would not think her weak. She was the Lady of Holdenworth, and she would make him proud. She was also the daughter of Belgar and Serina, who had set an example for her.

Chanity quickly composed herself by the time Derek crossed the room to join her. She greeted him with a forced smile that she hoped looked normal. "Sir Knight, have you been summoned to join your King? I could tell by the look on your face, the message was not to your liking."

"Aye my love, I am to leave at first light on the morrow. I am sorry I must go, but as you know I have no choice in the matter. If I had a choice, I would never leave your side. It breaks my heart to have to leave you, even if for a brief time. I will do my best to return as quickly as I can to your loving arms."

"Promise me Sir Knight that you will return safely to me. You must take care, and not take any chances with your life. You know how much I need your love, and how happy I am at your side. You fill my heart with love, and you are now a part of me."

"I promise that I will be as careful as possible, Chanity. I want a promise from you as well. Promise me you will stay inside Holdenworth's gates and walls. If you should need to go beyond the gate, make sure Bram and his men are with you, and do not go out unescorted. Please give me your word on this, Chanity."

"Derek, my dear husband, I give you my word I will not venture out alone." Derek reached for her and encircled her with his powerful arms as if protecting her from an unknown harm that she might come across while he was away. She felt secure within his arms, and would certainly miss that feeling while he was gone.

Chanity tried to show strength by not shedding a single tear. She did not want Derek to know how frightened she was for his safety. She knew Derek wanted her to feel confident in his abilities as a warrior. She also did not want him or their people to think she saw him as weak.

He had been her hero ever since the first day she met him. She reminded herself that Derek was a great warrior. He had even defeated Garth, the King's champion knight. In the back of her mind though, she realized that even the best warriors sometimes fell in battle. She had to have faith that God would watch over her husband and send him safely back home to her.

They made love twice that night, then again the following morn. Derek could not get enough of her, knowing it could be months before he saw her again. He held her in his arms, breathing in the scent he knew belonged only to her. Her scent was a mixture of her own essence and fresh jasmine. Her smile was like sunshine that brought warmth to his heart. They held each other until dawn, till he had to rise and ready himself for the journey.

Chanity dressed quickly and followed Derek down to break their fast. The dozen or so warriors that Derek chose were already at the table eating when he sat down. Derek's men knew how strict he was about being ready to leave on time, so they were always ready before hand.

Bram was waiting to see Derek when he arrived at the table. "Derek my Lord, friend, and brother, I wish I was going with you, but I know I will serve your purpose better here. This is the first time that we will not be going to battle together."

Ortaire spoke up as well. "Are you sure you do not want me to go Derek, for I can be ready in a moment's notice. All a warrior needs is his helmet, sword and shield."

"I can just imagine Ortaire, the mighty warrior, standing on the field of battle with nothing on but his helmet, sword and shield," Gunnar said in jest. They all roared with laughter except Ortaire, who smacked Gunnar on the back.

"Besides he does not need you," Gunnar continued. "He will have Sean and I to watch his back."

"I do not need you nursemaids fighting over who is going to watch over me," Derek said. "Bram, you serve me better by staying here and watching over Chanity and Holdenworth."

Derek turned to Ortaire. "I need you here as well. I know you will help Bram see that everything is secure. With the two of you here I will have less to worry about while I'm serving King William. Gunnar, Sean and the rest of my warriors will have my back, and I will have theirs as well."

After they finished their meal, Derek gave the order that it was time to leave. He knew Chanity would follow him outside, so he scooped her up into his powerful arms. She felt light as a feather as he carried her out of the great hall. He bent down to kiss her as they went through Holdenworth's huge wooden doors.

The warmth of spring was upon them. The birds sounded their calls, and the scent of blossoms hung in the air. As the sun rose, Chanity would have thought it a beautiful day, but now her heart was troubled over Derek's departure.

Derek noticed the frown on her face, and Chanity quickly gave him a brilliant smile to mask her sadness. She did not want him worrying over her while he was away. She wanted his thoughts to be on protecting himself and did not want him distracted.

The horses awaited their riders in the courtyard, so Derek set Chanity on her feet as he reached Rollo.

"Sir Knight, 'tis no reason to worry about me," Chanity said. "You have seen to it that I and Holdenworth are well guarded. Other than you, there's no better warrior than Bram or Ortaire to see to my safety, as well as Holdenworth. So worry not dear husband, for everything will be fine. I will stay busy, and not just sit around pining. I am now your wife as well as Lady of Holdenworth, and I find pride, strength and courage in that fact."

Chanity looked like an enchantress, and her strength and confidence were evident. "Chanity, I am so proud of you, and thankful to God that you are my wife." He drew her into his arms, and gave her a long sensuous kiss, not wanting to let her out of his embrace. He finally let go, mounted his steed, and shouted the order to ride out.

As Derek rode away, he turned to take one last look at his wife. Love and pride filled his heart. She truly looked like a regal queen guarding their kingdom as she stood there. He could not wait to get back home to her loving arms.

Though she had sorrow in her heart, Chanity was determined she would not show weakness as she had done when Derek first left to battle Garth. She still remembered Bram's lecture on how she should act as the Lady of Holdenworth. She had appreciated it, even though it hurt her feelings at first. After that they became close friends.

She trusted Bram with her life and knew she could count on him if she needed anything. She trusted Ortaire as well, but Bram was like a brother to her. Bram had been willing to sacrifice everything to take her to Derek's family if Derek fell in battle to Garth. Derek thought of Bram as family, and so did she.

She walked into Holdenworth with strength and did not let anyone see the sadness in her heart. She made it through the day without crying, but that night the tears flowed freely as she crawled into their bed. She could smell Derek's scent, so she closed her eyes and pretended he was beside her. It was a futile pretense, though, for she could not feel his body heat, or his arms around her.

She would allow herself to cry this one night, but afterward would permit no more self-pity. She told Derek she would not lie around crying, and she intended to keep her word to him. She would do as he wished and show the people her strength by being the Lady Holdenworth needed.

Bram walked past the master chamber on the way to his own. He knew Chanity would be weeping her heart out, missing and worrying about Derek. He wished he could take her in his arms and hold her to help ease her sorrow, but knew that could never be.

He had come to love Chanity, but he also loved Derek as a brother and would never betray him. He had tried to think of Chanity as a sister or friend since he first realized his feelings, but so far that had not worked. He would never tell anyone the way he felt for Chanity.

Instead of giving Chanity loving support, he would have to be stern with her at times so she would be the strong Lady that Holdenworth needed in Derek's absence. He had heard stories of the great fearless lady her mother Serina had been. He would have liked to have known her.

Feelings or not, he still would be spending a great deal of time with Chanity. He enjoyed their conversations as they played chess and didn't even mind so much that she won most of the time. They often went riding but were never alone. There were always a few guards following several paces behind. He would never risk any gossip, and would slay the man that dared suggest she had been unfaithful to Derek.

Bram realized he would have to leave Holdenworth one day if his feelings for Chanity did not change. At one time, he thought he would always be with Derek and Ortaire. They had been together since their youth and always watched out for one another. If someone insulted or attacked one of them, they had to face the wrath of all three.

Bram wished he and Ortaire were riding to battle with Derek. It was strange being apart from him, since they had always ridden into battle together.

Gunnar and Sean would be with Derek, but it wasn't the same. He was a warrior, and felt he should be riding into battle. Lately, he had to admit he enjoyed settling down at Holdenworth and helping run the place.

Derek treated him and Ortaire like his own blood and given them bedchambers inside the manor. Ortaire had just recently moved into Leva's cottage with when they wed, and it felt strange not having him right down the hall.

The next morning to Bram's surprise, Chanity marched into the great hall and greeted everyone with a smile on her face. She showed no signs of tears or weakness, but had a strength about her that showed she was the Lady of Holdenworth. She looked like she was ready to take on an army. Bram nodded his head at her and smiled his approval.

Chapter 20

A month went by without any problems at Holdenworth. To Chanity's amazement, it had taken only a week or two for Marla to become close to her grandmother. Her Grandmother was spoiling her with jewelry and little trinkets she had brought with her.

She made Marla all kinds of promises about what would happen when they returned home. She told Marla everyone would love her and could not wait to greet her when they returned.

Another week passed, till one night Chanity became very sick after she supped. She returned to her bedchamber and tried to lie down, but became so nauseated she couldn't hold down anything she had eaten that night.

She slept late the next morn, since she had been up all night. Alma came to check on her and told her to stay in bed, then left to fetch Etta to see what the malady was.

Etta arrived to find Chanity sleeping, so she felt her head for fever, then slipped out of the chamber. Nausea indicated it had been something Chanity ate, but it was strange that no one else had been sick. She decided to let Chanity sleep for now, and check on her after she woke up.

Etta went downstairs to ask Alma who had served Chanity the night before. Alma thought long and hard but could not remember who took Chanity her trencher of food.

"Keep a close eye on Chanity's food, and do not let anyone else serve her," Etta advised Alma.

Later that day, Etta went to Chanity's chamber to find her sick again over her chamber pot. "Have you had your monthly flow lass?" Etta asked her.

"Aye," Chanity replied, "It had stopped a few days before I became ill."

By her answer, Etta knew she was not with child, so that did not cause the illness.

It took nearly a week for Chanity to get over the nausea. Most meals she could hardly eat anything except bread and broth.

Chanity felt famished when the nausea finally broke, but Etta warned her not to eat much at first. She did as Etta had instructed, though she felt she could eat a meal for three. Etta told her she could eat a little more in a while if she still felt well.

Bram took Etta aside privately and asked her what she thought was wrong.

"It seems as if Chanity had ate something spoiled, but 'tis puzzling why no one else had taken ill," Etta replied.

Bram knew a few girls that would like to take Chanity's place. Some village girls were infatuated with Lord Derek, and some dreamed of taking Chanity's place as Lady of Holdenworth.

One was Alice, who seemed the most devious and determined. When she set her mind on something, there was nearly no stopping her. He thought he could rule out Alice, for she didn't have access to the kitchen, unless she had a friend that worked inside Holdenworth's walls.

He didn't think the other village girls would stoop so low as to poison Chanity, but Marla was still a mystery.

Marla had feelings for Derek not long ago. Perhaps she might be capable of such an act. For now, it seemed that she had taken to her Grandparents, and was ready to accompany them to Normandy. But was it an act? He didn't think she was acting, but decided to assign someone to keep an eye on her just in case.

Bram went to find Alma in the kitchen. "I want someone to oversee Chanity's food at every meal," he ordered.

"I understand your concern, and I agree, Sir Bram. I will be watching, and Elspeth will as well."

"Be sure only you or Elspeth prepare her food. Do not allow it out of your sight, no matter what happens. It would be easy for someone to create a commotion so they could slip something into her meal. Make sure you explain this Elspeth as well, because I will hold the two of you responsible."

"If anything should happen to my Chanity, I could not bear it," Alma said.

Bram saw the love in Alma's eyes for Chanity and wished he hadn't spoken so harshly. "Of course," he replied. "I just want to see to her safety."

It did not take Chanity long to realize people were keeping a close eye on her. She thought it was ridiculous since she was feeling better. When Alma came to check on her that night, she asked what all the fuss was about, since it was only something she ate that did not agree with her.

"Chanity, this was no small nausea. You were very sick, and no one else became sick from the food," Alma explained. "It could not be because of a babe in your womb, since you just finished your monthly flow. Bram is suspicious as well. We just want you to be watchful for a little while, and only eat what Elspeth or I serve you."

Chanity agreed but did not take it too seriously. She focused her attention on Holdenworth and left it to Bram and Alma to ferret out the issue.

Two weeks went by without incident, and soon Chanity thought nothing else of her illness. She was heading down to the great hall one morning, when she tripped on something and fell. She tried to right herself, but fell headlong, and landed midway down the stairs with a sickening thud. Chanity tried to rise, but felt the light fade, as darkness enveloped her.

Bram was on his feet running as soon as he heard Chanity scream. Instantly his eyes went to the stairs to see her lying in a motionless heap on the steps. He bounded across the room and crouched by her side.

She looked lifeless, and Bram feared the worst, but then he saw her bosom rise as she took a breath. He gently scooped her into his arms, and yelled for Alma to fetch Etta, as he took her straight to the master chamber. He eased her limp body down on the bed, and Alma was there by the time he straightened back up.

Alma held a wooden horse in her hand. "Sir Bram, this was on the stairs, and was probably what made her fall." Bram frowned as he took the toy from her. "Chanity's father carved this for her when she was but a small child," Alma told him.

He imagined Chanity as a little girl playing with the toy horse, and his heart ached to see her lying there lifeless. The knot on her head was the size of a hen egg, and it looked like she was going to have a bruise also. She looked so pale that he was afraid for her.

"If anything happens to her, I will slay the person who caused this with my bare hands," Bram said through clenched teeth. He did not want to leave her side, but he had to find out who did this, and make sure they could not strike again.

Bram took one last look at Chanity, then turned to Alma and Etta who had just arrived. "Let me know if there is any change, or if she awakens. There will be two guards outside her chamber. If you have any news, send one of them for me. I don't want her left alone."

"Do not worry about that, there is no way we will leave her alone," Alma replied.

After Bram left, Alma and Etta undressed Chanity, then checked her body for broken bones and bruises. Luckily, they did not find any broken bones, but there was a lot of bruising up and down her body from tumbling on the steps. Not only was her head bruised, but her face was as well. Fortunately, the bump on her head had not grown any larger, but she still had not awakened.

Bram descended the stairs, and spied Ortaire, who had just entered the hall.

Ortaire's concerned expression revealed that he had already heard what happened. "I came as quickly as I could," he said.

"We must gather everyone from servants to guards into the great hall," Bram told him. "Everyone is to be questioned immediately. I want to know how this wooden horse ended up on those stairs, or if anyone was seen with it."

"Is she alright Bram?" Ortaire asked.

"I do not know, Ortaire. She has not awaked. She has a bump on her head at least the size of a hen's egg. They are checking her now for bruises and broken bones."

Bram had talked to Ortaire about his suspicion that someone had tampered with her food a couple weeks before. "Do you think the two incidents are connected?" Ortaire asked.

"Aye, I do," Bram replied. "But I can't imagine why anyone would want to hurt her. She is so kind hearted, and is always nice to everyone. She goes out of her way to help people."

"Bram, do you suspect anyone in particular?"

"Not yet, but for them to single out Chanity, it must be over Derek. Someone must want Chanity out of the way for the sake of Derek or to be the Lady of Holdenworth. Perhaps even both."

"Three months ago, I would have said Marla was behind these incidents," Bram continued. "However, she seems closer to her grandparents now, and has accepted the fact she is going to Normandy with them. She and her grandmother are always huddled together talking. The old woman constantly spoils her with jewelry and little gifts. She promises Marla she will spoil her even more when they return home."

"Bram, there is no denying that Alice wants Derek," Ortaire reminded him. "She waited unclothed in his horse stall for him to return from riding one day. That's only one of many times she has tried to seduce him."

"She does not come to the Manor except to bring eggs, so I don't see how she had the opportunity," Bram replied. "If she wanted to hurt Chanity badly enough, I guess she could have slipped something into her food, but she had no way of knowing it would make it to Chanity, unless she has a friend or relative in the manor to help her."

"That is a possibility," said Ortaire thoughtfully. "I will check into this with Alma's help, that way it won't make her or her accomplice aware that we suspect them."

They questioned everyone, but no one knew how the carved horse ended up on the stairs, and there had been no children playing inside that morn.

After Bram spoke with everyone, he went to check on Chanity.

"Chanity placed the horse in an old chest of her special things," Alma advised Bram. "There was no way a child could have gotten it unless she gave it to them to play with. The horse was very special to Chanity, so I doubt she would have done that. We will ask her when she wakes up."

Alma hoped Chanity would revive soon. She was so worried for her. She loved Chanity, and it brought tears to her eyes at the thought that she might not recover. She held Chanity's lifeless hand and prayed for her to be alright. She had lost Serina, and could not bear the thought of losing Chanity as well.

Alma slept in Chanity's room every night to watch over her. Some nights Etta and Elspeth stayed also, but even then Alma never left her side.

Bram checked on Chanity each night on his way to his chamber. Bram was so worried about her that he would have stayed himself, but knew that would have caused rumors. He still had feelings for Chanity, but would always treat her like a sister.

Late one night, Bram climbed the steps to retire, and found Marla and her grandmother talking quietly in the hall. They looked up as he approached. Marla went into her bed chamber, and shut the door.

"Do you think it is wise going into my nephew's bed chamber with his wife, especially while he's away?" Tilly asked sternly. "I do not want my nephew hurt because of rumors that his wife is being unfaithful to him."

Bram shot Tilly a look of contempt that would have frightened most people and said, "then don't start any rumors. Alma and Etta are tending to Chanity as we speak, and they are with her still. Seeing how Derek left me in charge, it is my job to protect Chanity while some mad person is trying to kill her."

"Oh, I seriously doubt that anyone is trying to kill her," Tilly said incredulously. "Chanity was probably just clumsy and did not pay attention to what she was doing."

Bram had enough of her, whether she was Derek's uncle's wife or not. He bent down practically in Tilly's face and said, "Chanity is the Lady of Holdenworth, and will be spoken of with respect. If you can't speak nicely of her, then it is best you say nothing at all."

He stared directly at Tilly, daring her to speak another word. Finally, she turned and headed for her chamber. Tilly's face was filled with anger, but she said nothing else as she stormed off. Perhaps she had wanted Derek to marry Marla, but it did not work out the way she had hoped.

The next morning Bram decided to investigate Chanity's previous illness more thoroughly and went to speak to Cook. "Has Alice been bringing eggs every day?" he asked.

"Aye, she brings them with her when she comes to work."

"A few weeks ago, you said she only comes to bring eggs," Bram recalled.

"That was true then," Cook replied. "Now she is filling in for her cousin who just had a babe."

Bram realized Alice had the opportunity to put the wooden horse on the stairs. Since her cousin sometimes helped clean the bedchambers, she may have asked Alice to help. That would have given Alice the opportunity to look in the chest and discover the wooden horse.

Also, Alice had motive because she disliked Chanity. She had always been envious of her even in their youth. He knew Alice wanted Derek, and to be the Lady of Holdenworth. At one point, Derek could not even go into the village without Alice chasing after him. Derek began sending someone else to do his bidding in the village whenever possible.

Most young village lasses dreamed of catching the Lord's eye. Alice did not know Derek though. If a wench threw herself at Derek it repulsed instead of attracting him.

Chapter 21

Derek and William poured over the map, planning strategy for the next battle. It seemed with King William, there was always a battle to be fought.

If only the battles would end, and usher in an age of peace. He had been a great warrior, but now his place was home with his beautiful lady wife. He thought of her all the time. He woke thinking of her, and fell asleep thinking of her. He dreamed of holding her in his arms again, and hearing her soft moans as he pleasured her.

It was difficult to leave so soon after they wed, but he could not deny his King. He wanted to get this battle over with, so he could go home to Holdenworth. But most of all he wanted see his Enchantress.

King William could tell Derek's heart just wasn't into battle any longer. He knew Derek would not defy him if he needed his service. He had great respect for Derek. He was a loyal knight who served him well over the years. Besides, he owed Derek for saving his life, and would always remember that. When Derek took a sword in the side, it meant certain death, but he did it anyway. It was a miracle that he survived. As soon as this battle was over, he would send Derek home to his wife.

Three days later they thought the battle over, but enemy reinforcements arrived. King William's barons were the cause of most of his trouble. They overtaxed the Saxons and burdened them so that they revolted. Malcolm Canmore, King of Scotland backed the Saxons, so the battles kept going.

Derek was dismayed and thought he would never get home to Chanity. Gunnar and Sean tried to cheer him up, but it never lasted for long. The only thing that made him happy was thoughts of going home to his beautiful, loving wife. His warrior heart had grown soft even though his body had not, for he had the cuts and scars to prove it. He never complained, but dressed the wounds, then went on no matter the pain. He kept telling himself he would soon be home to his love, his enchantress.

Chanity finally awoke after four days. "It's about time you decided to wake up and join us again," Bram said with relief. She took his hand and gave it a light squeeze, since her mouth was too dry to try to speak. Her lips were dry and cracked, but she managed a small smile.

"Some were afraid you were not going to survive this, but I told them they didn't realize the strength of the Lady of Holdenworth. Seriously though, Chanity you must be more careful. You gave us all a fright."

Alma was almost crying with joy. "Gracious my lady, don't ever give us such a fright again. Bram is right; we were all worried about you." Alma went to the table and poured Chanity a mug of water. Bram and Alma lifted her up, since she was still very weak.

"Take it slow and don't drink too much at first," Alma advised, "I will give you more in a little while. Etta put an herb in the water to help with the pain from the lump on your head, and the soreness your body suffered."

Chanity finally realized why she was so sore and why they were making such a fuss over her. She remembered tripping over something and falling down the stairs. Her voice strained, she said "I tripped going down the stairs, didn't I?" She asked softly.

"Aye," Bram and Alma replied at the same time.

"Do not try to speak, it is too soon yet." Bram said. "It seems you tripped on a carved wooden horse. The horse on the mantle, is it the one your father carved for you?"

She turned to look at it and shook her head "aye," to answer.

Did you give it to someone?

She shook her head "nay," to that question.

"Was it put away in your chest by the wall?"

Chanity shook her head "aye," to answer him again.

"We will talk about it again when you are feeling better," Bram said with concern in his voice. "For now, get some rest. If you need anything tell Alma to send a guard for me. There are two guards outside your door, and will be until Derek returns."

Chanity stirred at the mention of Derek's name. "Everything is fine with Derek," Bram said, realizing instantly what she wanted to know. Derek asked the King's messenger to swing by here on his journey to London to let us know that all was well. He still does not know when he will be home, but he sends you his love."

Chanity's eyes welled up with tears, but she managed a small smile. She put her hand over her heart, as if to say she loved him also.

Bram went downstairs to let everyone know that Chanity had finally regained consciousness. There was a loud cheer from the people in the great hall. They had all been praying for their Lady Chanity.

"Bram, I will go check on Chanity and Etta to see if they need my help," Leva said.

"Remember, Chanity is still very weak, and does not need to speak yet," Bram advised her.

Leva thanked Bram and headed up the stains.

Bram was grateful that Leva had been staying with Chanity from time to time when Alma and Etta needed help. He was in and out all the time but did not stay long. Leva was one more witness that he was never alone with Chanity. The last thing he needed was any rumors getting started.

Marla and her Grandmother had visited occasionally, but never stayed with Chanity long. It seemed they had become inseparable. Bram had never trusted Marla or her grandmother. When Chanity first became ill, Bram told Alma to make sure Marla and Tilly were never left alone with her.

Bram overheard Marten tell Marla her grandmother was forty and nine years. She looked older because of her losing her children, but she had a commanding personality. Marla was proof of that, for she listened to her grandmother, and did her bidding without question.

Regardless of how Marla changed, he was not taking any chances for another accident to occur. Chanity's safety was his responsibility, and he cared what happened to her. He had to keep her safe no matter what.

A week after Chanity regained consciousness, she was up and about performing her duties as Lady of Holdenworth. Bram, Alma or Etta were constantly telling her to slow down and take it easy.

Chanity was just glad to be out of bed again, and able to do her work. Staying busy helped her keep from worrying about Derek.

She missed Derek very much and ached to hold him. She was unhappy without him, but tried hard not to let others see it. Instead, she buried her feelings deep inside and tried to look happy.

Chanity remembered her mother doing the same thing when her father was away. Serina would be smiling for everyone during the day, but Chanity would catch her weeping when she went to her bed chamber at night. She would let Chanity crawl in bed with her for a little while, then carry her back to her own chamber when she fell asleep.

She imagined what it would be like if she and Derek had children. She pictured a son who was a smaller version of Derek, and a daughter with golden hair like her and her mother. Chanity hoped that when Derek returned she would become with child. She wanted to start their own family, and hoped they would have a large family like Derek's parents. Derek wanted a big family, and she wanted to give him that.

Chanity was so lost in thought that she jumped at the sound of Leva's voice. "You look like you're daydreaming, and I bet I know who you are dreaming of," Leva said smiling.

Chanity blushed and confessed what she had been thinking about. She enjoyed her conversations with Leva. They always seemed to find something to laugh about. Chanity felt like she could be herself with Leva, and not have to hide her feelings. Leva had become the best friend she had never had before.

"I'm looking forward to being a mother as well," Leva told Chanity. "I will be so excited when that time comes. I've told Ortaire he will make a great father, but he acts hesitant when I mention it."

"Perhaps he just wants more time with the two of you before you have children," Chanity reassured Leva. "Give him a little more time, and I'm sure he will be ready for them."

Chanity rose to begin work again, but Leva stopped her. "You've done enough for today, lass. Now go upstairs and get some rest before Bram has me flogged."

"Thank you, Leva. I'll get a little something to eat, and head upstairs to rest."

Not far away, in another corner of the hall, Marla sat at a table with her grandmother. Marla talked often with her grandmother, and finally confessed her feelings for Derek while he was away aiding King William. Her grandmother had already known by the way Marla watched him.

"Chanity has always been good and tried to be a sister to me over the years, but I was always envious of her. Now I can't help having feelings for him still, even though they are wed," Marla said.

"Oh, my dear, I've known your feelings for Derek from the moment I laid eyes on you both. But don't fret so, lass. You are a beautiful girl. You will find someone when we get back to Normandy."

"As for Derek, I don't know why he wants to live in this country with these people. His place is at home with his real family and his own people. He should have taken on running our farmstead instead of this place. I know your grandfather is disappointed that Derek is staying here, though he would never say it. But you know, things can change in a moment. Who knows what fate might have in store for us," Tilly said thoughtfully.

"Let us go sup my dear, I'm getting hungry," Tilly ordered. "I am sure you must be as well. You didn't eat much at the noon meal. As I said, you're a beautiful young girl, but you need some meat on your bones. Men do not want their woman too boney. You should trust your grandmother on this matter."

They rose to fetch trenchers and mugs, and Marla took a seat by Chanity, Bram and Ortaire, while Tilly took a seat on the opposite side.

"Chanity, you are starting to look better since your accident. You must be more careful on those stairs," Tilly cautioned.

"Thank you, Aunt Tilly. I am feeling much better, and I will be more cautious," Chanity replied. She did not like how Tilly had implied that she was clumsy, but thought she probably didn't mean anything by it. From the time she arrived, it was obvious that Tilly was a very outspoken person.

Chanity decided to change the subject by talking about the weather. "The weather has been so nice lately. I think spring is my favorite time of year. I pray Derek returns home before summer is over." She did not linger on the subject of Derek, for she was afraid her sadness would show. She looked over to Bram and asked how the crops were doing.

"The spring crops are doing well, and we will begin planting the summer crops in a couple days," Bram said. "Do not worry Chanity, everything is going as planned and is on schedule."

"With Bram and I overseeing everything, there is nothing for you to worry about," Ortaire reassured her. "You just rest and mend from your accident. Derek will have our hides if he comes back and finds you not well. He told us to see to you first, then to Holdenworth. You are more important than anything to him."

The next morn was a beautiful sunny day, so Chanity decided to take a walk. The sun was shining brightly, and the blue skies were clear, except for a few white puffy clouds. Chanity could smell the blooms from the flowering fruit trees as well as the roses in the flower garden. Bees were buzzing all around the orchard, giving the impression that everything was coming alive after a long winters nap.

With spring over, the crops they had planted were growing well. As she walked around observing the crops, the guards sounded a horn signaling that riders approached. She hoped it would be a messenger with news from Derek.

Chanity walked toward the gates so she could meet the messenger herself. The guards opened the gate, and several riders came through. They were a dirty and scraggly lot, but as soon as her eyes fell on the head rider, she knew it was Derek. She dropped the wildflowers she had picked, and rushed to him.

Derek jumped off his horse and clutched her in his arms. Their kiss seemed to last for an eternity, neither wanting to pull away from the other. They stood just holding another without speaking for the longest time. Finally, Derek spoke. "I love you Chanity, and I never want to be apart from you again."

"I have loved and missed you so much," Chanity said, giving him another kiss. "I hope we never have to part again". She hugged him close to her once again and refused to let go.

There was a commotion off to one side, and Chanity looked to see Gunnar trying to help Sean off his horse. One of Sean's arms was bandaged in a sling, and he used the other to bat Gunnar's grasping hands away.

"I am a warrior, not an infant, just leave me be," Sean declared, as he slipped away from Gunnar and lowered himself to the ground.

"No fussing Sean. Let them help you to the hall to see to your wounds," Chanity ordered sternly, giving him a look that dared him to object.

"As you wish, Lady Chanity," Sean said, giving her a big smile.

They entered the hall, and Chanity began gathering the things she thought Etta would need when she arrived. "Lord Derek, I think you may have your hands full with your lady wife," Sean said teasingly so she could hear.

Chanity laughed along with everyone at his teasing. At least Sean was in good spirits, which should aid his healing. Soon both Leva and Etta arrived to tend Sean wounds so Chanity could be with Derek.

Chanity gave Derek her full attention again since Sean was being taken care of. She wanted to hear about everything that had happened from the time he left until he returned.

Derek told the whole story as Bram, Ortaire and Gunnar listened in. His uncle Marten arrived during the last few minutes of his story. As Derek finished, Marten gave him a hug, and patted him on the back.

"We are glad you made it home safely," Marten said happily.

Later, when they sat down to sup, Marla and Tilly came downstairs. Both went to Derek and gave him a hug to let him know they were happy he was home.

"You would not believe what a good job Marla did running Holdenworth while you were away," Tilly said. "She will make a great Lady someday. Bram was a great help also, and never left Chanity's side."

Chanity was hurt and angry at the lie. Actually, they had hardly done anything except give orders. Tilly's comment about Bram was a twisted truth meant to cause trouble. She held her tongue, not wanting to spoil Derek's return home. She would explain about Bram later, when she and Derek were alone.

Bram refused to let the slight stand and glared at Tilly as he spoke up. "Chanity ran Holdenworth well, and she only needed help while she was ill and hurt. Anna and Elspeth helped out in the great hall while Alma, Etta and Leva aided her. One of them was by her side constantly, and I checked to make sure Chanity was safe."

"It seemed like she was sick the whole time you were away," Aunt Tilly said with disfavor as she looked at Derek.

"Having some deranged person trying to kill Chanity is not the same as being sick all the time," Bram retorted.

Derek looked to Chanity then Bram, waiting for an explanation of his last statement.

Chanity explained in detail what had happened while he was away.

"Well, it sounds more like clumsiness to me than malice," Tilly chimed in. "I told Bram as much before."

Derek's uncle Marten turned to his wife and looked at her sternly. "That is enough of your assumptions, dear. This is their home, and their matter, not ours."

Tilly returned Marten's gaze, and said, "Come along Marla, it's obvious my opinion matters not a whit here. Besides, we have things we need to do. We can have our meal sent up to your chamber." With that, Tilly took Marla by the hand, and pulled her from the room.

Derek's uncle apologized for his wife's behavior. "She has been through so much the last few years after we lost the children. She is overprotective of Marla now, because she thought all was lost to her. Maybe life will be better when we get home."

Derek saw the doubt in his uncle's eyes as he spoke. He hoped things would work out well for Marten, because he had not only lost his children but his wife as well. After their sons were slain and Marta taken, Tilly pulled away from Marten, and locked herself away in her chamber for a couple of years.

When she eventually came out, she was not the wife she had been. Marten knew she blamed him because they had visited his sick brother that day in a neighboring village. Tilly had wanted to take the children that day, but the boys didn't want to go, so he let them stay. Since the boys got to stay home, Marta wanted to stay also, and he relented. If only he had made them go along that day, life would have been so different.

Marten bid them a good night, but by the way he slumped down and carried himself, it looked as if he had aged ten years in a moment. Derek could only imagine the guilt Marten felt, but knew there was nothing he could say to make Marten feel differently. He prayed things would get better for him.

The hall fell silent, and Derek took Chanity's hand and asked if she was ready to go to their chamber. "Aye," she replied, with a tired look on her face.

Derek scooped Chanity into his arms and carried her upstairs to their bed chamber. There was a tub of hot water waiting on them when they arrived. They enjoyed watching each other bathe. He was tired after the long journey, but all he could think of was making love to his lady wife. After they made love, they fell asleep in each other's arms.

Chapter 22

The next morn, they awoke, still in each other's arms and made love again before starting their day.

"I'm off downstairs to speak with Bram and Ortaire while you wash and dress," Derek said, smiling at her as she lie in bed.

Chanity gave him a sleepy smile in return. "Go on ahead. I'll be down in a little while," she replied.

As Derek made his way downstairs, his Aunt Tilly met him. "I am so pleased you are home. Now maybe the rumors will stop."

"What are you talking about?" Derek asked.

"Well for one thing, people have been talking about how Bram and Chanity rode their horses every day. I have been told they would ride a good distance ahead of the guards, and were always laughing and talking. I saw Bram coming and going from the master chamber at all hours, well into the night. Even Marla saw him. No wonder Chanity did not feel well the next day, and poor Marla had to run the place. I suppose you noticed how defensive Bram was last evening, when I mentioned all the hard work Marla had done."

Derek gritted his teeth in frustration. Bram had tried to say he was never alone with Chanity, but he never said anything about riding alone with her. What part of Bram's defense was true, and what was false, he wondered.

Derek stalked off, and left Tilly talking as he went to find Bram. As he came into the hall, he saw Bram and Ortaire sitting at the table about to break their fast. "I want to speak with you outside," Derek told Bram angrily, as he stormed out the door.

"What do you think is wrong with him?" Ortaire asked.

"Most likely something his old crow of an aunt, Marla or Alice has made up," Bram replied.

"I'm going with you," Ortaire said, as they left the table and went outside.

Derek waited alone in the tree line away from where the guards could hear. Ortaire let Bram approach first and hung back a little to see what would unfold.

"Have you seen bedding my wife while I was away?" Derek demanded.

"Derek, have you gone insane?" Bram asked. "You know I would never do anything to hurt you. I care for you and Ortaire as if you were my brothers. You know yourself how much Chanity loves you. She would take a rod, if not a sword to me if I suggested such a thing."

Ortaire saw Bram's prediction was right. "Derek, I never saw anything out of the way from him or Chanity while you were gone," Ortaire said. "If I had to guess, I'd say it was your aunt that told you these tales. I think she wants you for Marla."

"Aunt Tilly knows I am wed, so that is not possible," Derek replied. "She said you and Chanity rode out together every day, laughing and talking as you rode ahead of the guards. But the worst part was Tilly and Marla saw you coming out of our bed chamber more than once, even at night."

"That part is true," Bram replied, and had barely finished when Derek drew back to hit him.

Ortaire quickly jumped between the two warriors. "Derek, hear Bram out before you jump to any conclusions."

"Chanity was very ill Derek, more so than what she told you last night," Bram explained. "We were all frightened for her life. It was like she was poisoned; she could not eat or hold anything down for many days. She was the only one who fell ill, no one else. Chanity was so ill; I would go by and check on her before going to my chamber at night, and then check back on her as often as I could."

"There was always someone else with Chanity, as I told you before when Tilly first brought it up. Alma would not leave her side, and slept on a pelt beside the bed. Etta and Leva also stayed some nights with Chanity when we thought she might not make it. I gave you my word that I would watch over her while you were away, and I meant to keep that promise. Nothing has happened between us, nor will it ever."

"I am certain that everything that happened to Chanity was from malice," Bram went on. "She told you she tripped on her wooden horse at the top of the stairs. It was no mere child leaving a toy behind. Chanity had put it away in a trunk in the master chamber. Someone must have taken it out and placed it there just before she descended the stairs."

"Why would anyone want to deliberately hurt Chanity?" Derek asked.

"Maybe because they have feelings for you, or they want to be the Lady of Holdenworth." Bram answered. Bram could tell by Derek's expression that he was skeptical about what he had heard. Perhaps it was because Derek did not want to face the truth.

"I have not heard you say that you do not have feelings for Chanity," Derek stated.

"Derek, she is your wife. I care for you as a brother, and I will care for her like a sister," Bram replied. "Would it matter if I cared for her? Her heart belongs to only one man, and that is you."

"What Bram tells you is the truth," Ortaire spoke up. "Leva and I also feared Chanity would not make it. Leva was there some of the times that Bram stopped by, and he never behaved in an unseemly manner with Chanity. Bram made sure there was always someone else in the master chamber, so no idle gossip would take place. As for their rides, I also accompanied them sometimes. Everyone tried to get Chanity to laugh and stay in good spirits while you were away. It seemed like riding Lily was all that helped to ease her worries."

Ortaire was uncomfortable at the conflict between his two friends and tried to change the subject. "Derek, we should ride around the fields after we break our fast. I am sure you want to see how well the crops are doing," Ortaire suggested. "It looks like we will have a bountiful harvest this year."

Derek and Bram did not reply, and both seemed lost in thought.

"I don't know about you two, but I am starving," Ortaire finally said. "I am going back inside to break my fast." He turned and headed back to the hall, and was relieved to see Derek and Bram following. The three of them had little disputes over wenches over the years, but it was never serious. This time it was over a wife, not a wench. Ortaire hoped they would quickly get over this.

"Has anyone seen Derek?" Chanity asked, as she entered the great hall.

"He went outside with Bram and Ortaire," Alma said. "Perhaps they went to look at the new plantings. They have not broken their fast yet, if you want to eat with Derek."

The three returned to the hall, and Chanity rushed to Derek's side to plant a kiss on his cheek and give him a hug. She was surprised that he felt unresponsive to her affection. Perhaps he had something on his mind. As they ate, he spoke with his men, but did not speak to her unless she asked him a question. When he did answer, it was brief and to the point.

While they were eating, Marla joined them. "Good morning, what a beautiful day it is" she said, smiling broadly as she took her seat.

Chanity noticed Marla wore a new gown that her grandmother helped make. She also had taken great care styling her hair. Marla's hair was pulled up high, and her braids were fashioned like a crown upon her head. The style made her look a year or two older.

"Marla you look very lovely today. It seems you have matured while I was away," Derek said, trying to hurt Chanity out of his jealousy. "The men in Normandy will be dueling over you."

"Thank you, Lord Derek, but I don't think there will be any dueling," Marla replied, giving Derek a seductive look, and smile to match. Derek returned the smile before returning to his meal.

Bram and Ortaire glanced at each other after the slight. Both wanted to slug Derek, as Chanity hung her head as if she had just lost a long battle. She rose, and started clearing the trenchers and mugs from the other tables. A little while later they saw her headed up the stairs.

Ortaire went to find Leva in the kitchen, and pulled her aside. "Would you go upstairs and check on Chanity?" he asked. "I don't have time to explain right now, but I am sure Chanity needs someone to talk to."

Leva readily agreed, and went upstairs to find the door to the master chamber closed. She knocked on the door, but no one answered. She knocked again, and this time she said "Chanity, it is Leva." Slowly the door opened and Chanity bid Leva come inside. Leva could tell she was upset and had been crying. "What has happened Chanity?" she asked.

"I do not know, nor do I understand. Everything had been going so well. Derek was happy when he left the chamber this morn. After he came back inside the great hall he was like a different person."

"I will see what I can find out from Ortaire later," Leva reassured her. "Ortaire did not tell me what was going on; he just said you might need someone to talk to. So of course, I came right away. Please tell me what happened."

Chanity explained all that had transpired that morn. "It is just as before we wed, when Derek pulled away from me, and started paying attention to Marla. I forgot you were not at Holdenworth at that time."

"Derek rescued me from Vorik, and we were close at first, then he pulled away for a time. It took another warrior asking the King for my hand for Derek to finally confess how he felt for me. Derek said he was distant so he could be sure it was love he had for me, not lust. Now he has treated me the same and flirted with Marla to my face."

"If everything was fine when he left your chamber this morn, then something happened between then and when he came back inside. Do you know who he was with while he was outside?"

"When he returned, Bram and Ortaire were with him," Chanity told her.

"I will come back later, and let you know what I can find out from Ortaire. I'm sure, 'tis nothing but a misunderstanding," Leva said, trying to comfort Chanity.

"I will try to speak to Bram later to see what he knows," Chanity said. "I was so happy yesterday when Derek returned home. I just don't understand what would cause him to flirt with Marla. My appearance was somewhat haggard yesterday, since I had no idea he was returning, and Marla did look beautiful today. She looked the Lady of Holdenworth instead of me."

"Why don't you dress up tonight in the gown you made while Derek was away. The burgundy color looks so good on you. It will make you feel better. Derek would be blind not to see how beautiful you are. I have to go now and get my work done, but we will talk again later. I will see you at sup tonight. Cook is going all out for Derek's return. Some of the men are out hunting and fishing for the feast as we speak." Leva gave Chanity a quick hug, and hurried out the chamber.

Chanity realized she better go see what she could do to help prepare for the feast. She had been talking with Leva awhile, so maybe no one could tell she had been crying.

At the noon meal Derek spoke to her occasionally, but mostly to his men. Chanity was slightly relieved to see he did Marla and his aunt Tilly the same way when they tried to draw him into a conversation. At least he is not openly flirting with Marla this time, Chanity thought to herself.

Derek noticed how quiet and sad Chanity seemed at the table. He felt a little guilty about how he had treated her that morning. He should have never flirted with Marla to make Chanity jealous.

From what Bram and Ortaire told him, his aunt was either mistaken, or exaggerated what she had seen. The thought of Chanity being happy and carefree while he was away disturbed him. He could imagine her and Bram riding their horses and laughing merrily. Surely she had missed him, and had not been won over by Bram. Everyone had said there was nothing untoward between them, but the thought of Bram touching Chanity made him want to beat him. If Bram ever touched her, he would slay him, even if he was like a brother.

Derek noted that when he asked Bram if he cared for Chanity, he never denied it. He just said he would think of her like a sister. So whether anything happened or not, he knew Bram cared for her. Deep down, Derek knew Bram would not do such a thing as bed his wife. However, if he had been in Bram's place, he knew he would have done anything to have Chanity. He had to be careful how he handled this. If he hurt Chanity again, he might lose her love forever.

When Derek walked into their bed chamber that evening, he froze in his step. Chanity stood there in her new burgundy gown like a regal queen. She looked too beautiful to be real, more like a dream than reality. Her hair was pulled up and back from her face then long blonde curls cascaded down and around her shoulders. Derek did not know he had not been breathing until he spoke to tell her what a beautiful enchantress she was.

Chanity turned and smiled at him, and he thought his heart would explode from the love he felt. Then doubt settled back on him again as he wondered if she had feelings for Bram. Instead of walking to her and taking her into his arms, he said "I better change and wash up, then get ready for the feast."

"While you ready yourself, I will greet the villagers as they arrive," Chanity said. She hid her sadness and left the chamber.

The villagers had already begun to enter the hall, and Chanity told them Derek would be down soon. Ortaire and Gunnar had seen to it that extra tables and benches were brought in. The food was brought out, and everyone was taking their seats as Derek came into the great hall.

At the sight of Derek, everyone shouted 'hail to the Lord of Holdenworth!' In keeping with ceremony, Bram raised his mug, saying "Hail to Lord Derek of Holdenworth and to his Lady, Chanity of Holdenworth. Long life to you both." Everyone cheered once more before sitting.

Derek thanked Bram for the speech, but Chanity thought she heard sarcasm in his voice. What is wrong with him? She wondered to herself. Is he angry at everyone? He was upset with me then seemed to be upset with Bram. Perhaps someone said something to Derek about her and Bram? There were only two people she could think of who would do such a thing, Marla and her Grandmother.

But why would they be so cruel? She thought Marla had changed, but after her grandmother arrived, the two were inseparable. Would Derek believe them over her? Did he not trust her any more than that? It hurt that he believed she could or would do such a thing. She was hurt now, but the thought of Derek believing their idle gossip made her furious. She had not felt fury like that since her father was slain.

Derek asked her to dance, since it was tradition for the Lord and Lady to lead off. She was still furious with Derek, and did not even want him to touch her at the moment, but she accepted his hand as was expected of her. They danced in silence, then parted and she went on her way.

She watched as Derek danced with his aunt, then Marla, and now was headed to the floor with Leva. She danced with Ortaire, and Sean, then accepted a dance with Gunnar. She noticed Bram was nowhere to be seen and wondered where he was. She wanted to find out what was going on with Derek, and speaking with Bram would either confirm or allay her suspicions.

Derek took a break from dancing and went to sit at the table. He drank some wine while talking to a few of the villagers. Bram came in and sat with them as well.

After a while Derek spied Chanity across the room and headed back to dance with her. Before he made to Chanity, Alice marched over and practically dragged him to the floor.

Chanity looked on in frustration. At the last dance, Derek had promised her he would not dance with Alice again. Chanity approached Bram and asked him if he would like to dance.

"I would never say no to you, but do you think it's a good idea?" he asked.

"How would I know?" Chanity asked in return. "I have no idea what's going on. I'm the last one my husband seems to talk to."

"I suppose this as good a time as any for us to speak," Bram replied, bowing to her as they began their dance. He moved to a place in the hall so they wouldn't be overheard, and told Chanity what had happened.

"I had guessed it was something like that," Chanity said sadly. "Bram, I am so sorry that you have been put in this situation."

"I am the one who should be sorry, Chanity. I'm older and more experienced. I should have expected them to have made up such tales." Bram told her about the night he ran into them in the hall coming from her room. "I explained to them I was checking on you before going to my chamber. I even told them that Alma was in there with you. I don't know what they thought could happen with you unconscious, or what kind of person I could be to take advantage of someone in that condition."

"Bram, they knew nothing like that was going on. They just want to tell their wicked tales. Marla wants Derek for herself, and her grandmother wants her to have everything she desires." The music stopped, so they had to end their conversation and go their separate ways.

Bram noticed a lovely village girl glancing his way. She was standing alone, so he went and asked her for the next dance. He noticed Derek glared at him while he danced with Chanity, so he made sure to ask someone for the next dance, even though he just wanted to go to his bed chamber.

Chanity did not notice Derek glaring until she and Bram finished dancing. At the moment, she did not care if he was jealous or not. She was still furious with him for believing such tales about her. He of all people knew how devious Marla could be. This was the second time he had withdrawn from her for no good reason. Frankly, she was getting tired of it. He was no longer a wet behind the ears lad, but the Lord of Holdenworth. She wanted someone she could love and grow old with, someone who trusted her as well as being able to trust him.

Derek stood at her side before she knew it. "Did you enjoy your dance with Sir Bram?" He inquired.

"Of course I enjoyed my dance with Bram, as well with Ortaire, and Sean. Gunnar stepped on my toes occasionally, so I didn't enjoy dancing with him as much, even though the conversation was enjoyable. How about you Lord Derek, how was your dance with Marla and Alice? I bet the conversation was very stimulating. I can hear Marla now, 'Oh what a horrible wife you have. Just get rid of her, and marry me.' Or Alice, 'Stay with her if you wish, just come and bed me in the hay. I will be unclothed, and in the stables waiting.'"

Derek laughed at her imitations of the two, then picked her up in his strong arms and took her to their chamber. She demanded that he put her down, but Derek just ignored her and continued on his way. "You are so adorable when you are angry and jealous. Your eyes become a darker green, with flecks of gold. They look like they could shoot sparks from them."

He laid her on the bed and covered her lips with his before she had a chance to protest. He continued to kiss her until he felt her go soft in his arms. "I have missed you so much my little enchantress. I dreamed of being home and having you in my arms. You are mine and only mine. Never forget that, Chanity."

"Derek, I think you are the one who should remember we are wed. You seem not to remember that when you were with Marla or Alice. You believed Marla's falsehoods about me, and let Alice touch all over you. Afterwards you bring me up here thinking to bed me as if nothing has happened."

"Is that really why you are angry, Chanity? Or is it because it is me here with you instead of Bram?"

"Are you insane, or did you hit your head while you were away?" Chanity demanded. "What sort of person do you think I am? When we wed, was I not a maiden when you bedded me? Did I not say a vow to keep only unto you? Now you accuse me unjustly of such a horrible thing."

Chanity had fury in her beautiful eyes, and he saw hurt and anguish there as well.

Chanity did not stop there. "Derek, has Bram ever betrayed you in any way? Has he not loved you like a brother? Why do you think he watched over me while I was so ill? Because he didn't want to have to tell you that I was gone, and cause you such grief."

"Chanity if you think that's the only reason Bram was so attentive, you are daft," Derek replied. "He would not deny he cared for you when I asked him."

Chanity's face showed look of shock and puzzlement for a moment. Derek was surprised that she was unaware of how Bram felt.

"He only cares for me as a friend or sister," Chanity argued in return. "You were probably accusing him at the time. He was angry and wanted to hurt you. I can't blame Bram for not saying anything since you accused him. He was just letting you stew in your own words. At the time, would it have mattered what Bram said? You would have been too angry to listen to him."

Derek thought on this for a moment, then replied, "You are right. It would not have mattered what he said. I am sorry Chanity. It was foolish of me to think such nonsense. I know that Marla makes up tales, and she managed to convince my aunt of this foolishness."

"I think we need to plan our journey to my parents. We will let my uncle and aunt know in the morn that we will see them home. Then Marla will not be here any longer to cause trouble between us. I need to visit my family anyway, as I planned to do before King William called me back to battle. Since I just returned home I will need a few days to get things in order and we can be on our way."

They did not make love that night. Though Derek held her in his arms, it did not seem the same. He had hurt her before they wed by pushing her away, and even though he promised it wouldn't happen again, it did. It was hard for her to trust him once more. Would he reject her every time he thought someone paid her any attention? She finally fell asleep, but it was not restful.

Bram was on his way to his chamber, when he overheard Chanity's heated words. He was proud of Chanity for speaking up to Derek. He wished he could see the fire in her eyes as she angrily told Derek off. She had the spirit to handle his friend, and now she was finally letting him have it. She had become the Lady of Holdenworth in every way. If Derek didn't realize what a wonderful Lady he had, then he soon would. He had heard many legendary stories of her mother Serina, and the strong, beautiful, and graceful Lady she had been. Chanity took after her in many ways it seemed. He was envious, but still wished Derek and Chanity happiness.

Now that it seemed everything was right between Derek and Chanity, it was time for him to leave. He did not want Derek to always wonder if something had happened between him and Chanity. When Derek accompanied his uncle and family home, he would see them safely to Normandy. Then would go on to visit his own family, and journey back to England to rejoin King William.

It would not seem the same without Derek and Ortaire since they had been together since childhood. He could make new friends, but ones he loved like brother were hard to come by. He decided to tell Derek his plans on the morrow.

Bram awoke the next morn, and went downstairs to break his fast. "Alma, have you seen Lord Derek?" He asked. "If I know him, he's seeing to his horse."

"I was outside earlier, and saw him go in the direction of the stables, Alma replied.

"Thank you, Alma. I am sure that is where he is," Bram said, making his way outside.

Bram found Derek coming out of Rollo's stall. He asked if he could speak with him for a moment and told him of the plans he had made the night before.

"I wish you would stay at Holdenworth. You have been a great help," Derek replied. "You know you don't have to leave. I was tired and worn out from my journey, and should have realized it was just Marla's tales. She convinced my aunt to believe her, and I should have known better. I know you and Chanity would never betray me. I am sorry I spoke before thinking things through."

"You have helped me a great deal, Bram. I don't know what I would have done if you had not been here. I would have been sick with worry, but I knew you would take care of Chanity and Holdenworth while I was away. I must have been foolish to even consider such a tale. I wish I could make it up to you somehow."

"You don't have to make it up to me, my friend. Just worry about making it up to Chanity. I don't have tender feelings, but she does. Besides, Derek, we knew one day we would have to part ways. Even real brothers must. You, Ortaire and I have had many years together filled with great memories. We will always have those memories even though we are apart. I'm sure we will see each other from time to time during our journeys." They clapped each other on the shoulder as they headed back inside to break their fast.

Chanity, Ortaire, Gunnar, Sean and Marten were already at the table when they went inside. A few moments later, Marla and her Grandmother arrived and took their seats as well.

"We will be leaving for Normandy in a few days," Derek announced. Everyone should begin preparing for the journey. We will need six of our long boats, since we have some trading to do along the way. The Dragon ship will be used to transport the family."

"Ortaire, I need you to stay and see to the running of Holdenworth," Derek said. "Sean will also stay and help since his wound is still healing. Bram and Gunnar will be going with me, and I trust their judgment on what men to take along."

"Be sure not to speak of our leaving to anyone. I do not want anyone outside Holdenworth to know of our journey. Ortaire, speak with all the guards and tell them to keep silent. Chanity will speak with Alma, who will swear the household servants to secrecy. The last thing we need is for a raiding band to hear a loose tongue in the village tavern spreading word of our departure."

Derek was surprised to see his aunt and uncle did not seem excited about going home. His aunt had seemed happy to be taking Marla, but seemed a little hesitant now. Maybe she saw things in Marla's nature that worried her. Still, she was always at Marla's side. As always, Marla went along with her, and never complained about her grandmother's close attention.

Derek was still angry that Marla had influenced her aunt to believe that Bram and Chanity had betrayed him. Marla thought he was furious with her, since he barely spoke to her, and continued to shoot angry looks her way. She avoided him and wouldn't come to the table at meals unless her grandmother insisted.

Derek's uncle and aunt were kindhearted, and he hoped Marla would not be too much for them. When Derek was young, he enjoyed staying with them. He visited more often after their sons were slain and Marta was taken by Vorik. He spent as much time with his uncle Marten as he could, since his aunt stayed secluded in her chamber for years after the loss of their children. His parents visited often to make sure everything was going well, and see to their holdings.

Chapter 23

Summer was upon them, and it was a beautiful day, so Chanity thought she would slip away after the noon meal and go to her favorite spot. She had been going at least twice a week since early spring. That was the one place she found peace and let herself dream of Derek's return while he was away. This was the first time she had visited since his return home.

Thinking about meeting Derek's family in Normandy made her remember her parents and brother. Her secret place seemed to beckon to her at times, and she could almost sense Gerald's presence here. She closed her eyes imagined him running around the large boulder laughing.

Her heart ached at the thought that Gerald might be dead, but he must be, or he would have sent word by now. As she descended the hidden path, an uneasy feeling came over her. She paused for a moment, but thought it was because of the memories of her parents and Gerald.

Chanity took a seat on the rock and looked out over the sea. Her eyes closed slightly to rest for a while, as she listened to the sound of the waves and seabirds. Suddenly, she caught movement out of the corner of her eye. A large object swung toward her, and she had just enough time to lean back and move her head to keep from being struck. As she recovered her balance and sat back upright, she saw Marla's grandmother standing on the ledge with a limb in her hand.

Chanity sprang to her feet and moved away. "What are you doing?" She demanded. "How did you know about this place?"

"I have been following you, and biding my time. Derek needs to be with his own kin, and back home where he belongs. You are the reason he stays," Tilly said menacingly.

"He stays because he is Lord of Holdenworth, and this is his home now. He always wanted his own lands. Even if I die, he will never leave Holdenworth," Chanity retorted.

"You are wrong there, little lass. He will if you die. He will not wish to remain in a place that reminds him of you. He will return home to be close to his family, especially if he can inherit our estate. Marla will be there to help him get through his grief, and he will come to realize what a treasure she is."

"Tilly, your brain is addled if you believe all of this," Chanity replied, as she stepped back further to put as much distance as possible between her and the madwoman. Deep down, she wondered if it would happen as Tilly had described.

As Chanity looked down to make sure she didn't trip, Tilly charged, and violently swung the thick limb directly at Chanity's head. Again, Chanity managed dodged the blow, but lost her balance and fell over the side. She managed to grab a bush as she slipped over the edge, and held on for dear life. The bottom of the cliff was a great distance away, and she had no chance of survival if she fell.

The old woman bent over the side of the cliff and tried to strike at Chanity's hands so she would release her grip and fall. Tilly swung the limb wildly and missed. As Tilly prepared to deliver another blow, Chanity was able to slip her foot in between some rocks to help support her weight.

When Tilly swung again, Chanity grabbed the limb with one hand and jerked on it as hard as she could. The old woman screamed as she slid over edge of the cliff, and grabbed the same bush that Chanity was holding! Chanity watched in horror as the roots of the bush started slipping from the cliff. The gnarled roots seemed to catch for a moment, but they surely would not hold for long.

Chanity was relieved for a moment to hear a voice calling from above. Her relief turned to dread, as Marla peered over the edge.

"What happened?" Marla asked. "I heard someone scream and came as quickly as I could."

"Chanity tried to throw me over the ledge," Tilly cried. "I grabbed her as we fell. Give me your hand my dear, and help me up."

"Marla, she is lying," Chanity said, looking into her eyes. "She tried to kill me! Please hurry! The bush is about to give way from all the weight."

Marla was confused but knew she had to decide quickly. Marla reached down and grasped Chanity's hand just as the bush pulled free of the cliff. Tilly looked at them in disbelief as she fell, still clutching the bush.

Chanity was too heavy for Marla to pull up, but Marla's grasp gave Chanity time to make her foothold more secure. Chanity clung to the ledge where the bush had been, and Marla released her hand.

"Marla, I need you to go get help. I can hold on for a little while, but you must hurry. Go quickly and get help," Chanity pleaded.

Marla nodded, and disappeared from sight.

Chanity could not believe Marla had saved her instead of her grandmother. She prayed Marla would return with help soon. Her hands were growing numb from grasping the jagged rocks, and her legs were beginning to tremble.

It seemed like an eternity before Derek and Bram arrived, though she knew it had not been long. Derek reached down and lifted her up with one hand. She almost fainted as he pulled her up and into his arms. She was finally safe, but her arms and legs were trembling from fatigue, and the fear of falling.

"Thank God Bram and I was riding by when Marla ran out of the woods. What happened here?" Derek asked, as he held her tightly in his arms.

Tears ran down Chanity's face as she told him what happened. He held her, and did not let go until she finished. He could not imagine his aunt doing such a thing. He knew she had not been the same because of Vorik, but this was insanity. He dreaded telling his uncle about what Tilly had done, and how she died.

When they arrived back at the hall, Derek took Chanity to their chamber, so she could lie down and rest while he went to talk to his uncle. As Derek emerged from the master chamber, Marla was standing outside. He had talked to Chanity about what happened, but not to Marla. "How did you know where they were?" he asked.

"I did not know where they were until I heard a scream. Then I found a pathway down to the lower ledge. Grandmother had been acting very strangely since she heard we were leaving. I saw her head out the gate, and was going to walk with her, but she told me to stay and pack. I was about to tell her I had already packed, but she had a wild look in her eyes. I watched for a moment to see what direction she took, then followed her. I tried not to follow too closely, and didn't see her take the path beside the cliff. When she disappeared, I looked around for her, and was about to give up when I heard a scream."

Marla's eyes welled up with tears as she continued. "At first I did not want to be close to Grandmother because she was older. My great aunt was older, and she was cruel to me. Grandmother kept on until I became close to her. But then I started to worry, because she kept acting like you and I would be together. I was afraid she had placed the wooden horse on the stairs. I saw her coming out of the master chamber the day before."

"When you announced we were going to Normandy, she began acting even more strangely. I even heard her talking to herself a few times. One day she said 'Everything is going to be fine, just fine, Marta. Our Marla will be happy. I will make sure of that! Then they will come home where they belong.' I thought she was talking about you and me, so I started following her," Marla explained. "I was afraid she had tried to kill Chanity twice, and would keep on until she succeeded."

"Thank you Marla, for saving Chanity. You can't imagine how much that means to me. I only wish you had told me of your suspicions. I better go find Uncle Marten before he hears about this from someone else," Derek said as he departed.

Chanity heard Marla's voice, and asked her to enter. "Thank you for rescuing me today, Marla. I thought I would certainly fall to my death. I hate you had to choose between your grandmother and me. I know that had to be hard for you. What made you decide to save me?"

"How could I not?" Marla asked, as her tears began to flow again. Even though she thought she would never tell anyone, she confessed everything to Chanity.

"I loved Serina. She was the closest thing I ever had to a mother. Even though I acted like I didn't care, I looked forward to her visit every night. She would rub my hair, sing, or tell me a story, and never left without giving me a hug and a kiss on my forehead. That was the only time in my life I was ever showed any love and attention. I came to see you as a sister even though I never showed it. It meant a lot that you came to visit every day when Derek made me stay in the hut by myself. I would not have blamed you if you never spoke to me again after what I did. I must admit that experience changed my life, and I never want to be that person again."

Chanity looked at Marla with happiness and sadness in her eyes. Marla had truly grown and matured in a short time.

Marla could tell Chanity was getting sleepy, so she told her to rest and she would check on her in a little while. She bent down and kissed Chanity on the forehead as Serina had done so many times when she was alive. She looked at Chanity one last time before closing the chamber door. She realized then just how relieved she was that Chanity was safe now. She had been keeping an eye on her grandmother ever since Chanity fell on the stairs.

Marla dreaded facing her Grandfather as she went down to the great hall. She hoped one day he could forgive her for not saving her grandmother. Either way, she knew she would still save Chanity if faced with the decision again. She wished Vorik had not hurt her grandparents in such a horrible way. He had been a terrible person, and she was glad he was no longer living. There was no love for him left in her heart.

When Marten saw Marla enter the great hall, he swiftly went to her and hugged her close.

"I am so sorry, Marla! I can only imagine what you must be feeling. I have always loved your grandmother, but she has not been herself for many years now. She was a good woman before Vorik came, and I hope you know she cared for you dearly. When she heard you were alive, it was the first time she had been happy in many years. I hoped I was getting my wife back, but her mind must have been worse than I thought. I hope you can forgive her."

"I know she was addled Grandfather, and did not realize what she was doing. I just hope you can understand why I grabbed Chanity's hand instead. I care for you very much, and I care how you feel about me. If you still want me to go to Normandy with you I shall, but I understand if you don't."

"Of course I want you to go with me," Marten replied as he hugged her close again. "As a matter of fact, I don't think I could stand to go home without you. You are my granddaughter, and I love you very much. Everyone is looking forward to meeting you."

Marta smiled with relief. She saw the love in Marten's eyes, and for a moment, the pain he was feeling from his grief.

"We will delay the trip a few more days Uncle Marten," Derek said. "You and Marla need time to adjust to what happened."

Chapter 24

The morning they were to depart to Normandy approached rapidly. There was a whirlwind of activity at Holdenworth as Chanity made sure everything was readied for the journey. She made a list of the food and supplies to be taken on the trip, and spoke with the servants on how things should be carried out. She was confident that Alma could take care of anything that arose, since she had always been at Serina's side while she was Lady. Ortaire was in charge while they were away and Leva would be helping as well, so Alma would have all the help she needed.

While Chanity was taking care of things inside, Derek was outside doing the same. He had ordered the long boats loaded with trading goods, and directed the placement of the food and supplies that Chanity was sending out. After the last cloth sack was loaded, he stopped to rest a bit before they departed.

Everyone gathered by the shore to say their goodbyes. Derek went to speak to Ortaire one last time.

Ortaire clasped Derek's shoulder as he approached. "Don't worry about Holdenworth while you are gone, Dragon," he said smiling. "The volunteer guard have trained well, and Sean will help with anything else I need.

"I know you have all well in hand, Ortaire," Derek replied. "'Tis truly a relief that all I have to concern myself with is our journey to Normandy."

Derek's gaze swept over the dragon ship and longboats lying in Holdenworth's harbor. He smiled to himself as he thought back to the time when he purchased his first longboat. When he wasn't fighting for King William, he was busy trading, and storing up coin for another ship. Before he knew it, he had six of the craft. Even more than Holdenworth, his many longboats were the true measure his wealth and power.

He captured his dragon ship and two more long boats on a trading expedition when raiders tried to rob him of his cargo. Fortunately, Derek had seen a glimmer of their wake across the water and warned his men.

When the raiders attacked, they encountered a band of ready warriors, instead of the sleepy merchants they expected. Still, it was a lengthy battle, and one of his warriors fell to a raider blade. His men were fiercely loyal to him, as he was to them. He never hazarded the lives of his men needlessly, and deeply regretted any loss of warriors under his command.

Thinking back to that incident reminded Derek of the many dangers on the route. In past battles, Bram and Gunnarr and he had taken on a dozen men and defeated them without so much as a scratch. This trip would be different, for he had Chanity, Uncle Martin and Marla to watch out for as well. He felt relieved to have Bram and Gunnar, along with several of his best warriors guarding them.

Chanity felt a little sick the first couple days of their journey, but never lost her meal. Marla though, had been sick for several days. When they pulled to land the fifth night to set up their makeshift tents, she was still sick. Gunnar told her that it would help to watch the ocean where it met the sky.

The next day Marla tried to keep her eyes on the horizon, and finally began to feel better. One of Vorik's men had told her to do that on her voyage to Holdenworth, but she had forgotten until Gunnar mentioned it.

That was an awful voyage, but at least it allowed her to escape her horrible great-aunt. It also brought back memories of her jealousy of Chanity, and the love she eventually felt for Serina. She hoped if she ever had a child she would be as loving as her stepmother was, and that her babe's father would be more loving than Vorik was to her.

Marla wondered what the future held for her in Normandy. Would she ever find true love, someone that would love her as much as she loved him? She dreamed of having the same kind of love that Chanity and Derek shared together. She still cared for Derek, but she knew he would never love her like he did Chanity. If she couldn't have Derek, then she was glad Chanity did. It took her a long time to realize that.

It scared her when Chanity was sick and they thought she might die. That was when she realized she thought of Chanity like a sister, not just a stepsister. She would miss Chanity when she returned to England.

Marla chatted with her grandfather a lot on the voyage. She felt like she had really come to know him. He told her about his childhood growing up with his parents, two brothers and one sister. Derek's father was Marten's older brother, but only by a year. Marten told her they had always been close, and he was grateful that they stood by his side when the boys were slain, and Marta taken by Vorik.

The voyage was rather uneventful until the sixth night. Some raiders saw them go ashore, and decided to relieve them of their cargo later that night. Derek set up camp, unaware they had been seen. He posted guards as everyone got ready to turn in that evening. They were just about to retire, when the shape of longboats loomed out on the water.

"Marten, stay with Chanity and Marla," Derek quietly ordered, as he sent them running for the cover of some brush. "You must keep them safe, naught else matters."

As she ran toward the brush, Chanity grabbed a big piece of driftwood that she saw lying in the sand. Marten unsheathed his sword, and lay it beside them so he would be ready. He would use it only if the raiders came close to their hiding place.

Derek took an estimate of raiders, and they seemed to be equal in number to him and his men. Derek gave a mighty battle cry as he and his men charged toward the oncoming raiders. With any luck, the battle would be joined as far from where Chanity and the others lay hid.

The raiders leapt from their boats, and quickly closed with the warriors. The battle began instantly, and one of Derek's warriors fell in the initial onslaught.

The other warriors circled around their wounded comrade as the others continued the fight. Chanity was grateful to see he was only injured.

The battle seemed to go on a long while, and as it progressed, Derek and his men seemed to be holding their own against the raiders.

Suddenly one of the raiders fell, and looked to be injured quite badly. A few of Derek's men were bleeding from their wounds, but were still in the fight.

Chanity watched from her hiding spot as Derek and Bram fought two or three men at a time, as the raiders continually moved around trying to gain an advantage. The two warriors seemed to fight in unison and were unfazed by multiple attackers. They battled back fiercely and forced the raiders to shift around again.

One of the large raiders took on Gunnarr. With his great strength and mighty blows, he seemed to deal with his opponent well.

Sean's opponent was larger than he, but his youth and quickness gave him an advantage. He was the youngest of the five knights, and not as large as his fellows. The practice battles had honed his abilities and made his body muscular and lean. Sean's movement and lightning speed showed he learned much from Derek, and had taken on his fighting style.

Chanity was grateful that all Holdenworth's warriors had been training daily. Still, anything could happen in battle, and prayed that none of the warriors would come to harm. She had grown to care for these men as if they were her own family. Though she missed her brother dearly, having them around had helped.

Derek maneuvered his opponent around and tried to keep the fighting away from where his family was hiding. They tried to be as still as possible, but one of the raiders saw some movement in the brush and rushed toward it.

Derek broke away from his opponent and intercepted the raider before he reached Chanity. Derek lay on blows so thick and fast, the man had to stop his advance and fight for his life. Derek was so intent on dispatching his foe, that he turned his back to the main battle. His first adversary saw an opportunity, and ran to attack Derek.

Chanity saw that Derek seemed to be unaware of the danger bearing down on him. As the raider passed, Chanity leapt from her hiding place and smashed the driftwood against the back of the raider's skull. Derek heard the man approaching, and whirled like lighting to skewer him before he fell.

The raiders saw Chanity, and let out a bloodcurdling yell. Chanity realized she had made a big mistake. The thought of capturing a woman made the raiders fight even harder. They looked at her as if they had not seen a woman in some time. Chanity crouched back in the bushes, as the battle heated up again.

Raiders desperately tried to reach Derek's family so they could take them hostage and stop the battle, but they had lost too many men. Eventually they realized they had lost, and decided to run while they still could.

With the battle over, Chanity ran to Derek to throw her arms around him. Instead, Derek seized her arms with a tight grip and held her back.

"Do you know what those men could have done to you and Marla?" Derek asked angrily. "Do you not have any confidence in my skill as a warrior? Why did you come out when I told you to stay hidden? Chanity, you do realize I was Knighted for a reason." Derek looked furious as he walked away without staying to hear her explain.

Derek yelled to the men to break camp immediately. If the raiders had reinforcements at their camp they would attack again soon, in the hope of capturing the women. Some raiders had rather capture a beautiful woman than to loot cargo.

Chanity didn't know whether to be angry or hurt by Derek's reaction. The worst thing was that she felt foolish. She knew her father would have reacted the same way as Derek had.

Her mother would have tried to protect her home and children, but would not have ran into battle. Her mother loved her father dearly, but Belgar would have never tolerated Serina running into battle to save him. Men and their pride, she would never understand them completely. Deep down, she knew what she had done was wrong even though it seemed right at the time.

As she played the scene back in her mind, she noted that Derek had turned and thrust the raider through with his sword immediately after her makeshift club struck his attacker. Derek attacked so quickly, the man hadn't even begun to fall. She realized he would have slain the raider without her help. She decided to apologize later after he calmed down.

Derek was still angry when they broke camp. He didn't even go to Chanity to help her into the dragon boat when they cast off. Bram saw Derek was not going to assist Chanity, so he helped her into the boat so she wouldn't get wet.

"Derek will calm down in a little while," Bram explained quietly so no one would hear. "His pride is just a little wounded. Go make a bed of pelts and get some sleep, for it's going to be a long night. We need to put some distance between us and the raiders, in case they get more men and return."

By the time she had arranged her pelts into a bed, the men had oars in hand, and the longboats and Dragon ship were on their way.

A little before dawn they guided the long boats into a secluded spot so they would be shielded from sight. Derek knew the men needed rest after rowing all night and the day before, not to mention the battle with the raiders. He decided to camp the rest of the day and the following night so everyone could get some rest.

Derek saw Bram and Gunnar had the camp arrangements well in hand, so instead of stepping off on the shore, he lay down beside Chanity on her bed of pelts. She had not slept well, and tossed and turned through the night. She had been crying some also, by the way her body quivered. He wanted to go to her, but was needed at the oars since some of the men were injured.

Chanity awoke as Derek pulled her into his arms. He kissed her on the forehead as she snuggled into him. "I'm so sorry, Derek. I should have not done what I did. I hope you can forgive me. I should have shown more faith in your skill as a warrior. When I saw the raider running at you with your back turned, I reacted without thought of what I was doing."

"Chanity, it scared me, because if he had sensed you coming, he could have turned and killed you, and I could have done nothing to stop him. Let us forget what happened, but promise me you will never do this again."

Chanity gave him her word she would not interfere in battle again, but did not say she wouldn't try to protect him.

With the boat gently rocking in the warm breeze, they soon fell asleep in each other's arms.

Chanity was excited when they came to the first trading stop. She loved all the wares, vendors and merchants. Bram and Uncle Marten escorted her and Marla around. They looked at all the carts and tables overflowing with treasures.

Chanity picked up some ribbons and admired the various shades of each color. She had never seen so many shades of the same color before. She picked four out, but laid them back down because she didn't bring any coin.

Bram saw that she liked them, and when Chanity turned away, he picked up the four ribbons and paid the merchant. He quickly caught up with Chanity and handed her the ribbons.

"Thank you Bram, you didn't have to get me these. Chanity wanted to give him a kiss on the cheek to thank him, but thought better of it since Derek had been so jealous of him before. She truly loved Bram like a brother, since he had been there for her when Derek was away. He helped her face reality instead of letting her wallow in self-pity.

"'Tis nothing but a few ribbons. Think of it as a thank you for all the times you advised me with a problem at Holdenworth while Derek was away. I miss my younger sister, and you remind me so much of her. If she were here, I would want her to have the prettiest ribbons of any girl around. They laughed and she hugged his arm as they joined Marla and Marten at the next table.

Derek was coming through the crowd and saw Bram hand Chanity some ribbons. He stopped and watched them for a few moments. He saw Chanity hug Bram's arm, then walk to the next table to join his uncle. He had hurried to get through with his business so he could join her, but it seemed like he wasn't missed. Derek spun on his heel to leave when he heard her call out to him.

"Derek, you made it after all," Chanity said happily as she threw her arms around him. "I am so glad you finished in time to join us. I have never seen anything like this in my life!"

Derek had stood stiff and tense for a moment, but his body relaxed as she held him.

"I am glad you have enjoyed it, wife," Derek said as he looked toward Bram.

Bram couldn't help but notice the stress on the word 'wife' and knew Derek had been watching them earlier. He just hoped he was mad at him and not at Chanity. Derek was addled if he didn't see how much she loved and adored him. She would never betray him with another man. He knew Derek would never harm her, but he had ignored her before, and that had hurt her badly. When Derek was angry he often responded by pushing the other person away. He observed that during the many years they had fought at each other's side.

Chanity and Marla were busy talking to a merchant, so Derek walked over to confront Bram. "'Tis my place to buy what my wife needs or wants," he said gruffly.

"That's true Derek, but you were not here, and did not leave her with coin. If it had been my wife, and I was not close by, would you not have bought her something as simple as ribbons? I hope that you would have. I had thought this matter was cleared up by now. You are like my brother, and I think of her as my sister. She is such a kind person that you can't help but like her, but she is your wife and I realize that."

Derek's face showed the guilt he felt for being so jealous, but he did not say anything in return. Finally, Bram spoke up. "Derek, this is why I made the decision to go my own way. I never want to hurt our friendship, or cause trouble between you and Chanity. It seems there will always be little things come up to stir your jealousy. I am going to visit my family a while, then rejoin King William. It's time for us to part Derek, and you know it deep down. You have found your place in this life, and now 'tis time for me to do so as well."

Sadness replaced the guilt on Derek's face. "You will be greatly missed Bram. It will never be the same without you around. I love Ortaire like a brother, but somehow I seemed closer to you. I hope you will visit us whenever you have the chance. You know you always have a home at Holdenworth." They grasped each other on the shoulder, then went to join the others.

Chanity was saddened by the news that Bram would be leaving, and she was frustrated at Derek because she knew it probably had something to do with his jealousy. When she was with Bram, it was almost like having Gerald home again. She had lost Gerald, and now she was losing Bram as well.

Why couldn't Derek see how much she loved him, and not be jealous? Surely he could see how they both loved him, so how could he not trust them, she wondered.

She had been dreading Bram's departure ever since he first mentioned it at Holdenworth. She hoped Derek would get Bram to change his mind, but it was clear he had not. It hurt losing her friend, but she did not want anything coming between her and Derek. She would just have to accept losing Bram, who seemed like a second brother.

Chanity was grateful they were getting rooms that night, instead of staying in the makeshift tents. She asked the inn keeper's wife to have water sent up for a bath. After the dirt and grime of travel, she was really looking forward to it. Derek had surprised her with some wonderful scented soap, and she couldn't wait to try it.

As soon as the tub was filled with warm water, she hopped in, enjoying the soothing feeling. After she spent a short time relaxing, she washed her hair, then washed herself with the soap. She loved the sweet smelling scent of it.

After a thorough scrubbing, Chanity settled back in the bath to relax again, and did not get out until the water was turning cold.

As she stepped out of the tub, Derek walked into the room and his eyes instantly fastened on her. The air in the room felt cool, but his searing gaze warmed her all over. They had not been together intimately since they left home. He walked over and helped her to dry off, then he picked her up and carried her to the bed. Derek laid her gently on the bed, crawled in beside her, and took her into his arms. This would be a night they would not soon forget.

They left early the next morning on their journey. Derek had done well with his trading, and still had two more trading stops on the way. He would do quite well if the other two stops earned him the coin and treasures this one had.

On the last stop he would purchase items to sell when they reached Normandy. Derek carefully arranged the trading goods in the boats, so they held as much as possible, but still rode high in the water.

Chapter 25

After a couple of weeks spent traveling, they finally made it to the last trading stop. In a short while, Derek finished all his trading, so he and Chanity decided to walk around and explore the village. Bram and two of his warriors accompanied them as they headed down to the sea. On the way, they passed a slave market, and stopped when they heard a sudden commotion. Derek looked down toward the market and saw one of the slaves being dragged to a whipping post.

Derek turned to a man nearby who had been watching the scene and asked him what happened. "That slave spat in his new owner's face after he purchased him. The man was furious, and ordered his guards tie the slave to a whipping post," the man replied.

Derek glanced at Chanity to see if he should escort her away, but remembered she had seen the same scene play out at Holdenworth.

Chanity watched as they strung the man up, and for some reason she wanted to go help him. He was tall, with stringy dark hair that looked not to have been washed in a while. The guards ripped his shirt down the back and began the lashing.

The slave looked toward the crowd, but never made a sound. As his eyes swept over the onlookers, Chanity's eyes locked with his for a moment. Her knees buckled as she saw his amazing blue eyes, and she quickly grabbed onto Derek to keep from falling. Chanity steadied herself and started to run toward the slave market, but Derek caught her and drew her back to him.

Chanity looked at Derek with anguish in her eyes, then said in a low voice, "Gerald! 'Tis Gerald." She started toward the slave market again, but Derek held her tightly.

"Nay, Chanity, be still," he said quietly. "If I am to rescue him, you must remain here and tell no one he is your brother. Bram, keep her here no matter what. Chanity, stay silent, and I will see what can be done."

Derek and the two warriors walked into the market to stand by the whipping post. "Cease your whipping for a moment," Derek bade the guard with the lash in his hand. "Who is the man that owns this slave?"

"'Tis Lord Walsh," the guard said, holding up his hand to point out a man making his way back to the post.

"What is the meaning of this, young man?" Lord Walsh asked Derek as he approached. "This is my slave, and I gave the order to whip him for his insolence."

"Lord Walsh, I am Lord Derek of Holdenworth. I am in need of new slaves, and was late getting to market. I was hoping you might be interested in making a small profit by selling me this one. I need large men for the toll I have in store for them."

"Nay, this one I want to keep, and make him pay for what he did to me. I will break him of his insolence, or he will die," Lord Walsh responded.

"'Tis your right sir, and probably this slave's good fortune. After a while spent doing the tasks and labor I have planned for him, he will want to die. Every day he wishes he was back with you, I will remind him of his insolence here. If you will accept double what you paid for him, fine, but if not, then he is yours."

Lord Walsh hesitated for a moment, but was greedy for the extra coin. He accepted Derek's bargain, counted out the coin, and left the market.

Derek was sure he paid a little more than double, but did not care. He cut Gerald down, and led him away from the crowd. "You are a free man now," Derek told Gerald, whose eyes opened wide in amazement. "But I have one request before you depart. There is someone here who wishes to speak with you."

As they walked up the hill to rejoin Bram and Chanity, Gerald's eyes looked ahead and saw a familiar face. "Mother!" Gerald cried, surging forward to meet her. He drew closer, and saw green eyes where he expected blue, and realized it was Chanity.

Chanity ran to him, but was careful not to touch his back, for he had received a few lashes before Derek could stop the guards.

"I prayed so long that you were alive and well," Chanity said through her tears. "I can't believe I finally found you. I missed you so much. What happened, and why did you not return?"

"Some time ago, I sent a messenger to Holdenworth to tell everyone I was well. When the messenger arrived, Vorik told him that my family had died from an illness that swept through the village. I began to gather men to help me take back Holdenworth, but was captured during battle, then put in cell to rot for over a year. Finally, I was sold as a slave. I escaped a few times, but since I didn't speak the language or have any coin, I was quickly recaptured. Now, tell me the news of Holdenworth. Are Mother and Father alive and well?"

Chanity hated to tell Gerald of their fate, but it was best to get it over with now. "Father was slain by Vorik when he took Holdenworth. He forced mother to wed him by threatening my safety. She wed him to protect me, but died four years later. I will tell you all about it on the way to Normandy. We will not be in Normandy that long, then we will head back to Holdenworth."

Derek approached, and grasped her shoulders gently. "This is my husband Derek, who slew Vorik, and is now Lord of Holdenworth. I am so sorry that you have lost Holdenworth, but you will always have a home with us if you want to stay. I know this has been much to take in for one day."

"I will go to the inn and get us rooms for tonight," Derek said. "That way you can get cleaned up, and Chanity can see to your wounds. I know you have a lot of catching up to do, and you will have the privacy to do it at the inn."

Back at the inn, Derek was able to get the rooms they needed, and had hot water for baths sent to both rooms.

Bram and two of Derek's men made pallets in the hall and took turns sleeping so the rooms would be guarded.

Gunnar and all the other men stayed with the boats to keep the cargo safe.

After Chanity bathed, she donned clean clothes and headed for Gerald's room. She found him dressed in some clean clothes provided by Derek.

Gerald removed his tunic so Chanity could apply some of the healing paste Etta had sent with them. She cleansed the wounds first, since she Gerald could not reach them when he washed himself. She knew he had to be in agony, but he never uttered a complaint. After she applied the paste she began to tell him what happened after he left.

Gerald listened quietly as Chanity told him the whole story from Vorik's arrival to when they discovered him at the market. She left out nothing, though some of it was embarrassing. She even told him that when Derek rescued her from Vorik she was bare from the waist down.

Gerald did not speak a word until she was finished. "I wished so many times I had not left home," he said sadly. "I am sorry I was not there for you. It may have been different if I had been. I will have to live with that regret for the rest of my life, knowing I wasn't there for my family."

Chanity hugged Gerald gently so she would not hurt his wounds. "I'm so glad you were not there, because you would be buried also. There were just too many raiders. Father and his men held them off for a long time, but they just kept coming. I give you my word, as good of a warrior as you are, it would not have made any difference. Please believe me, brother. There was nothing you could have done."

Gerald pulled her to him and cried for the first time since he was a youth. Even when he had been captured and rotting in a cell, he had not shed even a single tear. Somehow his little sister had helped to ease some of the guilt he held inside for so long. She kissed him on the head and told him she would let him rest, since they would be leaving early in the morn.

The next morn, Chanity rose early and borrowed a razor to cut Gerald's hair and beard. "Look what I have for you," Chanity said as she entered the room. "When I first saw you, I only recognized you by your eyes."

Chanity set to work, and soon Gerald's hair and beard were neatly trimmed. He looked like a different man with his hair and beard set in order. His old clothes were so dirty and tattered they had to throw them in the fire. Derek's clothes fit a little loose, but Gerald looked fine in them. She made sure to clean his wounds again and apply more paste before he donned his tunic.

"This is for you," Chanity said as she handed Gerald a large pouch full of coin. "Don't even try to refuse it. You deserve something from Holdenworth, and I made sure to keep this safe from Vorik.

Now, let us go break our fast before we leave. Derek is downstairs waiting for us."

"Thank you for keeping this for me," Gerald said gratefully. "I am glad you never forgot about me and were looking for me in your travels." Gerald kissed Chanity on the forehead, took her arm and escorted her downstairs.

They set out early that morn. It looked like rain at first, but the sun finally came out and it ended up being a beautiful day. The day went by quickly, now that Chanity had Gerald to talk to. Derek joined their conversation when he could and seemed to really like Gerald.

Chanity thought there might be some resentment on Gerald's part toward Derek over Holdenworth, but he seemed at peace with it. He told her as much, when she hinted at the subject one day.

"How could I resent Derek when he avenged father's death, rescued and married you, and saved me from slavery?" Gerald asked.

After that, Chanity felt better, for she seen the sincerity in his eyes as he spoke.

When they had stopped to make camp at night, she noticed Marla always sat next to Gerald and tried to draw him into conversation. She often touched his shoulder, or rested her hand on his arm.

Chanity watched Marla trying to flirt before, but this was clearly different. She wasn't sitting close enough to hear their whole conversation, but from the tidbits she heard, they were opening up to each another about their lives. After several days of serious conversation, they lightened up and laughed some. For days after that, there was more laughter, but they always sat just far enough away that no one could listen in.

A few days later they arrived in Normandy. Gerald, Marten and some of the guards escorted Chanity and Marla around while Derek sold and traded his cargo. Chanity and Gerald had learned the language from a cousin, who stayed with them many years ago. It was the only other language they knew besides their own.

Gerald and Marla spoke constantly on the journey to Normandy. Chanity had been afraid Gerald would hold it against Marla for what Vorik had done to their parents, but he soon put those fears to rest. He reminded Chanity that Marla was not responsible for Vorik's actions.

Chanity could see Gerald was starting to like Marla a lot. He sought her out at every opportunity and seemed to look forward to their conversations.

The sea journey was over, and now the land journey began. Derek assigned half of the men to stay behind and guard the boats. The remainder would travel north with them on horseback. Next, Derek went to seek horses for him and his men, along with a wagon for supplies. He decided to get a coach for Chanity and Marla. His uncle Marten and Gerald would probably want to ride with them as well. It did not take long to get everything they would need for the trip.

While Derek was gone, Chanity listened to Gerald and Marla talk. They laughed and talked so much she could hardly get a word in. She would have been jealous, but she was just glad to see her brother alive and happy. Plus, she had never seen Marla open up to anyone before. They suited each other well.

Chanity wondered how Marten would feel about Gerald since he was from England. He had treated Gerald kindly so far, but if Gerald and Marla loved one another, then Marten might feel differently. She decided to talk to Derek about this the first chance she got.

Derek finally made it back with what the horses, supplies and carriage. As they set out on their journey, Derek and his men took the lead on horseback, while Chanity, Gerald, Marla and Marten rode in the coach. Since they had gotten a late start, Derek decided to push on through the night to arrive at the homestead in the morning.

Gerald and Marla resumed their conversation as they traveled along. Night fell, and Marten fell asleep first. Chanity dozed off, but a rut in the road jolted her back awake. Now that she was awake, she was too anxious to go back to sleep. She was worried about meeting Derek's family, and wondered if they would like her or not. She listened to Gerald and Marla chatter on, until Derek called out to let them know his family's home was coming into view.

Chanity looked out the coach window and was mesmerized by sight of a castle coming into view. It was a like a masterpiece to behold, though no canvas could do it justice. It was large and grand enough for a King. The rising sun shone down upon the castle, giving it a magical, enchanted look. She knew his parent's home was going to be grand by the way he described it but had never expected this.

Derek opened the coach door to help Chanity out. She tried to straighten herself the best she could. She hoped she looked presentable, since she was meeting them for the first time.

They had hardly dismounted from the carriage before Derek's family rushed out the front door. Derek had sent a messenger as soon as they got to Normandy, letting his family know he would be arriving early in the morn if trading went well.

Chanity was relieved to see some of the ladies had hastily dressed, so she didn't feel so bad about her appearance after the long journey.

Derek introduced his father Geirr, and Mother Elina. Everyone took turns hugging her and welcoming her to the family. They all seemed nice and made her feel welcome. Chanity was glad they greeted Uncle Marten and Marla also. They welcomed Marla, and told her how much they had loved her mother. Derek's mother even hugged Bram and told him how nice it was to see him again.

After Derek introduced Gerald as his brother-in-law, his mother hugged him and welcomed him in the family also. Tears came to Chanity's eyes, and at that moment she realized she loved his mother already.

Chanity imagined Derek's father would resemble him, but his features were different. He did resemble him in size, for both were tall, with a muscular build. Derek's older brother resembled his father more, and was very pleasant to the eyes, but Derek was the best looking of the two. She loved how his family laughed together, and all tried to talk at the same time.

Chanity saw that Marla was smiling, but did not say much. She had always been quiet and kept to herself. It was clear that Marla's smiles were mostly directed to Gerald, and his to her. Marla had talked more to Gerald on the journey than she had spoken to everyone the whole time she lived at Holdenworth. Chanity hoped neither one would be hurt over their feelings for one another, nor how Marten reacted to it. She pushed the worry aside for the moment. Right now, she just wanted to enjoy her new family.

Out of all of Derek's siblings, Chanity really liked Derek's youngest sister Reyna. It was amusing to see Derek's surprised reaction at how much Reyna had changed. Derek had probably pictured how she looked at when he was home. He should have realized Reyna was almost Chanity's age now.

Mirana had married in the springtime, so Chanity would not get to meet her right away. Derek's mother sent a messenger to her as soon as she received word that Derek had arrived in Normandy. Mirana sent word in return that they planned to arrive on the morrow. Chanity hoped she would love her as much as she did the rest of the family. They all had gone out of their way to make her feel a part of the family, and had done the same for her brother and Marla. Of course, Marla was their family, even though they had not known of her existence for years.

After they ate and talked a good while, Elina kissed Derek and Chanity on the cheek and bade them retire to their chamber. I had our chamber maid ready your bed chamber for you. Be sure to let me or the maid know if there's anything you need. She told them again how glad she was they had come, hugged and kissed them both, and sent them on their way.

Derek led Chanity to their chamber, and closed the door. "What did you think of my family?" He asked.

"I love them already, especially your mother. They are all so kind and loving. I know how proud you are to have such a wonderful family."

"Yes, but I'm even more proud of my lady wife. I enjoyed showing you off to everyone, my beautiful, intelligent, enchantress. They adore you already, and how could they not? They know I am a blessed, besotted Knight. He scooped her up and carried her to their bed. Even exhausted, he wanted her, and she him.

The next morn, Derek ordered water for their baths. Chanity pulled out her best gowns she had designed and made herself. She had made two similar in style to the green one she had been wed in. One was in a sapphire blue fabric with silver embroidery, and the other in a beautiful rich burgundy with gold embroidery. She put them back though, and chose the green gown she had worn to be wed in, which was still her favorite.

After Chanity bathed and washed her hair, she donned her gown, and styled her hair. She wanted to look more presentable than she did last night. She made a small braid on each side of temple, then pulled them back and tied them with a green and gold braided ribbon that matched her gown. She let the rest of her wavy blonde hair flow down her back.

Derek admired her as she dressed. He had always thought she looked like an enchantress. He thanked God every day for sending her to him. He knew he could never love anyone the way he loved her.

They had slept through the noon meal, but Derek's mother had food prepared for them while they bathed. It was waiting at the Lord's table when they went down to the great hall.

As Chanity looked around at the furniture and décor, she thought it should be called the grand hall. The wall tapestries were incredible, and must have taken years to complete. There were even rugs on the floor that matched the tapestries. The tables, benches, Lord's chair and four chairs around the fireplace were crafted from a rich mahogany wood. She could not wait to see the rest of the castle.

The food was very good, but since it was after the noon meal, Chanity didn't eat much. A little while after she ate, she became ill and could not hold down her food. Even after emptying her stomach, Chanity still suffered from dizziness, so she went to lie down.

Chanity was feeling better by the time they supped, and enjoyed the rest of the evening. It was fun listening to the tales of Derek growing up. They laughed and talked for hours. She didn't want the evening to end, but knew they needed their rest.

The next morning, Chanity became ill again after they broke their fast. It felt the same as the previous day. After a couple hours of rest she felt better, and got up to enjoy the rest of the day. She met Derek's mother, who was coming to check on her.

"How do you feel, Chanity?" Elina asked.

"I'm better now, since I had some rest," Chanity replied. "Still, I wonder what is causing me to feel unwell."

"Tis probably the long trip," Elina reassured her. "Mirana will be here soon. We will sit down to a meal when they get here."

A short while later, Mirana and her husband arrived. Chanity was feeling better and was glad to sit down to sup. Mirana and her husband sat across from Chanity and Derek, and began to catch up on all that had gone on.

Chanity took an instant liking to Mirana, as she had with Derek's other siblings. She was a year or so younger than Mirana, but since she and Mirana were both newlywed, they had more in common.

After everyone had eaten and talked for a while, Marten rose to his feet. "Derek, thank you for your hospitality at Holdenworth, and for the company on the journey home. I have enjoyed being together with everyone again, but I am anxious to show Marla her new home, and she is ready to go as well."

Derek offered to send some of his men to ride with them, but Marten told Derek he had plenty, and they would be fine.

"Marten, I would like to come with you, if you and Derek don't mind," Gerald said.

"That is a good idea," Derek said thoughtfully. "Gerald could help you at the estate."

"I would welcome your company," Martin said smiling.

Chanity had told Derek that morning of Gerald's and Marla's fondness for one another. He must have been too preoccupied with the trading and journey not to have noticed it himself. He was skeptical at first, but seeing the beam on Marla's face told it to be true. Then he noticed Gerald looking at Marla to see her reaction to him accompanying them. Aye, Chanity had been right about their feelings for one another. He needed to talk to Marten before he left.

Gerald and Marla went to pack up their belongings, while Marten headed down to the stable to see about the horses. Derek met him at the stable and asked if he could speak with him for a moment.

"Of course, what is on your mind Derek?"

"From what I witnessed, 'tis clear that Gerald and Marla have feelings for each other. I just wanted to let you know, before you took him along."

"How long has it taken you to notice?" Marten asked laughing. "I have known myself before we reached Normandy."

Derek confessed he had not noticed. "Chanity told me after we arrived here. I guess I was too caught up in the trading and journey," he reasoned.

I know Gerald's English heritage might cause a problem," Uncle Marten told him. "But our family has influence with King William, and Gerald is your brother in law, so no one will dare say anything. Especially since your father has the second largest estate in Normandy, and I the fourth largest. Gerald is strong, and I could use the help since I'm getting older. He did not know my worth, nor Marla's, so I know he cares for her, not for what she has."

"Besides, Derek, have you ever seen Marla truly happy before Gerald came into her life?" Marten asked.

Derek had to admit he hadn't, though she pretended to be happy at times, especially when she was chasing after him.

"After spending a few days with Gerald she was beaming," Marten said happily. "I enjoyed seeing her talking and laughing with him. I had worried she would never be truly happy, but now she is. That is all I want for her. It's been a long time since I've had any gladness in my home, and I want it now."

The stable hands saddled the horses, and Marten checked them over carefully before heading back to the manor. He said his goodbyes, then they were on their way. There was no coach this time. Gerald rode on one side of Marla, and Marten rode on the other. All three of them were laughing and talking as they headed toward home.

Chanity watched as they rode out of sight. Saying goodbye to Gerald was hard, but they would stop by to see him on the way back to the village where the longboats awaited.

Bram planned to leave with Marten, so he began making preparations as well. He would be traveling faster, so he let Marten get a head start. Besides, Derek asked him to delay as long as possible. Chanity had come to care for Bram as a brother, so both he and Gerald leaving at the same time would be hard on her. He hoped visiting with her new family would keep her from being too sad. Derek's family seemed to love her, and she loved them in return.

Soon Bram was packed and ready to ride after Marten. Chanity hugged Bram, and gave him a quick kiss on the cheek. "I will miss you dearly, brother. Thank you for helping me those times when Derek was away. I don't know what I would have done without you". She tried to fight back the tears, but it was a losing battle, and she wiped eyes frequently.

"Thank you for the couple times you lost at chess just to give me hope so I would keep playing," Bram responded. He tried to get her to laugh to lift her spirits, and so he could see her smile before he left.

Chanity finally smiled, and he kissed her on the top of her head, then turned and clasped Derek to him in a tight hold. "Take care of her and yourself, my brother. I will miss you, but will visit when I can."

"You better come to Holdenworth whenever you get the chance. You know you will be greatly missed by all. There will always be a place for you there."

"Then 'tis not a fair well, but a take care until I see you both again." Bram nudged his horse with his knee and took off toward Marten's group. He was glad Marten's group was far ahead of him so they couldn't see the look of anguish on his face. It broke his heart to see the pain in Chanity eyes from both him and Gerald's leaving. At least Derek would be there to soothe her and take away the pain.

Chanity clung to Derek's side with tears in her eyes, but tried to smile for everyone else. She had just lost both brothers. She knew Derek was sad also. He and Bram had been together since they were lads. "I hope Bram will find love and happiness as I think Gerald has," Chanity said wistfully.

After so many years of praying, she finally found Gerald, only to lose him again. At least now she knew where he was, and that he was happy. They would visit and see one another from time to time. She was happy for him and Marla. She would have never dreamed she would find Gerald, and that one day he would wed Marla of all people. Life held many surprises and fate controlled the outcome. What did fate hold for her, she wondered?

Chapter 26

Over the next two days, Chanity was ill again for a couple hours each day. Derek's Mother Elina sent their healer in to talk with Chanity. The healer mixed up some herbs for her to take each morn when she arose, and packed a basket full for her journey back to Holdenworth.

"You will probably have to take these for two or three months, but after that you will be fine," the healer told Chanity. "If not, your healer should know what to give you. If you become sick in the evenings on the journey, take about half what you do in the morning. The babe should be fine."

"The babe," Chanity whispered. "I am with child?"

The healer laughed. "You did not guess?"

"Nay, I had not guessed," Chanity replied.

"I will send Derek upstairs so you can give him the good news. Do not fear; he is going to be thrilled. I know him well, and was even the one that helped his mother bring him into this world."

A few moments after the healer left, Derek came into the chamber and sat down beside her. "Agnes said 'tis going to be alright, but you would tell me all." He picked up her hand and kissed it. "What did Agnes tell you was wrong?" He asked, with a look of worry on his face.

"'Tis nothing serious, husband, I will be feeling better in a few months."

"A few months of illness sounds serious to me," Derek replied.

"A babe can be serious, but my Mother had no problem with me, and I'm built like her, so I shall be fine." She saw confusion, fear, and then joy, come across his face.

"A babe, you are? We are? Truly, we are having a babe?" He drew her into his arms and started planting kisses all over her face. "I'm not hurting you, am I?"

"Nay, I am fine. It will not be much difference in me, except I will get big then bigger. I hope you won't mind a big wife."

"I will love you no matter how big you grow. After all, it will be my babe that makes you grow bigger." He bent down and kissed her stomach where he thought the babe might be. "Whether you are lad or lass, you are going to be so loved," he told the babe inside her.

A little while later, they went downstairs to tell the family about the babe. Everyone was overjoyed when they heard the news. "We are finally going to have a grandchild," Lady Elina said joyfully.

Elina and Geirr had been after Olen for the last three years about getting married and having an heir. Olen hoped this news would make them leave him be for a while. He would thank Derek, if it did, but was afraid it might even make his mother more determined.

Derek's mother had told Chanity on their first day to call them mother and father, if she would like to. Chanity had been trying to remember to do so. At first it seemed awkward, but it was getting easier as the visit went along.

"'Tis wrong to follow happy news with sad, but we will have to depart in a few days," Derek told them. "There is much work to be done at Holdenworth. With winter approaching, we need to gather the harvest and meat provisions, stock wood, and repair cottage roofs before the first snow. Holdenworth is well guarded, but working hands are few, since I had to bring so many. We have yet more buying and trading to do on the trip back home as well."

Derek asked his parents to visit after the babe came, and they assured him they would. He and Chanity had enjoyed the time they spent with his family. She thought of them as her family now and loved each one. She would miss them when they left for home.

Three days later, they rose early in the morning to begin their journey to Marten's estate. They hired a driver to return the rented coach. Derek's parents offered the use of their coach for Chanity, but she declined. She explained that she wanted to ride while she still could, and had rather be on horseback than tossed about by ruts in the road.

They said their tearful farewells, then mounted and set out. Marten's land bordered Derek's family land, but it was still a full day's journey. They arrived at Marten's home in time to see a beautiful sunset.

Marten's home was a little smaller than his brother's, but still quite large. It looked good from a distance, but as they drew near, Chanity noticed some things had been neglected. Still, it was beautiful to her, and had a charming quality to it. As the sun set behind the home, it took on a magical, enchanted, look.

Derek noticed her looking over the home and thought to explain the state of disrepair. "Uncle Marten has plenty of coin to repair the home, but as of late hadn't seemed to care if it was kept up or not. After the loss of his children, and his wife giving up on life, he had felt no need to repair anything. For years he felt alone, with nothing to look forward to, and no hope. Now, he wants to restore everything for Marla. When I sent word that she was alive and well, he began some renovations immediately."

"Uncle Marten has great plans for Gerald," Derek continued. "He wants Gerald to help oversee the place and help with the restoration. He promised he would speak with him about it on the journey here. This will give him time to see how Gerald and Marla's feelings progress toward one another. If things go well between them, then they will have his blessing. He asked that we not mention this to either of them, but let it progress on their own time."

Chanity smiled and nodded her head in agreement. More than anything, she was overcome with joy, and prayed everything would go well between them. She wanted to see them both settled happily. When her brother came back, she worried he could be devastated over losing Holdenworth. He had surprised her though. He had been through some horrors, and was just happy to be free again. Chanity was glad she would get to see him before they set out for England.

Marla welcomed them at the door, followed by Uncle Marten. She called one of the servants and asked him to let Gerald know they had arrived. "We are about to sup. I know you must be famished after the long ride here."

"We stopped for a bite around noon, and ate quickly so we could arrive before nightfall," Derek said. "We have not eaten since then."

Gerald walked in from outside, and hugged Chanity in a warm embrace.

"Not too tight, you don't want to hurt the babe. She is carrying your future niece or nephew," Derek advised, smiling.

Gerald held Chanity at arm's length for a moment, then hugged her to him again. "I can't believe my little sister is all grown up and going to have a babe. If 'tis a girl, I hope she will resemble you, like you did our mother. If 'tis a boy, then he should resemble me," Gerald declared then looked at Derek and laughed. "Nay, your first son can resemble his father, but the second should resemble me."

"I do not think I have a choice in the matter," Chanity said lightheartedly. "Who the babe resembles will be left up for God to decide. We do have a choice in names though. If 'tis a girl, we like Serina Elina after our mothers. Since you and Olan are firstborn, you probably want to name your first son after your father, so we decided if 'tis a boy to name him Derek Gerald." Chanity saw the big smile on her brother's face, and was glad to see he was pleased to hear his nephew would be named after him. It touched her heart to be able to see him smile after all he had endured the last few years.

The next day Gerald asked Chanity to take a walk with him so they could talk in private. As they walked, he told her of his decision to stay in Normandy. "I have missed you so much little sister, but I see you are well and happy. I know Derek loves you, for it shows in his face every time he looks at you. He will protect you and the babe with his life. I know you don't need my protection, or I would go with you. I love Holdenworth dearly, but 'tis not mine any longer. I know I will always be welcome, but I could not be happy there. The memories of all the bad things that happened after I left would haunt me."

"Here, I have a chance here at happiness, and I am looking forward to a new beginning," Gerald continued. "There are no sad memories for me here. Marten needs help to get over the tragic loss of his wife. I hope Marla and I can help him get through that. Marla and I like each other a great deal, but I will take it slow, to make sure we suit one another. We love each other's company, and we can talk for hours. Marten is kind, and treats me like one of the family. I hope you understand why I must stay."

"I already knew you were going to stay Gerald," Chanity said, giving her brother a big smile, as she hugged him to her. "I have never seen either of you talk to anyone the way you do each other. I pray you find the happiness you seek. You deserve to be happy after all you been through. I'm glad Marla found someone that will show her love and kindness. She had a hard childhood before she came to Holdenworth. You and Marla should be good for each another."

They stayed two more days before setting out for the village where Derek's men and the boats waited. Derek purchased items for trade, and after the boats were loaded, they set out on their journey homeward. They would only make two trading stops on their way home. Derek was becoming a wealthy man between what he had saved and what he had made before he reached Normandy. The goods he sold in Normandy and on the way back would make them wealthy for years to come.

Derek debated on whether he should do the trading or let Gunnar do it for him. He had been training Gunnar in what merchandise to buy, sell and trade for the last few years. Sometimes he would stand to the side and let Gunnar pick the merchandise, then watch as he sold and traded. Gunnar had not let him down and had chosen wisely the last two years.

Derek did not want to ever be apart from Chanity or their children to come. He would stay close so he would always be there to protect them.

As Derek thought of Chanity, he looked over to make sure she was comfortable on her pelts. She looked like an enchantress, sitting there with sunshine on her face while looking out to sea. He had never seen a woman more beautiful than she, nor as sweet and kind. Every time he looked upon her, he was thankful he had found her and made her his wife.

Now this beautiful, sweet woman was about to give him their first child. He hoped they would have many more children. They had talked and dreamed about having a big family. Derek smiled, thinking back to the day they had sat on the big flat rock, overlooking the sea from Chanity's favorite spot on the ledge. He could almost smell her hair, as she leaned back against him that day, talking about all the children she hoped they would have one day.

Derek completed his trading, and the days sped by. Soon their journey was almost at an end. They should be home on the morrow if all went well. Chanity had only been ill a few mornings and a couple evenings. Thankfully her spells of nausea did not last for long. The herbs Erina's healer provided definitely helped. She was thankful the healer had sent plenty for the trip. She could not wait to get home to Holdenworth. She had not realized how much she had missed home until they started back.

Chanity still wished Gerald and Bram were coming home with them and tried not to be sad. Thoughts of their babe helped with that. She could not wait to tell everyone about the babe. She and Derek decided to announce it to everyone at their return feast. It would be hard not to shout it as soon as they entered the gates, but she could manage to keep it a secret for a little while longer.

Chapter 27

They returned home before nightfall just as they had hoped. Everyone was glad to see them, and they were glad to be back at Holdenworth. Cook shouted orders to the kitchen to put on more food. It was a simple meal, but very good. Cook told them he would prepare a return feast tomorrow night.

As they supped, Ortaire filled Derek in on all that had taken place at Holdenworth while they were away. Chanity listened with interest as well. She had always loved her home and the people. There were some dark days when Vorik came, but thankfully they passed with Derek's arrival. Now, it was like home again, except for her family not being there. She would soon have more family to fill their home, starting with their babe, then hopefully many more to follow. She let her mind wander for a moment, then started listening to Ortaire and Derek's conversation again.

After Ortaire finished telling about what went on at Holdenworth, Derek stood and pounded on the table to get every one's attention. "We have great news," He told them. "On our journey we found Gerald, Chanity's brother. He is well, and has decided to stay in Normandy with Uncle Marten and Marla. It seems he and Marla took a liking to each another. Uncle Marten needed help overseeing his estate, so Gerald decided to stay and help." He drew Chanity to his side and gave her a hugged her tightly so she would not dwell on Gerald not coming home.

All those from Holdenworth that had known Gerald applauded when Derek finished speaking. They crowded around Chanity and let her know how glad they were that he was alive and well.

After they supped, Leva sought Chanity out to speak with her. She asked about their trip, and what she thought of Derek's family.

"I wished Gerald could have visited home before staying in Normandy," Chanity told her. "But what matters most is that he is well and happy. I hope he and Marla find the love and happiness they both deserve."

"I love Derek's family, and felt they loved me in return. Hopefully, they will be able to visit next year in the spring. The trip went well, except for one night when we rowed ashore to make camp. Some raiders decided to relieve us of our cargo, and there was a battle."

"You must have been terrified," Leva said.

"Aye, I must admit, I was a little scared, but tried to stay calm," Chanity admitted.

Derek laughed, as he walked up and heard some of their conversation. "My brave Enchantress tried to take them on, one by one," Derek said, speaking loudly so everyone could hear him. "The raiders all had swords, and Chanity only a piece of driftwood, but that mattered naught to her. She attacked the nearest one, and knocked him out with a single blow.

"My Lord husband is exaggerating the truth a little," Chanity said shyly. "I only felled one man with my piece of wood." Her cheeks flushed from her embarrassment, and she knew Derek would never stop teasing her about what she had done. Perhaps he was teaching her a lesson never to interfere with battle again. She was relieved to hear Derek's next words.

"We are exhausted from our long journey, and now we must bid everyone a good night," Derek exclaimed, as he pulled Chanity close. They climbed the stairs arm in arm to the master chamber. As they lay in bed, they discussed the babe, and how they would tell everyone at the feast the next evening. It was hard not to tell everyone about the babe earlier, but they wanted this news to be exceptional, and announced by itself. Besides, the whole village would be invited to the feast tomorrow, so that would be the best time to tell everyone.

The next day dragged on, and it seemed like the feast would never begin. Chanity stayed busy all day, hoping it would help time pass quickly. Finally, it was time to get ready for the feast. She went upstairs to change out of her dirty work gunna, and into her mother's best gown. She wanted to wear her mother's gown, so she could feel close to her. It would also make her feel like her mother was sharing in the news of the babe.

Alma sent hot water up to master chamber so Chanity could bathe and soak a while. She thought it would help her rest, so she would not be too tired at the feast. Alma was the only one at Holdenworth that Chanity told about the babe on their return. Derek asked the men who had journeyed with them not to speak a word about the babe until they announced it.

After the bath, Chanity lay down on the bed to rest, and ended up drifting off to sleep. Alma sent Elspeth upstairs to check on her, since she had not made an appearance. Chanity awoke when she heard Elspeth knock on the door. Elsbeth helped Chanity style her hair, and don her gunna. Derek came up to their chamber just as she finished. Seeing Derek arrive, Elsbeth excused herself and went downstairs.

"You look beautiful wife. I hope you not overly tired from our journey."

"Nay, I have rested for a while, so I feel ready to go downstairs to greet everyone."

Derek took her by the arm and escorted her down to the feast. The great hall was overflowing with people, since they had invited the whole village. She felt a little guilty for not being in the hall to greet the villagers as they arrived, but she needed the rest for the babe, and for that, she could not feel guilty.

The smell of food had made her sick that morning, but it did not seem to bother her this evening. She had made sure to take some herbs before she went upstairs to bathe.

After everyone was seated, Derek banged on the table with his mug to get their attention. He pulled Chanity to his side with one arm and held her tightly against him. "We have great news! We are going to have a babe! My lady wife is with child. Our first babe will arrive in the spring." He pulled Chanity close and kissed her on the lips. Everyone cheered at the happy news.

Ortaire banged on the table with his mug for attention as well. After the hall quieted, he shouted "Hail to the Lord and future Lord of Holdenworth," as he held up his sword high in the air with his right arm then smote his chest with his left fist three times. All the other men did the same, repeating the words "hail to the Lord and future Lord of Holdenworth" as they held their swords high and smote their chest three times as well.

Derek was proud of his men, and grateful for the honor they showed him. He saw Chanity was moved as well, since she had to wipe a couple tears away from her eyes. He could hardly wait till the birthing day so he could hold his lad or lass up for all to see.

The feast went well. They had the usual entertainment of music, dancing, jugglers, and a troubadour. The troubadour spun a tale of their meeting and how they found true love. His tale did not end until the moment when they announced they were blessed with their babe. He spun two more tales, one of a Prince and Princess, then one of a king who died in battle.

Derek only danced with Chanity, Leva and two elderly ladies from the village. Alice tried to get him to dance but he refused. He did not want to encourage her in any way, and actually had to remove her hands from his arm twice before she finally went away in a huff. He wished she would realize he wanted nothing to do with her, and that she would just stay away from him. He had many other offers, but the rest took "nay" for an answer and left him alone.

On Derek's next dance with his lady wife, Chanity said "I see Alice still has not given up on you, my Lord".

"So it's 'My Lord' now, is it?" Derek said with a laugh. "My dear, lady wife, I can tell when you are miffed about something." He drew Chanity close and kissed her, as she looked up at him. She gave him an enchanting smile that warmed his heart and made him wonder what the night would bring.

"Are you getting tired?" Derek asked.

"I am ready to go to our chamber, but not to rest" Chanity said, as she gave him another enchanting smile. Derek lifted her in his arms, and carried her out of the great hall, up the stairs and into their chamber, as they laughed along the way.

The people who witnessed their sudden departure laughed as well, and looked admiringly on the couple who had true love for one another.

Alice, however, was not happy, and had a look of hatred on her face. She wondered how Lord Derek could prefer Chanity, seeing she was much prettier and more deserving to be a Lord's wife. The thought of Chanity expecting a child made her smile slyly. Soon Chanity would grow fat, and then his lordship would seek her out.

She would be the one to warm his bed and find favor in his eyes. She would please him well, and there would be nothing he would not grant her, Alice reasoned to herself.

Chanity woke the next morn with a smile on her face. She did not feel ill at all, so she dressed quickly, and went down to break her fast.

Derek sat at the table with Ortaire, as they discussed how to reap the harvest and prepare for winter. They eventually decided to split the men up in two groups. One group would bring in the harvest, while the other repaired roofs. Chanity took a seat at the table, and broke her fast while listening to their conversation. When she was through eating she began helping Alma, Elspeth, and Leva clean up as the men finished.

Once the cleanup was done, Leva asked Chanity if she could have a word alone with her. "Let's go down to the orchard," Leva suggested. "There are quite a few ripe apples. I'll pluck them, while you hold the basket."

Chanity grabbed two baskets as they left the hall. At the orchard they would have privacy for the personal matter Leva wanted to discuss.

They arrived at the orchard, and Leva told Chanity about the gossip Alice had been spreading. "Last night at the festival, I heard Alice tell one her friends that she hoped the babe were truly Lord Derek's and not Sir Bram's. She told the village girl that you and Bram were always together when Lord Derek was away. I hope I do not upset you by telling you this, but I felt it was something you would want to know."

"Thank you, Leva," Chanity replied "I will think on this, and decide what I must do. I dread telling Derek, since he was already jealous of Sir Bram, as you know. 'Tis the reason Sir Bram did not return, because he did not want to hurt their brotherly bond. Bram became like a brother to me as well, and I miss him dearly. I only had feelings for him like a brother, and my love for Derek has never changed."

"Ortaire told me he would speak with Lord Derek and tell him about the gossip Alice was spreading around, if you wanted him to," Leva advised.

"Nay, 'tis best I speak with him about it myself. Tell Ortaire I truly appreciate his offer." Chanity hugged Leva and said, "Now if you don't mind Leva, I need to be alone a while to think."

"I understand. If you need anything Chanity, just send for me." Leva lifted her basket of apples and headed back to the hall.

Chanity gathered her basket and headed home as well. Back at the hall, she gave her basket to one of the serfs and asked them to carry it inside. She still had not decided what to do, so she headed to her favorite spot at the cliff.

The bright sun filtered through the autumn leaves, warming the cool air as Chanity walked down the familiar path. Soon she reached the cliff and climbed down to the ledge. With a deep sigh, she sat on the warm, flat rock and gazed out to sea.

Chanity sat and pondered for what seemed like an hour. She must have sat a lot longer than she thought, because Derek showed up looking concerned. He sat beside her on the rock and held her close to him. "It seems something is troubling you, my lady wife. What is troubling you so?"

Chanity broke down and told him what Leva overheard Alice saying. "It is so unfair. I never looked at Bram in that way, and only felt for him as a brother. I have never been untrue to you, and my love has never faltered. She is the wanton wench, not I."

Derek held Chanity in a tight embrace, as he kissed her temple, forehead, and cheek. His rough hands softly stroked her hair as he tried to soothe her. The last thing he wanted was for Chanity to get upset. It was not good for her or their babe. "I will take care of Alice," He reassured her, as he kissed her forehead again. "As soon as we get you safely home, I will have a talk with her father. If he can't control her, then I will banish her from our village."

Chanity was relieved. At last Alice would be made to understand that Derek did not want her, and he would never be hers.

True to his word, as soon as Derek saw Chanity safely home, he headed for the village. He barely got his horse tethered when Alice ran up and began stroking his arm.

"Lord Derek, you have the strongest arms," Alice cooed.

Derek grabbed her wrist and pulled her hand away.

"I see you like it rough," Alice said, as she grinned wickedly at him. "That's fine by me."

"Let's see how much you like it when I string you up from my whipping post, and the whip lashes down on your flesh," Derek said with rage in his voice. He set off at once for the smithy, dragging Alice in tow. She almost had to run to keep up, and stumbled as they went along. Everyone in the village stared at the spectacle with their eyes wide, and mouths agape in curiosity.

The noise of their approach must have echoed over the ring of the Smith's hammer, for Alice's father rushed out as they reached the smithy. "What has she done now?" he asked.

"'Tis best we go to your cottage so your wife will hear this as well," Derek advised.

Derek released Alice's wrist, and the Smith led the way to the cottage, with Alice and Derek close behind.

As they reached the cottage, the Smith flung open the door, and ushered Alice and Derek inside.

"What's the meaning of this?" The Smith's wife asked, alarmed at the sudden entry.

Derek told them about what Alice had done, showing up unclothed in the stables and starting rumors about Chanity at the feast. "I will not tolerate her saying anything about my lady wife and my babe. If she ever says anything about them again, I will tie her to the whipping post and order ten lashes from the whip. She will also be banished from the village."

"To make amends, Alice must publicly tell everyone that she has been spreading lies, and is sorry for doing so. She must admit she was jealous of Chanity, and made everything up," Derek demanded.

"Everyone saw them out riding together," Alice's mother said, as she spoke up in her daughter's defense. She soon realized she had made a mistake, as Derek turned his anger on her.

"You are the reason your daughter is the way she is. You never taught her to respect herself or others. Apparently you did not teach her to value the truth either. Can either of you rightly say that Chanity was ever alone with Bram, or did you just decide to spread gossip?" Derek demanded.

When neither spoke, Derek looked at Alice's mother with rage in his eyes and continued. "I ordered Sir Bram to see that Chanity rode Lily everyday so she would not sit around worrying over me. It was his duty to see to her safety. There were always guards to accompany them, and they did not let her out of their sight. When

Chanity was sick, there was always a lady in attendance when Bram checked on her. I better not hear these lies again."

The Smith's wife glanced at her husband for some aid, but the look on his face told her to shut her mouth and keep it shut.

The silence in the room made it clear to Derek that he had made his point. As he left, Derek told the Smith to send for him if needed, then walked out.

Derek closed the door behind him and heard the Smith's interrogation of Alice begin. "You showed up unclothed in his stables?" Derek did not hear Alice's answer, but she must have denied it, because her father said, "do not lie to me," followed by a loud slap.

The next day, Alice showed up at Holdenworth and apologized to Chanity. Chanity nodded as if to accept her apology, and Alice turned to go. Suddenly Chanity drew her mother's dagger from her waist and held it to Alice's throat. "If you ever tell lies about me or the ones I love again, I will slit your throat. I also suggest you never lay another hand on my husband, or show up unclothed. Do you understand me, Alice?"

"Aye, I understand," Alice replied, her eyes wide with fear.

"Then I accept your apology," Chanity replied, as she returned the dagger to its hiding place, and smoothed out her dress.

Alice practically ran from Holdenworth, and nearly headlong into Derek.

"Sorry my Lord," Alice stammered, then ran away as quickly as she could.

Derek noticed one side of Alice's face was slightly bruised, and she clutched at her throat. That was the first time she had not thrown herself at him, and he was glad of the change. He wondered how her apology to Chanity had gone, and why she left in such a hurry.

Derek went to check on Chanity, to make sure Alice had not upset her. He was happy to find her smiling. She was even more radiant than usual since she was with child. "You get more enchanting every day, my beautiful enchantress."

Chanity thanked him and gave him a big smile. "You get more handsome every day, Sir Knight. If the babe is a lad, I hope he has your build and good looks." She pulled Derek to her and gave him a sensuous kiss. Then he picked her up and carried her to their bed chamber for an early nap.

Chapter 28

As the months went by, Chanity kept getting bigger and bigger. Etta and Leva kept a close watch on her. Leva and Etta's healing skills complimented each other well, and they learned even more as they worked together. A month ago, Etta advised Chanity not to do any work except to sew. Chanity was grateful for the time to sew a couple new gunnas, since everything had gotten too small. She tried to walk every day, but now even that was getting to be too much for her.

Chanity had seen others who were with child, but they had not been this big. She was only eating as much as Etta suggested. Etta finally told Chanity she had to remain on the second floor, since it was no longer safe for her to use the stairs. Derek spent time with Chanity each day during his breaks to keep her from being lonely. Alma spent a good deal of time with her has well, like a mother hen checking on her chick. All the attention was tiresome at times, but Chanity knew Serina would have wanted it that way.

The last few days, it bothered her that she could hardly get in and out of bed. She wished the babe would decide it was time to be born. Surely, her belly could not grow any larger. Except for the swelling in her feet and legs, only her belly had gotten bigger. Chanity asked Derek and Alma if they would help her up so she could walk around. After they helped her out of bed, Derek supported her with his strong arms as she walked around the room. Chanity stopped abruptly, causing Derek to stop as well.

"'Tis time for our babe." Chanity whispered.

Derek looked down and saw water on the floor. Derek told Alma to send word for Etta and Leva, but she was out the door before he could finish his request.

They sat with Chanity for the rest of the day, but she had not birthed her babe yet. Derek was getting worried, but they told him it takes some time for the birth to happen. When the moon was high in the sky that night, Chanity yelled out.

Alma told Derek he should go wait downstairs. They promised to send for him, if he was needed. He hesitated, but Chanity assured him everything would be fine.

Ortaire was waiting for him at the table when he entered the great hall. Since Bram left, Derek promoted Ortaire to second in command. Ortaire was seated to the right of the Lord's chair, and Gunnarr sat in Ortaire's old seat, since he was promoted as well. Chanity seat was always next to Derek on his left.

"There you are, brother," Ortaire said. "I wondered when you would be down to join us." He handed Derek a mug as he sat down. "I know the waiting must be maddening for you. Do not worry. Chanity is strong, and she will do well. You will be blessed with many children."

Derek agreed she was strong and beautiful as well. "Still, I can't help but worry for her, for I wouldn't want to live without her. She is like my life's blood; I need her to survive. She has made life beyond wonderful for me, and now with the babe coming; I can't imagine how great our life will be." Derek silently prayed that everything would go well with Chanity and their babe.

In the early morning hours, Chanity screamed loudly, and Derek ran for the stairs. As he reached the second floor, he heard a babe cry out. Alma went to the door and told him "you have a strong son, my Lord."

Derek shouted down to his men "I have a son, a strong son," and heard cheers coming from the great hall below. Ortaire followed Derek up the stairs and clasped him on the back in congratulations.

Derek started to open the door to their chamber, but another scream sounded from Chanity. He was too afraid to go inside. Then a babe cried out again, and he heard two babes crying in chorus. Alma came back into the hallway and said, "you also have a beautiful little daughter." Derek's legs began to tremble, and he was speechless.

With Derek speechless, Ortaire shouted "He has a little daughter also."

This time even more cheers erupted from below.

"I have a son and a daughter," Derek said to himself. He felt like he was in a daze. A few minutes later, Chanity screamed yet again, and moments later another baby cried.

"What did I do?" Derek asked as he looked at Ortaire. "They keep coming, did I do something wrong?"

Ortaire could give no answer but to laugh.

Alma came out and said, "You have another son, my Lord. Stay around; we may need you if she births another. We are running out of hands." Then she turned and went back into the master chamber.

"Does she jest?" Derek asked Ortaire. "Can there be another babe?"

Ortaire just laughed and told him, "You are truly blessed. I did say a little while ago you would have many children. But honestly I thought it would take a few years. Ortaire shouted down "He has another son! He is now blessed with three babes." There was another great cheer at this news.

After the women cleaned the babes and tidied the room, they bade Derek come inside. He entered, and saw his babes lying on the bed with their mother. He had never seen such a wonderful sight. It would be a sight he would always remember and hold dear in his heart.

Chanity was beautiful, even in her exhausted state, lying with the three babes. He sat on the bed looking at them, amazed at the love and pride he felt for his family. They tied a ribbon around the first-born son's wrist to mark him as the heir.

Derek looked at Chanity, who smiled at the love that showed on his face. He touched each babe's tiny hand, just wanting to feel each of them. Chanity was so exhausted; she fell asleep while watching him. He placed a kiss on her head and caressed her cheek.

"We will be staying with Chanity and the babes tonight," Alma told Lord Derek. "I made Chanity's old chamber up for you so you can be right across the hall from them. They will be fine, so go get your rest. If anything should happen, I will send for you."

Reluctantly, he headed for the other chamber, but not before turning back and looking at his family one more time. No one would ever know how thankful he was for them, and the love that filled his heart. As Derek gazed upon his beautiful wife, he silently thanked God as he did every day, for sending him to Holdenworth. Not for the house or lands, but because he found Chanity, his lady wife, his enchantress.

Epilogue
Holdenworth
6 years later.

Everyone sat around tables placed under the shade trees, as they enjoyed a sunny summer day. The breeze carried the scent of the nearby roses that were in bloom. Derek's parents, Gerald, Marla and Uncle Marten had journeyed to visit. They made the trip to Holdenworth every couple of years while on their trade route. Sometimes Derek's brother and sisters came along as well, but they were not able to make this trip.

Gerald wed Marla six months after they arrived in Normandy. They named their son Belgar Marten Livingston Holdenworth, who was born a couple years after they wed. To their great joy, they discovered Marla was with child again just before they left on their journey.

Uncle Marten seemed to be very happy, and was enjoying life again. He was proud of his great-grandson Belgar, and spent most of his time with him. Belgar looked just like Gerald with his blue eyes. The only thing about him that looked like Marla was his dark black hair.

Gerald's had filled out well, and was back to his handsome self. It had taken several months to get over all that happened to him emotionally and physically, but with Marla's friendship, love and support he had overcome it. Now he was happier than ever, since he had Marla and their son.

Chanity saw some sadness on his face at times as he looked around his old homestead, but she knew it was only regret from leaving home against his father's wishes. A few moments later, he would look at Marla and smile again.

Marla had become more beautiful with age, and now had the look of a woman instead of the girl she had been at Holdenworth. She had changed in other ways as well. She was always happy now, and laughed with everyone. She had blossomed under the love and care of Gerald. Chanity was sure the love and attention she received from her Grandfather had helped as well.

This was the third time Derek's parents had visited in the last six years. They were always anxious to see their grandchildren. Their first visit was not long after the triplets were born, then every two years after that.

Derek's brother Olen had never married, nor had any children. As for Derek's sisters, Mirana had two children, and was expecting a third. Reyna married four years previous, and was expecting their second child in the next few months.

Bram stayed in Normandy after he returned home instead of rejoining King William as he had planned. He was needed to take over as Lord of his family estate. He still served King William and would join him when necessary, but Bram's story is for another time.

About ten months after Bram left, Ortaire's wife Leva perished in childbirth as well as their babe. It was a terrible blow to Ortaire, who was consumed with guilt because he had not wanted a babe at the time. He and Leva had loved one another as friends and only married for companionship. After losing Leva and the babe, Ortaire left Holdenworth and rejoined King William.

Ortaire thought he would never find true happiness, and felt a life of war was all that lay ahead for him. But fate had other plans, and his story was far from over, a story that will have to wait for another time as well.

Derek and Chanity named their first born Derek Gerald Olan Livingston but called him Dirk for short. They named their second child Serina Elina Livingston after their mothers. The last of the triplets they named Bram Ortaire Livingston in honor of Bram and Ortaire, since Derek cared for them like brothers. His first name was a tribute to Bram, who had been willing to give up his way of life to protect Chanity if Derek lost in battle to Garth.

Two years after the triplets were born, Chanity birthed their second daughter. They named her Madeline Josette Livingston after two of her great-grandmothers. A year and two months after Madeline, Chanity gave birth to their third daughter, Sophie Lenora Ann Livingston.

Chanity had always liked the name Sophie. That was the name she had given her doll when she was a little girl. Her mother had made the doll with left over pieces of material, and she had always cherished it.

Not long after, Chanity found she was with child again. "Lass, this will be your fourth birth in seven years," Etta exclaimed in amazement. "I would wager the babe will be a lad by the way you carry yourself," Etta noted, as she studied Chanity carefully.

"You are probably right, Etta," Chanity agreed smiling. "You have been correct with many other births in the past. If the babe is truly a lad, we shall name him Geirr Belgar Livingston. Derek's older brother Olan never married or had an heir, so calling the babe Geirr will please Derek's father greatly."

Derek and Chanity made a pallet so their youngest daughter could nap and took a seat beside her. They watched as their children ran around playing with their little cousin, while the grandparents trailed along behind them.

Chanity could tell Uncle Marten was as proud of his great-grandchild as Derek's parents were of theirs. It brought joy to their hearts seeing the little ones they loved enjoying themselves so. Gerald and Marla sat on the pallet with them, watching the fun and laughter going on all around them.

For a while they sat quietly, just watching the children play. They were all thinking of how blessed they were as a family, and pondered what the future held for them. There was one thing they knew in their hearts, that their lives would be filled with lots of love.

About the Author

Diana Sherrill Richards was born in Athens, Al. She still lives in North Alabama with her husband Randall. She has a grown son Justin who lives forty minutes away. She found her love for reading books at age sixteen and wanted to be a writer shortly after that, but through the years kept putting it off. She finally decided if she was going to see her dream come true, she needed to get started on her first book. She hopes you love reading it as much as she enjoyed writing it.